Since childhood RAY GROVER has reg
as stories about people. His first novel *Another Man's Role*—a story about a
Korean War veteran—was followed by the highly acclaimed *Cork of War*,
which depicted New Zealand in the eighteen thirties and forties when the
country was irrevocably changed by European settlement. Although presented
as fiction, it went on to win the New Zealand Book Award for Non-fiction
in 1983. *New Zealand: A Bibliography*, a result of twenty years' work at the
Turnbull Library, won him a New Zealand Library Association award. He
also received an Anzac Fellowship that enabled him to identify New Zealand
historical materials held in Australia.

Ray Grover is a former Chief Archivist of Archives New Zealand and
Trustee of the National Library of New Zealand. Since his retirement as Chief
Archivist he has held advisory positions relating to New Zealand's history.
Currently he is the Honorary Archivist of the Queen Elizabeth II Army
Museum, Waiouru and is writing a sequel to *March to the Sound of the Guns*.

---

*March to the Sound of the Guns is the story of ordinary New
Zealanders trapped in the most horrible of wars, where the only
response is to live or die with quiet heroism. The events of Gallipoli,
the Somme and Passchendaele need no dressing up. Ray Grover takes
us into the trenches, through the mud holes, into the face of enemy fire,
not with clashing armies but with individuals the reader knows from
their pre-war lives. The writing is strong, elegant, witty, restrained, the
characters well-rounded and likeable, while the research underpinning
pre-1914 life in New Zealand and the events of the war is heroic in its
scope and depth. March to the Sound of the Guns is a triumphant
amalgam of scholarship and story-telling, and is likely to be judged
our best war novel yet.*

Maurice Gee, *January 2008*

Also by Ray Grover:

Another Man's Role, 1967
New Zealand: A Bibliography, 1980
Cork of War, 1982

NOTE

March to the sound of the guns enunciates the duty of a soldier to betake himself to the battlefield and fight. Allegedly it was first pronounced by the Duke of York (1763–1827) the same general who, it is also alleged, had ten thousand men and marched them to the top of the hill where, on reassessing his maxim, he marched them down again.

'The Great War' was aptly named: until then no other war had killed so many. Like most wars it was started by leaders who were as heedless of the human cost as they were uninterested in contemplating the economic and political consequences of their actions other than what they had dreamed up for themselves. Germany was the best prepared. New Zealand was among the least, but given the close personal, political and economic ties to Britain at the time—and the chain reaction that wars create—it is difficult to envisage New Zealand not becoming a belligerent. Indeed being part of the Empire in 1914, once Britain declared war, New Zealand was at war too—although it possessed the authority to decide how deeply it should commit itself. When the New Zealanders were shipped halfway round the world they were ordinary young men from offices, shops, farms and factories neither better nor worse than generations before or since. What happened to them might be of interest to those born since or elsewhere.

MARCH
TO THE
SOUND
OF THE
GUNS

RAY GROVER

Longacre Press

Acknowledgements

I have lived with this book for over twenty years, but particular thanks to Chris Pugsley who got me going and who since then, has offered encouragement, advice and information I could not have obtained anywhere else—and many impassioned arguments. Others who have been of great help are Maurice Gee, Ray Richards, Barbara Larson, Emma Neale, Nelson Wattie (for French translation), Brian Turner, Dave Cheer, Charlotte Williams, Vince O'Sullivan, Kevin Ireland, Don McIver, Rachel Barrowman, John Crawford, Bruce Ralston, Gerald Gliddon, Alex Starr, Jim McAloon, Ron Quince, Len Richardson, John and Phillida Russell.

I'd also like to extend my thanks to the staffs of: Alexander Turnbull Library; Archives NZ; Auckland Institute & Museum Library; National Archives, London; National Library of Scotland; NZ Defence Library; Queen Elizabeth II Army Memorial Museum Library & Archives; Wellington Public Library.

Thanks to Creative New Zealand for funding the initial trip to battlefields.

First published with the assistance of

ISBN 978 1 877460 01 2

A catalogue record for this book is available from the National Library of New Zealand.

First published by Longacre Press, 2008
30 Moray Place, Dunedin, New Zealand.

Typeset in 11/15.5 pt Adobe Garamond

Book design by Christine Buess
Front cover design by Nick Wright
Printed by Astra Print, Wellington

www.longacre.co.nz

CONTENTS

FOREWORD

I need to declare my vested interest at the beginning of this introduction. I have known Ray Grover for some twenty-five years. I worked for him at National Archives after leaving the army and regard him as a good friend and mentor. These last seven years we have walked New Zealand ground in Belgium and France, but not yet Gallipoli. Once a year we meet and retrace a New Zealand battlefield; taking the route the New Zealanders took up past the woods to Caterpillar Valley and the New Zealand start line on the Somme, 15 September 1916. We have done the same at Messines, Passchendaele and on the route of the New Zealand advance from La Signy Farm to Le Quesnoy of 1918.

Over the years I have read great chunks of this manuscript and thought I knew the story, but I was wrong. Reading it as a whole for the first time staggered me. I got the book on a Friday and devoured it over the weekend, finishing it on Sunday morning. I found myself transported into a vanished New Zealand pre-1914 and into the lives of a group of New Zealanders: Harry, Frank, Jim and Nelle, and for a time, Lieutenant Colonel William George Malone of Chunuk Bair fame, who by various routes and inclinations find themselves marching to the sound of the guns.

Each is his or her own character and while occasionally there are triggers to places, events and sometimes words familiar to me, Grover has used the realities of New Zealand in 1914 to create a fictional world inhabited by characters that breathe. Each speaks with their own voice, allowing you to see how background, upbringing, and occupation shapes them as people. They grow in front of your eyes, in turn letting you share their experiences and interaction with each other in New Zealand, Egypt, Gallipoli, Belgium, France and in training, leave and convalescence in England. We inhabit each in turn, sharing events in the chronology of war, and, as it is historical fact, losing at least one of the principals along the way, among the many New Zealanders who are killed and maimed.

Grover's descriptions of land and people stir familiar chords. His characters comfortably wear his meticulous research, giving them a rich, too often horribly believable setting to inhabit and explore, but his real strength is language. Jim is Jim as much as Harry is Harry, Frank is Frank and Nelle is Nelle: all New Zealand voices. You hear the conversations in your head and know the people, because you have met them before and know the type; even if they, as they do, still have the capacity to surprise you, as all good novels must. Grover's story ends in 1919, but you as reader are conscious that it is not an end but a beginning; much is not known and for each of them, as for New Zealand, there is no certainty of outcome.

The larger caste of characters includes General Godley and his wife, a young James Hargest, one of the outstanding soldiers of the Otago Regiment who would become a controversial figure on Crete in the next war, and Lieutenant Colonel 'Hoppy' Mitchell who ran the New Zealand Infantry and Base Depot at Etaples in France; each more than an historical figure, but flesh, blood and bias. We see them through the eyes of the main characters and are allowed to form our own judgements. As in life nothing is clear cut; different encounters in different situations, allow various sides to be seen. I put down the book seeing aspects of Godley, Hargest and Mitchell (whom I have researched and thought I knew), often in a light that I had never appreciated before; such is Grover's skill in using detailed research and words to skilfully paint nuances of historical character.

Like New Zealand, his characters lose their innocence over these years of war and are shaped by their reactions to that experience. Religious beliefs are strengthened and lost, cynicism grows, but in the trenches of Gallipoli and in the mud of the Somme and Passchendaele, in marriage, birth and loss, each in turn realises that survival depends on drawing strength from one another; not always from friends, but from those bonds that soldiers and comrades, men and women, find in the horror and waste of war.

This is a story of friendship, of fortitude; of young people from a young country, inured to hardship because life was like that; who went mostly eagerly to war; who quickly lost faith in bureaucracy, army and sometimes God, but found something out about each other and sometimes important things about themselves. But always in the background is New Zealand; small, distant, hard, Puritanical, parochial, a country to flee from to a wider world and one to escape back to from the world's hurts. But as Grover shows us, there is no escape, only the uncomfortable realities of growing up and facing a century with no certainties.

I can think of no other novel that captures individual New Zealanders in the war as skilfully as *March to the Sound of the Guns*. Grover's language has the richness of Vincent O'Sullivan's writing, matched with his and Maurice Gee's knowledge of human frailties, combined with an understanding of the times worthy of the most skilled historian. It stands alongside New Zealand's two other outstanding war novels: Guthrie Wilson's *Brave Company* and Rod Elder's *Deep Jay*, but inhabits a much broader canvas. It is the novel of New Zealand as it was shaped by the first cataclysm of the twentieth century—indeed I would argue that it is the New Zealand novel of the twentieth century.

Grover is intent on taking the story on into the 1920s and the Second World War. He is in his seventies, so he will have to get cracking, but what he has given us here will more than do for now.

Christopher Pugsley
Department of War Studies
Royal Military Academy, Sandhurst
Author of *Gallipoli: The New Zealand Story*
    and *The Anzac Experience*
March, 2008

To Tom

PREFACE

New Zealand's involvement in the Great War is tragedy on the grandest scale. A nation with barely more than a million people sent a hundred thousand young men to the other side of the world to fight under the foulest of conditions. Of these, over eighteen thousand were killed (a death rate of 1:5.5) and over forty thousand wounded, with many suffering psychological afflictions. In the years leading up to 1914, British decision makers identified Germany as the nation most likely to upset the balance of power in Europe and to become a threat to Britain and the Empire. Among the steps taken to counter this was the encouragement of the Dominions to modernise and increase their military forces. In New Zealand this led to visits by high-level British generals and the sending out of General Godley and instructional staff. Conscription for part-time military training was instituted, a territorial force organised, and purchase of new equipment commenced. With very few exceptions, New Zealanders went along with what was being done, although the creation of a professional fighting force, or conscription on the continental model, would have been unacceptable. As it happened, war broke out before the basic training of the territorial force had been completed.

Much has been made of the failures of the Great War and this book is no exception. We must recognise however, that it was the first war to be fought with millions of men equipped with modern, industrially produced weapons. On the Western Front there was a further complication: the greatest siege ever, where the defences stretched from the Channel to the Alps. There was no obvious precedent to guide the generals, and because of the embedded rigid hierarchy of the armies involved, and the relative stability of the belligerent governments apart from Russia, the conditions were not conducive for a Napoleon or a Cromwell to arise and impose their genius on the new situation. Each combatant eventually arrived at the solution, but it was a slow, and frightfully costly, process.

March to the Sound of the Guns commences with a view of New Zealand in the years immediately preceding 1914, when it was not uncommon to hear it called God's Own Country. Jingoism ruled and one cannot forbear quoting from Kipling's 'Epitaphs of the War' (1918): 'If any question why we died / Tell them, because our fathers lied.' The story then moves to Gallipoli where an ill-led, ill-prepared body of men are thrown against a tough, determined enemy willing to sacrifice itself in defence of its homeland. The Western Front follows; this is where they met the best-trained and equipped mass army in the world. Without wanting to idealise him, I would say it was the ordinary soldier that carried the New Zealand Division through — his quiet fortitude, adaptability, courage and loyalty to comrades.

Nearly all the events related have been based on close inspection of battlefields and material derived from detailed research carried out over many years. Findings from each were sorted, chapter-by-chapter, into a sequence for the imagination to work on to varying degrees. The book aims to tell not just what happened to people, but how and why it happened. As an attempt to cover significant aspects of the complex events that occurred, and to give a feeling of immediacy, five narrators tell their stories in the first person — a colonel, a volunteer nurse, and three soldiers. Apart from named historical personages (who have qualities that may be fictional), the characters do not represent anyone living or dead.

A broad-brush description of military organisation and the responsibilities of some ranks might be helpful. The smallest infantry unit was a section, more or less of ten men, led by a corporal or lance corporal. For most of the 1914–18 war, four sections generally made up a platoon, which was mostly commanded by a lieutenant, but sometimes by a sergeant. The second-in-command was a sergeant. Three infantry platoons, plus a 'HQ' (signallers, clerks, etc.) platoon comprised a company commanded either by a captain or a major, and which had a sergeant major as its senior Non Commissioned Officer. Four infantry companies comprised a battalion that was commanded by a lieutenant colonel who was addressed as 'Colonel'. Three battalions made up a brigade which, early in the war, was commanded by a full colonel, but who would soon be made a brigadier general. Three brigades normally comprised a division commanded by a major general. An infantry division, however, also had field artillery, engineers, medical corps, army service corps (i.e. logistics support) etc. Generally three divisions made up a Corps that was commanded by a lieutenant general. Varying numbers of Corps comprised an Army, commanded by a general. The British armies on the Western Front were numbered One to Five and their Commander-in-Chief for most of the war was General, then Field Marshall, Haig.

To give an idea of the context in which the New Zealanders fought: their division, although one of the largest in the British Expeditionary Force, was one among fifty-seven British and 'colonial' divisions. These were far outnumbered by French divisions, plus, in the final months, up to thirty-nine large American divisions, and vast numbers of medium and heavy artillery, cavalry, medical and service corps units, etc., and, initially few, but increasing, air squadrons.

Ray Grover
February, 2008

If, in those days of my adolescence, I had not enjoyed friendship,
what would I have enjoyed?
Victor Serge

Fortitude I take to be the quiet possession of a man's self,
and an undisturbed doing his duty whatever evils beset,
or dangers lie in the way. In itself an essential virtue,
it is a guard to every other virtue.
John Locke

NEW ZEALAND

MALONE
New Plymouth — 1909

'It is well that war is so terrible. We should grow too fond of it.' Robert E. Lee's sentiment crossed my mind as I contemplated the fiftieth anniversary dinner of the Taranaki Rifle Volunteers. By coincidence they and I were born in the same year and the same month. It was a convivial gathering that commenced with the calling of the original roll. There were men present who responded to it. One was old Colonel Messenger who told us how in 1860 they had prevented the local tribes from entering New Plymouth by holding them at Waireka, thus the Taranaki men became the first British volunteer force to engage in the field. After the toast to the Prime Minister and Parliament—when I sipped my glass of water with mixed feelings—'The Taranaki Battalion' was proposed. The first response was by our commander and, about to resign, he should have had the floor to himself. Reluctantly, I had agreed to make the second response. Rather than commemorating the past, I spoke of the future, of the coming war that would be on a scale not experienced since Napoleon. Although I spoke with respect to the South African veterans, I stated how this war, which would be fought sooner rather than later, would be against an enemy vastly more formidable than the Boer. After stressing the need for a sense of duty, and training at its most intensive, I resumed my seat, feeling my words had been contrary to the mood of the gathering. Although tempted I did not quote the words of the great American civil war general—they deserve a dissertation of their own.

New Zealand's Chief of Staff, Colonel Robin—the rank indicates the size of our defence force then — proposed the toast of the evening, 'The Taranaki Rifles'. He quoted John Ruskin.

'You may wonder,' said Robin, 'why a man of arts and letters, a man of peace, is being quoted at a gathering like ours. I beg you to listen:

'"Idleness is a thousand-fold greater sin in those learning to be a soldier than in any other profession of life, for the fates of those you have to command hang on your knowledge and wasted time now means lost lives then, and every instant given to careless pleasure will bring you blood then."

'Gentlemen,' concluded Robin, 'I cannot think of a more apposite statement for those of us gathered here: any time lost, or misused, will be paid for in blood.'

Other speeches followed and finally the Presiding Officer called for 'God Save the King'. Lingering to buttonhole Colonel Robin, I arranged to meet him for breakfast prior to his boarding the train for Wellington.

The dining room opened at 6.30 and we met as he reached the foot of the hotel stairs and I passed through the front door.

'Good morning, Malone.' With his carefully clipped moustache, shining clean-shaven cheeks and chin, he was as spruce and as spry as ever. 'A most pleasant evening.'

'Indeed, Sir, it was.'

We had breakfast. While I declined a plate of porridge, I agreed to join him in bacon and eggs although with me the latter was singular. I was happy to learn the Defence Bill was to be passed, and compulsory training brought in.

'The Prime Minister has given it priority. It will be enacted by the end of the year. Then it'll be all sails set.'

I remarked it had taken the Government long enough.

Colonel Robin smiled.

'You and the Prime Minister have had your differences?'

'Well-practised at trimming his sails,' I said.

'Don't be too hard on him, he can only move as fast as his members, and some take convincing. Massey and the Opposition are all for it, so there is a majority in the house, but the PM, for his own political future, can't afford a split in his party. But have no fear, it will be passed, come what may—thanks to men like you, Malone, who have never let the pot go off the boil.'

He was talking about the National Defence League. We had worked hard over the last three years. But it also needed a good man in Wellington to argue the case and we'd had that with Colonel Robin, and I said so.

He smiled again:

'It was a combined effort. We have much to do and little time to do it. It's not easy to implant a sense of urgency.'

'The quotation from Ruskin,' I said. 'It could not be more apposite.'

'Thank you.' He paused. 'Sir Ian Hamilton drew it to my attention. He's about to be made inspector general of Imperial Forces and you might meet him one day. After we have settled down, he'll probably come out to see how we're doing.'

'And what do you think he'll find? It's one thing to pass a law, a different matter to make it work.'

Another smile:

'I'm sure Sir Ian will have nothing to worry about when he comes to Taranaki. In the meantime we are likely to see Kitchener. The Government has learnt he is to visit Australia and advise there. Steps are being taken to bring him here. He should be out within a year.'

'Why wait? You know what's wanted; I know too. Another excuse for Government inaction.'

'But you and I are not Lord Kitchener, Malone. What he says will be done. In a year or two we might have the beginning of something worth calling an army.'

'And you will get your due reward.'

'That will be my reward, an army.'

'And the command of it,' I said.

Again the smile.

'Not me.' He noticed my surprise. 'It'll be an officer from Home: Sandhurst, Staff College, staff experience as well as in the field; chip off the old block who will know everybody worth knowing in the War Office and,' his smile widened, 'someone whom the locals will respect.'

'You've done all the work, you've had distinguished service in the field, you know the situation here and have worked with Imperial officers.' And a model to us all, I said to myself. His uniform, despite having been worn the day and night before, and most likely, the days before that, was immaculately pressed.

'Thank you, Major, but we're talking about integration with other Empire forces. To do that we will have to be made identical with the Home Army in every respect and commanded by men who will be known and trusted by the Imperial commanders.'

I could see the sense of it, and so, with the appointment of General Godley, it has turned out to be, although I hope Colonel Robin will replace General Godley when his term expires.

'Major Malone,' he went on, 'do you still yearn for the life of a politician?'

'I can assure you, Sir, that I have learnt my lesson.'

'Then may I offer my congratulations in advance,' said he graciously. 'There's no one as well qualified, and your promotion to command the Taranaki battalion couldn't come at a better time. Some commanders will be able to cope with the changes to come, some, I fear, will not.'

'Thank you,' I said, 'but I shall not take the position for granted. I'll do the best I can and I trust that will suffice.' I did not comment on the latter part of his remark, but I knew that too many Volunteer officers, including commanders, were there for the social life. Whether they would be dispensed with, though, was a different matter. I went on to say: 'I am cutting down on the law. It's served me well but its day has come. Soon we'll be returning to Stratford. I am, Colonel, ready for whatever service I am called to perform.'

'From what I saw last night, you've a sound base to build on.'

'Good men,' I said. 'And so will be the majority of the conscripts. Once disciplined and trained they'll be as good as any.'

'Does all of us good, a dose of discipline.' He was joking. If anybody exemplified a man whose first disciplinary concern was himself, it was Colonel Robin.

Changing the subject, I said:

'I have a feeling, Sir, that you've read more of Ruskin than what you quoted.'

'A little.' He looked at me as if from one conspirator to another. 'The fact is I play around with art myself. Could do better, but then we could all do better, couldn't we, Malone? Every so often, I take the easel out and brush away. Some of the daubs I even exhibit in our Society's annual show. The joke is that it's come from my field sketching.'

I was surprised, but who would guess I play Brahms or Schumann?

As a youth I heard Clara Schumann play whilst I was working in London. My father, who had crossed the Irish Sea to pursue a career in industrial chemistry, died when I was seven. With five children under her care, my mother did not have easy circumstances, but she managed to have me educated by the Marist Brothers, first in England and then Lille. On leaving school, I would have preferred an army career, but as there was no money for Sandhurst or Woolwich, I took up a clerical position and joined the Volunteers. My brother, Austin, however, came out here and enlisted in the Armed Constabulary. I followed, in search of a more exciting life and brighter prospects.

The latter were realised, and the former, not. The AC had become a mere field police force, not well disciplined. When not loafing around stockades and redoubts, we built roads. I cannot remember anyone over-exerting himself, but such is the nature of government employment.

In 1881 we were mustered for action. The Maori had been defeated and they knew it. But some local confiscated land had yet to be settled. Living on it, and attracting followers, was Te Whiti, a fellow who called himself a prophet. He denied the propriety of confiscation, called for passive resistance, and promised a day of reckoning for the white man. Surveyors were sent in. Their proceedings were blocked—and a general election was due.

Fifteen hundred Armed Constabulary and Volunteers were called out and issued with ammunition. The resistance we met was a children's choir and two young women obstructing our passage with a skipping rope. Their removal had a music hall character. We cleared the pa, herding six hundred women and children onto a hill. We had men who looted. The 'prophet' and his lieutenants were carted away under the eyes of our Minister of Defence, John Bryce, a vulgar man, mounted on a white horse.

The arrested men were in custody for three years and never brought to trial. Either the law had been broken, or it had not. If there was a case to answer, they should have been arrested, and a platoon would have been sufficient. I have little sympathy for people who stand in the way of a civilised society and none for transgressors of its laws, but laws cannot be respected unless those who enforce them abide by them. Still in my early twenties, I was uncomfortable with what had happened, but was not sure why. It was only recently, in a misguided attempt to enter politics, that I realised what it had all been about; why the blatant force, why the white horse, and why the abuse of the law. An election was due; the signs were the Government would lose Taranaki and with it, the election. Taranaki was held. Five years later, there was obstructive ploughing of confiscated land, and clear evidence of who did it. It was dealt with there and then, six months' imprisonment. No election in the offing.

I had landed in Taranaki by way of a surfboat at Opunake. When I tipped the boatman sixpence, he gave it back, remarking I would need it, epitomising much of what is good about the New Zealander. On taking a discharge from the Constabulary it was to the surfboats I went. Riding the rollers came pretty close to the dreams I'd had of life in the colonies. Skill, judgment, a cool head, close cooperation by all concerned, and instant, correct, obedience to the helmsman provided a living where excitement and pride combined. Some days we loafed and other days it was up before dawn and to bed well after dusk.

When Taranaki was opened up, few settlers had capital, so the Government offered land on leasehold. This was a good stopgap measure, although on the brink of socialism. But more of that later. In 1882 my brother and I each took up a parcel of land near Stratford. They were small, seventy-nine acres, barely enough to scratch a living. Opportunities for business acumen being evident, however, I also established a land agency. I know it has a reputation for being one level above horse-trading, but I believe I am known for probity; there was no objection when I also took up local government duties. In the evenings, when not at a council meeting, I read law, eventually entering a partnership in New Plymouth.

As Colonel Robin mentioned, I also ventured into politics. To his later chagrin, the Prime Minister, recently *Sir* Joseph Ward, put me up to it. He is a fellow Catholic, in that he confesses, eats fish on Fridays and goes to Mass. A tubby little fellow who hops from twig to twig like a town sparrow, he happened to perch on me when a Taranaki by-election came up. Again, the Government might lose, and this time, I might be the agent for maintaining its fortunes. I agreed, but his relief on hearing this, quickly turned to wonderment when I added that, of course, I would vote according to my conscience.

'What, what do you mean?' For once his speech faltered.

'Exactly what I said.' Somewhat breezily if I remember correctly.

'But we have our policy.'

'Exactly,' I said, 'and there's much in it I would not seriously quarrel with.'

'Oh. And the issues where you ... would exercise your conscience?'

'Freehold and conscription,' I said.

'No problem with conscription,' he said quickly. 'No problem at all. We intend to bring it in anyway. All in good time, of course, all in good time.'

'Good,' I said.

'But freehold, now that's another matter.'

'It is,' I said.

He cleared his throat.

'We have members who hold views on that, who take the view that the land belongs to all and those who occupy it hold it in trust, and that the majority of leaseholders would not be there if the Government had not provided the wherewithal in the first place.'

'Socialists,' I said.

'I wouldn't quite say that, Mr Malone, though, as a party, we have tended to be broad rather than narrow, indeed yes. Because there are those, such as yourself, if I judge you correctly, who hold that every leaseholder should possess the right to buy himself out. You would not be alone, Mr Malone, and, perhaps, in good time, you and your fellow freeholders might be able to bring your colleagues around to your point of view. Indeed you might be doing the party a service by assisting the freehold faction. Indeed, yes.'

'By voting according to my conscience,' I said.

Another throat clearing.

'If only that might be so, Mr Malone, but we cannot give aid and comfort to the Opposition, who, I will whisper on the quiet, are breathing down our necks. They would seize on it, Mr Malone, seize on it, for their own ends. They are no respecter of persons, not at all. They would pounce on you and pounce on the Government.'

'I could bear it,' I said.

'But you would be voting with them.' Shaking his head more in sorrow than anger, he added, 'In politics, Mr Malone, one sometimes has to keep one's personal views to oneself.'

'We will have to differ on that, Prime Minister,' I said.

'Would you think about it?'

'I have,' I said, 'I'll stand as an Independent.'

'Mr Malone!'

'Independent Liberal. I'll vote with you when I agree and against when I don't.'

That, I discovered later, caused mirth amongst my acquaintances. 'Independent', yes; 'Liberal', not quite. My views might have more in common with Mr Massey's Reform Party, but I could not associate with them, not with the Protestant bigots who dominate it. In my simple belief that an honest man who spoke his mind could get voted into Parliament, I stood twice: first at the by–election and then the general election. My own fault for not having learnt the lesson I witnessed in 1881. All, however, has turned out for the best. The successful candidate (Reform) not only shares my views on freehold and conscription, but also was the commander of the Taranaki Rifles and thus, following his success at the polls and believing it proper to resign, created the vacancy to which I am to be appointed.

Settler communities are raw: jerry-built townships straggling along roads deep in mud in winter and dust in summer, burnt-over stumps and logs wherever the eye might turn, women haggard at thirty, dirt and grime everywhere—you can smell a dairy farmer and his brood at a hundred yards. And the curse of drunkenness—it was no great sacrifice, ten years ago, when I swore off liquor and tobacco. To gain relief from this, I bought a piano—cheap, and in the nursery now—and I made time to play. I still do, gathering the family in the drawing-room to sing old favourites like 'Rule Britannia', 'Soldiers of the Queen', and Stephen Foster melodies, but when the family is quietly occupied elsewhere, I sit at the keyboard, put Brahms, Schumann or Chopin before me, and do the best I can.

There was the matter of the children's education. At elementary level, Mater, then our governess, taught them at home. My neighbours believed this was because there were, as yet, no Catholic schools nearby: but parish schools that have come to my notice have not impressed me. My old schoolmasters, however, have founded St Patrick's in Wellington and lately the French Sisters of the Order of the Sacred Heart, Sacré Coeur, also in Wellington. You can count the good families in Taranaki on your fingers, and most are Protestant. Of substance, they work at maintaining the manners and traditions of Home.

The children will need to exercise discretion in their choice of a spouse and not just because of the lack of Catholics of good family. My boys go amongst other lads as if indifferent to their origins. On the credit side they are fit, healthy young men, entering adulthood with more behind them than if they'd been raised at Home, and in discerning company, recognisable as young gentlemen. Moreover, my mother and sisters have been enabled to join us for a life commensurate with their standing.

I am grateful for what has been achieved, but my family has paid a price. More often than I care to remember, when I gave time to the boys, it was to be severe with them, exacting penalties for misbehaviour. Boys are natural barbarians. However energetic they may be, when it comes to cleanliness, incorrigible laziness is the rule. Years in the Volunteers have provided me with sufficient evidence of that. But I should have been with the older boys more. And even more with their mother, poor Elinor: we married with such hope. I hope I'm doing better with Mater and the two little ones; indeed I must do better.

HARRY
Upriver — 1894 – 1911

My daughter has suggested I write my memoirs. Always a kindly soul, no doubt she believes it will keep me usefully occupied in my old age and out of her mother's way. Tactfully she says mine has been an interesting life. It may have been, but I remember it as a happy one. Commitment to the Faith leads to a life where there is little time for anything else. It is only now, in my declining years, and in writing this memoir, that I have had the opportunity to delve more deeply into the events that afflicted my generation in the Great War. Some of my colleagues sincerely believe such study is at odds with Christian principles. It is a view I humbly believe to be mistaken. I know of no reason for evil to be studied only by advocates of the devil, and let us never forget, we are here telling a story of great suffering, great generosity of spirit, and great courage.

I was born in 1895 and brought up on a back-blocks farm about thirty miles inland from Wanganui. My father took it up in 1890 just after the district had been opened for settlement. As land, it was a mixed bag, good on the river flats but not greatly productive on the hills. Like his neighbours, Dad had little capital and survived because he initially took up government leasehold, and earned an income of sorts by working on the roads for six months of the year. On the farm, his time was almost entirely taken up with clearing bush. It was through this he met my mother. He was felling a tree, his foot slipped and slid under the tree trunk as it fell. His leg broken under the trunk, he lay there for two days until a neighbour, who wanted to borrow a saw, found him. He had intended to call on Dad a few days later, but something, he said, impelled him to go and see him just then. In his pain, Dad had prayed for help. He said he had felt the presence of the Lord during his ordeal. He was taken to Wanganui hospital where my mother was a nurse.

My grandfather was the minister of St Paul's, Wanganui. My mother inherited his vocation and intended to become a missionary nurse. When they met, and Dad told her of the Presence, it was two Christians coming together. Two years later, they married. By then my grandfather had moved to Wellington so my mother was very isolated. My father, however, made a commitment he never broke: no matter how little money we might have, she would visit Wellington once a year.

My earliest memory is of a two-room pit-sawn timber cottage. As time went on, another bedroom, a scullery and a bathroom were added and then, to Mum's great pleasure, a sitting room. Finally, a third bedroom was put on. In front there was always my mother's garden. The other memory is mud. Mud led from the back door to all parts of the farm and down the drive to the road. The cow yard in front of the milking shed was a sea of it, and as fences were built, so was every gateway. As a consequence the back veranda was always lined with boots. Not until my last year at home was a concrete path laid from the back door to the drive.

Burnt stumps surrounded the cottage. They were the first to be removed, a long and tedious job requiring blasting powder, timber jacks and axe work. Stumps on the river flats were the next to go and took a year or two. Those on the hills were left to rot and some are still there. In the early years, Dad worked at bringing the flats into production, the soil being better and ploughable. I left school to help clear the hills. He and I worked together, and after I left, Brian, who is still on the farm, joined him. We'd be up at 4.30, milk the cows, have breakfast, load the milk cans onto the dray for Dad to drive to the factory, and I, with an axe, whetstone and a slasher, headed for the hills. Dad joined me around mid-morning — sometimes a little later, as he liked a yarn with his neighbours at the factory. He would bring another axe, a saw, and lunch. I was always glad to see him, as I'd be ready for the fresh scones Mum had baked. Then we would get stuck into the big trees, scarfing one side for the saw and the other for the back cut.

By then Dad had become an expert at it and it was rare that we brought down only one tree at a time. We worked rain or fine, autumn, winter and early spring, so that what we had felled would have dried out considerably by late summer. In the depth of winter it was, if anything, easier. There was no point in rising too soon before the sun, and apart from the house cow, there was no milking. It was cold, but that doesn't last long when you are on the end of a crosscut saw.

The high point of those years was the burn. Neighbours in the valley joined together and burnt in a block. The first one went so well that even those who had not taken the care to fell as Dad had, finished up nearly as clean as we did. The next year it did not go so well. It had been a wet summer and on the day chosen, Dad had wanted to postpone it, as three weeks of dry weather beforehand were needed to get a clean burn. Then there was the wind. Dad liked to burn against it because there was less chance of it getting away. Most of the neighbours, however, were fearful the dry weather we had had would not last, and were willing to take a chance on the wind. For us it was the difference between a good burn and a very good one, but one of our neighbours had his burn sweep up over a ridge into uncut bush—and a year's extra work to clear up the mess.

The little township grew with the farms. First there was the school, then the dairy factory and the store. The pub followed these, alas, which, with its two storeys and large verandas upstairs and down, was the largest building in the district. Across the road, our little church came next. It was modest by comparison, but that did not worry us because it was built for the glory of God. Every part had been given, the land, the timber and the labour, many hours being put in by men whom we never saw again until their daughters' weddings or their own funerals. When it was dedicated, it was just a floor and unlined walls and roof. The pulpit was a table; there was nowhere to sit, and a concertina accompanied the hymns. In summer the sun beat down on the corrugated iron roof, and in winter it was best to be well clad. The minister rode in for afternoon service once a fortnight, and then rode on for evening service at the next settlement.

While I was not a studious boy, I enjoyed school. There were never more than eighteen or twenty there at a time, so, although our ages ranged from five years upwards we were all given individual attention, and I learned beyond my years. Soon I was making my daily Bible reading without assistance and I cannot remember the first of many readings of *Pilgrim's Progress*. There were books in the house, but except for Sundays, which were devoted to scripture, there was little time for reading. In Wellington, however, my grandfather had a copy of Sir Charles Firth's *Oliver Cromwell and the Rule of the Puritans in England*. Thus I learnt about one of the greatest Englishmen who ever trod this earth and how he came to be that. When I was thirteen I left school. It was a year earlier than I was supposed to, but I had reached its highest class. The schoolmaster said I should go on to high school; I agreed, as I had decided to be a minister, but it would have to be postponed. I have never wanted to be anything other than a minister of the Gospel, though my life has led me to other occupations. We were a strong Presbyterian family. My mother's family was Scottish and my father's, Northern Irish.

On Saturdays, after the cows had been milked, Dad was happy for me to play cricket and rugby. I was a fair batsman but rugby was more my game, as I could be useful as a halfback: being able to throw a decent pass from the back of the scrum or, when necessary, accelerate quickly and use the physique I had developed on the farm. I enjoyed the rough and tumble of the game, playing hard, and everybody being the best of friends at the end of the match. Too often, however, the after-match conviviality was marred by drink.

I was blessed with a good eye and a steady hand, which enabled me to supplement our farm meat with venison. Deer, recent arrivals, were few enough to be stalked in every respect. We had neighbours who shot stags to have antlers mounted on a wall. The more points, the better! In our family we would never kill a farm animal for pleasure and, likewise, never a wild one. When excused from milking, I would rise well before dawn and head for where the bush was untouched. Then, depending on the wind and where I had shot recently, I would select a ridge, sit until the sun came up, and watch. Sometimes I saw nothing but on other mornings one, or sometimes two, deer would browse in a glade or drink from a stream.

We had only one rifle, a single shot Martini-Henry. If I missed, no second chance—I had to be home for breakfast. Although the rifle was out-dated, it had been little used and the barrel was in first class condition. Dad and I had worked on the sights, so that if you judged the wind and the range correctly, you hit what you aimed at. When I had a choice, I would shoot the younger animals, as they were better eating and a lighter carry home. By contrast, a stag was plenty to carry—without bothering about the head.

One old man stag I remember more than any other. I would have been no more than fourteen and, having been told not to bother with anything too long in the tooth, I left him. Then I looked out for him because he was a very fine animal. There was a pool that seemed to be his favourite drinking spot and for a few months, if lucky, I would see him there and watch him lower and raise his huge antlers. A couple of weeks went by and I didn't see him until, one morning, after I had gone into the bush to retrieve an animal I had just shot, I smelt something that, alas, I was to become familiar with. The smell led to his remains. His twelve–pointed antlers had caught in the supple–jack. The more he had struggled, the more he had become entangled. I climbed the nearest tree and freed those beautiful antlers and lowered what was left of him to the ground. Then I dragged him to a hollow and kicked some earth over him and wished I had a spade. I told my parents and Mum said it was only a dead animal and I was just a boy. When I went back, someone had taken the antlers.

I came down to Wellington after the 1910 burn. My mother and Warwick, then the youngest, came with me. The only way out of the valley was by coach. It was not like what you see in a cowboy film, more like a four wheel sprung wagon with a tied down canvas hood. At the rear were folding steps, which passengers clambered up to sit facing each other on a couple of planks with a pile of mailbags, sacks and cases of stores in between. The hood extended out the front and a lucky lad was able to sit alongside the driver and another man—or two if there was a crowd. More than one visitor regretted being granted permission to sit up there. The hill at the end of the valley rose a good thousand feet in a smooth near-vertical slope. My father and his neighbours had cut the road when they first came in, and the Government had been unwilling to pay for anything more than a surface wide enough for a wagon or a coach with a passing bay in the odd furrow of a gully. As you neared the summit it seemed there was nothing between you and the river, which, at that height, had alarmingly diminished in size. Depending on his frame of mind, and assessment of the visitor beside him, the driver might launch into an account of what had happened to a recent English immigrant who, having partaken of the hospitality of the pub, misjudged the width of his wagon. 'The only thing not broken,' he would conclude, 'was a brandy bottle, half full. Amazing when you think of it.' The Englishman, who had left no record of his relatives, was the first to be buried in our little cemetery.

We caught the train at Wanganui and arrived at Wellington in the early evening where we were met by my grandfather and taken to where I would stay for nearly four years. The old couple were kindness itself; at their age it would not be the easiest to have an active, and not always quiet, fifteen-year-old in the house. We shared a commitment to the church and they were delighted to encourage my studies and church activities. They introduced me to St John's in Wellington and its remarkable minister, Rev. Dr James Gibb, a man who was to influence me greatly.

Born of humble parents in Aberdeen, Gibb became the most prominent clergyman in this country for the first twenty years of this century, having the ear of anyone from the Prime Minister downwards — not that Prime Ministers always wished to hear what he had to say. A great advocate of Bible in Schools, an inveterate enemy of gambling, drinking and vice generally, he fought tirelessly to make this country as close to the Kingdom of Heaven as it is possible to be. Although a great Empire loyalist, he preached vigorously against the opium wars in China and lambasted the local politicians for acquiescing in the French annexation of the New Hebrides. One of the few who voiced doubts about the Boer War, he tepidly supported it because the natives might have a fairer deal under British rule. Within the church it was he who united Presbyterians in New Zealand and improved the lot of their Home Missionaries. During his years at St John's, if you did not arrive early you were likely to stand in the porch or even outside, so admired was his preaching.

The youth work at St John's was equally vigorous. There were two

Young Men's Bible Classes and two Young Women's; with classrooms, a social parlour, gym, tennis court, and a swimming pool at Kelburn. I suffered none of the loneliness of a newcomer, being welcomed immediately into stimulating fellowship. We raised money for foreign missions and sent young men to the Boys' Institute; which Dr Gibb had founded to help poorer boys. Apart from night school, and an inability to withdraw from the rugby field save on Sunday, my free time was almost wholly devoted to the church and Bible Class. It was at St John's that I met my dear wife, Janet, whose loving and constant support has sustained me for so long. It was also where I met Frank Butler.

I came to Wellington to commence my studies, but I also had to support myself. In those days you came by a government job through the influence of a politician. The Reform Party, which was in power, was a farmer's party and my father supported it. He visited our local member. My needing a job coincided with the introduction of compulsory military training—which, like most citizens, I did not question—and the Defence Department was expanding. A letter was delivered stating I would be employed as a temporary junior clerk, in other words, a message boy. Although I would have swapped places with the carters who were bringing building materials and taking away spoil for the construction of Parliament Buildings, it was work suited to a young lad not used to the confines of an office.

The other messengers were older men, well past their prime, and employed to repay a minor political debt. They did not have the mobility of youth and were not averse to tarrying at pubs or stopping off to place bets in Chinese gambling dens. I never tired of the trips between Mt Cook Barracks at one end of town and Government Buildings at the other, nor the tram rides out to Fort Dorset at Seatoun. Indoor work included delivering and collecting files and distributing mail within the Barracks. The Department was a benign employer. When it became known I was studying at night school, I was not discouraged from studying if there was a lull in duties; so to gain more time, I ran from one office to another. The job took me into all levels of the Department and Government.

Before long I was working for General Godley. His arrival caused a stir in the Department, and his standing was evident when he and his wife immediately went to Government House as the governor-general's guests until Mrs Godley (she became 'Lady Godley' just before the war) found a house fit for them to live in. Godley was connected with Irish aristocrats. He called his autobiography *Memoirs of an Irish Soldier*, but he was far from most people's idea of an Irishman. English born, sent by his better-off relatives to an English public school and Sandhurst, he spent most of his life in England. Closer to seven feet than six, slim, immaculately groomed no matter what, clipped in speech, and directing his gaze down to other men, General Godley did not fade into the colonial landscape. In peacetime he was as successful as any man could be in organising a territorial force in a very short time. Although distant, he was a considerate superior. Once you had gained his confidence, whether a boy messenger, officer or divisional general, you were left to get on with your job; although I once overheard him berating a staff officer — a lesson in how to humiliate with courtesy. Once or twice I was present when the general was called to Mr Allen, the Minister of Defence. Mr Allen, who was also Deputy Prime Minister, had once been a colonel in the volunteers. General Godley never addressed him as anything other than Colonel Allen, and Allen could not call Godley by any title other than General. Mrs Godley found Mr Allen exasperating.

I met her about six months after their arrival. He was working at home and I delivered a message to their house at Oriental Terrace, overlooking the bay. Set well back from the road, it was two storeys high, flanked on one side by a three-storey tower, and it looked along the harbour to the Tararuas. I bowled up to the front door and rang the bell. A maid appeared, the first I had ever seen. I gave her the message and said I would wait on the steps for a reply, being happy to sit there and take in the view. It was late autumn with a southerly so light that the harbour glistened, a day to glory in the works of the Lord.

'Young man!'

A tall, striking woman with dark swept-up hair stepped out.

I stood up.

'Hello,' I said.

'Who are you?'

'Harry,' I said.

'Harry! Harry who?'

'Harry Patterson,' I explained.

'What are you doing *here*?'

I looked at her with curiosity. She spoke similarly to the general but in her case there was a hint of Irish in it.

'Waiting for the general,' I explained.

'Waiting for the *general*!'

'I sometimes work for him,' I said.

'Sometimes? What do you mean, sometimes?'

I did not want to over-rate my importance so I said, 'When there is nobody else, I do things for him. Like now, help out.'

'Are you a soldier?'

'No,' I shook my head. General Godley had yet to get the Territorial scheme going.

'You're not an *officer*?' The scepticism was apparent, but, for a reason my tender years could not fathom, she wanted to be sure.

'Oh no,' I laughed. 'I've thought about it, but I'd rather be a minister.'

'If you are not, what are you doing here?'

'I have brought General Godley a message from Colonel Heard and I was told to wait for a reply.'

'But you say you are not a soldier.'

'Sometimes I work for the general, sometimes for Colonel Heard, sometimes for other officers, and sometimes for the Head of Finance or the Chief Clerk.'

'You are a message boy!'

'More or less,' I said.

'Are you or aren't you?'

'Yes, I reckon you could say that.'

'Then what are you doing at my front door?'

Seeing I had already told her what I was doing there, this puzzled me.

'It's a good place to wait,' I suggested.

'Indeed it is and I wish to know what you are doing here.'

'Like I said, just waiting.' I was at last beginning to feel she didn't want me there.

'The general's very quick,' I added. 'He won't keep me waiting long.'

'He won't? I'm sure you're the last person he would wish to keep waiting.'

I laughed, but she did not.

'Why did you not use the Tradesmen's Entrance?' There was an early limit to her patience.

As I had never heard of such a facility, I was again puzzled.

'For goodness' sake, have you no idea of a Tradesmen's Entrance?'

I shook my head.

'There,' she pointed to a far corner of the house. 'Around there, is the Tradesmen's Entrance.'

'OK.' Halfway down the path to it I turned back. My conscience was clear so she did not upset me. 'Nice meeting you, Mrs Godley.'

The back door led into a large kitchen where a woman, about my mother's age, greeted me. By now, my experience led me to conclude she was a paid cook. She looked as if she enjoyed her vocation.

'Hello,' she greeted me. 'I've heard about you. Have a scone.'

You don't see them often nowadays, but it was a wedge of girdle scone made on a hot plate. About half an inch thick, it was crisply browned with melting butter and raspberry jam. With a cup of tea, and the warmth of a kitchen, it wasn't too bad a consolation for being sent to the rear.

MALONE
Stratford — 1911

The school summer holidays are drawing to a close. I shall miss Norah, Brian and Maurice, but the house will be more under control. The older children show respect to Mater, but they do it for me, not her: it's a veneer, and because the application is youthful, it's thin. For them, she is still the governess; the look on their faces when, after our wedding, I asked them to call her Mother, was close to dumb insolence. Hence Mater: the compromise. It counts for little that she was of great help and comfort to Elinor, that Elinor would have departed this earth earlier if Mater had not been with her and that it was Mater who suggested I rouse the Postmaster before daylight to telegraph St Patrick's so the boys might catch the day's train. They have no more than the barest notion that I could not have carried on if I had not known that everything at home was in the most capable hands. Mater had my respect from the first day she entered the house; a respect that became love.

Elinor: she needed me more than I knew. But where would we have been if I had not been so heavily engaged? In our early years, she was eager to chat: whom had I met, where had I been, what I intended for the morrow, and what I thought of what she had to tell me about the children. But she became less and less interested, not asking, but telling: what she needed from me for the children and for the house, no curiosity about my work, and quiet when any but relatives were present, retiring early. May the Lord forgive me, but I did not question why.

Leading up to her sixth confinement, she had become a semi-invalid.

But I never expected I would be running the streets for a priest. 'For the sake of her immortal soul!' cried Bridget, 'Mr Malone, a priest, for the sake of her immortal soul!' Not long from County Mayo, her dialect was thick and I, half-awake, had asked her to repeat. The first impulse was to rush to the bedroom, but I stifled it; if I was to be any use, it was to fetch a priest. I ran, a forty-five-year-old respectable solicitor, running the wet streets like a fugitive, after midnight, muddy, splashing into potholes, in the rain, in the morning's early hours. At the presbytery, wanting to pound the door down and exercising more restraint when the priest appeared, taking his time, it seemed, until one brought to mind it was no novelty for him to be so awakened.

The Lord be thanked, we were in time for her and the baby to be anointed and absolution recited. After seeing the priest and doctor out of the house, I paused in the hall, for how long, I'm not sure, but when I came to myself there were tears in my eyes. Mater, the midwife and Bridget were upstairs, so there was no witness to it and I could pull myself together before repairing to the bedroom. The three women were waiting, and my self-control was sorely tested to see mother and child. Bridget was about to speak but Mater touched her arm and the three left quietly. The tears came again.

I sat beside the bed until I heard the first stirring of the children. They had gone to bed expecting to meet their mother in the morning and a new sister or brother. It helped they knew Elinor had not been well. Maurice, nine, took it the hardest, worse than seven-year-old Norah whom one would have expected to have been tearful for a day or two.

After each of us had sorted matters out to the best of our abilities and the older boys had returned to school, Mater and I saw more of each other. She was still the same self-contained person—as Elinor, God bless her soul, never had been—but she took an interest in my affairs that showed she knew what I was about. And we now have a third piano, in the music room. From four to six, weekdays, it is out of bounds. Previously a music teacher, Mater has returned to her profession. The money is inconsiderable, but it is hers. It was after Maurice had gone off to school, and Norah the only child at home, that I realised my life would be empty and unfulfilled if Mater did not continue to live with us. I could see myself as an old widower, like a priest without a vocation, perhaps taking to the drink again; joining other bores propping up the bar at the Club. Moreover I am still an active man. It was one of my greatest joys to learn that such a beautiful and capable woman reciprocated my feelings.

As Elinor's boys reach manhood, Mater is inclined to recognise them as men, and they to see her as my wife. No great love lost, but they rub along. There is no sign, however, of Mater treating Norah as anything other than a girl, or Norah regarding herself as any other than Elinor's successor. The latter, Mater won't tolerate, and I have made it clear she is not expected to. The only girl amongst boys, Norah might have been indulged. Although not amenable to discipline, she responds, for the time being, to a frown or a coldness of manner. She is generous, warm-hearted, and although most determined, I am not giving serious consideration to her current announcement that she intends to take the veil. But she loves the little boys and I am trying to persuade Mater to appreciate that.

A combination of Elinor's passing, a wish to spend more time on the land and an increased concern about the military preparedness of what has become my native country, has impelled me to return to Stratford. Although I have sold my partnership in New Plymouth, I have not surrendered the law altogether; indeed I represent some of the leading businesses in Stratford, but it no longer plays such a large part in my life. While neither conveyancing nor mortgages are great stimulants of the intellect, they can bring in a steady income. Criminal law is of no interest to me whatsoever. On the occasions a miscreant has sought my advice, I have questioned him closely, and when there is hedging, as there mostly is, I have told him to go find somebody else. If there is a plain admission of guilt and clear evidence of mitigating circumstances, I have been willing to argue accordingly.

Although I also work at developing and maintaining my properties, I am spending an increasing amount of time on military matters. As I have mentioned they have always been of interest and concern to me. When war broke out in South Africa, I raised and trained the Stratford Volunteers even though I was unable to serve there myself. Our men appear to have been capable scouts on the veldt, but would they have stood a hard campaign such as the Japanese fought in Manchuria, 1904–05? I ask this because I am currently working at thoroughly absorbing Sir Ian Hamilton's *Staff Officer's Scrap Book*; a highly instructive account of his attachment to the Japanese army in their war against the Russians; indeed I have sketched maps and the scenes of battles to make myself familiar with the topography that dictated tactics. More than South Africa, the Russo-Japanese war may have lessons for us. But it is a chancy business, predicting how the next war will be fought. All we may claim with any certainty is that much of it will be unforeseen and that we should plan, and train, accordingly.

It is no secret that our Imperial general staff believes a war against Germany is more than likely — something I could not say at a public gathering like the Rifles' commemorative dinner. For this we are woefully unprepared. Our officers' reading, for example, rarely extends beyond the current edition of *Infantry Training* and other manuals, sufficient for passing promotion exams, but no more. I have plugged on alone, spreading my reading widely, studying any major conflict in the past hundred years: in particular, the late Colonel Henderson's biography of the great Stonewall Jackson; Napier's wonderful account of the Duke of Wellington's defeat of the French in Portugal and Spain; Count von Sternberg's *My Experiences of the Boer War*, which presents the Boer point of view; and, what has just come to hand, Colonel Henderson's collection of his last essays, *The Science of War*.

Henderson taught at the Staff College at Camberley. Nearly all the generals in the Imperial Army today sat at his feet, including, for a brief period, General Godley. Henderson studied the American Civil War closely, where citizen soldiers predominated at all except the highest levels. Again and again American troops fell to ambushes and surprises because officers and men lacked the discipline to rise above harsh conditions. 'So far as history can tell us,' he wrote, 'no army, however high the standard of education, has become really efficient until obedience has become an instinct. The presence in the ranks of men accustomed to think for themselves and to reason before acting, however weighty the authority which bids them act, renders the acquirement of such instinct a long process.' Not a bad summing up of those who will comprise our raw recruits.

In my opinion, the principles for the training of light infantry, practised over one hundred years ago by Sir John Moore, are best suited to cope with the unexpected. His officers were trained to assume command at any level without hesitation. When officers were lost, NCOs were expected to take over, and private soldiers to lead in the absence of NCOs. Moreover, when the common methods of attack were either in line or column, Moore's light infantry were trained to fight in any formation. Field exercises were carried out rigorously; it became second nature to concentrate behind cover, disperse after leaving it, advance by rushes, by creeping, and dividing into sub-sections, with one covering the other. In contrast to the armies of other civilised countries, Moore's men were expected, when ordered, to be capable of selecting their own targets and firing independently. All were trained to report on enemy movements. His discipline was strict, but it recognised that the training that strove for mechanical perfection was inimical to the free exercise of intelligent initiative. New Zealand has the potential for such infantry. But it won't be easy to realise it.

Myths that engender complacency about the character of the German army are current. Their training reflects several of Moore's principles, and not, as many affect to believe, those of the marionettes of Frederick the Great. Moreover, the Germans have two years of full-time compulsory military service, and, for each of those years, eighty days are spent in field exercises. Here, in New Zealand, our men will serve one week full-time a year, plus the equivalent of another fortnight served in half-day and evening parades, for seven years. Better than nothing, but no more than that, and who can guarantee the Germans will give us seven years?

HARRY
Wellington — 1913

Before Godley was brought here, there were hardly any regular soldiers worth speaking of apart from the coastal artillery. Territorials took the form of Volunteers who elected their officers. Some, like those under Malone in Taranaki, were recognisable as military units, but many were no more than social get togethers in fancy uniforms. General Godley brought an entourage of English officers and NCOs, who regularly reminded us we would never equal the British army at Home. Owing to the shortage of local regulars, I was given duties normally performed by an orderly.

In 1910, hardly anyone, from Prime Minister downwards, had any idea what the compulsory training legislation would entail and it was left to Godley to present the scheme to the public. Godley, having fought in South Africa, was not unfamiliar with colonial society. That, and jingoism, helped him greatly. A lot of people turned out to hear him, but boredom might have prevailed if it had not been for lantern slides and the interjections from the pacifist community. The interjectors, although morally courageous, had little effect on the outcome of the meetings. Only when the call-up notices went out did more citizens look at what the country had landed itself with. Godley quickly devised a routine of responses to raise a laugh and imply greater intelligence among the scheme's supporters. Moreover, the majority of the questioners were mothers seeking reassurance their sons would not be corrupted or wear wet clothes, or farmers and businessmen worried about how long the boys would be absent from work. I believe he came to enjoy what he had, at the start, regarded as a necessary but uncongenial task for a general.

The orderly initially assigned to the magic lantern couldn't work it—he was, however, a first-class groom—and I was drafted to take his place. I looked forward to it as an opportunity to travel round the country. Arrangements were made between the night school and the Department to enable me to study whilst away. After being informed of the dire consequences if I showed the slides out of order, or the gravest crime of all, upside down, I was ready. In the early part of the tour, the general would tap with his pointer when he wanted the next slide to come up, but soon I knew his routine off by heart.

An issue that arose was Sunday observance. My grandfather, a Christian patriot, suggested I discuss it with Dr Gibb. A tall, heavily built man, he had the rectangular face and broad forehead often seen amongst Scots. He spoke two varieties of English, one to the world in general, the other to his wife and fellow Aberdonians. When I first heard the dialect, I thought it might be Gaelic until a Highlander brusquely put me right. Apart from the occasional English word tossed in, for the uninitiated, it could be Hungarian or Hindustani.

'Harry, my lad, it's time we had a chat. I see glimpses of you at Bible Class and Christian Endeavour, and I hear that you coach the Institute boys in rugby football.'

'It's fun.'

'It's never been a sin to enjoy working for the Lord, Harry; the devil has no monopoly on pleasure. But you haven't come here to talk about rugby football.'

'It's about duties on Sundays…'

'Where do you work?'

'Defence.'

'The New Zealand Government is making its employees work on Sundays!'

'Well, not quite, or rather, sometimes, you see, it's like this…'

'Like what, Harry?'

'Ever since General Godley arrived, I've been put on to doing jobs for him.'

'And they've told you to attend him on Sundays?'

'Well, more or less, not often, but sometimes.'

'You had better explain, Harry.'

'It began when they asked me to go with the general when he makes an inspection or takes officers on a staff ride.'

'I'm just a humble Presbyterian minister, Harry, what's a staff ride?'

'It's when staff and command officers go out into the country to fight a battle without any soldiers.'

'Really!'

'They select ground, look at the maps they have, plan an attack or a defence, more often an attack, and then see how the plans turn out if they'd had to move troops over the ground. Sometimes, at an annual camp, they go back to where they had the staff ride and see how it works when they have real soldiers.'

'I think I follow you, but go on.'

'With staff rides, weekend and annual camps, it's not possible to return home of a Sunday. I know the general would rather be with Mrs Godley, but she doesn't travel with him all the time. Sometimes, at the annual camps, there will be a church parade on Sunday but there is just as likely to be normal training. Sometimes we travel on a Sunday.'

'How often do they expect you to do this?'

'Well, it's only just begun. It will really get going when they hold the annual camps, April and May, when the milking season is tailing off. Getting up to nine or ten a year, I guess, separate ones for Mounteds and infantry and then camps for those who couldn't make the regular ones. The general likes to inspect every camp himself.'

Dr Gibb sat back in his chair and steepled his fingers.

'Harry, the desecration of the Sabbath is taken far too lightly. We call it God's Own Country but too rarely are we willing to render unto God what is God's. The Sabbath was made for man and not man for the Sabbath so we have, before God, a great responsibility to observe the Sabbath as He would wish. It is one of the greatest gifts endowed upon man: six days thou shalt labour and on the seventh thou shalt rest. Even the heathens amongst us observe our day of rest because they know that if it were not for the Christian Sunday, life would be one unremitting drudgery for all who provide for their sustenance by work. It would be the poor who would suffer most, Harry, if the Sabbath observance were allowed to lapse. However, you did not come here to hear a sermon. I have seen enough of you to know that you never forget to remember the Sabbath and keep it holy.'

Here lies one of the reasons for my admiration for the man. For him there was no doubt about the necessity of Faith but along with it came a recognition of how it should be applied here on this earth to better the lives of all, believers or not.

'Indeed I would say that you don't have the *time* to break it, though—' and here he allowed himself a smile, 'I suspect you find it hard to walk past a football field of a Sunday afternoon.'

My response was a rueful nod. I must confess it has not been unknown, then and since, for me to linger and watch and, at that age I only barely managed to stay on the sideline.

'I have no fears for you, so we are able to look at it without taking your spiritual condition into account. A Christian may be a soldier. The great Emperor Constantine converted because Christians were his best soldiers. Onward Christian Soldiers we sing because we know that Christianity has to be defended and, on occasions, by the sword.'

And with what gusto we sang that hymn. As for Constantine and the exemplars that brought about his conversion, it was a tale told with pride.

'It has been by God's providence, and only by God's providence that the English-speaking race has fulfilled its destiny to gain supremacy on this earth. It is a supremacy that is not without its flaws, but no other people have been a force for such unparalleled good. I pray otherwise, but our Empire is day-by-day coming under challenge. It will need the help of all of us.'

We really believed in the mission of the British Empire. Those who didn't were as few as those who were unable to connect Christ's love with going to war.

'Harry, no other body of men needs godly men more than the military.

It grieves me to say so, but for a lad like you, I only can say that if you are called on a Sunday, I can see no choice: it is your duty to serve.'

If I had known then what I know now (and how often as the years progress does one repeat that phrase) I am sure I would have suspected Dr Gibb did have a nagging doubt to advise me so, not just about serving on a Sunday, but also about the Empire and Christians as soldiers.

'That's what Grandfather told me,' I said.

'Pray, seek guidance, as you have done, and do what your conscience dictates. The general seems a worthy man, though a little too English for an old Scotsman like me.'

'He's not so bad once you get to know him,' I said.

When the annual camps were under way, I combined the duties of messenger and holding horses for the general and his staff. He rode his own and, like its master, it tended to be highly-strung. I soon set about organising myself a horse. This led to a rather comic conversation. I had ridden off to deliver and receive a message and on the way back, after trying out my mount over a couple of logs, boy-like, I took him over fences before cantering up to the knoll where Godley and his officers were standing. As I dismounted, I realised I was attracting more attention than is usually accorded to a holder of such a lowly office as mine, and as a boy does, it was then I remembered that I had probably been breaking all sorts of orders and regulations as well as putting Government and private property at risk. Making the best face possible, I saluted and handed the message to an aide.

'Do you hunt, Patterson?' The question came from the tallest man in the group, the general.

'Yes, Sir.'

'With whom do you hunt?'

I was puzzled at this, and said, 'Just at home, Sir.'

'And where is home?'

'Back of Wanganui, Sir.'

'You mean there is a hunt beyond Wanganui?'

'Lots of deer there, Sir.'

'You hunt deer?'

'Yes Sir, all the farmers do it.'

'Well, well, a stag hunt in New Zealand.'

If I remember correctly, one of the officers thought an explanation might be required but before he spoke, I said:

'Good eating, Sir, especially a young spiker.'

'You hunt to eat!'

'Yes Sir, I wouldn't do it otherwise. Doesn't seem right, killing for sport.'

The officers were now standing very still.

'Really!'

I have never seen any point in denying something I believe, so I quietly and, I hope politely, said: 'Yes Sir.'

I must have been polite enough because his face changed from its usual aloof demeanour almost to a smile.

'So in New Zealand, people ride with the hounds for the table!'

'Oh no, not hounds at all, Sir,' I explained with enthusiasm. 'Just an old Martini-Henry. If you don't get him first shot, Sir, you've lost him. Where we are you really have to stalk to get a hit.'

'So you'd recommend the back of Wanganui for the keen stalker.'

'If you know what you're doing, I would, Sir.'

'But not otherwise?'

'Not really, Sir.'

'Thank you, Patterson; I'll bear that in mind. And Patterson?'

'Sir?'

'If you want to hurdle fences, seek permission first or join a hunt. Yes, Patterson, join a hunt.' He turned. 'Well, gentlemen …'

You might have noticed I saluted when handing over the message. By then, I too had been conscripted into the Territorials. Some months after I had been issued a uniform, I was ordered to wear it when accompanying the general. I was also taken aside by a sergeant instructor and given a private lesson in saluting, and other quaint customs practised by the military to lessen the possibility of the general suffering distress by civilian demeanour. My presence in his entourage caused comment; on my sleeve I wore the Red Cross flash of the Field Ambulance, giving credence to the rumour that the general was not in the best of health and was always accompanied by his medical attendant! Although I had no doubts about conscription and the military, a still small voice suggested a unit dedicated to saving lives, rather than taking them, was an appropriate place for a future minister of the Gospel.

When the general advised me to join a hunt club, I and everyone with him took it as a joke, but about three months later there was a staff ride on an extensive property at Takapau, where the owner, Mr Walter Johnston, permitted military exercises. The staff ride was a preliminary to the manoeuvres to be held at that year's annual camp. The general and Mrs Godley and his staff were invited to stay for a hunt the following day. It was when I reported to the general's aide, and asked if there were anything I was required to take back to Wellington on the next train, that I was told I would not be travelling back.

'You'll be staying for the hunt.'

'Me!'

He grinned. 'False modesty will get you nowhere, Patterson. Wait.' He went off and returned five minutes later.

'The general says youthful enthusiasm should be encouraged and Mr Johnston instructs you to call on his foreman who will find you a horse and a bed in the bunk-house.' The aide also passed on directions to the foreman's house.

I entered a sort of dispersed village where there were cottages for married men, a bunk-house for single men, shearers' quarters, a huge shearing shed, other sheds and stables, and vegetable gardens, all dominated by Johnston's house, the biggest I had yet seen.

After I knocked on the door of the cottage, a kindly soul appeared.

'A soldier boy!'

I explained why I was there.

'You can stay here.' She turned and spoke to her husband as he came to the door.

'There's a soldier boy here who's with the general. I told him he could stay here.'

A face appeared that could have belonged to one of our neighbours at home.

'Good-day.'

'I was told that Mr Johnston said you could fix me up with a bunk.'

'If the missus says you're staying here, this is where you'll be staying,' he said.

'Come in,' she said. 'Anyway I think the bunk-house is full and you don't want to go down to the shearers' quarters all by yourself at this time of year.'

When we sat down to tea, which could have been cooked by Mum, I told them about Mr Johnston saying I should be given a horse, but that I would not mind if they didn't as I was not a hunting man at all. He said he was not either, having enough of horses mustering sheep, but how was it that I was to join in with Mr Johnston and the general and their crowd? When I told them they had a laugh.

'Sounds you were too clever by half,' he said.

'You could say that.'

'Reckon you can handle it? Clearing fences and creeks with a bit of mud thrown in?'

'I'd do my best, but I wouldn't want to risk a good horse.'

'Nor would I. We'll see how it goes in the morning.'

Before breakfast he took me out to a paddock with hurdles and half a dozen horses.

'Johnston keeps a fair enough string. The best looking ones will be given to his crowd, but come over here.' We went across to where a smallish mare was grazing, rather stocky, not like the obvious hunters in the paddock. I looked her up and down and knew she was to be trusted. Now I had to show I was to be trusted, so we saddled her up and I took her for a walk, trot, canter, and a short gallop so that she was nicely warmed up before I took her over the hurdles. Or, rather, she took me. I trotted her back.

'You'll do,' I was told. 'Just let her go, and she'll see you right. She could do with a bit of a run.' We led her back to the cottage just in case anybody else might have ideas about her.

It was a crisp morning with a blue sky coming up. Hawke's Bay at its best. Along with his staff, Godley had brought his mount up from Wellington, as was always the case when there was a staff ride or a camp.

Mrs Godley was as well-mounted as her husband so I guessed hers had been railed up too. She was riding side-saddle and I wondered how she would take the jumps.

'Boy!'

I trotted across. The mare and I were given the once over.

'Shorten your leathers,' she said and turned away.

I did, because I knew that if I did not, she would notice and make me shorten them more than I was used to.

I was wearing my uniform (I didn't have anything else) and a couple of the officers were wearing theirs. As for the rest they all wore hunting outfits, though I don't remember a pink coat: most were grey, or, like the Godleys, black. Most of the riders were farmers and their families from around the district, who were better off than the farmers I knew, but I was more interested in what a hunt would be like. I enjoyed the day for its novelty. After milling around, we trotted off, following a man (he *might* have worn a pink coat, now I come to think of it) with a pack of dogs. Then we stopped and milled around again. I was getting bored when there was a yell and everybody was off, I later than the rest, because I hadn't been expecting it. Doing as I'd been told, I let the little girl go — and go she did. Each jump was careful and precise, she being more of a show jumper than a hunter, but in no time we were at the tail of the front bunch and that was good enough for each. From time to time I caught a view of Mrs Godley sailing over the jumps almost as though she were in an armchair. I was not in at the kill when some poor hare was quickly made dog tucker. I could see why people liked it, but it seemed a lot of time had been spent hanging around. I probably could have worked things to get a horse and train it but I had better things to do with my time, and, we were into 1914.

Besides, when visiting the camps, I had another diversion. Much time was spent training the infantry in the use of the rifle, it being the British Army view that accurate rifle fire was nearly as important as close order drill. To keep my eye and hand in, I would hang around the butts, and prevail upon the tolerance of the NCO in charge to let me have a go. I was a little bit cheeky doing this, as I knew they would not expect much from a Field Ambulance man. Mostly they allowed me to fire off five rounds and then, when they saw how I grouped them, gave me five more to see what I was like at adjusting my aim to hit the bull's-eye. Sometimes there would be a further five just to make sure the first ten had not been a fluke. After a time I was sent to marksmanship competitions—the general might have been involved in this—and did well enough to qualify for a crossed rifles badge, but in the hurly burly of late 1914 I was never awarded it, which I didn't mind, being unsure about wearing crossed rifles and the Red Cross together.

In late 1913 the country went through the upheaval of the waterfront strike. Its implications I was unaware of, until Dr Gibb publicly stated the Government was being intransigent. I was, however, uncomfortable with the Government stance that the army was playing a minor role only, knowing this was not so. Generally the regular soldiers disliked being in-volved, believing themselves defenders of the nation, not its policemen. Godley was on a visit to England and we soon sensed his Chief of Staff, Colonel Heard—who, like Godley, was also English—had doubts about Massey's instructions to bring the army in. And there was a small, but increasingly prominent, anti-militarist movement, one of its arguments being that the purpose of universal military training was to create a force of strikebreakers. Also, up and down the country came reports of local parades being disrupted by anti-militarists and pacifists, and declining at-tendance. Nevertheless, being on the public payroll, there was a limit to Colonel Heard's resistance to the Prime Minister's wishes.

A compromise was reached. Local military commanders were to re-cruit special constables. Although territorial officers and rank and file were in the majority, farmers and businessmen were also recruited. The railways supplied trains to transport men and horses from country districts. The farming community was especially incensed with the strike. They were the ones who would suffer if the wharves were not worked. After years of hard toil and little income, my family would come very near to bankruptcy if our butter, wool and meat were not loaded and shipped for sale on the British markets.

In Wellington the first group of specials rode in from the Wairarapa. The Government had planned to house them in the waterfront buildings, but when a riot erupted, Colonel Heard had no option but to agree to their being billeted at Mt Cook Barracks. They were undisciplined and, in an attempt to keep law and order among those who themselves were not always orderly, officers and NCOs—instructed to wear mufti—were detailed to drill them. Our future divisional general, Russell, who had come down from Hawke's Bay with a contingent of Mounteds, was put in charge of the specials.

My brother Brian was one who came down to Wellington and I was at the railway station when he arrived with others from Taranaki, Wanganui, and Manawatu. After they had detrained and saddled up, they rode up the Terrace where they had their first, and relatively light, introduction to the sticks and stones. As they rode into the Barracks the cheers of earlier arrivals greeted them loud enough to equal the cries of the crowd outside. By then there were upwards of nine hundred men and their horses in the Barracks. I spent the night with Brian, in the Garrison Hall along with four hundred others, though those who brought beer did not improve the atmosphere.

The day after, in civilian clothes and wearing no armband, I slipped out of the Barracks to perform the unusual task of visiting all gunsmiths and ironmongers to enquire about the possible purchase of a revolver. There were grave faces when I reported to Colonel Heard that all shops were sold out. I was also able to sneak Brian in and out of the Barracks to visit our grandparents. To do this it was necessary that he wear my clothes, as like other specials, he had come down in his farm clothes and thus was likely to be challenged by those with sharp eyes and keen noses. Others only went out in parties with their batons. The possibility of being victimised led some city relatives to warn them to stay away.

When the country boys rode out they were subjected to foul abuse and missiles, some of an unmentionable nature, especially when they were riding past upper storey windows. Unable to control themselves, some responded harshly. Many on each side were under the influence of liquor. After ten days, Brian tired of it. He was not alone in this. All had work to be done at home; they had left their farms to get the wharves working, not to play politics. And the city people treated them with either indifference or resentment.

Three or four days before the wharves were opened again, a large crowd gathered outside the Barracks. The Police Commissioner was there. His early days had been spent in the Royal Irish Constabulary and he thought he was back home. He ordered fire hoses to be turned on the crowd, but all that did was to make it retreat the length of a cricket pitch. Two squadrons of Mounteds charged with their batons. They and the crowd were equally inflamed, causing injury to people on each side, some merely onlookers. Shots were fired. The Mounteds returned and so did the crowd. Brian would have been in the next charge.

But Major Hume, a gunner officer, went out alone. Standing in front of the crowd, he raised a hand. Missiles were thrown, and maybe one or two hit him, but he stood firm. When he spoke, his voice was calm, measured, sounding quiet, but heard well into the crowd. To carry on, he said, will profit no one and hurt many. Nobody has been killed yet. If we do not stop we may well cause the deaths of some of us here. So far we have been lucky. Don't let us put it to the test.

A short message, his gaze directed at what he judged to be the most dominant man in front of him. There was a long pause. Then a voice said, 'Let's go,' and men turned away. Voices were raised in protest, but more were saying it was time for bed, a beer, or there was another day tomorrow. Hume stayed until the crowd had dispersed. I have seen other acts of courage since, and under terrible circumstances, but Hume's remains in my memory.

FRANK

Wellington — 1900s

My parents were born in England, like many of my generation. My mother was twenty when she landed in Wellington with her parents. They came from Falmouth, and, like many men of that town, her father was a seafarer. When my grandmother coaxed him to take a shore job, he was canny about it. Using his master mariner's ticket, he sought a position as a harbour pilot in the ports he had sailed to. Wellington was the first to respond positively. The second was Durban — and I am forever grateful that luck deprived me of becoming a South African. Sharing a propensity for conviviality, common amongst professional sailors and soldiers, he enjoyed company, including that of his grandchildren. He had a limitless fund of stories about the sea and strange ports — the latter, I guess, discretely censored, and the former, tidied up. I loved hearing these whilst sitting on the veranda, looking over the harbour with its ships, and south to Cook Strait, where there was nothing between us and the Antarctic. Remember, we were of a generation that recited John Masefield: 'I must go down to the seas again, to the lonely sea and the sky…' It was the Boyhood of Raleigh all over again.

My mother inherited much of the old man's conviviality. My father was reserved at times to the point of coldness. Looking through old photograph albums I see a tall, handsome, and apparently confident young man. More handsome, probably, than my mother was beautiful; their attraction, at the time, was that of opposites. As the years went by they lived, as the saying is, their own lives; yet they shared the same house, the same bed, the same church and the same friends—except my father shared my mother's friends. They visited her and spoke with my father as a matter of common courtesy. In a time when families tended to be large, my sister and I were the only children. Born in 1900, she was five years younger than me.

When he was very young, my father's family emigrated to Australia, but came to New Zealand during a slump in Australia in the 1880s to settle in Palmerston North. My paternal grandfather was clever with his hands. This, combined with a business sense acquired during Australian peregrinations, was sufficient for him to open a bicycle shop in Palmerston North. They were strict Calvinists, having been Congregationalists in England, but changing to Presbyterians along the way. My mother, again like many Cornish people, was brought up a Methodist. Never being concerned with theological niceties, she didn't mind becoming a Presbyterian on marrying my father. She missed the Methodist singing, saying, with a smile, that Presbyterians were well suited to funerals, but was as involved in the women's organisations at St John's as my father was in its management.

After he left school, my father, having no desire to work in his father's bicycle shop, took a job as a clerk with the Wellington Harbour Board. It was while he was there that he met my mother and it was through her that he went to work at Parliament. A frequent caller on my maternal grandparents was Mr Edward Tregear. From him my father learnt of a vacancy in Parliament. With Mr Tregear as a referee, he was appointed to it. Initially he took the job because working there would enable him to study law. Although he completed his legal studies he never went into practice. Instead he became involved with law drafting. Such work demands a particular cast of mind and my father, to a satisfactory degree, had it. He had great respect for Mr Tregear because of his position (Secretary of Labour) and because he engaged in informed conversation about my father's work and any other topic my father might raise. Moreover, when my father caught himself on a conversational hook—as he did now and then—Mr Tregear appeared not to notice it.

After surviving a skirmish or two in the Maori wars, Tregear spent several years as a surveyor in remote Maori communities. By temperament and conviction he believed it was a man's duty to care for those less fortunate than himself. His wife shared his feelings and each of them was the despair of friends as being the two softest touches in town. Tregear is a Cornish name and he was proud of his heritage. He also enjoyed the company of women and was happily married to a stately beautiful woman. (My office-holding mother of the Presbyterian Women's Missionary Union (PWMU) was not unduly fussed that he was a freethinker and his wife was a divorcee.) There was one daughter of whom he was also very fond. He missed having a son and I was a beneficiary of this. It warmed my childhood heart to walk into a room and be greeted with the same interest and respect as any adult received. The oldest book in my small library is *Fairy Tales and Folklore of New Zealand and the South Seas* inscribed by the author. Published three years before my birth, it is probably the first children's book published in New Zealand. Like much of his other writing, it reflects his curiosity about the original people of his adopted land and their fellow Polynesians elsewhere. His *Aryan Maori*, however, is more of an embarrassment than otherwise and similarly, when he tried his hand at science fiction and satirising feminism. He was, at his best, a lexicographer of Polynesian languages. One or two of his poems, such as 'Te Whetu Plains' where his English origin confronts a landscape alien to it, bear more than one reading. He also wrote much about labour law and relationships in New Zealand. He refused to accept that a colonial society is necessarily a crude society. As I grew older, he tailored our conversations to become less about events and more about their implications.

During his term as Secretary of Labour, New Zealand became a healthier and safer place to work in. Unions were officially recognised and conflict between labour and capital was expected to be resolved before a labour court, but this did not always happen with the larger unions. Tregear was critical of their propensity to confront employers with strikes. At the turn of the century, his duties necessarily involved dealing with Seddon. My relatives were surprised Tregear had a kind word to say for him. It was difficult to imagine the slightly built, ironical, quietly spoken Tregear, finding common ground with the man we knew as the fat, cunning, loudmouthed Prime Minister, associated with petty corruption and vulgarity. Now one wonders whether there was more to Seddon than his public face. Especially as after he died, his party declined and Massey's Reform party became the Government. The hard men on each side increased their following.

I left school in 1910 when I was sixteen. For the next two years, I went to university part-time and worked as a pupil teacher: serving a sort of apprenticeship, assisting teachers in the classroom. It was a good system because you learnt if you were suited for the job and had practical experience to build on if you went to Teachers' College. Towards the end of my first year at Teachers' College—where I had generous time off to attend university—all the men students were called together and told that, as we were on the public payroll, we were to volunteer as special constables to assist in the restoration of law and order disrupted by the waterfront strike. It was thought to be a lark and a welcome diversion from the demands of the College—which were not onerous. I was surprised, never thinking it would involve me.

When we reported to the Town Hall, I was uneasy. A crowd had gathered. Police ringed it off but that didn't stop the assembled populace stating what they thought of us. Once we were inside, various dignitaries addressed us on the firm measures to be taken against pernicious foreign doctrines. We were sworn in after being congratulated on our public spirit and issued with armbands and batons. Remarks were heard about taking a crack at the beggars. (The language of the respectable class in those days tended to be spotlessly clean.) Although the only uniformed men were police, Major Beere of our territorial unit, supported by its officers and NCOs, was in command. The city was divided into four sectors, and each sector had four units. I was lucky to be posted to the northern sector. We were put under a keen NCO, but 'escorted' by an aged constable. All his life he'd been arresting the drunk and the disorderly. With a hard look at the NCO, he announced that, so long as he was around, we would do what *he* told us. 'If anyone is looking for a fight, bugger off now. Do I make myself clear?' Only the NCO seemed not displeased by this instruction. We would, said the constable, leave by a side door, ignore the abuse, and carry the batons *under* our jackets. We filed out with our heads down, one of the last parties to leave, as the crowd was rushing off elsewhere.

Our stint was guarding Government Buildings. Nobody bothered us and we bothered nobody. We were out of the rain and had coal fires, day and night. When we were on duty we lounged in doorways, otherwise slept, studied for exams, encouraged the constable to reminisce, or slipped off our armbands and sneaked out for home cooking.

It was on one of these trips, as I was walking up Molesworth Street, that I ran into Mr Tregear. He said hello and that it was a sorry business.

'And what's going on over there is scandalous.' He gestured towards Parliament grounds.

I was puzzled. Several things were happening about Parliament, and the most obvious was the building of the new Parliament House, manifested by a sea of mud in winter and a dust bowl, liberally dispersed by northerlies, in summer.

'It's not so bad today,' I said. And it wasn't. There'd been enough rain to lay dust, but not enough to spill the mud beyond the site.

'Not so bad? It's outrageous! The unions went there to negotiate with the Prime Minister and were told, *by the employers,* that nothing short of compulsory arbitration would do. Massey then declared the meeting closed.'

'But, but …' I was more puzzled. Here was the man who had denounced unions not accepting arbitration. 'Surely accepting arbitration is what we all want,' I said.

'With them? You know why they talk arbitration? To smash the big unions now and the small ones later. The last thing they're interested in is social justice. It is appalling!' His eyes focused, as if seeing me for the first time. 'But, we'll talk about that,' he glanced over at Parliament, 'in happier surroundings. You're obviously on your way home. Please pass on my kindest regards to your dear mother. I trust in the midst of all this tumult that you are not neglecting your studies.' He smiled. 'Not that I've ever had a high opinion of universities.'

'The year is pretty well finished,' I said. 'It'll be exams soon.' I paused. 'Mr Tregear, I have just come from Government Buildings.'

'Yes?'

'I'm a special. They signed us on at the College. All of us.'

'I see.' His expression had changed and it was one I had not seen before. He had slipped back into the guise of the public servant who had spent years taking care not to reveal his feelings, practised in running options through his mind before making a response. 'I'm surprised so many acceded.' The pause was barely noticeable.

'We were told that all men on the public payroll had to.'

'Is that so.' His tone was even.

'You used to say,' I said, 'that strikers are no more than anarchists.'

The smile on his face was wry. 'Yes Frank, I did say that. And maybe I was more right than I knew. When faced with irresponsible authority, anarchy may be no bad thing.' He put his hand on my shoulder. 'Frank, you're all but a man now. I can't tell you what you should and should not do, but I can ask you to keep out of the way of what's happening as much as you can.'

'It's pretty quiet where we are,' I said. 'No one's interested in Government Buildings.'

The smile became a little wider. 'Having worked there for many years, I can understand why.' He held out his hand. 'Good-bye, Frank. If you would like, we might talk about this further.'

He might have controlled his feelings with me, but it was Guy Fawkes the following night and he really lit the city up. At a meeting, organised by the Federation of Labour, before an audience of women, and at the height of the tumult, he made a scathing attack on 'farmers and their sons who were outcast scum from the country brought down to bludgeon citizens into submission to the Government ... as mounted scab constables scouring the streets and cracking people's heads.' In Parliament he was called a political skunk, a provincial Chamber of Commerce condemned him for slandering the 'sons of the soil' whose taxes paid his pension, and demands were made for his removal from Justices of the Peace and the Wellington City Council. The few MPs who defended him were Labour, and did him no good at all. He claimed he'd actually said 'outcasts from the country', but only he saw the difference. My most enduring memory of that year is of that quiet, sixty-seven-year-old retired public servant, overcome by an intensity of passion generally associated with people fifty years his junior.

Slightly less than fifty years his junior was Harry. My first meeting with the Reverend Harry Penrose Patterson MC, Order of the White Eagle of Serbia (Third Class), was on the forecourt of St John's. It was in the spring of 1910, with a light southerly, the air sparkling, and with me envying sinners who had not spent the morning in church. I was waiting for my mother, who was holding an impromptu meeting with other members of the PWMU. Beside me was a Joint Leader of the Senior Bible Class — who, almost exactly six years later, was to be killed on the Somme. Not having much to talk about, we were reduced to looking over the city and kicking the gravel. The minister, James Gibb, hurried up. 'Alec,' he said to the Joint Leader, 'I would like you to meet Harry Patterson who has come to Wellington to study for the ministry.' As Gibb hurried away, I introduced myself. He looked as he always looked — straight off the farm; the trunk of a six foot four weight lifter supported on a five foot four's legs, and a garb best described as roomy.

He became a keen member of the Bible Class and, midweek, of Christian Endeavour, and was never diffident at asking questions and making comments. He was friendly to all, never varying from one person to the next, whether or not they were affable in return. Some people became uncomfortable at this; most took him at face value. An enthusiast for charitable work, he enjoyed working at the Boys' Institute with the boys from the Te Aro slums. Although his aim was to spread the Gospel — where, if so few responding saddened him, he did not show it — he also liked taking them to the nearest park to coach cricket and rugby, especially the latter. Rugby was one of the few occasions when Harry took time off to indulge — his word — himself.

Harry was a remarkable halfback. Indeed the term fits him well, being half a back and half a forward. He knew when to pass, or kick, and when not to — especially near the other side's line. As I was to learn, it was there he used his build and strength. When he came down to Wellington, nobody knew much about him except that he looked as if he could take care of himself. Maybe the club he joined would have had to displace somebody to put him in a more senior team because they tried him in my grade first.

I was tallish for my age, quite light, with fair hands and a good sprint, adequate for a wing in my grade. The two of us had a brief friendly chat in the changing shed, trotted onto the field, spread out and took off when the whistle blew. Little ball came my way. I learnt why after we had knocked it on near our goal posts. Harry fed the scrum, got the ball, bent low, slammed me to one side, and scored. Sometimes it takes a while for the penny to drop. In the second half we were close to their line and it was our put in. Again I was on the blind side, and this time, keeping a close eye on my opposite number, I was ready. Our halfback did a quick turn to the left, the ball was in my hands and I was off. A swerve to the touchline dealt with their wing and Harry was next. I grinned, did another swerve and the last thing I noticed were his eyes, pale blue and no recognition, his shoulder hitting my hip, and me on the ground winded, with a hip and shoulder tender for the best part of a week, and the ball across the touchline with the throw-in for Harry's side.

We lost and when the match was over he came up with a big smile and said what a great game it had been and that he looked forward to playing us again. 'I dare say you do,' I said. 'Oh,' he said, 'your team just had a bad day.' His face suddenly became grave. 'You're OK?' 'Just bruised,' I said. He smiled again and said he would see me tomorrow. We didn't play each other again, as Harry was immediately promoted to senior grades where he invariably became captain.

When I was eighteen, I was conscripted into the 5th (Wellington) Regiment. It took only a couple of evening parades for the novelty of soldiering to wear off and for the instructors and I to agree that my military potential was average. Until then there had been nothing more adventurous and ennobling than being a soldier or a sailor. When I was four, I was the proud possessor of a sailor suit, which had a hat with *HMS Conqueror* on it, and a collar edged with three lines, each of which, it was explained, signified Lord Nelson's three victories. When we went to primary school we had the *School Journal* put before us every day with its stories of brave soldiers and sailors of the Empire on which the sun never set. At high school there were annual essay competitions, set by the Navy League, on our great naval heroes and victories. Kipling was the poet of all this — although one of our class caused an uncomfortable silence when, after being instructed to commit a poem to memory, recited, 'For they're hangin' Danny Deever, you can hear the Dead March play... the young recruits are shakin', an' they'll want their beer today...' Then there was Sir Henry Newbolt. His lines I cannot forbear to quote at length:

> The sand of the desert is sodden red —
> Red with the wreck of the square that broke; —
> The Gatling's jammed and the Colonel dead,
> And the regiment blind with dust and smoke.
> The river of death has rimmed his banks,
> And England's far, and Honour a name,
> But the voice of a schoolboy rallies the ranks:
> 'Play up! play up! and play the game!'

When we sang 'Rule Britannia' and 'The Empire is Marching' the school hall shook.

War was the Boer War. Soon after I'd started school, the First Contingent embarked from Wellington. I was envious of the boys whose parents let them run alongside the soldiers with their slouch hats and rifles at the slope as they marched down to the wharves. At the wharf entrance, Seddon seized yet one more opportunity to exercise his not inconsiderable lungs. People were there from all over the country, totalling just about the population of Wellington. Nine more contingents went and the crowds still gathered to see them off and gathered again to see them return after their eighteen months' tour. Over six thousand men went away and seventy were killed in action.

A favourite pastime was to visit their camp in the weekends. As the contingents were nearly all country boys, their relatives turned up too, with cakes and butter and eggs. Recruits were assessed on their ability to ride and shoot. Necessarily, civilians were kept away from the butts, but riding was open to view. Two men would gallop down a slope, a rifle in one hand, clear two hurdles, gallop up the facing slope, turn, gallop down, hurdle, and up again, each all the time dressing in line with the other horseman. As for their parades, even we could see why they were called Roughriders;

but they seemed to perform well enough on the veldt—though, with twice as many dying of disease as were killed, one wonders where the real enemy was. At any rate, by the time the Boers were beaten, just about everyone believed New Zealanders didn't have much to learn when it came to fighting a war.

JIM
Before the War

The mine owners killed my dad. It was on the fourth of December 1910 and he was forty-four years old. He was extracting pillars. When you extract a pillar, you put props in the place of the solid hunk of coal that has been holding the roof up. Then you cut it out. Mostly it is safe to do this. In mines where getting the tonnage out is put first, and miners second, it is not so safe. Ironbridge at Denniston was one of those mines.

In some ways Dad was like Harry. Dad was religious and a teetotaller too. But Harry was a tougher man than Dad. And a leader. Dad was like a lot of working men I've known. Honest as the day is long, they don't expect too much. When they put their trust in people, they like them to be people like Harry.

His name was John McDonnell and he was born in Scotland. His family was cleared off the land when he was a boy. He went south looking for work and found it in Yorkshire where he went down the mines. There he became a Methodist and joined the union. When he was seventeen, he came out with his Yorkshire mates to work at Denniston. The passage was free. When he was trucked two thousand feet up to the mist, rain and the slapped-up township, he knew how free the passage had been.

A lot of the men who came out from Yorkshire were chapel and union. The first President of the union was John Lomas who preached in the chapel when the parson couldn't make it. In those days, men like Lomas and Dad were the ones who fought the battle. Because it's been a battle right from the start. Straight after they asked for recognition of the union, customary miners' holidays and employment of experienced colliers at the face, the Company cut the hewing rate. So they stopped work. Families were turned out of their houses, people went hungry, and scabs were brought in. There was no strike fund and people like Dad had to leave the plateau. He went down to Westport and met Mum at the church there. She had not been out from England long either. He found just enough work to keep himself alive. He got it from people in the church. He was six months at Westport but for once there was a sort of victory. The miners went back at the old rates and the scabs were driven off the plateau.

When Mum went up to the plateau, she would never come down again. She died of TB twenty-two years later when I was twelve. She wasn't the only one. Before she passed on she became what they used to call melancholy. Again she wasn't the only one and if she'd lived longer they would have taken her away as they did the others. A lot of people came and went, single men especially, and families who had somewhere to go. Mum never left Denniston. One ride on the incline and she knew it was a ride she would never do again. It was a cable railway for bringing the coal down from the plateau. Each truck was filled with coal and then fell by its own weight down the track that a lot of the way had a forty-five degree angle or more. Full trucks going down pulled empty trucks up. For boys it was a game to ride it and some were killed. They found one poor little bugger beside the rails with his leg cut off. When Mum and Dad first went up it was the only way to the plateau. It took years to get the Company to cut a bridle track. People like us didn't have much use for bridles so Mum would've had to use shanks's pony. And if she had gone down to the bottom there would have been no one she knew that well. Her family were in England and I can't remember either side being great writers. Neither were Dad and his people.

At the top, the incline changed over to what they called the rope road. It was like the incline, but crossed the plateau to the mines. It also ran between houses through the middle of Denniston and other townships. Kids whose legs were cut off there had a chance of being saved, as there'd be people around. You knew about the townships before you went into them, though you noticed them sooner if you were heading into the wind. The stink became thicker the closer you were. It wasn't the coal smoke, that only sharpened it up a bit. Apart from the coal, the plateau was rock, so it was hard work sinking drains, and the company wasn't wasting money on sewerage pipes. It was all out in the open, running over the edge of the plateau into the nearest creek. The houses weren't up to much either. When I was old enough to notice things, our house was a big as it would ever be. When Mum moved in and Dad's mate moved out, it was a twelve-by-twelve single men's hut with a door and a couple of windows you couldn't open. In his off time Dad added a lean-to at the back, which he lined with packing-case timber he'd seen around the mine. It became a kitchen, and washhouse for when he came home from a shift. Then he bought, or picked up, some corrugated iron. That became a lean-to added to the lean-to because the family was growing. Around the same time he divided what had been the hut into two rooms. Packing-case timber lined the walls with names like Manchester and Machinery blacked onto them.

The year of the great Maritime Strike was 1890 and the Denniston men stopped. Typhoid hit the town; food ran out, and the strike was lost. When the men at the face went back, they were made to tender contracts. Not even the best geologist in the world knows what a seam will do in this earthquake-riven country, so what a man might earn became chancy as well as low.

I was born in 1894. It was the year Parliament passed an Act that tried to be nice to both bosses and workers. It made it illegal for a boss not to recognise a registered union. It also made it illegal for a registered union not to go through all sorts of merry-go-rounds in the 'Arbitration' Court and to go out on strike. The Lord giveth and the Lord taketh away, as Mum used to say. For men like my dad, who had been through two hard battles, it was something to have a recognised union, and it seemed worth-while to give the new system a go. Some quiet years at Denniston followed but it was during this time that Tom Mann visited New Zealand and rode up the bridle track to see us. Everybody went to his meeting. I was only a kid, but I was there, along with other kids too, as well as a lot of women. He was a big handsome man with a handlebar moustache who could work a crowd. I remember hearing words like 'Union', 'One Big Union', 'Capitalists', 'Christian Socialism' and 'Marx'. I wondered what sort of marks they were, and my dad had to wise me up. It was a big thing in Dad's life for a great union leader to come all the way to Denniston. Mann said one reading of *The Communist Manifesto* was enough to make him a Marxist. It didn't stop him from being a Christian; it made him a Christian Socialist. He spoke of the London dockers' strike; the first time ever a strike of unskilled labourers had won. It was because they had made One Big Union. But it was only the first stage along the way. One Big Union was not just about getting better wages and conditions. It was about overthrowing the capitalist system.

Tom Mann was not forgotten, but the next three or four years at Denniston were on the quiet side. With their memories of 1890, Dad and other older men had become gun-shy of taking the bosses front-on if there might be another way of getting better conditions. Even though it might be bit by bit. But younger men were coming in and 1890 didn't mean much to them. One who stirred the pot was Paddy Webb from Australia, where mine owners had blacklisted him. The other was Pat Hickey.

Pat already had a local reputation. He had worked in Denniston before he tried his luck in America. He'd gone to the Klondike, and after not striking it rich, had worked in the mines in Utah. There he learnt what bosses did when there was no one to stop them. Whatever you might think of Pat—and like my dad I thought him a mean bastard, though Dad would never have put it like that—in America he put his life on the line when he became an activist in the Western Union of Mineworkers. Or had he seen the way the wind was blowing, and run away?

The Western Union of Mineworkers though, was the foundation of the Wobblies—the Industrial Workers of the World. I've always had a soft spot for the Wobblies. Like Tom Mann they were for One Big Union. The closest to this in America was the American Federation of Labour but it had become more a corporation of working men, like a business corporation. The Industrial Workers of the World (IWW) did not want that. It wanted what Tom Mann wanted. The opening lines of its Constitution are clear enough:

> The working class and the employing class have nothing in common. There can be no peace so long as hunger and want are found among millions of working people and the few, who make up the employing class, have all the good things of life...

The IWW was ahead of its time in opening membership to anyone: black, white, yellow, man or woman. The membership, not union bosses, ran it. Nobody cared if you belonged to another union, a political party, or anything else. The IWW was for everything that anybody with any power in America was against. Wobblies were beaten up, jailed and murdered. The song 'I Thought I Saw Joe Hill Last Night' was about a Wobbly who, before he was hanged, said don't mourn me, organise. And there were many more than he who fell before the power of the capitalist state. Maybe their principles and honesty doomed the Wobblies from the start. But they gave it a go.

That's what Pat claimed to come out of. The stories, and the literature he brought, set me off. We listened when he said there was no future in being nice to the bosses and their Arbitration Court. Soon the Company sacked him and he moved on. Before he left, he set up the Denniston Branch of the Socialist Party. I was only thirteen but I joined: a foundation member. It didn't take me long to get hold of *The Communist Manifesto*. It made sense then and it makes sense now. Our victories have been seldom and defeats frequent; the few still exploit the many. It will continue so long as the workers of the world fail to unite. In those early days, we believed the masses were being awakened and the Revolution not far off. Some laughed then and some laugh now, but the world will be here for a decent life when people give up being fooled.

Our first battle was compulsory military service. When the Government said all boys and young men had to register, we heard the boys at Addington Railway Workshops had formed the Passive Resisters' Union. We formed a branch and the first thing we did was to pass a motion that:

> We, the young men of Denniston liable to serve under the Conscription Act of New Zealand, decline to comply with the regulations of the Act, because we regard all war as merely a ruse of the capitalist

class to set the workers of this country and the workers of other countries at each other's throats. We recognise no enemy except the hereditary enemy of our class — the employers and exploiters of labour in this and other countries.

In Denniston I can't remember any of us being pacifists. We fought conscription because it would make a standing army. A standing army would oppress workers. Early 1912, when I was eighteen, I went across to Christchurch. I'd been down the pit four years and I'd had enough. Nineteen twelve was the year when Frederick Evans, a gold miner at Waihi, was murdered by the police, and union men and their families were run out of town. The Wobblies called for a general strike but our so-called leaders said the time wasn't ripe.

I headed for the Addington Workshops. On the way I stopped at Otira, where they were drilling the tunnel. But not for long. The pay was better than Denniston but it took only one shift to learn why. Two hundred inches of rain a year that channelled into the tunnel through rock fissures. In winter, icicles as thick as your thigh. Our huts never dried out. I crossed over to the Canterbury side and took a job in a shearing shed for the run holder, R.M. Macdonald. The pay was shit but the work didn't worry me and the gang was friendly. It was the first time I'd come face to face with a capitalist. It's one thing to hear about the rich but it's another to see them. I learnt later he was a great one for compulsory military training. With his acreage that made sense.

At Addington I stoked in the boiler house and joined the local Socialist Party. Its secretary was Fred Cooke. Fred's son, Harry, had already gone to jail for not registering. Thousands of others had not registered, including me, but Harry was arrested because of his father. A public meeting was called with nine hundred inside and twice that outside. A crowd from the university and colleges tried to get in. They broke every window. None were arrested. When Harry Cooke came out of jail a Welcome Home was held at the King's Theatre. It was packed out too, but this time the organisers had three hundred peacekeepers ready. On Show Day, the big day for farmers and their bagmen, the police marched the peace campaigners off the grounds. They had paid for a stall but who cared about that?

When Alex Cooke, another one of Fred's boys, was sent to jail, two thousand of us got together in Cathedral Square. We put a resolution calling for the repeal of the Defence Act. The majority for it was huge. The next day we caught the Lyttelton train—with extra carriages. On the way we sang, 'We'll Set Our Children Free' to 'John Brown's Body'. In Lyttelton they could hear us as we came out of the tunnel. We went to the jail. We marched around it more times than I can remember and held a meeting in front of it. Boys who had registered were playing up too. It was all in the papers. From Whangarei to Invercargill they disobeyed orders at night parades, stood in silent insolence or just didn't turn up. At Westport no one turned up at all. At the first annual Territorial camps thirty per cent were absent.

For the Christchurch City Council, it was time to give the Government a helping hand. The Passive Resisters' Union and the National Peace Council had been holding meetings in the Square. The City Council said we were obstructing traffic and our President, Reg Williams, was arrested and jailed for it. Next meeting, we hired a taxi. It drove round the square, no trouble. Also the mayor had spoken, and councillors, and a preacher. Students, farmers, and soldiers in civvies, broke up our meetings and you couldn't see a policeman for miles until only the speaker was left. Then they'd turn up and arrest him.

One day I caught a cop eyeing me. I thought they'd pick me up at the meeting but it was six o'clock in the morning of Wednesday 11th of June 1913. You remember dates like that. I was handcuffed and taken to the station and then to court where I found there were seven others from the workshops. Reg Williams was up for the third time and Tom Nuttall and Jim Worrall up for the second. Reg and Tom were not just anti-militarists; they were pacifists—the first I had met. Tom was no older than me but he was a lay-preacher and Sunday School Teacher in the Linwood Baptist Church. We said we wouldn't pay our fines. They said we were military defaulters and took us on the train to Lyttelton where a Sergeant's Guard was waiting for us, fixed bayonets and all. We hadn't known we were so important. They marched us down to the wharves and the watersiders jeered them and cheered us.

We were taken to the fort on Ripa Island in a steam launch where, in the army way, they set out to show us that we were shit. After we had refused uniforms and orders to drill, they locked us up, the CO saying his men were looking for a fight and they'd knock the stuffing out of us. Then he gave us twenty-eight days CB (Confined to Barracks). We were again ordered to wear uniforms and to clean guns and practise semaphore. We wouldn't and were sent to solitary confinement. We were on half-rations. As this was five-eighths of fuck all, we went on a hunger strike and were up before the CO again and given seven days on top of the twenty-eight. General Godley said no boy was going without food. We were, and some were sick, one seriously. At the sick parade, the doctor said they were malingering.

Halfway through all this we were joined by five more — miners from Runanga who hadn't paid their fines for not registering. They'd taken to the bush. When Paddy Webb ran for Parliament they came out to help and were picked up. He won and they lost. Jim Worrall and Reg Williams wrote a letter to Fred Cooke. Nowadays it'd never get through, but the Government was still learning. Fred Cooke was in Wellington at the Labour Unity Congress. The letter was read out to the four hundred delegates and before the hour was out, the Government had all those four hundred outside Parliament. The lads didn't muck around and before they knew it, Massey and his Minister of Defence were faced with a deputation. Webb and Semple were there and a couple of others. If it had been left to the Defence Minister, we would have been allowed to rot. But Massey, that pig-eyed Ulsterman, was fly enough to know that, just then, enough was enough. Suddenly the sick boys were looked after; we were locked up only at night and were fed full rations. They tried to make us do non-military work but it was too late — I didn't let on, but I was curious about the military side — and they were glad to get rid of us. We were lucky.

We were taken on a tour of the country to speak of our experiences. One of the places was Wellington. I stopped off there. Just in time for the riots. It began when the bosses took away the shipwrights' travelling time. They went out on strike and the watersiders came out in sympathy. The watersiders held a stopwork meeting — and were sacked. The strike committee decided not to go back until the men were reinstated. Next day there were reports in the paper on 'this offence against the amenities and decencies of social and industrial life' and advertisements for scab labour on the wharves.

The Wobblies were in it up to their necks. But not enough to unite the workers to act as one union. We learnt the hard way. There was no agreement in the union leadership. And the bosses had picked the time for the fight. The rush export season was a month or two off, and it was a quiet time for farmers. It was here I came across Pat Hickey again. By then he had become the secretary of the United Federation of Labour. Now that the chips were down we saw the man neither my dad nor I had time for. He, with the UFL president, Tom Young of the Seamen's Union, thought it could be sorted out by talking tough in public and negotiating in private.

I was an honoured guest of the left-wingers in Wellington and put up at the Albemarle Hotel. It became the headquarters of the strike commit-tee. It's still there today, and if you walk past it, you will see it is not all that large. For a young fellow like me, it was sleeping on the floor. I joined the picket on the wharf the next morning. The first and easiest I've been on. More of us than scabs, and a fine bunch they were. Businessmen it was claimed, but I remember tuppeny-hapenny-clerks, bookkeepers and the like, who'd never raised a sweat in their life. No sign of the courage of their convictions. Not when, for once, the odds slanted towards us. We stood in a U at Queen's Wharf. Anyone who wanted to get on the wharf had to walk into that U. None made it that day.

That was on the Friday. Saturday morning we heard a bunch had got through and were unloading. Police were on the gates, barricades were up, but we just went through. The *Evening Post* wanted to know why the police weren't protecting 'men who were willing to work'. On the Sunday over a thousand were on the wharves and again no work was done. A crowd of thousands came out to protest and we joined and marched to the Basin Reserve. The gates were closed but we just poured through. Harry Holland stood up. A hard honest man. He never fooled himself about the class war and cutting a deal was his last option. His plain speaking had twice put him in Australian jails and he'd see the inside of ours twice more. That day he repeated what the Australians had jailed him for. 'If they hit you with a baton, hit them with a pick handle and have a pick in it.' As he spoke, the call was going out for special constables and horses.

As usual more were on our side than the papers said. But there were more who didn't know what we were fighting for. A couple of days after the Basin Reserve meeting, HMS *Psyche* berthed. We were alongside with placards. When a sailor yelled 'Whatcha fighting for, hours or wages?' We yelled 'Neither—Workers' Solidarity, Industrial Democracy.' Hitching up his trousers, he spat over the side, 'You're on your own.'

A hard lesson. Maybe we didn't get the message because of the good news coming through. The Huntly mines had gone out, the West Coast miners wouldn't go down the pits until matters had been settled at Huntly and Wellington, and no coal was being unloaded in Auckland. Soon all watersiders in Auckland, Lyttelton, Port Chalmers and Nelson were out. We thought the big day had come and gathered at Post Office Square, opposite the Queen's Wharf gates, to hear Harry Holland again. He said the farmers would never invade Wellington. Unusual for Holland. About the only time he let optimism get the better of him.

Next morning there they were. A mob on horseback. That's how they came in, that's how they went about it, and that's how they left. We'd heard they were coming and were waiting. Their batons were like fence battens except they were of hardwood and a handier length for belting people. This lot was the first thirty. They tethered their horses at the Post Office store across the road from Pipitea Quay. Twenty of them went to Lambton Quay Police Station to be sworn in and the other ten were left behind to guard the premises. We made use of a paling fence and they were soon running to join their mates. (If we'd known then what we knew later, we'd have got rid of those horses there and then.) We heard there was a fancy swearing in at the Town Hall. This time it was 'foot specials'. I knew their kind; the same bastards who'd busted up our Christchurch meetings. There was a bunch in khaki shirts, breeches, riding-boots, and armbands. Big boys, who'd have been welcomed by the man with the little moustache twenty years later, no questions asked. Come to throw their weight around.

They met their match. A bunch of pansies against our lot. One had a go by himself. He finished up in Whitcombe & Tombs's bookshop. Guess who he was face to face with. Maybe we were evenly matched because I had a baton too, one of his mates having lost interest in it. He was big all right, rugby forward, I guess, maybe a lock, but he hadn't been swinging a pick for years like I'd had. I smashed his knee, something he hadn't expected. He'd have learned other things he didn't know if the shop manager hadn't come out with a pistol. The most useless weapon ever invented except at a yard or two—and I was. The police took him away, not too gently, and took a couple of walking wounded out too. As soon as they went, the crowd took it out on the shop and next door. Once back at the Albemarle we hung the baton up as a souvenir, and for future use.

Lambton Quay cleared, word came that the specials were at the Army Barracks. A crowd went up there but they had regulars with a Maxim machine gun at each end of the street. It was back down to Post Office Square and late in the afternoon along came fifty specials flanked by police. Abuse was hurled, but not much else, when they rode through at a trot. When they were well clear of us they turned and made a sort of charge. We scattered, some shots were fired, and not all from the crowd. They said a police horse was hit in the shoulder. One of the police was injured too, but not by a bullet, otherwise we would have heard more. In the crowd there was a bruise here and there. The specials didn't come back. We did. Downtown Wellington was ours. For the time being.

That night, specials rode in from the Wairarapa. The Wobblies took action, just as it was a Wobbly or two who set alight the wharf shed where they were making batons. Once it gets going, Australian hardwood has a glow. We lot went to the Hutt Road. Where it was narrowest, we stretched barbed wire across. We didn't have enough but did as well as could be done. Then we shinned up the hill and collected rocks and bowled them down.

The next day, armed sailors from HMS *Psyche* marched onto the wharf. There was no way to take them on. In his no bullshitting way, Holland stood up and told them to use their arms in their class interests. Specials were riding around like in a Tom Mix movie, abusing people and having a swing at them if they answered back. Shopkeepers who didn't want to serve them got hit and so did their shops. The specials were into the booze too. They'd come to town to have a party and they were having it, rough as guts. The police had no control over them. Whatever happened, if you were hauled up before a beak, it was their word against yours, and you were for it. Cockatoo Constables, they were called at first, and then Massey's Cossacks, and that has stuck. The longer they stayed the more they were hated: it wasn't just us on the wrong end of the batons.

Another Sunday, it rained hard, but five thousand headed for the Basin Reserve. This time they were ready for us. We arrived in bits and pieces; each bit and piece small enough to be sent away. Word got around to meet at the Opera House, but it couldn't take the crowd so it was 'Back to the Basin Reserve'. The Watersiders' band struck up, and down Courtenay Place and along Cambridge Terrace we went, rain in our faces and banner carriers using their muscle. But, if they wanted the Basin Reserve, they could have it; we went on to Newtown Park. We were soaked to the skin, boots squelching, but everyone stuck it out.

Tom Young had his say. He was a different man from Holland. Harry did what he did because he was a socialist. Young was too but saw it as another way of becoming a boss. As president of the UFL, he was supposed to act for the watersiders and the miners. But they were a way ahead of him. In his own Federated Seamen's Union, only Wellington and Auckland seamen were solid. So we were given bullshit, in the rain. 'If Massey continues to use specials and the army to support the bosses, and supplies any other reason to incite people, I'll incite them and lead up to fifteen thousand armed men against the authorities.' The watersiders had already rejected the motion he put for settling the dispute, but only they knew this. Young declared it passed by acclamation.

Banjo Hunter was a different kettle of fish. He'd been at Denniston a year before I left. Always a union man, he was soon on the union executive and when police murdered Fred Evans, he was one who called for a general strike. He was up in Wellington representing the Buller Miners' Central Strike Committee, and he told us how strikers had seized control of Buller and the West Coast. In Westport, the mayor had been set aside and they had the freedom of the town. Banjo gave a special invitation to the specials; they would be matched man for man up to a thousand and if this was going to be a contest about who was in control, then a contest it would be. The Government already had blood on its hands and no workers had caused bloodshed. Why should we offer no retaliation? Banjo spoke truly. There were a thousand out or ready to go out at Buller and the Coast. And they were to be the last to go back. But even as he spoke, Hickey was making plans to go south and head the miners off.

Young and Hickey carried on their two-horse act the next day. There were a lot of ships waiting to load and unload, and five hundred seamen turned out to hear them. Webb, who'd stopped Banjo's general strike call in 1912, and the blow-hard Bob Semple, on his way to Labour Party fame, also spoke. After the seamen had heard these prize four, they were all in favour of Young keeping his two jobs. Young had let them think he could handle the branches that weren't coming out. Which he couldn't. The seamen passed a motion they'd walk off if scabs worked cargo or bunkered ships. But they were walking off anyway. The next afternoon, Young went to a meeting with the employers and Prime Minister Massey. He thought he'd gone to negotiate. He offered terms worse than the wharfies had already rejected. The answer he got was arbitration or nothing.

In the evening a large crowd gathered near the Army Barracks. The ground was thick with tents, and the Barracks and the Garrison Hall were crammed. Here was proof of what we'd been fighting against down south. The crowd wasn't just workers and sympathisers, but had a sprinkling of lads and lasses from Te Aro, glad to get out of the slum and have a crack at the bastards who put them there. Not too long before, the Barracks had been a prison and a few of them, if they hadn't known the inside of it themselves, would have had dads who did. At first there was only yelling across the wire. It became riper as the sun went down and the crowd grew, maybe a couple of thousand or more. The Commissioner of Police arrived. He ordered his men to clear the road but they were met with rocks and gravel and stuff from a scrap-yard. They didn't have the numbers and their hearts weren't in it. They'd just been stopped from having a union themselves and they knew it was the specials we were after. When a couple of women told a pair of them where they could go, they just walked away.

The Commissioner turned the fire hoses on us. It was our turn to pull back. Not too far—the knockdown range wasn't that long—but long enough for the mounted specials to form up and charge. More like a mob of bolting horses. It was the sightseers who were hurt, they were not ready for it, and some went to hospital. We'd learnt a mounted man couldn't touch us under a shop veranda. The specials had no idea of working as a unit. I was lucky not to have my head bashed. I was interested in a girl at the time. I'd told her not to, but she'd come too. She was sticking to me, and when we ran for a veranda, she wasn't quick enough. She was hit and on the ground. As I hauled her up, the special had a go at me. He missed because someone fired a shot and his horse shied.

Two of ours went away with bullet wounds. Someone from a first floor window had a go at the Commissioner in his fancy uniform. He also missed, but when arrested they couldn't prove he'd fired. So they gave him the maximum for participating in a riot. The specials cleared the street, but when they returned to the Barracks, the place was packed again. It was the Army who stopped it. The O/C Artillery came out and said it was time to go home before someone was killed. That was not quite the end of it. The Royal Tiger hotel was close. It had been an army pub since the eighteen forties and the specials had taken it over. As the proprietor had liked their custom, we thought its windows good for getting rid of the rocks and brickbats we'd picked up. A policeman on a horse was in the way but he lived to tell the tale. As for the girl, when I took her home, I was blamed for her bruises.

The fifth of November was fireworks day all right. Racehorses were brought down from Trentham to be shipped to Lyttelton for the Riccarton races on Canterbury Show Day. If there'd been negotiations they'd have been let through, no trouble. Horseracing is too serious a business to be held up, strike or not, and by then the UFL executive had caved in though they hadn't told anybody yet. Instead over a thousand specials were put on the street. Mounted, flanked by foot, maybe they'd learnt you don't send in cavalry without infantry. Our people were learning too and the windows of upper floors were manned to pelt them and tell them to get back to their cows. A tram driver slammed his tram into the rear end of a horse. Two army-issue Webley revolvers came out, one covering the driver, the other the crowd, and the specials let rip on the driver and the conductor. In Featherston Street the Mounteds tried a charge. Featherston Street was lined by verandas and they didn't do so well. And by then the foot specials had thought of better things to do. It was us versus them, fair and square, the roughest free-for-all in the whole business, and the fewest arrests. The word had gone out to leave the blues alone. We did, and they didn't care too much what happened.

But the strike was as good as over. When the horseboxes came down from Trentham, and were shunted onto the wharf, the pickets stood aside, as they would have done anyway, and other cargo went in and out. No more big dust-ups with the specials—though they were still out. The girl and I were pretty keen on each other and she was seeing me even though her parents thought I was a dangerous character. They were decent working class people and at another time we probably would have got on OK, but they didn't want their daughter getting bashed up again. Whether she was seeing me because she believed I was like her mum and dad thought I was, I don't know, but I hope not. I'd told her often enough it was the cause that took me where I went and that I had no time for roughnecks, rich or poor. We'd been to a picture show and I was walking her home to Newtown. The quickest way would have been past the Army Barracks but we kept clear of it and were heading for the Basin Reserve. We were coming up to the Basin, and were under a streetlight, when we were jumped by a couple of foot specials. I yelled at her to run. She did and that was the last I saw of her. I kneed one below the belt, got hold of his baton and laid into the other. I knew what would happen if they took me. Not just a cracked head and broken ribs. If I was up before a beak, it'd come out about being an army defaulter and shipped off to Ripa Island, the hunger strike and all that. It'd be me for a stretch inside for sure. I wasn't interested in a fight. Just in getting away. But I had to be sure, so I swung the baton across the second one's head again. He dropped and I faced the other. He was still sore between the legs. 'Look after your mate,' I said. 'Look after your mate,' and backed away with the baton at the ready. He had a view of me, because I was looking straight at him, but that's what was needed at the time. The footpath was clear behind and I backed for a good dozen yards. When he bent down, I took off.

I made it back to the Albemarle, a frightened boy. I told myself I wasn't, but I was. The special on the ground might be dead. He wasn't, but I didn't know that. I'd become friendly with a couple of watersiders, and when I said what had happened, they knew what to do. The *Athenic* was sailing for London, loaded by scab labour. A couple of the crew had jumped ship. One from the black gang. I didn't like the idea of serving in a scab-loaded ship, but I was told it was either that or take my chances here. I signed on. Nothing unusual about that, they'd signed on worse than me in the stokehold. I'd become a trimmer. Not the lowest of the low, but getting near it. Shaw, Saville and Albion the company was, or as better known, Slow Starvation and Agony. I wouldn't argue with that.

NELLE
1913–15

While I waited for Father to arrive, I did not feel at all guilty. That I did not, maddened the Headmistress who, with eyes that might have reminded me of a viper — if I had ever seen a viper — claimed that the gravity of my offence compelled her to use the telephone to inform Father he was to remove me from the school *at once*. Now that I have reached what is termed 'a certain age' — a delightful expression for a condition not quite delightful — I have some sympathy for my seventeen-year-old self. For the first time I was aware of being on my own. There were people near, oh yes. The Headmistress stood over me like a prison warder and, not as discreetly as they thought, a fair portion of the school had taken up their observation points. It was a hot, windy Rangitikei day, less than a week before the end of term, with grit from the gravel drive blowing in the air.

Father drove up. A new car, I noticed, and, thank goodness, he was alone. As he swung in a U–turn and skidded to a stop, the Headmistress and I were equally covered in dust. Leaving the motor running, he jumped out, seized my suitcases and threw them onto the rear seat. With barely a pause and the briefest of greetings, he received an envelope from the Headmistress, heard what she had to say, said something, and jumped back behind the steering wheel. Ignoring the audience behind twitching curtains, I hitched my skirts up and jumped in too, fearing if I didn't hurry I might be left behind.

'Your mother is upset,' he said as he swung the car out of the drive onto the road. And that was the sum total of our conversation as we bounced along thirty miles of very dusty road. For the only time I can remember, we went past the farms without slowing to look at stock and having a word with the managers. When we turned through our front gates and stopped in front of the veranda, Mother was sitting in the front bay window. She had her back to us but I stepped down carefully, cars were high in those days and skirts were low. I entered the house, distantly aware of Father putting the car into gear and driving round to the stables.

'I'm in the drawing room!'

'Yes, Mother.'

'Nelle! We are ashamed. Deeply ashamed.'

She pointed to a chair, lower than hers.

I sat.

'I beg your pardon!'

I looked up.

She was offering a cheek.

I stood, put my pursed lips on it, and returned to the chair, the most uncomfortable in the room.

'Look at me.'

Given where she had placed the chairs, I had no option.

'You have disgraced your father. You have disgraced me…'

Past her I could see the drive curving through the garden.

'I said look at me!'

I did.

'And you have nothing to say?'

'No, Mother.'

'You have disgraced us before the school, our relatives, our friends, everybody.'

'Yes, Mother.'

'Your equanimity does not impress me.'

'No, Mother.'

Her lips sealed together and she slowly shook her head. Then:

'I really don't know. I really, really don't know.'

'No, Mother.'

'Don't say "Yes, Mother, No Mother" all the time!'

'No, Mother.'

'Don't!'

I sat there and noticed that, despite the care she took, the lines on her face were deeper.

She shook her head again and I watched the folds in her neck rise and fall.

'I don't know what to do with you. Your father, he doesn't know what to do with you.'

She looked from my shoes to my hat.

'You're filthy.'

Really, I thought.

'Why didn't you put on a dustcoat? And a scarf over your hat?'

'Father was in a hurry.'

'And now you're blaming him. I have told you again and again. Whenever we travel in the motor car, we wear dust coats.'

'Yes, Mother.'

'*Don't* start that again. Go up to your room and change. At once.'

Thankful to be released for the time being, I went to my bedroom. It was tidier than when I had left it. I ran a bath. Luxury, after school, the dust, and Mother. I made sure to be down to dinner early but at the head of the stairs I met Mrs Browne, the housekeeper. Her hug was much needed.

As was his wont, Father was silent over dinner. Mother was not, so for the most part we sat through a monologue. I shall bore neither you nor myself by repeating it save to mention that it served the purpose of exhausting her for the remainder of the evening and allowing me to retire early. Breakfast was pleasant. Mrs Browne and I chatted as we had done since I am capable of remembering and when Mother appeared, the morning was well advanced. The afternoon was spent in the sitting room, where I was presented with embroidery designed to occupy many hours. From time to time, Mother broke the tedium by sending me to the piano and correcting my playing.

If we had been Roman Catholics they would have locked me up in a nunnery. For the first month when Mother made her afternoon calls, she went alone. When she and Father accepted a dinner invitation I dined with Mrs Browne. Neither did dinner guests cross our threshold, and yearn as I did, no prince, handsome or otherwise, came to rescue me. Once the month was up, I was permitted to accompany Mother to afternoon teas with matrons no longer in the first bloom of youth. Nothing was said about *why* it was a month—if they only knew, the 'situation' discovered by the Headmistress owed considerably more to imagination than observation. Dinner guests appeared again—no man younger than Father, one of whom—according to Mother an epitome of respectability—I avoided being alone with. Boredom was not alleviated by infrequent musical evenings that included members of the younger generation who were no threat to anybody's reputation.

I don't know what I would have done if it had continued like this—gone quietly mad I suppose—but then it was announced we would be off to England. Mother was born there and had met Father as he was completing his medical training and about to return home. Her parents had died but as it was some years since her last visit, she was eager to have a holiday from 'the colony', and visit a sister, whom, we understood, had married well but was now a widow. Father went because he wished to gain an FRCS. As for me, I would be sent to a finishing school and out of circulation for a year. Three birds killed with one stone.

We were to sail in early November and during October, Father was busy finding a locum and making arrangements with the farm managers, etc. He was quite exhausted when we went down to Wellington to spend a night or two before embarking on the *Athenic*. Wellington, however, was in the grip of a wharf strike and we had to wait for a month. Mother was sure it was directed at her personally. It may have been exciting for others but not for me. Twice we saw farmers galloping and rioters running, but that was all. Father, although he went on about 'the country being held to ransom' and complaining about hotel bills, enjoyed the excitement actually, patching up the injured and helping General Russell bring the anarchists to heel.

At last the *Athenic* steamed out of Wellington heads, but relief was briskly dispelled. For a fortnight, we ducked and dived in a convincing imitation of a corkscrew. There was very little promenading on the promenade deck and the chief topic of conversation, when there was conversation, was about how marvellous it would be when the Panama Canal opened. I was a good sailor. Mother was not and I sat with her in the cabin. When I escaped, it was to risk life and limb along pitching passageways and swaying stairs. Once on deck and well wrapped up, I would hang onto the rail and behold nature at her wildest. After rounding the Horn, Mother was fit for a deck chair. Our neighbours and visitors were limited to a selection of fifty First Class passengers; Second and Third were definitely *out*. From our deck one looked down on them. No sooner would I position myself to cast an eye in one direction or the other, than Mother would appear and that would be that. With the vessel proceeding on an even keel, dances were held. I could never make up my mind whether they were too frequent or not frequent enough. I would sit at a table with Mother — Father repaired to the smoking room — and one of the few unattached First Class males, guaranteed not to set one's heart aflutter, would approach. Only after he had braved an encounter with Mother might he be permitted to issue an invitation, which, demurely, I would accept. The last week dragged dreadfully.

On our arrival we went with Mother to her sister in Norfolk. Father managed to plead business in London after the first weekend but I had a fortnight of it during which my aunt received an education on the severe demands living in New Zealand had made upon her sister. It was a relief when I was taken to a school near an old abbey in Hampshire: redbrick classical, formerly the home of an industrialist from Birmingham or some-where. But on a clear day one might see Southampton Water.

Apart from carefully supervised dances, the school was organised to keep chaps out and us in. It was weeks before the other inmates would talk with me. Coming from a family with relatively modest means and speak-ing 'colonial' — though at home occasionally I was accused of an 'English' accent — I was lonely. Matters improved when it was learned I was neither an 'awful' Australian nor a 'dreadful' American. We brushed up on our French, learnt some German — the latter quietly removed at the end of the year — and did a little painting and embroidery. How to keep a house, 'entertain', and please a husband capable of keeping you in a manner to which you were expected to be accustomed, figured large: save for the particular pastime with the said husband which no one dreamt of educating us about.

When war was declared the call was 'business as usual'—not difficult for the school to comply with. As the German dwindled away, increased instruction in first aid and home nursing took its place. A young doctor, whom, we agreed, was rather fetching, taught us first aid. When he demonstrated how to dress a wound, splint a limb or resuscitate the comatose, the poor man seemed bewildered by our rapt attention and willingness to volunteer as his patient. Home nursing, expounded by a well-seasoned battleaxe who made no bones about waterproof sheets, bathing the immobile and the less savoury aspects of caring for the bedridden, was less attractive.

Our return voyage was to have been mid-1915 but by then ships were needed for sterner stuff. Father joined the Medical Corps—in which he was a reserve officer—and Mother did her bit by renting a small flat in Marylebone she expected me to share. I had other ideas; but more of that later. Soon after I joined her we had Lady Bell and one of her daughters, Vi, for tea. She was the wife of Sir Francis Bell, Attorney-General, whose duties kept him in New Zealand. Although Sir Francis and Father met from time-to-time, Lady Bell had not been a frequent visitor at our house, nor we at hers. Not that one might have guessed at our meeting her again, as we learned from Lady Bell that although she found the English quite de-lightful, she had begun to yearn for old friends from New Zealand—and so on. Notwithstanding that, however, she had been moved by English hospitality to colonials during wartime; it had been such a pleasure to visit their homes.

'To call them stately is barely doing them justice.'

'I'm sure,' said Mother who hadn't gone anywhere much.

'And not all of them are ancient. For example there is Avon Tyrell, Lord and Lady Manners' residence, built only recently and in its own way quite remarkable.' She smiled at Vi.

'A "calendar house",' stated Vi.

Mother and I were duly puzzled.

'Three hundred and sixty-five windows, fifty-two rooms, twelve chimneys, seven outer-doors … It's quite hilarious actually.'

'You make it sound like an overcooked gingerbread house,' said Lady Bell. 'Really, although it is large, it is quite charming.'

'How remarkable,' said Mother.

'In his younger days,' said Lady Bell, 'Lord Manners was a prominent amateur jockey, and in eighteen eighty-two, he trained and rode the winner of the Grand National steeplechase. It was his winnings that built Avon Tyrell.'

'How interesting,' said Mother.

'Isn't it! Well you'll be glad to know that Vi and I have been invited down and we wondered if you might care to accompany us, and Nelle too.'

'We'd be most happy,' said Mother. 'Thank you.'

'Ten fifteen, the Bournemouth train; a return ticket to Christchurch. A car will pick us up and we should be back in London no later than eight.'

'We look forward to it,' said Mother.

'And how is Colonel Travis?' enquired Lady Bell.

'He is well, thank you, but we see so little of him.'

'The war?' asked Lady Bell who knew perfectly well it could be nothing else.

'One would think he is the only army surgeon in London.'

'Does he have many New Zealand patients?'

'More than one might expect. And, I gather, they are to be found in hospitals throughout the Home Counties.'

'You have heard that two hospitals for New Zealanders are to be opened up?'

'So they say,' said Mother. 'I haven't been told the details.'

'Because of our poor boys coming from Gallipoli, the New Zealand War Contingent Association has extended its work from simply providing comforts to establishing a hospital of its own. The army is establishing another.'

Lady Bell paused. Although she must have been in her sixtieth year and a mother of eight, she, with her broad brow and high cheekbones emphasised by her upswept hair, was a most handsome woman who carried with her an air of calmness and serenity, enhanced over the years by having a husband who was more often seen in Parliament and the law courts than at home, and who, although upright and generous, was not known for *his* serenity.

'Lord Plunket,' she continued, 'whom I'm sure you were acquainted with when he was our Governor, is its chair, and a committee with New Zealand affiliations ably assists him. They are taking over Mount Felix, a rather grand country house at Walton-on-Thames.'

'If what they are doing allows my husband more time at home, I will be most grateful,' said Mother.

'I'm sure you will,' said Lady Bell. 'But what has been so heartening for colonial boys has been the willingness of people with country seats to open up their homes for them. Some for a few days' leave in rural peace and others for convalescents.'

'Most generous of them,' murmured Mother.

'And among the most generous are Lord and Lady Manners.'

'Oh?'

'You shall see for yourself. They are in the early stages as yet but already they have a group of young men who will be so glad to meet and chat with Nelle and your good self.'

'Oh.'

'Avon Tyrell is but a few miles from Brockenhurst and when Lord and Lady Manners heard about the hospital to be opened there, they offered Avon Tyrell as a convalescent home for New Zealand officers.'

'I see.' Mother cleared her throat.

'It's so sad,' said Vi, 'when you see what awful wounds some of them have had.'

'Yes,' said Mother, 'I am sure.'

I enjoyed the trip down. Despite the parental presence, Vi and I were able to chat and share our experiences from the voyage over and in England so far. We alighted at Christchurch, just out of Bournemouth, a railway station with which I was to become familiar, from where we were conveyed in a very large car to Avon Tyrell. Although the house had all the attributes listed by Vi, it was not unattractive, being designed in the Arts and Crafts style. On the way I learnt that the Manners family had lost a son in France in the first months of the war.

After meeting and lunching with the family, one of the daughters, Lady Diana, whose mere presence was enough to turn every head in a room (or in this case, the garden, where a dozen or so soldiers were lounging in cane chairs), guided us out to them.

'I hope you don't mind,' said Lady Diana, 'but I mentioned your names to the soldiers. They don't have many New Zealand visitors and they like to know who they are in case they might know them. One, Lieutenant Branscombe, mentioned he had met you, and if you didn't mind, he would like to talk with you.'

'Who?' said Mother.

'Lieutenant Hugh Branscombe,' said Lady Diana. And then she added. 'He's blind now.'

'Is he … Well *I* shall see him. Nelle … '

For once I spoke up. 'I shall see him too.'

Not wishing for a scene there and then, Mother said nothing.

Lady Diana gave us a brief glance, called a servant to fetch two chairs, and led the way.

I hadn't thought a great deal of Hugh since the night of the ball jointly held by his school and mine. Actually my feeling for him hadn't been all that intense even on the night. He was handsome, and undoubtedly I found him attractive, but otherwise I was motivated as much by curiosity as anything else. What feelings I might have had for him were dissipated in the weeks after being sent home. As I remember, *his* school did not expel *him*.

He was sitting, as the blind so often do, as if he were gazing into the distance—which, I suppose, in a way he was. The glasses he was wearing were round and very dark. He was still handsome and still, apart from the glasses, had the look and build of the captain of his school First XV and a promising steeplechase rider—which must have given him something to talk about with Lord Manners. Next to him was another lieutenant whose crutches rested against the arm of his chair. His companion noticed us approaching and said something and Hugh moved his head a little but not to focus on us. When he heard our footsteps he rose from his chair. Even Mother thawed a little.

'Lieutenant Branscombe,' she said.

'Good afternoon,' I said. I was about to extend my hand then wondered what was the point if he couldn't see us, but then he extended his hand so Mother reached out and shook it. As he still held it out, I went up to him and held it between mine. I drew him a little closer and he took a step forward. I didn't care what Mother thought because although we were close to each other, his dark glasses still looked past me.

'Lieutenant Branscombe,' I said, 'I hope you are well. I hope you are very well.' I felt a catch in my voice as I said it.

'I am, Miss Travis,' he said, 'I am very well.'

I held his hand until the servant approached with the chairs. It wasn't love I felt; it wasn't that at all. It was remembering the happy confident young man who had believed he had the entire world before him. Tears were coming and I brought up my handkerchief and turned away but then I thought he wouldn't know and who cared what anyone else might think.

'You must miss your home, Lieutenant Branscombe,' said Mother.

He made half a smile. 'I must say I do, Mrs Travis, and that is why it is very kind of you to visit. People from our part of the world are rather rare around here. Thank you for coming down. And thank you too, Miss Travis.' His gaze into the distance did not shift.

When I had recovered myself I joined in the chat about everything except the war and his wounds. Mother and I raked our memories to bring up names of common acquaintances and we even worked hard at remembering what Father had reported about news from New Zealand and how prices were on the rise for meat and wool — he came off a sheep farm in Hawke's Bay. Not really our topic but we did our best. His companion joined in and it helped that although we had not met before, he also knew people we knew. So the afternoon passed. The good news was that Hugh would be boarding one of our hospital ships for the voyage home within a fortnight. In later years he was to marry and do a remarkable job managing his farm.

GALLIPOLI

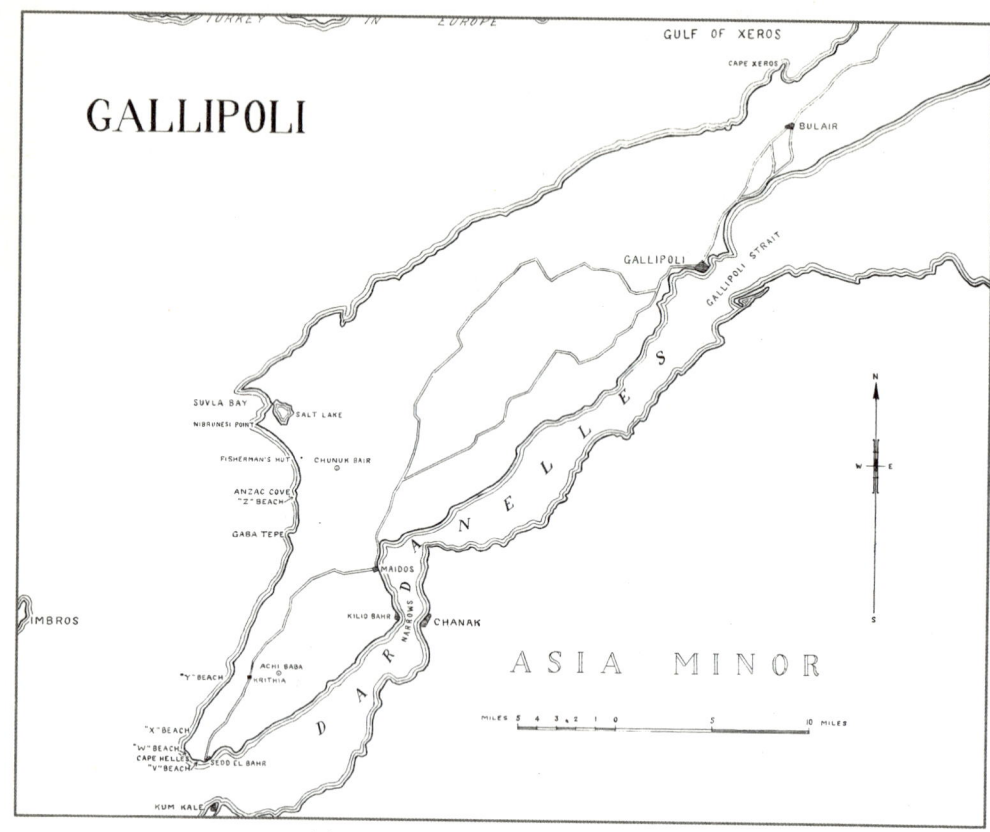

The Gallipoli Peninsula. *Source: Byrne, A.E.*

MALONE
Lemnos

It is night and there is the unnatural quietness of a ship at anchor. We shall make our landing in a couple of days. The Australians will go in first to clear the lower ridges of the Sari Bair range and we shall sweep across the five miles of the Maidos plain to the Dardanelles and cut the Peninsula in two. The Turks at the south end will be at the mercy of the British and French, and the Narrows will be opened to the Navy. The enemy's aeroplanes have been overhead so he should have a fair notion of what he will have to deal with. Our own aerial photographs show he has been entrenching and building emplacements. It is doubtful they will stand up to the massive naval bombardment to be showered upon them. There is no doubt the landing will be a success. It may well be easy. All of us, from general to private, are impatient to proceed.

The general has told us that the New Zealand Brigade is equal to any other in the British Army. He is not alone in saying there is no better battalion in the brigade than that of the Wellington Infantry Regiment.

We are called the Wellington Infantry Regiment even though we are but a single battalion. Each company has been drawn from one of the territorial battalions in the Wellington Military District. Taranaki Company, for example, is from my own Taranaki Battalion. The other companies are thus named Ruahine, Wellington West Coast, and Hawke's Bay. Wellington City does not have a company as most of its men went away with the Samoa Force although one or two of them managed to join us.

When Serbia rejected Austria's ultimatum after the assassination and

Russia mobilised, it was inconceivable to me that Germany would not seize the opportunities it appeared to have been offered. I at once set about organising my affairs for when war would come. My offer of service to Defence HQ was drawn up and telegraphed on the morning of Britain's declaration of war. To my joy the appointment to command the Wellington Regiment was received the day after. Recruiting offices were immediately opened in the Drill Halls. We had more than enough and took only the keenest and the fittest.

In the interim, between receiving my appointment and going into camp, I waited on the mayor of New Plymouth in the expectation of receiving his assurance that he would seek to persuade other mayors of the province to raise funds together for the purchase of comforts for the men. It was as though I was asking for additional luxuries for a Cook's Tour. The editor of the *Taranaki News* was more positive but most people believed that those who volunteered for a life of hardship, rigour and possibly to sacrifice their lives for king and country, were about to undertake no more than an adventurous jaunt.

All ranks were to assemble in Palmerston North at the Awapuni Racecourse. A special train was laid on. There were few dry eyes among the

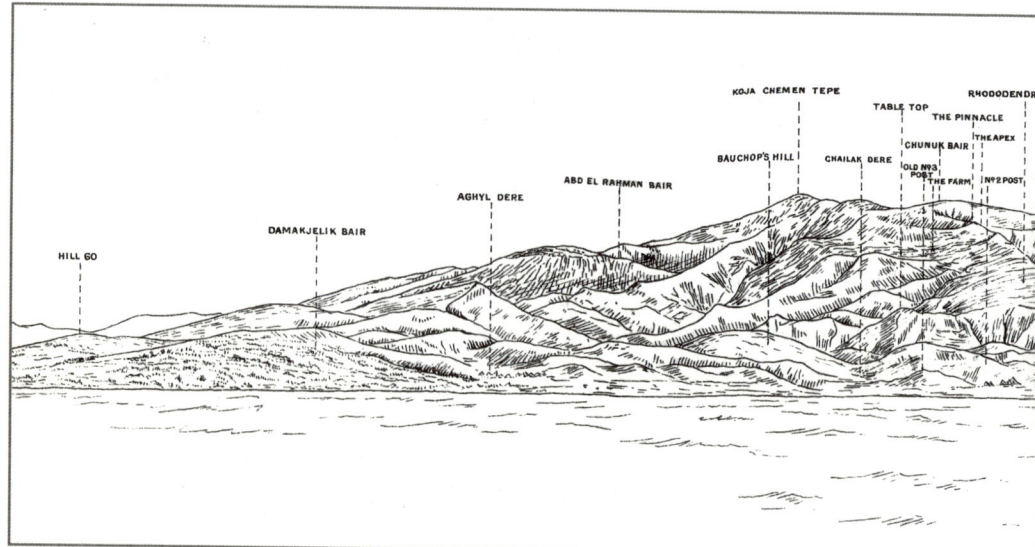

mothers, wives and sisters, and fathers blew their noses vigorously. The three of us, Edward, Terry and I, took our farewells at home. I'm glad we did. The little ones would have been overwhelmed at the railway station and our feelings would have been exposed to the eyes of many. It was especially hard saying goodbye to Mater and the little ones, who sensed, but did not understand, that this was a parting different from any other. I was to return twice, before going down to Wellington, but they were fleeting visits. The parting on that day would change us forever. Nonetheless I felt more alive than I had since I first came ashore at Opunake.

War is a serious business, but few of the young men knew it when they rushed to join the colours. It was my task to disabuse them that they were about to enjoy a great adventure. From the start it was made clear that any officer or man who did not meet my standards would be removed. Some were, and it made no difference whether they were officers or rank and file. Apart from the manuals they had studied for promotion and their parade ground work, the officers were tyros who did not know their ignorance. Hart, my second-in-command, who had served in South Africa, was one of the exceptions. A goodly proportion of other ranks had territorial training, but of these, the most experienced had no more than six or seven

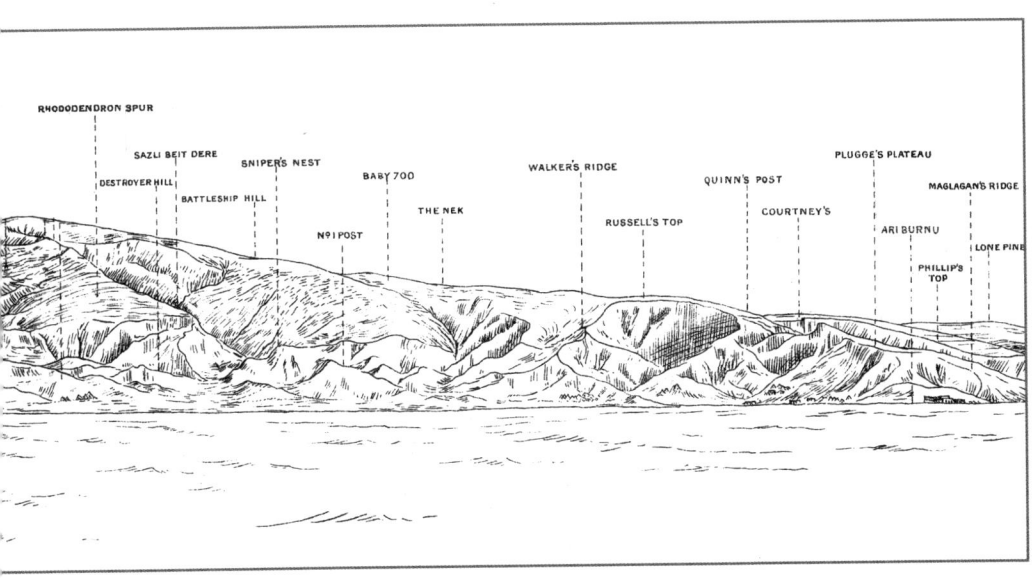

Panorama from Anzac Cove to Chunuk Bair. *Source: Byrne, A.E.*

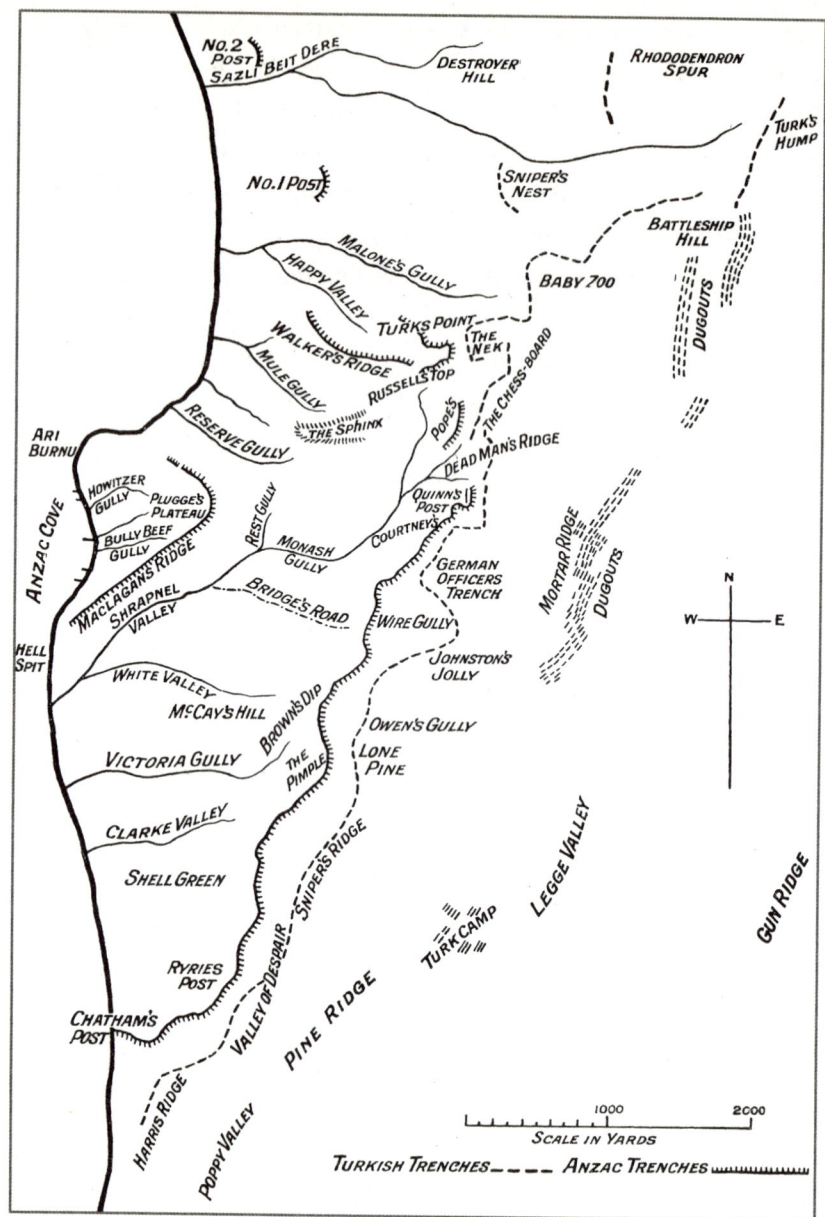

Anzac Area. *Source: Waite, F.*

weeks at parades or in camp. Some recruits came with no training at all and it points to the general standard that they did not stand out.

An ill-disciplined, untrained army is a band of cutthroats. In attack it is but a charging mob; in defence it is ready to run. It knows nothing of manoeuvre. From the moment we entered camp, I was determined that we would begin at the beginning. During the first week I inspected each man, closely. Every day began with a half hour's physical exercises in which I participated myself. For the rest of the day it was drill, varied by a little musketry and route marches up to twenty miles a day. Nothing equals a route march to toughen a man up. Contrary to what you may have heard, the New Zealander is no more a 'natural' soldier than a Chinaman.

New Zealanders tend to be careless about dress. From the first, it was made clear that those who were incorrectly dressed were punished and their sergeants and platoon commanders admonished. If there were too many in a company who were not up to standard, the company commander was also admonished. I also regularly inspected the men's rifles and always after they had fired them on the rifle range.

There was too much toleration of slackness if an officer was thought to be a good fellow. My first experience of this was when Hart reported the adjutant was no good. Colonel Johnston, our brigade commander, after hearing me out, said he did not like the idea of shifting him. The next day I had the officer before me and tested him. On seeing Colonel Johnston again I said he would be receiving my written report on the officer, requesting his removal. A battalion can't function efficiently without an efficient adjutant. I was allowed to have my former Taranaki adjutant although he too had to be brought up to scratch; indeed he has survived only by the skin of his teeth.

Early on I had to call an officers' parade and have a go at them for not ensuring that the men had facilities to wash their clothes. On the voyage we used to see the *Ibuki* regularly decked from stem to stern with the washing of its crew. Remarks were passed about a floating Chinese laundry. I suspect the Russian Navy in 1905 might too have shared the Chinese laundry sentiment as their fleet complacently steamed to its destruction by Togo's guns at Tsushima. (I admire the thoroughness of the

Japs. Just before we sailed I noticed a party of them going into Whitcombe & Tombs, buying maps. We'll be at war with them in twenty years or so. They will be a formidable enemy.) Arabs aside, Europeans are amongst the dirtiest races in the world.

Shocking evidence of this was presented when we embarked aboard the *Arawa* in Wellington last year. If anybody had bothered to inspect her or the other vessels, there was no sign of it. I could not understand how those who had boarded before us had done nothing about it and berated myself for not having travelled down a day earlier. On putting in a requisition for sand-soap, deck scrapers, tea towels, scrubbing brushes and other essential items, I was told the Government had not supplied them and I would have to spend our regimental funds. I have great respect for General Godley but his staff is known for their nonchalance and superior airs. (How different it was when we boarded the *Itonus* at Alexandria a fortnight ago. There we dealt with naval transport officials. Our requests were listened to, a plain question or two was asked and our needs granted.)

Our departure was delayed owing to recent reports of German naval activity in the Pacific. Three weeks passed before more escorts were supplied. During the interim the hills of Wellington were used for manoeuvres. They revealed a lack of cohesion that demonstrated we were not ready for more advanced training. Our deficiencies were so evident that I had to have a go at my Company Commanders. I decided there would be no more fancy stuff until we had the basics right.

Edmund and Terry were also on the voyage. Being Mounteds they were on a different vessel. We are lucky they are in Colonel Meldrum's regiment. He trains his men thoroughly and tolerates neither slackness nor behaviour unbecoming a soldier. The latter brought him into conflict with the Imperial authorities in Egypt when one of his men severely beat a native. Meldrum imposed an appropriate sentence but then found it had been commuted. It was clear it was because the victim was not white. A lesser man would have left it at that, but Meldrum protested vigorously.

We were six weeks at sea. The master of the vessel and I made sure we had a clean ship. Hundreds of men were crammed into the holds. The weather was mostly warm and when there were heavy seas, they were no place for weak stomachs. I insisted they were kept clean. We worked on the horse accommodation too. With the help of some carpenters amongst the men we hacked out vents in the horseboxes so that each could be flushed out frequently so the effluent would no longer be walked into the holds.

Heavy seas did not bother me. Across the Great Australian Bight we rose, fell and rolled with majestic regularity, the great billows reminding me of the countryside to the south of Lille where I was sent as a boy to be educated by the Marist Brothers. In the middle of my first year, the Franco-Prussian war broke out. We were never at risk in Lille, even though we did not know it at the time. Echoing with bugle calls and marching men, Lille was an exciting city for an eleven-year-old, but it was more than that. I saw the raw recruits march out for the glory of France. Across the rolling slopes of the Somme, they attacked the Prussians, each with two years' service under his belt. There was no glory in the ghastly mob that returned.

The confined space aboard the ship did not stop us from training. Half hour physical training sessions for all ranks continued followed by six hours of parades. In the evenings classes were held for officers and NCOs. Many were devoted to tactical matters, but we also looked at past conflicts. I conducted many of the latter myself, drawing on my studies of the American Civil War, the South African War and the Russo-Japanese war. Some questioned the relevance of such work. They failed to see that the principles of war change little in substance and that there is much to be learnt from studying how those principles were applied in widely different circumstances. Very few officers have a real knowledge of military principles, without which the science of war is a mystery.

The desert was an ideal place for training. Plenty of room, the heat takes off the fat, marching through sand strengthens the legs and tightens the knees. Each morning there was a four-mile march to our training ground where there'd be drill, musketry, the manoeuvring Colonel Johnston wanted, and then the four-mile march home. Route marches were resumed; the sand and the heat enhancing the men's endurance. Stonewall Jackson's men were known as 'foot cavalry' and so will mine be.

On medical grounds I was told not to march the men out in dust storms. If I had had support from above, I would have marched them. It would have been intolerable but war is intolerable.

On our arrival in Egypt I was disappointed that we were to follow British Army garrison practice of ceasing training at two p.m. and allowing the men to do what they liked until ten at night—going into Cairo if they wished. If I had had my way we would have been up at daylight and everyone kept busy until 4.30 in the afternoon and only men of good character permitted into Cairo. Nobody could stop me, however, from adding two hours of extra training for the battalion. It did not make me popular, but it made a good battalion.

It is here I must mention Colonel Johnston. At heart he is not a bad chap. He comes from a respected Catholic family. His father is a well-known politician and his uncle, who owns the Takapau station in Hawke's Bay, made it readily available for army manoeuvres. Colonel Johnston was sent Home to be schooled and from there to Sandhurst after which he joined the North Staffordshire regiment. Much of his service was in India. He owes his current appointment to visiting his parents when General Godley was looking for a regular officer of sufficient seniority to command the Wellington Military District. Although I was acquainted with his father and uncle, Johnston and I first met at Awapuni. His most notable features are his protruding eyes and florid complexion. He is tall and, for a man in his early forties, stout. He is popular in the Mess; but I don't think he seeks popularity for its own sake, however he is not keen to take action when he should, as I also discovered about my adjutant. Until recently he has been generous in letting me command my battalion as I thought fit. On the infrequent occasions I had a little time on my hands, I had no hesitation in seeking out his company.

On the first day of battalion training, during one of our musketry periods, when the men were split up into sections under their NCOs, I was visited by our Corps Commander, Lieutenant General Birdwood, and Major General Godley. Each had a yarn with me, asked what I was doing, and when I asked straight out what they thought of me enhancing the training schedule by spending more time on instructing the men on the care and use of their rifles and on drill, they approved it. Soon after they had left, Johnston appeared.

'Colonel Malone!'

'Colonel Johnston.' I saluted.

'Why are you not obeying my orders?'

'I am, Sir.'

'General Birdwood and General Godley were here and the men were doing squad drill. Why are they doing squad drill now?'

'Musketry, Sir.'

'Musketry, squad drill, why are they not training as ordered?'

'They will follow your orders, Sir. They will follow them exactly: in time, place, and formation.'

'You shall immediately order them to cease what they are doing now and set them to follow my instructions.'

'And so they shall, Sir.'

'Now!'

'If you care to stay and observe, Sir, you shall see your orders will be followed to the letter. If you send one of your staff to observe, he shall see likewise.'

'Do not prevaricate, Colonel.'

I then spoke quietly and evenly.

'I do not prevaricate, Sir. This parade is mine. I am responsible for the efficiency of this battalion. I know better than anybody else its weaknesses and I shall rectify them. I give you six hours a day, Sir, and during those hours I follow your orders to the letter. The other two hours are mine, and it is my responsibility to determine what my battalion shall do during those hours.'

'You shall do as I say!'

'As I will, Sir. The men will exercise precisely as you have ordered.' I still kept my voice low and even, but it was becoming difficult.

'Are you defying me?'

'Sir, the standard training procedures they are undergoing occupy the additional two hours.'

'By heaven you shall do as I say!'

Surprised at the indignity he had inflicted on himself, I did not respond.

'You shall do as I say and that shall be the end of it.'

'Sir, permission is requested to see the general.'

'Refused.' He spurred his horse and was off.

He might refuse permission to see General Godley, but he could not stop me from sending, through him, a letter to the general. I was confident of the outcome, but the incident irritated. An hour later, while my men were busy with the work Johnston had ordered, an orderly delivered a message that he wished to see me. The irritation returned, his visit and that of the generals had taken up time, and I could not afford to engage in a further argument.

'Colonel Malone?'

'Colonel Johnston.'

'I have reconsidered. You may do as you want. So long as you do the battalion work as ordered.'

It is never pleasant to see a man whom one has respected climb down, so I thanked him warmly. I also felt it would be common courtesy to tell him that the generals had approved what I was doing. He did not seem surprised by this.

He is highly strung and does not keep good health. Currently laid low, he will not be landing with us. For a while it was mentioned that I would take over the brigade, but that will not be; the general prefers regular officers when he can get them. We shall land under the orders of Brigadier General Walker, General Birdwood's Chief of Staff. He should be capable of handling us for the landing, but we know little of him and he knows little of us.

Colonel Johnston does not seem to hold a grudge. After an extended tactical exercise, he told me we did very well — more than I would have said — and when the Turks made a sortie against the Canal, it was Wellington and Otago that were sent under my command. We saw a little action but nowhere near as much as we had hoped for. The prisoners we took were a poor lot, Arab conscripts, old men and boys. While our landing should not be too difficult, it will be tougher than the Canal.

Our commander is Sir Ian Hamilton himself. We could not wish for a better. I have admired him since reading his meticulous account of the Russo-Japanese war where he was an attaché with the Japanese. Many of our tactics have been modified because of his close and keen observations of that war, particularly that a charge, with dispersed but controlled and committed men over a short distance, can still overcome entrenchments. And while one appreciates Sir Ian's distaste for entrenchments and siege warfare generally, it must also be remembered he has also stated that in modern war the spade is second only to the magazine rifle.

So far as training is concerned, Sir John Moore is the model I have sought to emulate. My aim has been to train disciplined, thinking soldiers able to deal with the unpredictability of battle and fight on when their commanders fall. Unfortunately, we must not be surprised if we come up against such troops when we meet the Germans. Don't let us be fooled by what we hear about field grey automatons with no other thoughts than what their drill sergeants have instilled. Their discipline is harsh, but it is not rigid and their doctrine takes into account the unpredictability of battle. Let us not forget it was the Germans who instructed the Japanese.

As for what I have seen of the British Army during the last six months, I am sad to have to admit that I have had to modify some of my views. When we first went into camp I believed that, however hard we worked, it was not to be expected we would match the British regular. Unfortunately that does not seem to have been entirely correct. I have already mentioned how few of our staff have exerted themselves. Nearly all are regulars brought out from Home. Many, like Temperley, our brigade major, who has far too much influence over Colonel Johnston, can be downright patronising. A day or two ago, I had a good look the at the 29th Division, the one regular British division that will be landing on the Peninsula. I had a yarn with some of them. Most had worked in cotton mills as boys, and they looked it. I haven't seen them at work so they could be good stuff, but, for the present, I would have one and a half of them to one of ours. Our men seem giants, and gentlemen, beside them. As for the Australians, with their baggy Garibaldi outfits and slackness all round, I can't like them. I've tried, but I can't.

The last nine months have been as demanding as any I have spent. I miss Mater and the young ones deeply and no sooner have I read their letters than I reply and then read them again and again and wait for others to follow. I was able to spend the last night with Mater, but in the morning, she broke down. Who can blame her; she had kept such a brave face for two months. I trust that the last eight months will be the longest separation we will suffer. She, Norah, and the children are now on their way to England. Once the landing is completed and the Bosporus opened up, we will surely be on our way to France. Once there, we shall be able to be together much more frequently. It cannot come too soon. Yet I would not be anywhere else than I am now. May the good Lord forgive me but the declaration of war was the happiest day of my life. For thirty years I have been stodging away making money. At last I am able to do something for my country.

MALONE
The Landing

'You won't need them,' Colonel Johnston said when I asked that our picks and shovels not be stowed in the hold. It has become a war where the obvious is preached, the foolish is practised and the means to fight it are just not there. To begin with, the Navy failed to land the Australians where Hamilton had planned. It has since fabricated a tale that its boats were dragged north by a current it hadn't known about. Nobody else knows about it either. The Australians were to land on a broad strand of three thousand yards with easy rolling country behind. Instead they were put ashore into a cove barely six hundred yards long, a cricket pitch deep, with a tangle of ridges and gullies beyond. They went in before dawn. Until late afternoon, we cruised up and down, leaving the Australians to it, and our units divided, half of mine on one ship and half on the other.

We landed in the midst of a mêlée of men, mules, donkeys, supplies, ammunition, dead, wounded, naval beach parties, malingerers, and the genuinely astray. I was ordered to send two platoons to reinforce the Australians. It was in this piecemeal fashion that reserves were sent forward, detached from their battalions and put amongst those who knew them not. Taranaki men, fifteen I have never seen again; men who have been with me for years and whose families, if I return, I will have to face. The beach being lit up by star shells, I set my men gathering picks and shovels left lying around by the Australians as they rushed into the hills.

To serve a useful purpose I patrolled the foot of the beach, which, being protected by a cliff face, was well populated by sleepers. Some were there because they didn't know where to go; others did know but would rather stay put. They were sent on their way. I came across a cosy group, deep in slumber, oblivious to the big guns of the warships and the Turk artillery. When I asked one who he and his mates were and gave him a not too gentle a prod with my boot, a bursting Turk star shell illuminated the face of General Birdwood.

'Malone,' he said.

'Sir!' I said.

'You're a dedicated officer, Malone.'

'Thank you, Sir.'

'And what may I do for you?'

'One or two stragglers down here, Sir. Some genuinely lost, others not.'

'Thank you for telling me, Malone. The provosts, no doubt, will deal with them in the morning.'

'I'm sending them on, Sir.'

'Oh! Excellent, Malone, excellent.' The general looked his group over. One of them I noticed was General Godley. Like the others, he did not stir. 'I think, Colonel. That here we're all accounted for.' His hand went up to cover a yawn. 'If we are harbouring anyone who shouldn't be here, I'll send him to you. Indeed I will.' This time the yawn went uncovered.

Another star shell went up and I saw a pile of picks and shovels behind him.

'With your permission, Sir, I shall relieve you of those tools.'

'Tools?'

'Picks and shovels, Sir, behind you.'

'Really!' He half turned. 'Quite so, Malone, dig, dig. Can't go wrong.'

'Thank you, Sir.'

I summoned half-a-dozen enthusiastic Hawke's Bay men to retrieve them. Eager to demonstrate their enthusiasm before their general officer commanding they were, perhaps, more boisterous than they needed to be, but the sleepers remained undisturbed.

'Malone!'

'Sir!'

'Get some sleep. You'll find it a benefit.'

'Yes, Sir. I shall when all my men have landed.'

'Not yet?'

'Not yet, Sir.'

He sighed.

'In the meantime, get some sleep, and those boys of yours too. You'll be needed tomorrow, have no doubt about that, Malone, have no doubt at all.'

With that he eased himself back and rolled over.

General Birdwood cannot be blamed for what his commander decreed, or for his troops being landed in a place where he had no intention of fighting. Nor can he be blamed for his plans. His failure has been to ensure his staff was capable of putting them into effect. He is not alone in this. There is slack staff work wherever you look.

Several hours later the balance of my men waded ashore but it was not until 4 p.m. the next day that we were sent around the northern point of Anzac Cove to report to Brigadier General Walker, who, in the absence of an ill Colonel Johnston, was acting commander of the New Zealand Brigade. An English regular, Walker is what an Imperial officer should be: a man who talks plain, expects plain talk in return, rewards competence and has no hesitation in getting rid of incompetence. When we first met he ordered me, when a roar for reinforcements came down the ridge, to send a company up. 'What are they to do?' I asked. 'They will be met at the top and put where they are needed,' he replied. Wellington West Coast was sent off and when the next yell came, Hawke's Bay.

With yells for more, I went to see for myself and I came upon a fat Australian major with about forty men and a couple of machine guns.

'Why are you yelling for reinforcements?'

'They're calling from above.'

'Why don't you go yourself and take your men with you?'

'I have orders to stay.'

So I went on, passing Australian wounded, until I reached a Colonel Braund who said he was in command. Because of Turk snipers, my company commanders had ordered their men to dig in, but Braund, on the grounds he was the senior officer, overruled them. It was murder. I asked what his plan was, where he had placed his defences, and why he had left his own men on the ridge and yet called for New Zealand reinforcements. He replied men were needed on the neck of the plateau.

I told him my company commanders were commanding my men, not he, and made him bring up all the Australians. When I reported to Brigadier General Walker, I was ordered to take my remaining companies and man the line as a reserve where the fat Australian major had been. Sending Hart ahead to reconnoitre, I brought up the men and set them digging. When an Australian yelled, 'Fix bayonets, the Turks are coming!' I deployed our defences but Hart reported there wasn't a Turk in sight. Braund demanded more reinforcements and I refused. He said if I did not send reinforcements, he would have to retire to his first position. I replied he should never have left it. He claimed that if he hadn't tried to push on, his men would run away. *That*, I said, was no reason to sacrifice *my* men and I returned to Brigadier General Walker. It was heart-rending to pass so many of my wonderful men, who had been sent up in the first hour, lying wounded. They were very brave. I'd been hard on them but they spoke like old friends. 'Well, Colonel, I've got it.' 'Good luck, Sir.' 'Could be worse.' One muttered, 'Oh Daddy, Oh Daddy.'

'I want all the Australians removed, Sir,' I said. 'As soon as possible.'

'Can you hold without them?'

'They are a source of weakness.'

'I will come with you.'

Up on the crest we met Australians hiding in the scrub. Some I kicked up the backside, others I pelted with stones, but they went forward. I took the general to Colonel Braund and left him there. Soon afterwards he called at my headquarters.

'Colonel Braund and his men will have left their positions by dawn.'

They spent the night firing at Turks they could not see. By doing this they drew fire on everybody. I tried to stop them, failed, and when, at 1 a.m. Colonel Braund came and asked for more ammunition, I refused.

'All you're doing is telling the Turks you're scared.'

'I insist. You have ammunition and I must have it.'

'No.'

'Then it is on your responsibility.'

'Yes,' I said, ' unless the brigadier orders me.'

I heard no more of it. War is war and casualties are part of it, but to lose good men, in the face of my officers' objections, by plunging them into a barrage of hidden machine gun and rifle fire was murderous stupidity. But the Australians are not entirely to blame. They were plunged into the worst possible country with nothing to guide them. The maps issued have been no more than cartographic cartoons. Royal Engineers mapped the Peninsula during the Crimea and, by one means or another, their maps were updated. Why weren't they issued?

We dug through the night and the day, our casualties dropped to a fraction of what they had been, and we settled down to giving as good as we got. My officers are loyal and obedient, but they are not unquestioning. Indeed on the voyage over, I got so fed up with their questioning, I was tempted to issue orders without hearing what they had to say. I never succumbed to the temptation—though I was most sorely tried—but my reward is they are able to use their initiative when carrying out their orders. This has permeated into the rank and file. The day before we went to Hellas I decided I would borrow a rifle and go out and see things for myself. Creeping through the scrub and well beyond our trenches I suddenly felt a grip slowly close around my ankle. To raise my head would be to lose it, so little by little I turned it and was glad to see that the hand did not look like a Turk's. 'Sir, don't turn. Backwards, carefully.' I obeyed and found myself lying alongside my corporal scout. 'Sir, follow me.' I was going to ask why, but he shook his head and we headed back. In a safe position, he quietly said, 'Sir, you were in Turk country. The boys know about their mates up here, but they don't know about you.' He looked me straight in the eye. 'Sir, they'd have got you—and if not them, the Turks.' 'Yes, Corporal,' I said. After we parted in the trench I could hear him berating the sentries for not stopping me! Less than a year ago he had been a ship's stoker. I am both proud and humble to command men like him.

About a week after the landing we heard that a prominent knoll a little to our northwest was to be seized. Called Baby 700, it was seven hundred feet high and smaller than another seven hundred foot rise. Fire from it covered many of our positions. With artillery support, my battalion was in a position to seize it by a night attack from the flank. Instead Godley and Johnston decided to mount a night frontal rush at the strongest point by the Otagos. Otago's commander, Colonel Moore, is a British regular. He was originally seconded from General Godley's own regiment, the Royal Dublin Fusiliers, to assist in the training of our territorials. The general chose him, it seems, because he knew him. Early on, the original Otago commanding officer had fallen sick. It seems that General Godley promoted Moore to command Otago because he was a regular officer. To get the Otago battalion into position, Colonel Moore had to take it on a long and difficult march. Once in position, the Otagos then had to make an attack at the precise moment the artillery and naval gunfire opened up and the Australians created a diversion. Because Colonel Moore did not reconnoitre his route, he arrived late. It was half an hour after the barrage had fired and the Australians were shot to pieces.

Otago was sent in alone. It met concentrated fire and I saw something I thought I would never see — New Zealanders who turned and fled. Enough were rallied to make two more charges but they too failed. We could do little but give covering fire and watch the disaster evolve. Johnston was beside me. When Otago did not show, he cursed and when they did, he cheered them on.

In my years studying military matters, either by the great captains or in the baldest instruction manuals, two tenets were forever present: never reinforce failure and never attack the enemy at his strongest point if there is an alternative. Yet a combination of the two was what a battalion of the Royal Marine Light Infantry, brought up as a reserve, was ordered to do — at dawn. By then the Turks had the ground so well enfiladed that the RMLI were hit from every angle including the back of the head. They broke, were rallied (by General Godley I am told) and broke again, and because they were neither New Zealanders nor Australians, they were blamed for the failure at Baby 700.

The New Zealand Brigade was next sent down to Helles where, in open rolling country, I believed at last we would be engaged in a battle that would be waged scientifically. Not even the sight of the shattered *River Clyde,* an old hulk that had been run ashore with troops spilling out onto the beach in the face of point-blank machine gun fire, suggested second thoughts. We bivouacked near a British battery of 18-pounders, which was rationed to two shells a day and not allowed to stock up for attacks.

The following night we were ordered up to reserve trenches behind the 29th Division, which, for past two days had attacked at 10.30 a.m. Morning revealed ground gently rising to the village of Krithia. Spring wheat had sprouted and here and there were clumps of immature pines and bundles of barbed wire but none of it systematically laid out. It looked ideal fighting country. Although there were shrapnel bursts, no Turks were seen. Early in the morning, I sent out scouts. They reported on no man's land and its lack of cover. It called for a night attack.

Johnston called his battalion commanders together at 10.10 a.m. We too were to attack at 10.30 a.m. He'd left no time for briefing. But then he knew nothing of where we were to attack from, where we were to attack to, artillery support, cooperation with other troops, or if other attacks were to be made. Our reserve trenches were half a mile from the front line. We took casualties moving up. In the meantime our artillery fired a fifteen-minute bombardment, warning the Turks about another 10.30 a.m. attack.

Never have I been more proud of the men as on that day and never have I been so appalled by the stupidity that sacrificed so many of them. When they went to ground, they had gone further than any other battalion.

During the afternoon, Johnston called his commanders together.

'At five-thirty you are to go through the Turk lines and clean them out,' he said. 'We will really show them this time. Cold steel.'

'My forward line is less than one rifle per yard. The forward support line is two hundred yards to the rear, the next three hundred yards, and the furthest, five hundred yards.'

'So?'

'So it's not war,' I said.

He almost seemed amused.

'It is for the rest of us, Colonel.'

'I cannot advance, Sir.'

'Cannot, what is this "cannot"?'

'I am three hundred yards in advance of the battalion on my right. We are enfiladed from there and we are exposed on our left.'

'Then Auckland will come up and cover your right as it advances.'

'We were badly cut up, Sir,' said Plugge, the Auckland colonel. It was the first time I had heard him differ with Johnston. 'We are down to less than half and I have very few officers left on their feet.'

'Very well, we'll bring up Otago to reinforce you.'

Because of their losses after Baby 700, Otago had been made the reserve battalion.

'Sir,' said the Canterbury commander, whose battalion was to the right of Auckland. 'We are left with less men per yard than Wellington and are no more forward than Auckland. To attack is to destroy the New Zealand Brigade.'

'It's true,' said Plugge.

Johnston looked across at Moore but he was looking at the ground.

'Gentlemen, we have been sent here by Sir Ian Hamilton and put under the command of General Hunter-Weston, commander of one of the finest divisions in the Imperial Army. We cannot disobey; the honour of New Zealand is at stake.'

Nobody said anything. Before it had been only me who would differ with Johnston. Then Moore looked up.

'Would you put the position to the general, Sir. Explain we don't have enough men to get through.'

This was the outlet Johnston needed. He looked at his watch.

'Very well, I will tell him. See what he can do about it.'

He went and returned with the message that our concerns had been passed beyond Hunter-Weston to Sir Ian. The attack was to go ahead.

'You will advance at five-thirty.'

I was shocked, but not surprised, by the fatalism I saw in the eyes of my fellow commanders. Whatever initiative they might have exercised to make the best of a very bad job had been dulled; they were accepting the pointless destruction of their battalions.

'My men will hold until their flanks are covered,' I said.

'Colonel Malone, they will attack at five-thirty as ordered!'

I looked him in the eye.

'Yes Sir,' I said.

'You must push on! Fix bayonets. Go right through.'

I did not respond. There was a silence. Those who were not gazing at the sky were examining their boots. Then Moore said:

'Would somebody show me where my men are to advance?'

'I will,' I said.

I was angry and when one is angry one is careless. As I took the Otago commander up to where his two companies (all he had left) should go, a bullet passed between our heads and through the lobe of his ear, as clean as a shepherd's earmark. I bound it up and decided to be more careful; we were losing far too many officers. Auckland, I was to learn, had only two left, Colonel Plugge being soon wounded. As for me, I seem to be immune. On the same day, when I was up in one of the clumps of pine trees, a shell burst close enough to feel the shrapnel pass. There were a couple of other close shaves. It would have been safer, and I might have exercised more control, if I had sat in my HQ beside the telephone, but it is hard to sit there when the men are up front.

At 5.30 my right flank made another one hundred and fifty yards but had been hit too heavily to advance beyond that. Ten Otago men and a few Aucklanders joined them. A platoon of the Essex Regiment, sent up as reinforcements and not liking it, went back, leaving our right flank in the air. If we had attacked at night we would have succeeded; few of my good brave men would have suffered for it.

The next day I managed to get four machine guns and took them and their squadron up to the front myself. I returned to find Johnston waiting and demanding I relieve the Royal Fusiliers.

'Sir, I can't.'

'You can't! What do you mean you can't?'

'They are twelve hundred yards behind me. And, Sir,' I went on, 'I want them moved up. They're not in touch with me and are no more than moral support. And we must have engineer wire detachments. We have no wire and a decent counter-attack would come right through. Sir.'

He turned away muttering I was more trouble than the other three battalion commanders put together.

The next day I was ordered to relieve the Essex battalion—also behind me.

Although my men were dead tired, had lost heavily, and been ill used, they had not lost their esprit de corps as had Auckland and Otago. The Dublin Fusilier Moore, no longer the cocksure British regular, blamed his men. Nonsense; when they first marched into camp, they were no different from mine. Indeed many were Wellington men drafted south to make up the numbers.

We were withdrawn four days later, having to make our own arrangements, in the rain, with greatcoats yet to be issued. Down on the beach, in the pitch-black night and I dripping wet, I noticed a bivvy with only one pair of legs. I crawled in. The occupant was a true Christian for he willingly shared his blanket. We kept each other warm. In the morning I was astounded to find I had been in bed with a Hindoo! I went back later to give him a tip and have our photo taken. He was a mule driver from Madras. A very clean man.

My other interesting meeting was to dine with General Paris, GOC the Royal Naval Division, arranged through Colonel Richardson, whom I had known in Wellington as a hard working instructional officer from Home. He is now on General Paris's staff. The general was interested when I presented a plan to break the deadlock on the Peninsula by attacking, under cover of darkness, the lightly held Turk defences on our left flank, using the rugged terrain to our advantage. It is simple and speed would be of the essence. The general said he would carry it further.

I also learnt that Sir Ian Hamilton had suggested a night attack on Krithia to Hunter-Weston, also responsible for the *River Clyde* massacre. Hunter-Weston turned it down saying it was too complicated. For that murderous buffoon anything other than a bayonet charge would be too complicated.

HARRY
War

When war was declared the Defence Department expected all young, fit, and able in its employ would be going. Our church had a similar view. There must have been some young men in the Bible Class who did not volunteer, but they would have been few. We did not question that our duty to King, Country and Empire was less only than our duty to God. When Dr Gibb preached on the matter, as he did frequently, he articulated our feelings and those of the community we belonged to. I was disappointed not to go off with the other Wellington men sent to occupy German Samoa, but it was well for me personally that I was held back because it enabled me to sit my first university exams. I had commenced as a part-time student at the beginning of the year. It was November when I was marched into Trentham camp.

There were, in the Field Ambulance, as fine a group of chaps as any I have had anything to do with. Except for one or two, the officers were all doctors, and for the most part, they were doctors first and officers second. Many were recent graduates and not much older than the rest of us. As for the rank and file you could, broadly speaking, divide us into two: those who had volunteered for the Field Ambulance and those who had volunteered for another arm and had been told it was either go with the Field Ambulance or not go at all. Those of us in the former group shared a disinterest in promotion and achieving even a modicum of military glory. Most were practising Christians and a fellowship was quickly established. Among those who were worried the war might be over by Christmas, were the NCOs who instructed us to form fours and other quaint practices essential to a soldier. Mostly old sweats who had served in those parts of the Empire where drinking was heavy and service was light, the declaration of war had presented them with an unexpected opportunity to revert to a life they had feared they had lost forever. Such was our innocence that we felt we were in the hands of those who practised the military arts at their highest.

There must have been a belated recognition that our overseas troops were deficient in medical personnel because we were sent overseas after two months. The highlight of the voyage was sailing into the Gulf of Suez. I was up early, and in the clear morning air, I beheld, on the horizon, Mount Sinai where Moses had received the Ten Commandments. Then we passed where the Red Sea had opened up for the Israelites. Somewhere near was Carcamesh where Solomon's ships had discharged their cargoes of treasure from Ophir. After we had disembarked at Suez, travelled across the desert by train to Zeitoun, and the pyramids came into view, I could not wait for the opportunities that must surely arise to see the country where Moses had been raised and where our Lord Himself had been taken to escape the massacre of the Innocents.

Imagine my disappointment when, on Good Friday after attending morning service, we learnt we would have less than a day in Cairo. After that, all leave was stopped. The reasons were two-fold. One was that training had to be intensified as we were to be sent to the front in less than a month. The other was because of a degrading and disgraceful affair perpetrated by the Anzacs. Of all days, it happened on Good Friday when, despite the sanctity of the day, men had flocked to the Wazir where every form of vice was practised. Over-indulgence in its grossest sense, led to an orgy of fire and destruction.

All were glad when we embarked for the voyage to what we believed would be glory and honour. I slept well the night before battle and when I woke up and looked across the sea at the hills that rose from the distant beach, I was startled to notice that I could have been looking across Wellington harbour to the Orongorongo range: the same ridges and spurs, the same colours. Of all the campaigns where New Zealanders fought in the First and Second World Wars, it is strange that the first was in country that could have been home. If we had landed first, we might have handled the terrain better, but I doubt whether, overall, we would have had more success.

Going ashore in a barge towed by a steam launch, we experienced shrapnel for the first time and one of our men, sitting on the gunwale, was hit. Stretcher-bearers were ordered to fall in immediately after disembarking. There was no hospital ship offshore and no hospital on Lemnos, just an Australian Casualty Clearing Station. Its job was no more than to patch up men so they might survive transfer to a hospital and it was not big enough even for that. No one had organised for anything like the battle around us. About a hundred feet high, curving above Anzac Cove, there was a forty-five degree slope that led up to a small plateau by the way of goat tracks. Our first job was to go up onto the plateau and carry down the wounded. It was swept by rifle and machine gun fire from the inland ridges with shrapnel bursting above. There was nowhere for a collecting post, so we doled out morphine and tied splints with rifles and bayonets on the spot before carrying down to the beach. A hundred feet might not seem much but when you take into account the steepness of the slope, that there were no formed tracks, and that soon darkness came and with it a drizzle that quickly turned the tracks into mud slides, you might have some idea of what the poor fellows we were carrying had to put up with.

The plateau having been cleared of wounded, we were sent up Shrapnel Gully. As the crow flies it is only about a mile from the head of Shrapnel to the beach, less, probably, but it took two hours to get a stretcher down it. The Gully twisted and turned in S bends, drizzle fell, and with the hundreds of troops going up and down, it became as bogged as a cowyard. Fit young Australians do not make light loads. They discovered, as we all did, that battle creates parched throats. Some, because of their wounds, could not be given water, but after a time we were not able to help those who could drink, as our bottles were soon emptied and water that had been brought ashore had been put in canvas troughs that were soon riddled with holes. As for the wounds: many were horrified by what a high velocity round does and thought the Turks were using explosive bullets. Because of the deer-stalking I knew a round could enter no wider than a finger's width and exit with a hole you might put your fist in. It is a terrible and a sad sight for a young recruit, only too recently from the love of his mother and home, to see men so shattered. And those poor fellows, their bodies torn apart, in their last moments on this earth, who do they call for? Their mothers.

Early on it was first come first served when the wounded were being barged off the beach, and there were cowards and malingerers who made their escape: not many, but they were there. Stretchers were soon in short supply and we had to improvise with rifles, puttees and blankets. Sometimes there was nothing for it but to drag a man along the ground with a ground sheet. When sheer fatigue overtook us, we fell to the ground and slept oblivious to all the noise and destruction until our mates, sympathetic but desperate for help, shook us awake.

Once evacuated, the wounded were crammed into one of the filthy cockroach-ridden former German cargo ships — seized in allied ports at the outbreak of war — that had conveyed us to the Peninsula. We sent out one of our bearers to retrieve stretchers. We didn't see him for a week and thought he was dead. The first vessel he boarded had impressed him to assist a vet, the only other man on the ship with any medical knowledge. His voyage to Alexandria was horrible.

After three days, connected dugouts were made for a facility with an operating table, making it possible for wounds to be re-dressed, urgent operations carried out, and for some poor souls, their last hours on this earth eased with morphine. Stretcher-bearers soon took off the white armbands inscribed with red SBs to identify them, like the Red Cross, as non-combatants, as they stood out on the battlefield and thus attracted the attention of snipers. Perhaps it was because they had many country lads in their ranks that the Turks had no lack of keen-eyed men. One poor fellow I was helping to carry was shot dead within ten yards of relative safety. There was talk that bearers working under such conditions were worthy of medals but the general said no, that was a normal part of our duty. He was right. Infantrymen do not get decorated for simply advancing under fire and neither should bearers for carrying men away from it.

To prepare for the Baby 700 attack an Advanced Dressing Station was established in a patch of dead ground beneath it. After the ADS had done what it could we carried the wounded down to the beach. It took four hours. When day dawned we saw bodies behind every bush and in every depression forward of the Otago position. It took all that day, the following night and the next day to bring the wounded in, so many that non-medical personnel were brought to assist. The snipers, making use of the star shells, slowed things down. In daylight they pretty well had things their own way. A mule is an easy target for an experienced rifleman and when killed on a track it takes time to be cleared and exposes men in the process. The engineers had to build overlapping sandbag barricades along the way so that men could shelter behind them and then dash forward to the cover of the next pair. When you take into account there would have been five or six infantry battalions up and along Monash and Shrapnel, plus engineers, service corps and medicals, you begin to have some idea of what the congestion was like.

There were Otagos in no man's land who tried to make their own way back. Some crawled, some ran and some who ran were demented. One, not all that far forward of the crest, rose to his full height, gripping the stock of his rifle and yelled at his comrades who cowered around his feet. It was a mad grotesque sight as he cursed them, the Turks, and it seemed, the sky itself. Barely a week previously he would have been a lad in the very best of health; utterly innocent of what lay in store for him. In his pocket would have been letters from his mother and his girlfriend. The shooting stopped as each side watched, but on rushing forward he was immediately felled. Another man, after crawling in, cried when we stopped him from going back to get his bayonet. When the Otagos finally pulled out, where they had fought over was called Deadman's Ridge.

Two Royal Marine Light Infantry battalions of the Royal Naval Division had been brought up to support Otago. Bernard Freyberg who would be governor–general and commander of 2NZEF made his reputation in the RN Division. The RMLI we called Run My Lads Imishi. They were not regular Royal Marines but leftovers from the volunteers for the Royal Navy. Nothing I saw changed my opinion that an average New Zealand infantryman would have outshone any two of them. I have never regarded

General Freyberg's military capabilities as anything other than average. He had great courage, but in my life the courageous have outnumbered the cowards. Not, however, on the day the RMLI made its attack.

When they moved into position it was with the rising sun behind them and artillery support falling short amongst them. They fell back, cramming the Australian fire trenches, which were little more than footholds cut below a crest and within range of Turk hand-grenades. To the Australians this was just one more torment to bear but the RMLI ran, spilling from the trenches and tumbling into the gully.

General Godley, who had come up to see for himself, stopped them. A man who long since had learned to control his fears, never for a moment tolerant of insubordination and having nothing to do with any form of theatricality, he drew himself up as he would on a parade ground and in his parade ground voice ordered the mob to halt. He held them, just as a dog holds sheep, by facing them down until their officers reasserted themselves and his staff mustered the strays.

Although it is unusual for a major general and a Field Ambulance private to be in proximity, I was close when it happened. But then it is unusual for a major general to put himself so far forward. My mate and I, after carrying all night and being deadbeat, were sitting in a cosy possie near the ADS. As the RMLI was sorted out I saw Godley's orderly get hit. From the way he was flung back, it was probable the sniper was not too far distant. As I said, I was tired, but I was still alert enough. By then, with the sun above the horizon and shining directly onto the hillside, it was possible to get a good sight of the scrub forward of the Turk lines and identify where the sniper might be. The general and his party took cover and had the fallen man with them. Near where they had been, another man was hit. Another shot following so soon told me the sniper's success might be going to his head.

I told my mate I'd be back in a couple of minutes and, taking care, went over to the general.

It not being proper for a private to shove himself in front of an officer, let alone a general, I put myself in line with the general's vision so that when he had finished berating the RMLI colonel and looked past him it would be easy to attract his attention.

'General Godley, Sir!' I saluted. Absurd behaviour in the frontline of a battlefield but that's how the army is.

'Good Lord, it's Patterson.'

'Sir!'

'What can I do for you, Patterson?'

'Your orderly, Sir. I think I can get his sniper.'

'You *think* you can get his sniper?'

'Yes Sir. I saw your orderly hit, and another man. The shots must have come from below the Nek. A fine shot, Sir, but maybe not as careful as he might be. I've watched the ground closely. He is in one of three positions. With your permission, I could deal with him. He's a dangerous man.'

General Godley paused. Dangerous men were hardly unique in the upper reaches of Monash and he may have been tempted to remark on the fact. Instead he said:

'You're very sure of yourself, Patterson.'

'Yes Sir,' I said.

'It is not a task for a Field Ambulance man.'

'I know where he is, Sir, and I can stalk him. You know me, Sir.'

He beckoned his aide.

'Rhodes, my compliments to Colonel Malone. Present Private Patterson to him with my recommendation that he is a first class marksman who may be of use to Lieutenant Grace.' He spoke to me. 'Colonel Malone will decide whether or not you are fitted for the work.'

Captain Tahu Rhodes, formerly of Canterbury and from a family of some wealth (acquired by the sharp business practices of a grandfather in the early days of settlement) was now a captain in the Grenadier Guards, no less, and General Godley's aide. Captain Rhodes did not appear over enthusiastic about being ordered to inform a CO known for eating junior officers alive (staff officers most definitely not excepted) that the general was of the opinion that a Field Ambulance private was possessed of the qualities required of a sniper and, moreover, was expected to present that private to the CO in person. He pulled out his pocket-watch, examined it, and said:

'Report to me at General Godley's headquarters at two p.m.' He turned away, thus insulating himself from the contamination of being addressed directly by a private so early in the day.

Being young I was disappointed, and puzzled, at not having had my offer taken up with the speed with which it had been given. I had arrived at an important conclusion: that if you are in the military, it makes no difference whether you are a stretcher-bearer, a pay-clerk, or a machine gunner firing at point blank range—each is part of the whole.

When the Turks made a mass attack it was a machine gunner who saved us from being overwhelmed. Major Wallingford originally had been brought from England by Godley as an NCO instructor. It was his deployment of our few guns that cut down the charging Turks like great sweeps of a scythe. In our innocence, we believed we would never see its like again. One of our young Number Ones, having never before fired at anything human, told me it was the worst day of his life tapping the gun as line after line advanced. 'It was murder,' he said. 'They came within yards and when dawn broke we could see their faces.' No man's land was carpeted with dead, dying, and wounded. It took nearly a week before an agreement was reached to allow the remains to be removed.

Being in a burial party was as unpleasant as expected but allowed our dead a Christian burial and put paid to the rumour that the Turk was using explosive bullets, there being evidence that our bullets too could rip large holes in a body. It was a new experience to be out in no man's land and like everybody else, we took time off to have a good look. The Turks benefited more than us because no man's land was above our positions. It was depressing to see we held not even the acreage of a decent farm. As if to make sure we would not forget what we were up against, within a week we saw the battleship HMS *Triumph*, while hurling its shells into the Turks, torpedoed and turning turtle. Two days later another battleship was torpedoed. From then on the Royal Navy was rarely seen in the daytime.

I must confess, however, that what I observed between our lines and those of the Turks at the head of Monash Gully was soon to prove useful.

'You're mates with General Godley, I hear,' said our sergeant. 'Why wasn't I informed of this? One word from you and I could've been back in the Wazir with all the sheilas. You're to report to the Wellingtons. Your choice and I wish you luck with that colonel of theirs. Turned down their rum ration. Though,' and here he gave me a wistful gaze, 'that wouldn't worry you much.'

There was regret in leaving. The mark of the stretcher-bearer in the months of May was plodding courage, drawn on day after day, with no expectation of reward except the thanks of a poor soul who, once he was on the beach, had a chance of coming through.

The officer I reported to was 'Army' Grace, a fine marksman and noted deer-stalker. His squad considered themselves the elite of the Peninsula. While it was not stated that General Godley's opinion only went as far as my being received into the unit, it was made obvious that it was not going to be he who would decide whether I might remain. This did not aggrieve me. Here I was, out of the blue, an unknown quantity.

Nevertheless you may imagine my pleasure when I saw the face of Jim McDonnell. With his blunt honesty and dour humour, Jim's Scottish forbears are never far away. Neither is John Knox, however vehemently he might deny it. If you wish to know more about Jim read *Rob Roy* or *Quentin Durward* or, if you want a change from Scott, try Conan Doyle's *The White Company*. And, despite his protestations of atheism, that great work, too often not read these days, *Pilgrim's Progress*. Jim too is a pilgrim. Although, when Grace paired us off, I knew Jim was carefully assessing my suitability. But he did it quietly. Likewise when it came to sharing a bivvy he did not complain about having a non-smoking, teetotal Bible-basher landed on him. As for me, as days and weeks passed, and we set about putting the upper reaches of Monash Gully to rights, I realised I was paired with a man of tenacity, steadfastness and courage.

To do the job properly one needed a German rifle and telescopic sight. The excellence of the German lens industry is well known and a Mauser is more accurate than a Lee Enfield. There was a further reason, however, for seeking a Mauser and that was because when it was fired, its sound was easily identifiable; if one was near Turkish lines a Mauser shot was less likely to draw attention. Although I could have acquired a Mauser easily enough by going through our arms dumps down on the beach, it was not where you would find a marksman's weapon. Eventually I obtained a quality rifle and sight and would lie out in the scrub in the gullies at the head of Monash. I was not alone in this. Our doyen was Jimmy Swan, a former miner, killed eighteen months later on the Somme. A hero of Anzac, he earned his DCM a dozen times over.

After the worst sniping had been dealt with, and I think, when General Godley decided his replacement orderly did not suit him, I was ordered to report to his headquarters. I entered a different world. It might have been no more than a mile and a half to the front line and shrapnel still burst overhead—a staff officer was killed while sitting down to lunch with Godley—but shrapnel was about all that staff and line had in common. I, a mere orderly, lived at a level superior to that of an officer at the front, being first in line for anything that landed on the beach. I was especially favoured as, being a divisional commander's orderly, I accompanied him to meetings aboard battleships and at General Hamilton's headquarters on Lemnos. I bought cheaply from ship's canteens and the meals I devoured in the seaman's Mess were princely compared to anything served at the head of Monash.

One of my jobs was to carry the general's map case and anything he might need when he made his regular visits to his commanders and the front lines. I observed Generals Russell and Birdwood at first hand. There was also Monash, Australia's most famous general. On Anzac his brigade was an unhappy one but he knew how to make his name; and was capable of sacrificing some of the world's best fighting men.

Being on the beach allowed me the privilege of opportunities to attend religious services more frequently than at the front. For the first time I attended a Roman Catholic Mass. While these days it would cause no more than a raised eyebrow, then it was a different matter. Except that at Gallipoli, in the face of death every day, it came upon me the absurdity of not joining others in worshiping the Living Christ, among them our Wellington colonel. There were also men from the Maori contingent and their singing moved me deeply. (Indeed it was hearing their singing at an earlier Mass which drew me to the one I attended.) Upright, righteous, and courageous, Father McMenamin was a fine example to any man.

Would that there were more Protestant padres to follow his example. I wrote home about my attendance at Mass, and on later occasions, but never received a comment. Ulster Protestantism dies as hard as Fenian Catholicism, more's the pity.

I served the general for about six weeks. Towards the end of July the Wellingtons were on their way to dig terraces for the August battles, and I could not help noticing how drawn and ill they looked. The more days that passed, the less I could justify remaining in the relative safety and comfort of my position.

'General Godley, Sir!' It had been a busy morning and he was leaning back in his chair contemplating the pile of paper on his desk.

'Yes, Patterson,' expecting me to hand him a dispatch.

'A personal request, Sir.'

'Would you delay it for a day or two, Patterson, we're rather busy at present.'

'I know, Sir, and it was that I wished to make a request about.'

'You consider yourself overworked!'

'No Sir. I enjoy the work very much. No complaints, Sir, no complaints at all.'

'I'm glad to hear it, Patterson.'

'Thank you, Sir. In fact, Sir, there is no better job than working here. And,' this I added in what I considered the most kindly way possible, 'I would be very sad to leave you.'

'Indeed!'

'Yes Sir, very sad. But,' and here, I looked him in the eye (it is amazing how tolerant an adult can be of youth), 'it is time I left.'

'Pack and go?'

'Yes, Sir. I do not feel it is right that I stay.'

'I wasn't aware you had any choice, Patterson.'

'General, there are other men who can do this job.'

'Really? Request refused.'

'With respect, Sir, the infantry, scouting, and the rest, I would be more use there.'

'Patterson, it has been reported that you have leadership qualities. You were about to be recommended for promotion. If you transfer, you will lose that opportunity.'

I smiled.

'Oh, that doesn't matter at all, Sir, the rank is but the guinea stamp!' It was to be some time before I realised that such a remark is not one usually addressed to the likes of generals.

'You sound like a socialist, Patterson.'

'Oh no, Sir, not at all. Our family votes solidly for Mr Massey.'

'Indeed.'

'Sir, there are good men, who are not as fit as they might be, who could fill my place very well. I am not asking for Mr Grace's squad, although he said he was sorry to see me go; anywhere in the Wellington battalion will do. If there's no room there, Field Ambulance is always short.'

'There is a limit to what I may tell you, Patterson, except to make it clear there will be very hard fighting under the most arduous conditions.'

I nodded my head.

'There is important work to be done here, Patterson.' He picked up a report. 'I cannot guarantee you a posting.'

I left, downcast he hadn't shared my enthusiasm. Consequently I was surprised, on the day the Wellingtons were sent to Happy Valley, to be ordered to report to them.

JIM
Volunteer

It took six weeks to get to the London docks. I could have signed on for the trip home but I didn't. Best to stay away a while, and the stokehold was not for me. Not in the tropics. I've heard of men going mad down there and I believe it. Not that I'm partial to cold. It was getting on for Christmas when I signed off and all I had on when I walked through the dock gates was a jacket and trousers. The rest of the black gang stopped at the nearest pub but I knew where I was going. I had a letter from the Wellington Strike Committee to Tom Mann at the International Federation of Ship, Dock and River Workers (IFSDRW). Tom was away at the time, speaking to workers in America and South Africa, but the letter did the trick. They sent me to a family in Stepney and fixed me up with a job of sorts. I guess I could have settled in England. They were good people. A lot had had the guts kicked out of them and just as many had been half-starved since they were born but they were always ready for a laugh and no matter how things were they didn't give up easily. But it was not my patch.

You'd never guess but in those days London was a centre of the socialist world. It began with Marx. Others followed and it became a centre for international conferences. It was in London that Lenin began laying down the law on what a revolutionary party should be. All I wanted was enough to keep me alive and catch up on what I wanted to know. I could do this at the IFSDRW; mainly maritime stuff, but I also learnt about 'Poor Little Belgium' and the King of the Belgians cutting off hands and heads of the

Congo people to line his pockets. Imperial Germany too, in South West Africa, wiping out sixty thousand of a seventy thousand tribe. Not bad for beginners and they improved with experience. I met people who had been through the mill: Spanish anarchists, French Syndicalists, American Wobblies, Independent Labourites, Bolsheviks and Mensheviks. One night I let myself be taken to a Fabian meeting. Felt I was back at school; heard George Bernard Shaw, clever and up himself.

The big let down for the Socialist International was after Sarajevo. We knew there was no hope with the Labour Party, but we thought there might be a chance with the Germans and French. But the German socialists lined up with the Junkers. And in France, after Jaures was shot, the French socialists went in with the bourgeoisie. It was three years before Lenin made his break but by then he'd had three years to organise, a full-blown revolution waiting for him, and a free rail ticket from the Kaiser's Government. When he called for workers to boycott the war in 1914 nobody took any notice.

The day war was declared you would have thought it was a free fiver for all. Crowds out in their thousands. Then it turned nasty. Some of it was in Stepney. There are always bad eggs and there are always those who will let their anger be used by the oppressing class. A couple of doors along from where I stayed there was a tailor's shop. The owner was a Jew who'd cleared out from somewhere in Eastern Europe after half his relatives had been wiped out. If anything he'd been born under the flag of our ally Holy Russia, but the word had got round he was German. He and the family he'd brought with him were as poor as we were. If I say that people like me went to him to get our clothes mended, it will give you an idea of how he was doing for himself.

A mate and I were on our way home one night when we saw a crowd outside his shop. Someone smashed a window and there is nothing like breaking glass to get a crowd worked up. There was yelling to get the German bastard, so we pushed our way through and stood in the doorway and shouted he wasn't a German. Not a nice thing to say, no man's nationality should be held against him, but when you're in front of a crowd who've been in a pub for the best part of a night, you can't be too pure. Besides it was true. I tried telling them that he was a worker like the rest of us, but all that did was to fire them up further—and not sounding like a local wouldn't have helped. You could see it all; they'd found an enemy they could take it out on. Staying safely away were two police.

We were told to get out of the way or get what was coming to us. When we didn't, two big fellows who'd just arrived pushed forward and told us to fuck off. They didn't care whether the family behind us were German or not. They were boozed and after a fight. There didn't seem much to use to belt them with but then I felt heat behind me. All this happened quickly. The two came at us; I leapt back to the stove, grabbed a flat iron and let the first one have it on his ear. It knocked him back and I let him have it again before he got over his surprise and put the boot in as he went down squealing. As for my mate, he'd grabbed a poker and laid into the other one. That downed him. Police whistles were blowing and we were off. Through the house, into the yard, over the fence, through a kitchen, and out through a gate where my mate went one way and I the other.

Turned a couple of corners and Stepney Green underground station was before me. Into it I went, no one behind just then so I made myself buy a penny ticket and then ran. A train came in as I hit the platform. I got out at Victoria, a main line station that might lead me out of London. I came up in the middle of the crowded hall and looked up at the destination boards. None of the names meant much. I looked around and there walking towards me was a New Zealand soldier. Where do I join? I said.

He was wary at first. Me popping up like that at that hour of the night and looking as if I'd been in a fight. I told him I'd just paid off a ship and had spent the day looking for New Zealand House to join up and not finding it, now had nowhere to go. I was lucky all right. He had just come from the office where they were raising a New Zealand contingent and was on his way to make a connection to Waterloo for a train to camp. I had enough on me to pay the fare and joined him. That's how I volunteered for king and country. It was no questions asked next morning after a medical, and I took the oath, but I know for the first week no one was very sure of me. They did not doubt I was a Kiwi. (There was an Englishman or two who'd joined us after manufacturing a New Zealand father because we were paid more than the poor old shilling a day Tommy.) It was a combination of my sudden appearance and that I was working class. There weren't many working class New Zealanders in England at that time because the only way they could get there would have been to work their way like I had. And of those, half would have volunteered first go, and the others only when the choice was conscription into the NZEF, or the British Army. And of those who had volunteered early I am sure that one had joined for the same reason I had. When he kept getting into trouble, others were sure too. But not me, I kept my nose clean. Army life did not bother me. Just then it was as good as a holiday.

So there I was amongst these clean middle-class boys: students, farmers visiting the Old Country, lawyers, teachers. When they learnt I wasn't interested in leave and would swap duties so they could go off to London, they didn't mind having me around. It didn't fool the old NCOs but they had enough to do, bringing us into line. But it was good to see England disappear into the fog when we shipped out early December.

Most of the English mob were posted to the Engineers and Service Corps. I was not. With some others I was marched to the Wellington lines. Heavy culling had been going on there. When we came to a halt, the colonel stepped forward and spoke and then a platoon drawn up nearby gave us three cheers. It took me less than two minutes to decide that the holiday was over. Others took a little longer. After we were dismissed they walked every which-way, taking a short cut across the front of the colonel's tent, having yet to learn the need for observation in a war zone. In front of his tent the colonel had a garden. The desert bloomed. Watered every morning and again at night. His flowers had not been walked on; they'd been murdered. He let rip and the boys, men, some of them, shook. After that, names were taken. 'I have your names,' he said. 'I have your names.'

In the Wellington lines every grain of sand was in place. The inside of every tent was like an old maid's bedroom and every button shone like gold. And out in the desert, in the heat, Wellington went an extra two hours. The old bastard never let up. No use a friendly corporal taking you behind a sand hill for a little rest. You'd be missed and found. Lunch was short and water likewise. In March we were issued with khaki drill. A sad day for the old bastard; nothing like New Zealand wool and desert sun to toughen a man up.

When it came to musketry I was not a bad shot. Not brilliant like Harry, but good enough if I were close enough. Neither was I too bad at seeing things and getting to places where there were things to be seen. Again, not as good as Harry, but good enough. Malone used scouts right from the first. He had us picked out before field exercises started. God help his officers if they went anywhere without using us.

Then we were sent to stop the Turks crossing the Suez Canal. The first shots fired by a New Zealand force in the Great War. We were down at Port Tewfik where vessels coming up from the Red Sea lay while waiting to go through the canal. Not even Malone could haul us out as we were *at war* and had to man the defences. So we spent days looking over the canal and watching the ships sail past. There were still passenger liners going to and fro and when they lay in wait for their turn, we organised boats to row out and collect the cigarettes and chocolates the passengers tossed to the brave boys below. The old man must have been beside himself. All I saw of the enemy was when we took over a hundred or so Arab prisoners from the Gurkhas. Even the Gurkhas felt pity for the poor buggers and when we went back to Zeitoun we were sure we'd beat the Turks any time we liked.

It was now towards the end of February and the days were heating up. We still did our two hours extra no matter what time of the day or night we'd been out and no matter how many sand hills we'd climbed or trenches dug. We dug in sand so soft that in five minutes the sides were forty-five degree slopes and in rock so hard the pickaxes bounced. And night exercises, there were plenty of those, cooler, yes, bloody cold in the desert at night and sliding and stumbling in the sand hills; you'd come back like a loose sack of potatoes.

In Egypt I was able to take as much leave as came along. Lenin had not yet written *Imperialism as the Highest Stage of Capitalism*, but what I saw in Egypt confirmed everything I later read. Just before we left we had to march through Cairo to celebrate Egypt being proclaimed a British protectorate and to remind the Egyptians who was boss. Egyptians like a bit of a laugh but I don't think they saw the joke. If you were British you could do pretty well what you liked to — as they said — a wog. I saw an Egyptian boy knocked down by a carload of drunks. The kid had been playing with his mates and the car swerved onto him and kept on going. I went to see what I could do but when the crowd saw my uniform they turned nasty so I cleared out. The Egyptian authorities went along with the British. That was where the cash was. The rest scratched for what was left. Some poor buggers used to follow us out into the desert, hawking bottles of soft drink. They carried them in bags or under their shirts. Some of us thought it a laugh to throw stones to smash the bottles. They didn't mind if they missed a bottle and hit a boy or got both at the same time. Then they'd moan about wogs ripping them off.

While I like a beer, I'm not a great boozer, so when my mates looked like settling in for a session, I'd most often go off by myself, or with some- one else who wanted to remember where he'd been. There was a club in Cairo at the Esbekia Gardens where soldiers could go if they wanted to read newspapers, have a cup of tea or write letters. I didn't have many let- ters to write but I liked to keep up with the capitalist press and now and again sit down in a place where there was some peace and quiet and have something with a cup of tea that didn't taste of an army cookhouse.

It was there, round about noon on Good Friday 1915, that I met Harry. He was writing letters and I was going through a week-old copy of the London *Times* — it was either that or the *Daily Express* — when he put down his pen and came over and gave me his big smile.

'Wellington, I see.' He pointed to my hat. At that time the Welling- tons were the only ones who pointed their hats lemon-squeezer style.

'I'm a Wellington man myself, glad to know you.' He held out his hand so I shook it. 'You're Wellington-West Coast.'

'Yes,' I said.

'You must know …' and he mentioned some names.

I said I knew one or two.

'You don't come from there yourself?'

'No.'

'You must be like me,' he said. 'Only in reverse, so to speak. I come from there but I've spent the last few years down in Wellington. Then did my Terry training with the Field Ambulance. Most of the Wellington city boys went off to Samoa. You didn't?'

'No.'

He nodded and held out his hand again.

'Good to have a chat.' He smiled again and went back to his letters.

But that was not the end of it. Later in the afternoon I ran into a couple of lads I knew and had a couple of beers with them. It was on the edge of the Wazir where the brothels were. They decided to go off there. I had better things to spend my money on and turned back down the street, along another, and there was Harry again with his big smile. He stepped in front of me.

'Think of your mother.'

'Eh!'

'Remember her,' he said.

'Who said I'd forgotten?'

'Have you forgotten it's Good Friday, the death of our Lord?'

'Who says so?' I said.

'Don't go. You're a good chap, I know that.'

'Thanks,' I said.

'And think of the women there.'

'I do,' I said.

'One might be your sister.'

I wondered about him saying that. There were men I wouldn't have said it to.

'Or yours,' I said.

''Tis only by the Grace of God she is not.'

He was lucky that when I did meet his sister, I never passed on that little line. I was getting fed up by then and was about to tell him to mind his own business when there was a roar from a crowd and breaking glass, lots of it, and smoke.

'Let's go.'

He didn't move. At the time I thought he wasn't sure what to do. Now I know he was working out the percentages of coming with me or poking his nose in.

Then we heard horses approaching at the trot.

'Redcaps,' I said.

He'd been in the army long enough to know what that meant so we walked away smartly. By smartly I mean smartly because anything less if you were sighted by the Mounted Military Police would be a baton on your skull.

The smoke became thicker, we heard shots, and we stopped only when we came to a café out of sight and sound. We sat ourselves down.

'You should be happy,' I said. 'They're tearing the place apart.'

He shook his head.

'It's terrible. And on Good Friday.'

'Like a beer?'

'I don't drink.'

'No,' I said. 'You wouldn't.' I ordered a lemonade for him and a beer for myself. We gave our names to each other, talked a bit, and then went back to Zeitoun. I found him hard to place. He had the manners of a middle-class boy but didn't look like one. Later I watched him in a rugby match and thought it was just as well he didn't booze.

At Zeitoun when we entered the camp all men were being stopped and told they'd be going back into Cairo as pickets to reinforce the redcaps. There was a lot of milling around and when I saw my chance I quietly wandered off.

All leave was stopped because of it. It seems half a block of buildings went up in smoke, the redcaps had to beat a retreat, a whole battalion had to be marched in to quieten things down and, apart from the breach of discipline, everyone thought it good riddance to bad rubbish. As for leave being stopped, it would have been anyway. We were off to the Dardanelles. The peddlers at the camp told us. Otherwise it was a big secret.

Sailing into Mudros harbour in the island of Lemnos we saw a huge fleet. It was big enough to make us think that if the Turks had any sense they'd give up straight off. Which shows just how ignorant we were. Likewise when a German aeroplane flew over we were interested because it was an aeroplane. That it was German only made us more curious. If we'd had any sense we would have wondered why no one was trying to shoot it down before it reported back the number and size of the troopships in the harbour.

When we went ashore, it was to march. One day we were allowed a couple of hours' leave. Never saw a good-looking woman. Just the old. When you've been under military occupation for a few hundred years, as the Lemnos people had, you get careful about things like that. They'd not long been freed of the Turks but a schoolteacher we met and who spoke English told us Greece had just been at war with the Bulgarians and it was them they'd rather have a crack at just now. Everyone was poor and about all we could buy were lemons, nuts, and black wine that laid out one or two.

April the twenty-fifth was spent cruising up and down the Peninsula and watching shell bursts over the beaches. They weren't far away, but we didn't connect them with something we would be facing ourselves. We were more interested in the firing from our own battleships. It was five o'clock the next morning that we were sent ashore and up a gully. We lay in the scrub, not too hot, just nice and warm, watching the shrapnel burst, hearing bullets go overhead and joking about Turk marksmanship. There was a lot of wild thyme and rosemary about and no one was crapping during the first day or two so it was the only time the place smelt OK.

By late afternoon of the second day they must have begun to wonder why the walkover hadn't happened because it was then we drew two days' rations and marched to Walker's Ridge. We climbed it in single file. As the first Wellington-West Coasters fell we changed our opinions on Turk marksmanship. I've heard it said that when you first go into battle you wonder how you will go. It didn't affect me like that. Maybe because of the raggedy way we went in: cruising along the coast, lying in the valley, going up the spur, and, one after another, attracting fire.

We came to a crest where there was an old Turk trench. Then came a yell from the Aussies that the Turks were coming and to charge. Our company charged, down a slope and up again. The Turks were not coming. They were sitting above us and had the downward slope well covered and at that angle could see us in the scrub. Going up the other side I tripped. I lay still and stayed until dark. Those who kept with the charge took the Turk position but were not enough to hold it. With them I crawled back after dark to the old Turk trench. We brought back dead and wounded.

We joined the other companies digging. By dawn we had a new trench with machine gun emplacements. After the last of the Australians had been pulled out, we dug for the next couple of days: reserve trenches and connecting saps. On the seaward side of the ridge, Wellington-West Coast dug a reserve platform with a fine view of the sea so that our colonel could walk under cover from his bivvy to the forward trench. It was tough going. The Turks blasted us the whole time, shellfire, machine guns, snipers, the lot, and then we heard the teetotal old bastard had turned down a rum issue from the general. Said *his* men didn't need Dutch courage.

Water and everything else had to be carried up from the beach. Hard, hot and a good chance of being hit. From positions higher or level with the slopes of Walker's the Turks shot us like ducks in a sideshow. And now I come to another thing that Wellington did right from the start; after you have dug your trenches, you deal with the other side's snipers. It takes a sniper to get a sniper and those of us with an eye were put on the job. We organised ourselves in pairs. One with a rifle with a telescopic sight and the other with a telescope to observe. We would leave the trenches and lie out in the scrub in good cover and wait and watch. Not a bad life in some ways. So long as you did your job you were left alone and didn't have to worry about getting the shitty jobs the army forever dreams up. The only thing wrong with it was that the enemy had men out there whose job was to get you too.

Because of our losses when first sent up to Walker's, I was made a corporal. Early one evening I went up to the forward trench when a couple of my mates were due back. A sentry reported the colonel had just gone out.

'Funny if they all meet up,' he said.

'Bloody funny.' I was out of that trench double quick.

The old bastard wasn't too bad for his age but compared to the rest of us he left a trail in the scrub an elephant could have gone through. On the way he'd taken a pack off a dead Turk and put it ready to pick up on the way back and had stopped beside a second to go through his pockets. They had slowed him down and I caught up with him, close enough to grab his ankle without his knowing. It was interesting seeing him turn his head and the look on his face. Curious rather than scared. He didn't argue, nor when I laid down the law about going into Turk territory without warning the rest of us.

It rained and drizzled at night and we still had no blankets. But even if we'd been warm and dry there wouldn't have been much sleep because we were blasted twenty-four hours a day: machine guns, heavy stuff and hand-grenades. They had more artillery and machine guns and, as for hand-grenades, at that time we didn't have any. Other troops returned fire whether there was anything to aim at or not. Wellington fired only at targets. Besides, every round had to be carried up from the beach, though we shot off a few when we gave covering fire to the Otago attack.

When we went down to Helles we were glad to be in farmland with water. There was shrapnel, but not as much as at Anzac and the olive groves gave us cover from the Turk observers. It was almost like a picnic except for the Turk corpses that had been out in the sun since the landing. It was early days and some of the lads found them hard to take. Late in the day the brigade was ordered up to reserve trenches. Before dawn the Wellington scouts went out into no man's land. We saw enough to be able to report that the country between the Turks and us was gently rolling and easy enough for a night advance. On the way we had passed through two lines of the 29th Division. They'd been trying to drive the Turks back during the last two days, charging in daylight. We wondered why they had been so stupid.

Most of us grow up some time and my growing up went into top gear that morning. The battalion advanced a fair way from the reserve trenches before the Turks woke up to it and those of us leading were in the 29th Division positions before much had hit us. The rear was not so lucky. We took a closer interest in what the 29th Division had to say than we had before, but we didn't have much time to listen as we dropped into their trenches no longer than to climb out the other side. But it was time enough to be told that if we were going to charge across what they called the Daisy Patch, God help us.

Our orders were to keep in touch with the Aucklands on our right. To do this, we had to go into low-lying ground exposed to snipers. This was the Daisy Patch. The Aucklands got it worse than us and we got it badly. Flat on the ground, we scraped away until we had holes deep enough to lie in. More were killed and wounded during this. We were out on our own, about four hundred yards in front of the 29th Division. The Aucklands had no show catching up and fell back to a dry creek bed that gave cover to those who made it. Hawke's Bay Company on our left couldn't connect with us either.

The high command must have decided not enough were dead yet because late in the afternoon we were ordered forward again. There was a patch of scrub one hundred yards in front and when some of us reached it, the CO said: 'This is it, boys,' and so it was. Some 29th Division men had obeyed their orders and joined us. Others stayed behind. This was interesting because being pommy regulars they were used to doing what they were told. Three days of it in a row had been too much. Fair enough, more than fair.

When it was dark we brought in our dead and wounded. No trouble. The day hadn't finished though. We were Wellingtons, picks and shovels were up and we dug in well and truly. The Turks must have been saving their shrapnel, but why should they bother at night when the Heads laid it on in daylight? It wasn't a hundred per cent quiet. Near us there was a gorse patch with wounded Sikhs. We could hear them when something set it alight. If we'd known about them before we might have been able to get them in, but by then it was too well lit.

Late in the day Lancashire lads relieved us. Poor little sods. From the cotton mills. They looked no more than sixteen. Maybe some were just that, but after Stepney I'd learnt the poor look younger when they're young and are old when they are forty. Volunteers, they'd answered Kitchener's call and the good feeds that went with it. Now they saw what they'd been fattened for. It didn't help it was raining hard. We told them it wasn't too bad and other bullshit.

After Helles we had a little rest. A real one, not what the army usually means by it. We dug a sap around the north head of the Cove and smoothed out a streambed for a road, but apart from that we lay in the sun, played cards, deloused, swam and tried washing in salt water the clothes we hadn't changed for a month. I remember a mate coming back from Anzac beach with bread, onions and dried potatoes. After boiling the onions and spuds with flour and water and getting into the bread I lay back like a bloated capitalist.

When the battalion went into Courtney's they called for men with mining experience. I kept quiet. It was enough to hear them underneath, never knowing which was Turk and which was ours and who was going to blow and when.

MALONE

Courtney's and Quinn's

Our return from Helles to Anzac was an embarkation disgracefully organised by Major Temperley, another regular who had been brought out to teach us how to run an army. As brigade major to Colonel Johnston he was responsible to him for the coordination of the units that comprised the New Zealand Infantry Brigade. That the position also carried with it being the eyes and ears of his commander was more to his liking — much more. Never overly impressed by the man, before the landing I suspected that if he had not been given a job in New Zealand, he would have been on the retirement list. Now my suspicions were more along the lines that his kind was not uncommon in the force from which he had been seconded.

It was just after our return that Johnston called a meeting at brigade headquarters. General Godley had just honoured me with a visit and I thought I was on my way to a proud and happy meeting to discuss sending in special mentions for bravery and devotion to duty. This indeed is what we did and it was an amicable gathering for all concerned. Yet when the meeting was over, Johnston signalled for me to stay. He was, he told me, 'unhappy' with my 'lack of compliance with orders'. Astounded, and unprepared, I said something about being surprised, saluted, left, walked a pace or two, thought about it, and went back.

'Colonel Johnston, Sir.'

'Yes, Malone.'

'Sir, you say I have not complied with orders.'

'I felt it necessary to state that.'

'I am at a loss, Sir. Would you please explain your concern.'

'Well … err, well … Malone, you always …' For a moment he looked past me. 'You always question.'

'And fail to comply, Sir, when?'

'Just one question after another. It never stops.'

'I do admit to raising questions, Sir, but the failure to comply?'

'You never just obey. You must always raise issues. No sooner is one settled than you raise another.' His face was not that of a well man, but he tried to smile. 'Sometimes I think you lie awake at night planning what you're going to question next.'

'I give our situation a great deal of thought, Sir.' Indeed, I have lain awake at night seeking how to deal with matters that brigade should have dealt with.

He leaned forward. 'Colonel Malone, as a battalion commander you worry above your rank. I am not talking about me, but those who carry the responsibility of high command. They know much more than us, much more. And they carry a terrible responsibility, a truly terrible responsibility.'

'Indeed, Sir.'

'Strategy, cooperation with the Navy, coordinating with the French, allocating reinforcements, the demands of the Western Front, matters like that. Supplies too, Malone, a terrible problem with supplies, everything coming by sea. We must make do with what we have, Malone.' He looked at me earnestly.

'Very difficult,' I said. Trying to be firm yet not insubordinate, I asked, 'Sir, when and where have I failed to comply with orders?'

'I hear it all the time, Malone … all the time!' He blew his nose.

'You *hear* it?'

'You're notorious for it.'

'Notorious! Would you please explain, Sir?'

His normally florid face was becoming paler. 'Malone, old chap, you're a hard man to satisfy. Hardly a day has passed when you haven't wanted something. You've wanted this, you've wanted that, you've wanted to go there, you've wanted to go here, you want this officer sacked, you want that officer promoted and,' here he paused, 'you question orders in the field.'

'With respect, Sir, questioning is not want of compliance.'

'There is a strong impression abroad, Malone, that, at times, you are a law unto yourself.'

'That is not true, Sir,' I said quietly.

'I am glad to hear you say so, but it is a view widely held.'

'By whom?'

'Just about everybody.' He pulled out the handkerchief again and wiped his brow. It was a warm day, but I don't think it was that warm. 'And it makes it very difficult for my staff. You are the commander they least like having to approach.'

'Sir, have I ever behaved incorrectly?'

'You put everybody's back up, Malone.' He tried to smile. 'You'll never get the promotion that's your due.'

'I was not aware, Sir, that popularity was a qualification for promotion.' (That, I must confess, was not wholly true.) 'But, I am concerned about the stories you seem to be hearing.'

'One hardly knows where to begin. On the day of the landing you circumvented my order on the stowing of picks and shovels by bothering numerous people, including our Corps and Divisional generals, no less…'

'Did they complain?'

'Did who complain?'

'General Birdwood and General Godley?'

'Colonel! The question is insulting to each of them.'

'I agree, Sir, because I would have been surprised if they had complained.'

'You refused to support Colonel Braund, or even supply him with ammunition. An officer who had been in continuous action for two nights and a day.'

'And unfitted by then to exercise judgment.' I now know that Braun had been thrown into a mess not of his making—but that was no reason to follow his example. 'Sir, did either General Walker or Colonel Braund make a complaint?'

'You know they didn't. But that is not all. There is Krithia. Twice you were ordered to relieve other units. Each time you failed to obey. Claiming each was behind you.'

'Which they were, Sir.'

'Nevertheless, it was an order: from General Hunter-Weston himself.'

'He seemed to be unaware that, if we had relieved those units, the ground we had gained would have been lost.'

'An order is an order. Moreover, an order given by one who could see the whole picture.'

'Sir, I cannot remember anybody complaining about us staying where we were. So far as I know, the position is still held.'

'It happened to turn out for the best, but it would be most unwise to count on that happening again.'

Although on first appearance it may appear otherwise, I was not unsympathetic to Johnston: I expect my orders to be obeyed and he has every right to expect his to be. But what do you do when you receive orders that bear no relation to the situation at the time? I let the matter rest. There was a more important issue. I did not like bringing it up because already I had sailed very close to the wind, but because it related to my integrity it could not be overlooked. And I was angry.

'If I have understood you correctly, Sir, you have received no complaints from Generals Birdwood, Godley and Walker, nor from Colonel Braund.'

'That is correct.' He sighed, almost as if he were sorry they hadn't complained, but I knew it wasn't that. The handkerchief came out again.

'The aspersions cast are unjustified. Sir, I request, through you, to discuss them directly with those gentlemen.'

'There is no need for that. I have raised the issues with you and so far as I am concerned they are settled.'

'With respect, Sir, we might differ there'.

'Malone!'

'I have been maligned, Sir.' I let him think about it for a moment before saying, 'Sir, apart from the incident at Krithia—which, I think we have cleared up...' Again I paused and when there was no objection,

I continued, 'I would like to know when you have witnessed my alleged failure to comply with orders.'

'I have never claimed to have witnessed any. Although you did not make things easy in Egypt.'

Tempted though I was, I did not suggest that those whose battalions made it 'easy' in Egypt were now, or rather their battalions, were paying for it. 'Thank you, Sir,' I said, 'it appears you might have been referring to *allegations* made by other parties.'

'I may have.'

'It cannot be otherwise, Sir.' I paused again. Court experience has never done me any harm. 'Major Temperley does not always get the full story,' I said as if we had been indulging in casual conversation.

'Major Temperley is a loyal officer.'

This was not the first time I had heard loyalty mistaken for cunning and it is unlikely to be the last.

'Sir,' I said. 'Is it fair that I be judged without my side of the story being heard?'

He looked at the ground and up again. My anger had not diminished but I felt sympathy for him. His face had become pale and his eyelids were drooping.

'No,' he said. 'It is not.' He paused again. 'Colonel, I apologise.'

So I had worn him down. That was not the way I would have liked it but he was in no state to continue.

'Sir, you have given me a fair hearing and I appreciate the generosity of what you have just said. If you hear more stories, would you inform me at the earliest opportunity?'

He nodded, so slumped in his chair that he seemed on the brink of tipping over.

'Thank you, Sir.'

I did not gloat. It is dishonourable, and whatever faults my commanding officer may have, he is gentleman enough to admit a fault. What disturbed me was that as soon as I was out of his bivouac, he would resort to the bottle.

A more positive event on our return from Helles was that Brigadier

Russell's Mounted Rifles had landed and occupied our former positions on Walker's Ridge. More than ever was I grateful Terry and Edward were with them. Meldrum had been ordered to send a hundred men to make yet another charge across open, enfiladed ground. Meldrum referred it to Russell, who went to Godley, and the order was countermanded. Terry would have been one of the hundred.

Soon after Johnston and I had spoken we moved up to Monash Gully to take over Courtney's Post from the Australians. Courtney's Post is on what is known as Second Ridge, which is the crest that bounds the southern limits of Shrapnel Valley and Monash Gully — which divides into three gullies at its head. There were other posts along the crest: Pope's, Steele's and Quinn's. Courtney's was the only one not immediately overlooked by its Turk neighbours. Each post covered the other and if one fell the others would go and if they went, so would Anzac. They were the military equivalent of hanging on by one's fingernails.

At Courtney's the nearest enemy trench was fifteen yards away and slightly lower. We took over a higgledy-piggledy show on the brink of being abandoned. Work at once began on the defences and digging terraces into the slope below the crest to accommodate the men in the second line. These enabled men who were having their forty-eight hours out of the forward trenches, to spend their time as restfully as possible, and yet close enough to provide instant reinforcements.

After having gone to much toil and trouble to clean up Courtney's, I was ordered to garrison Quinn's, the closest to the Turk. Running parallel to the lip of the crest before it drops down into Monash Gully, it curves like a reversed S. Half of it is a salient exposed to fire on three sides. Like Courtney's, Steele's and Pope's, however, it has one advantage: it is so close to the front Turk trenches that it is impossible for the Turks to shell it without hitting their own. There had been talk of abandoning it but nobody could come up with an alternative. I sent my second-in-command to inspect it. He reported shocking conditions. The Auckland garrison, thoroughly intimidated, slunk out like thrashed dogs. 'A death trap,' they muttered to my men, 'a death trap.' With portions of the forward trench abandoned to a total of fifty yards, so it had become.

Our front line defence works that protected the Anzac-held ground had been originally scratched out of the earth in the heat of battle. To prevent their breach they had to be consolidated. It was not possible to do this adequately without building materials. Requisitions for them, however, invariably received the response that none were available. It was our Regimental Medical Officer — who supported the need for latrines — who reported piles of timber and iron right next to divisional headquarters. I will forbear explaining how we acquired them, but acquire them we did. Although the work was fraught with difficulties, abandoned trenches were recovered, new sandbags set in place, parapets repaired, fire-steps made, trenches deepened, scraped and cleaned, overhead cover put up to bounce the grenades on their way and a solid traverse constructed where the forward trench ended at a gully. Soon it was possible to walk as safely as it ever could be from one end of the system to the other. Once this was completed, terraces were cut deep into a hillside with head-height, shrapnel-proof roofs and open fronts so that there was shade during the day and air circulation always. And, right from the first day, every shot fired at us was replied twenty-fold.

Hand in hand with the improvements to Courtney's and Quinn's, I proposed expanding our Wellington snipers to a brigade-wide unit. For once I had the full support of Headquarters. It was the beginning of the end of the Turk dominance of Monash and Shrapnel. Just the day before they went out, six Australians were killed and wounded within an hour, but within a fortnight, anybody could walk up from the beach to the head of Monash unmolested by anything other than shrapnel.

After matters had settled down at Courtney's, a revised training manual came my way. It discussed where one should entrench on a ridge and recommended below the crest on the reverse slope. Until 1914, a war of manoeuvre was anticipated and the rule had been to entrench at the foot of a forward slope because it would facilitate the attack. The fighting in France and Belgium, however, demonstrated that when you entrenched to defend, you would be less vulnerable to enemy artillery if you did so on a reverse slope. This change of view, *on the whole*, seemed correct to me.

One morning I was interrupted by a request that Major Temperley be shown around the Post. I summoned my second-in-command and had him do this. When the two officers returned I offered them a cup of tea.

'Thank you, Sir,' said Temperley. He sipped with the air of a man who was receiving no more than what he was entitled to. That a soldier had sweated his way up Monash Gully under fire so he might enjoy his cup would never have given him pause. 'You'll soon be ship-shape, Colonel.'

'We're getting there,' I said.

'Indeed you are, Colonel. The engineers must have been a great help.'

'Yes, some even know about field engineering.'

While considering how he might reply, his eyes alighted on the instruction manual. His first reaction was surprise; his second, concern.

'Colonel,' he said. 'We must be very careful here.'

'Really?'

'Oh yes. Sir, the very most that might be said about the new view is that if a lesson has been learned, it might well have been a hasty one.'

'You think so, Major?'

'Let me explain, Colonel.' His face took on the expression of a second-rate schoolmaster. 'The original doctrine that entrenchments should be dug on a forward slope was decided on the principle that a trench should be sited to provide as wide a field of fire as possible. Obviously this is best obtained on a forward slope, particularly as every defensive position should be regarded as, sooner rather than later, an attacking position. Moreover, the preferred position on a forward slope is the foot. The reason: the lower you are, the less exposed you are.'

'Thank you, Major. Here, at Courtney's, we are higher than the enemy and it is to our advantage.' My eyes met his. 'I have no intention of sapping out into no man's land to prove somebody's point.'

He glanced away. 'And neither would your field of fire be enhanced, Colonel. For the time being you have no option but to remain as you are.'

'And our support trenches, being on the reverse are well protected.'

'As support trenches, Sir. The manual discusses fire trenches.'

'The authors have paid close attention to our campaign in France,' I said.

'They have, Colonel, but Sir, the case they are trying to make has so far been demonstrated only at that particular time and place.'

'I would doubt that,' I replied. 'Entrenching on a reverse slope to prepare for an expected attack from the front, Major, can be to a defender's advantage. You might remember Jackson's destruction of the Union Army when it came over the crest at First Manassas.'

There was no indication he had ever heard of it. 'Colonel, we are talking of the twentieth-century here. This,' he held up the manual as if it were intended for an unmentionable use, 'is no more than an immediate reaction to circumstances that may well prove to have been abnormal. The view is derived from a weight of artillery unknown before or, as is not unlikely, since.'

'I see.' I paused. 'You seem very sure of that, Major.'

'Indeed I am, Colonel.' The tone was patient. 'Here we have a different kettle of fish entirely. The Turk artillery is light. No comparison with German capability on the Western Front. Our emphasis must be on the attack. If it is not, we will remain where we are. Remember Colonel, with the Navy alone we can throw a much greater weight than our enemy.'

'You are equating naval gunnery with field artillery? A naval bombardment of high-velocity shells that our ships are capable of throwing on these shore targets is like thrusting a fork into a haystack.'

'It's been of great assistance to us, here, Sir. And even more in the future.' His patience was coming to an end.

So was mine. 'I'm glad to hear it, Major. In the meantime I'll keep an open mind.' I stood up.

'Sir, we are planning a push. It will entail seizing Sari Bair Ridge preparatory to the next stage of attack. If we don't entrench on its forward slope, we shall find ourselves in difficulty.'

'We will entrench as circumstances dictate. Thank you, Major, it has been an interesting conversation.'

'Yes, Sir.' Brigade Major Temperley saluted and left, not quite as complacent as when he had sat down.

JIM
Sniping

Snipers can't work together without trust. You can't trust unless you know the man. All we knew about Harry was that General Godley had sent him. Godley hadn't been liked from the start and nothing he'd done since had changed our minds. It was all right for Mr Grace (as lieutenants are addressed in the army) to be told to send Harry back if he wasn't OK but you don't kick out a general's man unless you are very sure. There's only one way to be sure — see how he goes on the job.

When he turned up, he shoved out his hand and smiled his big smile.

'Jim, haven't seen you since Cairo. Been keeping an eye out, but seemed to have missed you.' You'd have thought he was my long lost brother.

Now Grace knew who to pair him with.

'OK, McDonnell,' he said. 'Take him down to the butts.'

I already had a mate, and a good one.

'He hasn't a rifle, Sir.'

'He can use yours.'

It might seem funny to have a range at Anzac because the whole place was a shooting gallery. But the armourers had to have somewhere for testing and so did we.

I had gone to a lot of trouble to get my rifle right and I watched his handling of it.

He lay down and put a round up the spout.

'I'll put one away just to see how she lines up.'

'Five rounds,' I said.

'One'll do,' and he fired. 'Let's have a look.' Something stopped me from bothering him to fire four more. It was a short range and a calm day and when we went to the target we saw he'd cut the edge of the bull's-eye.

'It's always hard to fix your sights that last little bit,' he said.

So I had found, though most men after one shot would wonder whether they might have been at fault.

Back at the firing position, he lay down again.

'How many would you like?'

'Five rapid.'

He rattled them off, not seeming to hurry but not wasting time.

This time there was nothing left of the bull's-eye and everywhere else was clean.

The armourers had seen the shooting and we took up their offer of a cup of tea with milk in it. When we'd drunk it, Harry boiled the water again and cleaned the barrel for me.

'He's just joined us,' I said to the sergeant armourer. 'What have you got for him?'

'The new Mark III has just been landed, he can have one of those.'

I looked at it. It was short for a rifle and the woodwork was wrapped around the barrel. We still had the Mark II from the Boer War and its woodwork covered only the lower half of the barrel. I was about to say OK when Harry said:

'Have you a Mauser, Sergeant?' We were surprised. He might be able to hit a target but you didn't expect a Field Ambulance private to ask something like that.

'You bloody well try this,' he was told, ' and count yourself lucky. It's brand spanking new.'

'I'd like to borrow your gear,' Harry nodded at a light hammer and a small punch. 'Ten minutes and I'll have it right.'

The sergeant armourer looked at him, wondering whether to send him on his way or not. He might have been the oldest NCO at Anzac and his hair was grey. There were not many grey heads on Anzac and there were even fewer who knew his trade like he did. Mostly it was only those who had some grey themselves who would ask to borrow his tools. I would, but he knew me, and I'd pick my moment. Harry had not just asked, he had asked because he wanted to work on a rifle the sergeant armourer had just given him. But the old man knew, whether he liked it or not, snipers only trusted what they had done themselves. And he'd seen Harry's shooting. He told Harry that if he wanted to fuck it up he'd do it right here and right now.

We borrowed a locking cradle, clamped the rifle in it and Harry went to work while I had a smoke with the armourers and another cup of tea with milk in it.

Harry came back.

'You were right, Sergeant. A first class job, only needed a tap or two.'

'You don't say,' said the sergeant.

We went back to Grace. He looked up, I nodded, and he said:

'He can spot for you tomorrow.'

We weren't there with Harry yet and this was why we were wary of newcomers. Snipers mostly work in pairs. Most sniping needs a spotter as much as it does a rifleman. Trust is there when the spotter is also a sniper. A spotter uses an ordinary telescope along with the naked eye. His job is to seek out targets for the sniper and then see if there are hits. A lot of those targets are enemy snipers, so if your spotter doesn't see them, you might be the target. It's not just the spotting; if your mate is clumsy in a possie, he'll give you away no matter how well you might have camouflaged it. A lot of concentration goes into spotting, so it's normal for the pair to take turns at the telescope and the rifle. You look through a scope there too, because we were getting issued with telescopic sights by then. You had to be careful because a sure way of getting seen was to have your scope flash in the sun.

But ten minutes out with Harry was enough to learn he could spot a louse on a Turk's head and send it on its way without cutting a hair. When you were paired, that was it; you shared a bivvy and your grub. He never gave up his Bible bashing—they never do, but when he pushed it I'd let him know and he'd shut up for a while. He'd eat anything put in front of him and when he cooked you didn't die although you wouldn't want him taking his turn too often. Hot, cold, wet, dry, mud, dust, wind, calm, it didn't matter to Harry. He only noticed things like that when there was something to be sized up.

He had the head of Monash sized up. He'd been up there often enough with a stretcher. Each time he'd have kept his eyes open, watching for where the bastards might be; not just for protection but because he was like that. His stretcher-bearer mates and he had been sniped since they'd landed. Along with all the rest, some of them had been hit too. But for Harry the Turk snipers weren't bastards. They were 'brave men only doing their duty'. I didn't argue, that was his call. I never asked if he said a little prayer before he squeezed the trigger and sent another true believer on a shortcut to paradise, but I wouldn't be surprised if he had.

Harry had to get his Mauser. The Short Magazine Lee Enfield Mark III is about as good an infantry rifle as you can get. Its bolt action has no equal, you don't get your left hand burned, it's a handy length, and so long as you cover the breech when you're in mud, it can stand up to the rough. But it is not a sniper's rifle. The distance between the backsight and the foresight is on the short side for fine shooting when you use the iron sights—as, horses for courses, we sometimes did. A Mauser has an awkward bolt action but its barrel is getting on to nearly thirty inches long and its backsight is not so far forward as that of the SMLE.

Our job was to clear Shrapnel Valley and Monash Gully of snipers. Like being a rat catcher; you'll never get them all, but if you work at it, you can keep them down. Our easiest possies were trenches along the southern edge of Plugge's Plateau but the trouble was distance. The farther inland you went, the better the shooting. We had more room than the Turk sniper. He was there to cut our supply line and couldn't wander from anywhere that covered it. We were there only to deal with him and had any amount of ground for roaming. But when you were close you were not too far away from their mates in the trenches.

The exceptions to sniping in pairs were one or two like Harry or Jimmy Swan. But unless you were like them, you weren't likely to do much good or come back. Mostly you're after a target that's no bigger than a head. It fills your sight when you're aiming and after you've fired it's hard to see whether it's been hit or just moved out of the way. It's not like shooting something standing up and seeing it fall. A spotter watching through his telescope can tell you things like that. He can also direct you exactly onto the target. One day a man below Courtney's was hit. Below Deadman's there was a patch of scrub. Harry put the telescope to his eye and watched like a cat outside a mouse hole. A party from the beach came up the gully, but the Turk knew there'd be someone like us watching and took his time. Harry lay there, the telescope up, one eye closed and a half smile on his face, the flies walking across his forehead like old friends. Then the Turk fired.

'See the dried grass with bushes around it?'

'Yeah.'

'From the centre of that grass go nine o'clock to the gap between the two bushes whose shadows meet to a V.'

'OK.'

'The bush below. If you look hard you'll see the right hand side, ground level, is darker.'

I watched and then I saw something like a shadow move.

'That him?'

'That's him.'

I fired. The bush shook long enough for me to get off another shot. After that, still.

'You were right,' I said. 'How'd you pick him up?' I had been watching too, but hadn't seen a sign of anything.

'He hid himself well enough, and his muzzle flash too,' said Harry, 'but forgot about the grass in front of his muzzle flattening when he fired.'

We watched to see if anyone tried to bring him in but not for long. They had a keen-eyed lad out there who'd picked up my shot. If he'd not been so keen and waited for a clear target, either Harry or me wouldn't be here. The round went between us and we dropped. Another followed. Nothing more. Maybe we'd been forgotten about. Maybe, and we didn't move till the sun went down. Some of the boys let the cowboy stuff get away on them. They fell for the challenge, fought duels, exchanged shot for shot until the best man won. Not for Harry and me. The other man was there because he could shoot the left eye out of a fly. Why take a chance against someone like that?

'It's not a game,' Harry used to say. Maybe, but whatever it might have been, he knew how to play it. There was a Turk in the gully below the Nek. The bastard covered upper Monash and if he had you in his sights, you were a goner. He had a possie in the shade and was covered by a trench above him with riflemen nearly as good. Stretcher-bearers were his specialty and Harry felt he'd been around long enough. And, about this we had no doubt; to be able to hit at the ranges he fired, his Mauser and scope would be the best.

He talked it over with me and with Mr Grace. It was risky but not stupid. Word went out that the gully below the Nek was to be left alone until further orders. If anything moved, let it be, but watch the loopholes in the trench above the sniper and when one looked darker than the last time you looked, let rip. I positioned myself farther down the gully to watch and make a diversion by firing when I heard Harry fire.

Harry knew where he was going because he'd been there. Between first light and dawn it would be bright enough for him to move in, but not bright enough for his movements to be seen by Turk pickets unless they'd been alerted. He calculated on having about ten minutes. With dawn, the Turks would have their eyes skinned for anything that moved. When it was full daylight and the stand-to over, their eyes would not be so keen. Then he would wait and, if he was lucky, he might see what he was looking for.

Something I didn't mention earlier: along with patience, a sniper needs to be able to send off a snap shot. Targets flick in and flick out. You wait, one hour, two, half a day, all day, and then see, aim, fire. No thinking, no second chance. And getting close, that's what sorted the men from the boys. Get close, wait, snap shoot. The only way for what Harry was after.

Lying in my possie I heard someone behind me: Malone.

'Where's your mate, Corporal?'

'Gully below the Nek, Sir.'

'Who authorised that?'

'Mr Grace, Sir.'

'OK. Where in the gully?'

'Seven o'clock from the Turk trenches; twenty to thirty yards.'

He turned to me.

'That's close. Who is it?'

'Private Patterson, Sir. From Field Ambulance.'

'Him!'

'He's not bad, Sir.'

'He'd better not be.' Malone looked at the gully. 'Can you see him?'

'Not yet, Sir.'

'What's he after?'

'Turk who's been giving us a lot of trouble. A clever bastard.'

'Mind your language, McDonnell.' So he remembered me. 'Where's the Turk?'

'Gully, below the Nek, but hard to place, Sir; thick scrub and a lot of shade.'

'I'll borrow your telescope.'

'Yes, Sir.'

He screwed up an eye and peered. Easy to see he wasn't used to it, and soon his eye watered, as mine would now.

He put it down.

'If he's there, he's well hidden.'

'He's there all right.'

He looked at me sharply. I kept on watching the gully. After a while I saw what might be something moving through a shadow.

'Sir, I might be onto something.' Keeping my eyes focused, I reached for the telescope. He handed it over. A bush up the hill moved a little. Above the bush there was the ridge of a small spur that would be about twenty yards from where we reckoned the sniper would be. The ridge might give Harry cover. I turned to Malone.

'Sir, you might give us a hand. I think Harry's moved into position. We should know, maybe in five, ten minutes. If you take the telescope and look where we think the Turk is you'll be able to see better than me whether Harry gets him first go. If he just wings him, you'll tell me and I'll know where to aim. I'll fire anyway and maybe they'll think he was hit from here.'

The telescope was up to his eye and I showed him where to watch. We lay and waited, me looking through my riflescope and he the telescope, each lifting our eyes now and then so we wouldn't see things not there. There was the usual rifle fire at the head of Monash and a machine gun would sometimes fire a burst. It was a lot longer than ten minutes, but Malone lay without a twitch. His eye was running like a tap. It was hard enough for me and I was young and used to it. It was a good possie and as well hidden from the rear as from the front. The colonel was happy, doing it himself for once. So we watched where the Turk should be and then Harry fired.

Malone: 'Half way, Nek/Chessboard, six o'clock.'

I'd seen it too.

The sniper had been thrown back against the hillside and was rolling half way out of his possie as I squeezed my round off. Seeing another movement I fired again. So did Harry. A machine gun opened up and Malone and I slid to dead ground. I couldn't see whether Harry had been spotted but they weren't leaving us alone. Wouldn't be able to use the place again. Not for a while.

'Fine piece of work,' said Malone. 'My guess is you'll be seeing him after sundown, but he was cutting it a bit fine going after the observer too. My compliments to Mr Grace and tell him I wish to see Private Patterson in the morning.'

'Sir!' The colonel was right. Harry was cutting it fine and should have left the Turk spotter to me. Only a Jimmy Swann or a Harry could have got away with a second shot when every other Turk in the Gully would have been alerted by his first shot. But he wasn't going to let the Turk spotter keep the Mauser and its sight.

'You're a good lad too, but I'd watch that tongue of yours.'

'Yes Sir.'

He looked across at me.

'We need good NCOs, McDonnell, and that's you. Don't spoil it.' He crawled away.

Harry waited until dusk before he collected the rifle and sight. He went through the pockets of the two. But there wasn't much; no plans, messages, nothing like that, they were snipers.

'They had photographs,' said Harry. 'Womenfolk. Just like our boys. Nothing to bring in.'

'Except one Mauser and one sight.' I picked it up. Harry had a prize.

The sight clear as crystal and no pits in the barrel.

I told him about Malone seeing him in the morning. He went and when he came back, he said Malone had wanted to know where his family farmed and which part of Ireland his father's people were from. When Harry told him that after the war he'd go back to studying to be a minister, the old man said good churchmen made good soldiers and quoted Oliver Cromwell: 'It is plain that men of religion are wanted to withstand these gentlemen of honour.'

We didn't do too badly at counter-loophole shooting. First you had to find them. Although they were small, it was not as hard as you might think. They were in plates of bulletproof steel, with a hole for a muzzle and foresight. If you have been keeping a close eye on a parapet for a day or two, you can sense when there might have been a rearrangement. A riflescope then comes in useful. Once you have found the loophole you wait until a shadow appears behind it and then you fire. Their loopholes quietened down and moved on once they had been hit. One way to deal with them was to aim just above the top edge so that chips of steel would fly into the trench and the hole made bigger. If you split the end of a round, it would branch out and make a bigger mess of the loophole. Harry wouldn't have it on; it's against the rules of war. When one of those rounds hits a man you can put your fist in at each end.

If they'd left Harry there, he would have collected a DCM. He didn't forget us. He turned up once a week with cans of milk and peaches. When we could, we traded too—down at the beach with sailors. You wonder how they got home alive with what they shoved into their kit bags: mountain-battery shells, unexploded Turk grenades, or, after a win at poker or pontoon, a pistol with rounds. Enough to sink a ship. I'm surprised they didn't.

Then we were packed off to Happy Valley—someone had been showing off his sense of humour—and who should turn up but Harry, condensed milk and custard powder in his pack, telling us Godley had been nice enough to let him go. The boys said he was off his head, right off, but when he showed up that morning, I said to myself, 'I know you, Harry my boy, I know you.'

FRANK
War

When war was declared I was of two minds. The Wellington City battalion was calling for men to volunteer 'for an unknown destination'. Some thought it meant an advance party to France and that especially appealed. In my younger days if, unlike Katherine Mansfield, you did not have a hard nosed banker for a father, you would have to impose years of penny-pinching and committed saving on yourself before you could buy a ticket to the northern hemisphere. We were curious about the place our elders called Home or The Old Country. It raises a smile if you hear that now but every second or third adult we met originated from there. Every book we picked up, apart from the few produced by Mr Tregear and his kind, originated in Britain. We were proud to be described as more British than the British. But it was not just our real and imagined connection with Britain that drove us. By the early years of the century, after the wars had been fought, the gold panned and the land explored, New Zealand had settled down to a solid and respectable country; there was not much to excite young men with the glint of adventure in their eyes apart from running around a rugby field. In the words of one of our poets—who in 1914 had only lived his first decade and was yet to compose what he called 'Dominion'—it was becoming a country where:

> In the suburbs the spirit of man
> walks on the garden path,
> walks on the well-groomed lawn
> among the manicured shrubs.

And in the countryside:

> … the land is
> the space between barbed-wire fences,
> mortgaged in bitterness, measured in sweated butterfat.

So you might say, for a lot of young men, whether of town or country, it was not all that hard to be enticed away.

On the other hand, the riots had taught me that one remove from the action was better than being there. Along with my lack of affinity for the army, there was also a university year to finish. But it wasn't easy to keep out. Fathers, mothers, girlfriends, uncles and aunts; they had no idea what their young men would be in for. White feathers made their appearance. I received mine from a woman with a flour-bag full as I was jumping off a tram: must have been the detritus of a Sunday roast. My mother was doubly shocked. She knew the woman and I was about to go into camp. Because I did join up in 1914. Belonging to a generation unfortunate enough to be born in the 1890s, I would have gone anyway, but what tipped the balance then was a young lady. I now know that beautiful eighteen-year-olds are not all that rare but it didn't seem like it at the time. We were in a Bible Class/Teacher's College crowd that lived in a state of not entirely blissful ignorance. In the summer of 1913–14 we played tennis together. We were even able to dance, but clandestinely: the Free Church of Scotland proclaimed dancing led to sin — not, however, in our case.

Helen, being a patriotic Christian, remarked she'd never seen me in my uniform. I took the hint. By then, the Wellington boys who had volunteered had sailed for Samoa. The remainder, who considered themselves lucky, were training at Awapuni, but I heard from Harry that the Wellington battalion had a colonel who sacked slackers.

'He's a Catholic,' said Harry. ' A hard man, but a good man. Speaks his mind. Last time he was in Wellington, he agreed to meet a bloke who wanted to join.'

Mr Tregear used his connections to arrange an appointment with Malone. My mother, a capable dressmaker, turned what had been not much more than a brass-buttoned sack into something almost smart. I practised rolling my puttees and, through Harry, had an old British regular show me how to mirror-glass my boots. (Sadly for Harry, immediately after I tipped the old fellow, he headed for the pub.) When all was ready, and looking in my mother's full-length mirror, I decided Helen and I would make quite a pair.

I went down to Defence HQ and presented myself in the corridor outside the office Malone was using, making sure I arrived army time — five minutes early. Dead on the minute an orderly came out and called my name. I marched in, came to attention, muffed a salute, and stood, feeling a flush creeping up my neck.

'Private Butler!'

'Sir!'

Although I was looking straight at the wall above his head, I glimpsed a middle-aged man sitting at a desk who would be about my height but thickset. Later I'd see that his face suggested the bulk was that of a fit man. His hair and moustache were black with a few flecks of grey. His eyes were dark brown under heavy eyebrows. I waited for an order to stand at ease. It did not come.

'You wish to join my battalion?'

'Yes Sir.'

'Why are you not in Samoa?'

A glimpse of those eyes indicated a qualified reply would not receive much sympathy. 'I had exams to sit, Sir.'

'University?'

'Yes Sir.'

'Have you sat them?'

'No Sir.'

'When will you be sitting them?'

'November, early November, Sir.'

'If you go to the recruiting office and state your reasons for having your call-up delayed, they will take notice.'

'I am willing to go now, Sir. I hear … I hear you sometimes have vacancies.'

'Not many, but they occur.' He looked down at what I realised must be my personal file. 'You've had three years' Territorial service. There's nothing negative on your record.' He looked up. 'There's nothing positive either. It's correct you attended all parades and camps?'

'Yes Sir.'

'But nothing more. There is nothing here that tells me you attended any course for prospective NCOs or officers, or anything else.'

'No Sir.'

'I expect more from young men such as you, Butler. It's obvious you come from a good family and are well educated. You have a duty, Private Butler, to serve your country to the best of your abilities.' He paused. 'To the very best of your abilities.'

Doubting he expected me to comment on that, I kept quiet.

He looked me up and down.

'Do you know what is the greatest virtue of a soldier?'

This time I tried. 'Discipline, Sir.'

'Discipline is a given, Butler. Without discipline there is no soldier. Fortitude. Fortitude is the greatest virtue of a soldier.' He looked at me hard.

'Sir!'

'Will you pass your examinations?'

'Maybe, Sir.'

'Maybe? What do you mean, maybe? You will or you won't.' He flipped the file shut. 'Have you worked?'

'Yes Sir.' No option but to put a gloss on the truth.

'Then you will pass,' he said quietly. He put the file down and looked up again. 'Do what I say, Butler. Sign up and explain your circumstances. When the examinations are over, they will call you up. If you pass the medical, we shall see you some time next year. Wherever that might be. The war will not be over by Christmas.' He paused again, his eyes still fixed on me. 'What are you studying?'

'This year, languages, Sir.'

'Le français?'

'Oui Monsieur, et …' here I hesitated because such an admission, to many people, made my patriotism suspect. 'Et l'allemand, Monsieur.' Only then did I realise I had replied in French.

'Combien de temps avez-vous étudié le français et l'allemand?'

'Quatre ans dans le secondaire et deux ans à l'université.' I was surprised, but he spoke with ease.

'Est-ce que la langue que vos professeurs vous ont enseignée, c'était leur langue maternelle?'

'Oui Monsieur, à l'université, notre professeur était une dame française. Nous étions très heureux de l'avoir.'

'Oui, ça s'entend. Votre accent est correct, meilleur que celui des gens qui ont appris ici, ou malheureusement, mais c'est général, on apprend toute chose en seconde main. D'avoir un professeur originaire du pays dont il enseigne la langue, c'est une immense chance. Comment est votre allemand?'

'Peut-être un peu mieux que mon français, Monsieur.'

'Avez-vous réalisé combien il a pu être important de savoir parler l'allemand à Samoa?'

'Oui, je le sais, maintenant.'

'Donc vous le savez. Voici l'enseignement que vous pouvez en tirer, Butler. La Nouvelle-Zélande n'a pas forgé sa réputation sur l'enseignement des langues étrangères, et votre allemand vous aurait été très utile. En complétant vos études, vous serez mieux à même de servir votre pays. Assurez-vous que toutes les langues que vous parlez soient mentionnées sur vos certificats.[1] Dismissed.'

I saluted, turned, and saw a clock on the opposite wall; it had taken ten minutes to the dot.

---

[1] Square brackets enclose the English version of the French text.
'[French?]'
'[Yes Sir, and ...]' here I hesitated because such an admission, to many people, made my patriotism suspect. '[And German, sir.]' Only then did I realise I had replied in French.
'[How long did you study French and German for?]'
'[Four years at school and two at university.]' I was surprised, but he spoke with ease.
'[Were you taught by native speakers?]'
'[A French woman, Sir, at university. We were lucky to have her.]'

I was disappointed and so was Helen, but we had more time with each other and when the call-up came, the location of Trentham Camp could not be bettered. A short trip down the valley and there she was and home too for a decent meal and a hot bath. When friends and families came out to the camp, there she was again, the more innocent of my brothers-in-arms rather envious, and the worldlier, after some observation, doubting there was much in it for me. It is fair to say, however, that if our leave-taking had not been so rigorously chaperoned, they could well have been proved wrong. Whether that would have changed our relationship in the long run, who knows?

It was less than twenty weeks between entering Trentham and clambering up to Quinn's Post. We steamed into Anzac on a beautiful calm night, the vessel gliding through the shimmering water, the only wave the bow wave. A raid was on and our introduction to a battlefield could not have been staged better. Muzzle flashes lit up the hillsides and the red parabolas of shells screamed up into the hills to explode in sheets of yellow and white. In the din of rifles and machine guns for the first time we heard the distinctive pit-pot of the Mauser and the thuds of grenades. Between artillery flashes twinkled the lights of hundreds of bivvies, which, if you ignored the noise (not possible) looked not much different from entering Wellington on an evening ferry.

We tumbled into barges. Overshot shrapnel splashed alongside and a voice remarked the Government should be told about bringing us here, as someone might get hurt. Disembarking, we stumbled along the pier, well cursed and shoved aside: supplies in and wounded out—blood-caked

---

'[You were indeed. Your accent is fair, better than most who are taught it here, who, unfortunately, generally have to learn everything second hand. Having a native speaker is a great advantage. How is your German?]'
'[Perhaps a little better than my French, Sir.]'
'[Are you aware that German might have been useful in Samoa?]'
'[I am now, Sir.]'
'[You are now. There is a lesson for you there, Butler. New Zealand has a poor record for foreign languages, and your German would have been useful. By completing your studies, you might be able to serve your country better. Make sure each of the languages is noted on your attestation form.] Dismiss.'

bandages, matted hair, stupefied faces. Passing stretcher cases and other wounded, we were guided to Rest Gully to shots and flashes of the fire-fight from Monash. The lucky ones had somewhere to sit, the remainder crouched with blankets across their shoulders muttering inconsequentially to one another. About a hundred yards long, a V cut out of the landscape, Rest Gully, with six or seven hundred bivvies hacked into its sides, could have been an encampment of down-and-out gypsies.

As dawn broke, we discerned its occupants. Hollow cheeked, gaunt, with eyes fixed on something over your shoulder, they made terse replies when friends and acquaintances were enquired after: some dead, more wounded and many sick. Further enquiries went unanswered: we had not been there on St Crispin's Day. A unique bond is formed between men who have little in common but associate closely when danger, tedium, and inhuman conditions combine. A relationship of mutual reliance and tolerance, it accepts human qualities to the greatest degree. There have to be very good reasons for that acceptance to run out. When it does you feel betrayed and deal harshly with the miscreant, but that didn't happen often, so strong was the need to maintain the bond. Which is not to say that, from time to time, each of us did not descend to silent detestation of our comrades—which is what they were. A comrade is thrust upon you, a friend is chosen. During their six weeks on the Peninsula the veterans had learnt the cost of making friends.

I was posted to Wellington-West Coast Company: mostly upcountry Wanganui farmers and bushmen. We'd been hanging around an hour when I heard a familiar voice. It was Harry. When he saw I had heard him, he waved but stopped to talk with someone and on the way stopped a couple of times more. He said hello as if we had run into one another after a long holiday, his smile as broad as ever. Again I noticed his light blue eyes. In one respect he was like the rest: down to tattered shirtsleeves and shorts, in keeping with a scarecrow Australian slouch hat.

'I'd have looked you up earlier, but we've been busy at Monash.'

'Many casualties?'

He paused, the smile still there.

'A few.'

'Well, that's not so bad, if it's only a few.' A stupid thing to say, I thought.

He slapped my shoulder. 'It's good to see you, Frank.' His gaze shifted. 'Just a minute,' and he was off to speak to another new chum. Harry shook his hand, asked him a question, seemed pleased with the reply, spoke a few more words, and was back to me again.

'Keith Fraser,' he said, 'His family were members of our little church. I told him about prayer meetings we hold and he said he'd be glad to attend and will look out for anyone else who might be interested.'

I must have shown my surprise.

'Yes,' said Harry, 'here in the midst of all this we have time to worship. You will join us, of course?'

I couldn't think of anything else but to nod.

'Excellent! I always try and contact the new fellows when they come in and I always find some to join our little group.' He looked around. 'Have you got a mate?'

'Well, no.' Hoping he would volunteer.

'You'll need one, for your bivvy. Need two for that.' He strode off to Keith Fraser and brought him back. 'You two know each other? Good. Come with me.' We were given a brief tour of unoccupied bivouacs. 'Best ones have gone, but …' pausing, looking around, and down again, 'this'll do. A bit far in and maybe a bit high up but pretty well sheltered from what Johnny throws at us and in a rainstorm no one's going to slide down on you. Here,' he grabbed my haversack and put it down. 'You've claimed it now. Tidy it up, put a couple of ground sheets across the top and when you've got time, go down to the beach and scrounge extra ground sheets and anything else useful and you'll be as snug as bugs in a rug. Just here,' and he kicked the hillside with his boot, 'is where you'll boil the billy.'

The earth was blackened from other boil-ups, but, on looking higher, I noticed what might be a better site, and began climbing up to it. My ankle was gripped and I was stopped right there.

'Far enough, Frank, or Johnny'll have you.'

Grateful and embarrassed, I slid down.

'Now,' he pointed. 'That's where Jim and I are. When you get your rations, come over and we'll show you what to do with them.'

Keith and I had shared Trentham and the voyage, but that was all. While we were together, I think I profited more than he as he could turn his hand to just about anything. He did not have a great deal to say but when he did it was brief, to the point and, on occasions, rather dry. He attended Harry's prayer meetings and services held by a Protestant chaplain but he never spoke about it. He was unwaveringly steady. When Malone praised the battalion he was thinking of men like Keith.

We took our lumps of bacon, hard biscuit and tea to Harry's bivvy. With him was Jim McDonnell. He said little, observing you from under his brow, leaving Harry to do the talking, which was a short course on what you might do with axle-grease bacon, bully beef reminiscent of the pampas it originated from, and biscuits whose scrapings off the sharp edge of a tin might be edible. But because Keith produced a tin of condensed milk and I a chocolate bar, the four of us had what I was soon to learn, was an Anzac feast.

Their bivvy had an air of permanence about it, different from others in the gully, cut deep into the hillside, with solid sandbag walls.

'You seem to have the pick of the bivvies.'

'We've been here a while,' said Harry.

'Field Ambulance stay put?' I said.

'I'm giving the infantry a try.'

'You are?'

'It's the infantry who take the brunt,' he said.

'A combatant,' I said.

'We're all combatants, Frank.'

I was puzzled. Then I noticed the butt and bolt of a rifle just inside the entrance to the bivvy, which was different from those on our Lee Enfields.

'What's that?'

'Mauser.'

'A souvenir?'

'No.' His tone was mild. 'Jim and I snipe.'

'You do!'

He smiled and nodded.

At a loss for words for the moment, I turned my head towards the Mauser and remarked it had a telescopic sight.

'All the way from Germany,' said Jim.

I looked closer. Rifle and sight were spotless, the woodwork gleaming with oil.

'When you go up tomorrow, there'll be one less Johnny than today.' Jim had found his voice. 'You can thank him for that.'

'A brave man,' said Harry.

Trying to cover my bewilderment, I asked, 'Why a Mauser?'

'Came with the sight,' said Jim.

Our corporal was yelling so Keith and I took off. Latrine fatigue: and having just arrived, we were the obvious choice.

Around midnight Wellington went into Quinn's for the first time. At Anzac, you did not descend into hell; you went up and it was Quinn's Post. You climbed the side of Monash Gully, the stench thickening, to enter a combined sewage and charnel pit: dried blood, flesh, guts, and rotting limbs. After a couple of yards up came my breakfast, the start of a chain reaction, back along the line. In no man's land, just out of reach, the corpses lay as they had fallen, inflated to frightful Michelin men.

It was eight days in and eight days out for the next two months. Once in, the routine was forty-eight hours in the forward trenches, twenty-four hours in support and twenty-four hours in reserve. But the first week was different. There were front line trenches where the parapet had been flattened. We started from the bottom of the trench, laying and inter-laying one sandbag over another, hoping, *praying*, we weren't in line for a Turk grenade. Trench floors were dust alive with maggots because, although we got rid of the carrion within, corpses in no man's land mounted up, crawling maggots their shrouds.

Folded greatcoats were to hand so that when a sentry yelled a grenade was on its way or landed, a coat could be thrown over it, the thrower ducking into the next bay. Some threw grenades back. More often than not, it worked, but when it didn't you were lucky if only your hand was blown off. Our grenades were homemade from tins, gelignite, and scrap iron.

The Turks had a German cricket ball type, but not an unlimited supply, so homemade varieties came at us too.

Quinn's was seven interconnected small trench systems, spilling down from the crest of Monash with numbers Three and Four fronting a no man's land seven yards wide. Number Four had a listening post sapped out to six feet from a Turk post, plus a manhole for tossing grenades. The one loophole was like a big keyhole and when I took my turn at it, I hardly dared blink. Grenades were attracted like flies and when we took over the roof was regularly blown in — once when Keith and I were in it. I envied the way he calmly worked in the chaos of shrapnel, grenades, flies and putrefaction, his humour becoming drier by the day. If, in our digging, there were a month old corpse to dig out, he would shovel seemingly oblivious to where his nose happened to be. One day I was laying sandbags at the base of a parapet. He yelled, I jumped, he threw the greatcoat, and whump! Shaking, I felt his hand on my shoulder and heard 'OK, you can come out now.' He shoved a sandbag at me, I took it, and crawled to the shredded coat.

We also learnt about rest at Rest Gully. Water carrying is what sticks in the memory. We did a lot of it and never had enough water: four pints a day when at Quinn's. We dug gun positions, bivvies for reinforcements and our share of the Main Sap, parallel with North Beach, and wide enough for mules — there were men who would jump out of the sap and risk being sniped rather than squeeze past a train of mules. It was done at night. During the day, you either slept while flies explored you or you didn't sleep. Mouth, eyelids and nostrils: they loved them. As for eating, wave your spare hand as you like, they rode into your mouth like an escalator.

'You never were a soldier unless you was lousy,' I heard an old dig reminiscing on the radio. Lice, an enduring memory; when recalled, the itch returns, a living hair shirt from top to toe. When swimming, hoping the shrapnel would not burst too close, we sank our clothes. Dried out, they'd be stiff with salt but free for the next hour or so. Every spare moment; shirt and pants off, we would be burning matches along seams and pinching the maddening pests between fingernails. Lice, as we were to learn, didn't stop at the edge of the Aegean. Just what they can do to you is recorded by the diminutive East End Jewish poet, Rosenberg—at least the equal of Wilfred Owen—when he recounts events he witnessed in some literally lousy peasant barn in either Belgium or France:

> … For a shirt verminiously busy
> Yon soldier tore from his throat, with oaths
> Godhead might shrink at, but not the lice.
> And soon the shirt was aflare
> Over the candle he'd lit while we lay.
> Then we all sprang and stript
> To hunt the verminous brood.
> Soon like a demons' pantomime
> The place was raging.
> See the silhouettes agape,
> See the gibbering shadows
> Mixed with the battled arms on the wall.
> See gargantuan hooked fingers
> Pluck in supreme flesh
> To smutch supreme littleness …

Well, it wasn't quite like that with us; we were on a beach in the sun and didn't have the energy. Whatever, lice were to be with us on whatever front we were to be shoved into.

Ranks thinned. You stayed until you dropped and too often returned too soon. I was lucky. I passed out. Coming-to: the sky revolved, nausea hit and, when hauled upright, my knees buckled, and passed out again. Twenty-four hours on the hospital ship *Gascon*, clean, *with no lice*, and a nurse with a smooth face and soft hands. Ashore to an Australian hospital on Lemnos where, with straw mattresses on ground sheets, as short of medicines as staff, the doctors and orderlies worked themselves to the bone. But reasonable food and rest, especially rest, allowed most bodies to heal themselves. After a fortnight I was transferred to a convalescent camp where I teamed up with an Aussie and walked the island for another fortnight, talking about everything except war and sampling the abominable wine.

Believe it or not, when declared fit, we had a job getting back to Anzac.

All was geared to the big push. It was only when they cleared out the hospitals and convalescent camps for the offensive that they put us aboard a destroyer carrying dispatches from Sir Ian Hamilton to General Birdwood.

MALONE
Happy Valley

We are lying up, north of Walker's Ridge, in Happy Valley. Triangular and shallow, it broadens to the sea between two spread spurs. The valleys we will need to penetrate tonight will be much narrower than this, their sides steeper and their scrub just as thick, and it will hide the Turk as it now hides us. From where I am there is a fine view of the sea. The hue and calm of the Aegean has not lost the beauty that inspired the ancients. I am not the only one who has gained comfort and strength from the sight of it. We lie back in the scrub, relishing the quiet and the scent of wild thyme. The men chat, doze, and gaze up at the sky and clean weapons already clean. Last night they wrote letters and sang. The songs were of home and sentimental. Afterwards I told them they had done their duty, will do it again, and that I am proud of them.

When you have had noise hour after hour, day after day, the quiet takes getting used to. We can hear birds. They were here when we landed, and the day after, but before we went down to Helles they had gone. A comfort they haven't fled us entirely; just moved out of our way. Although there is fire to the south, it is sporadic and distant, not enough to disturb us. Calm, but still vulnerable. We are overlooked by Sniper's Nest, its occupants yet unsuppressed, and above a German aeroplane drones. It would only need somebody to show himself and with him would go any hope of success tonight. It would be best if we could sit like statues, but that is impossible for all but very few. I do not know a man who is well. There seems no way to avoid it. We are the cleanest unit on the Peninsula and yet it is going through all of us. Night and day one runs to and fro. I need to now, but with the German aeroplane, I cannot move. Will I be able to control myself? ... I succeeded, but it was very close and, like my men, I used my entrenching tool. Would that other units did; the flies have found us again.

Because of Sir Ian Hamilton's demand for strict secrecy, only yesterday could I take my officers and NCOs to higher ground to view the Sari Bair skyline and the ridgelines below it. Afterwards I called my company commanders together to share what we had learned. It was very little. Although I told them of twice accompanying Godley and Johnston aboard a destroyer to study the approaches to the Sari Bair range from the sea, I was unable to add to what they already knew. Nobody can. Because Hamilton feared they might be captured, few scouts were sent out.

At Helles the plan I put to Paris and Richardson was a simple left hook through the Turkish right flank. As circumstances were then, the flank was in the air, the Turks having no option but to rely on its rugged terrain and a few outposts and snipers to defend it. The advance would have been a broad sweeping, closing door movement across the Suvla plain and up the northern spurs of the Sari Bair range. I am sure we had enough men to do it. So the situation remained for much of May. In June, once the Turks had secured the Anzac line they turned their attention to their right flank; every week since they have dug more trenches and deeper.

The mark of the great captain is never to let an opportunity slip. Sir Ian has. When he should have acted, he asked for more men. Now, two months later, they have arrived: three 'New Army' divisions. He inspired me for years but, now that I recall his definition of a commander, it lacked a key point. A commander, however professional he might be, must *lead*. Sir Ian did not mention this. His plan for the Sari Bair assault does not bear the mark of a general who has sized up the enemy and the terrain on which his battle is to be fought. It is a plan evolved by staff remote from reality and enveloped by paper. Sir Ian does not fight the enemy; his subordinates do.

Even if the country were easy and familiar it would still be a complicated plan. Each field commander of the thirty-seven thousand under General Birdwood's command has been given an objective and a time to gain that objective. The objectives and times are all interlinked and each dependent on the success of the other. A New Army division is to land at Suvla Bay, seize the plain, and advance to where the Sari Bair plain terminates: the topography of which is unclear. South of Suvla, four columns are to advance and converge on Chunuk Bair. They comprise two New Army Brigades, an Australian and an Indian Brigade, and the New Zealanders. At Anzac the Australians will make feint attacks. I have never been a lover of our antipodean neighbours but they are now hardened and experienced, and under the recently promoted Walker, ably led. Why are they being wasted on feints while the half-trained, untried New Army units—who at best might garrison Egypt—are given major roles?

When Johnston called his commanders together, he was not exaggerating when he said we had been given the prime task. With its two rounded peaks and saddle in between, Chunuk Bair on the Sari Bar ridge has loomed above us from the day we landed. Whoever holds Chunuk Bair dominates the Narrows. As if advancing in column up trackless hillsides were not difficult enough, Otago has been put in the lead and additionally tasked to secure Rhododendron Ridge, a spur that leads straight up to Chunuk Bair. Wellington has to secure Cheshire Ridge, a northern, and less significant, spur off Chunuk Bair. To do this, we will first have to pass *through* Otago. When Moore and I have secured our respective ridges, our battalions are to move on Chunuk Bair. If Moore messes up, all of us will.

I was reluctant to speak on the matter, but there was no alternative. I secured an appointment with Brigadier Johnston the next day—along with other brigade commanders, he has been promoted.

'It's a complicated plan, Sir.'

'It's not simple, no,' he cheerfully admitted.

'We'll be heavily reliant on the Mounteds and the Maoris to clear the foothills. What contingency plans have we if things do not go as expected?'

'With commanders like General Russell and Colonel Meldrum things *will* go as planned. Each officer is highly respected. I,'—a laugh—'have heard you say so yourself.' Another laugh. 'You're not always free with your praise, Malone.'

'Thank you, Sir. It was the terrain and the Turks I was concerned about. It is a night attack. And it will be without artillery preparation. We know so little of where we will be going.'

'Malone, you were the one pressing for a night attack at Helles. Now you're complaining about your wishes not being granted.'

'What we'll be going into here is different from Helles, Sir.'

'The scouts have been out. By now they'll know it like the back of their hands. They're good lads; you as much as anybody, Colonel, should know that.'

'They don't have cat's eyes, Sir, and they haven't been out all that much. And Otago, nearly all of whom are recent reinforcements,' as I politely put it, 'are to lead the rest of us.'

'Colonel Moore is an experienced officer. His men will be well whipped into shape by now. Just the fellow to lead a night attack. Give him a chance to rectify his bad luck at Baby 700.'

'The Otagos ...' I deliberately avoided saying Moore, 'The Otagos will be finding their own way. If they are held up, diverted, or lost, all of us will be compromised and, with no artillery preparation, at the mercy of the enemy on the heights.'

'Lost? Colonel, you speak as if we were a bunch of Boy Scouts. Do you really believe that Wellington is the only trained battalion in the brigade?'

It was with some effort that I kept my voice level. 'I'm concerned about the unexpected, Sir. No allowance seems to have been made for it.'

'I find it difficult to understand you, Malone. Auckland, our reserve battalion, is to deal with that.'

'Of course, Sir.' Not that I lacked confidence in Young, one of my former officers. 'But it is possible to envisage that matters might go wrong at different times in different places. There do not appear to be the necessary allowances to deal with these if they occur.'

'If there's any hitch, Malone, I'll go and take the place myself!' He really believed it. 'But we have an experienced brigade. All of us, since the day we landed, have had to deal with the unexpected.'

In more ways than one, with the likes of him. 'We have also deteriorated physically, Sir. Hardly a man would pass a medical examination and yet we have been given a key role in the attack.'

'Indeed we have, Colonel. And you may thank me for that. General Birdwood, although not as pessimistic as you, suggested that because we had done so much and been so knocked about, we should not participate.'

'He did?' I was amazed, not at what he'd told me about Birdwood, it was what I would have expected of him, but that we were still included.

'Yes, but I reassured him we would consider it to be a dishonour to be overlooked in what will be the major offensive in the campaign. He demurred a little, but I insisted, and I rarely insist with a lieutenant general, believe me. I insisted that we be given the lead role. My men may be colonials, I said, but they are well up to it.'

'I see.' He may have wondered why I slowly turned and looked out to sea, but if I had not, I would most likely have given him such a piece of my tongue that it would have been impossible for the two of us to have remained in the same army. It was mid-summer on Anzac and was a day that reminded you that the desert was not far away. A day that, even under the best of conditions, would give you a perpetually dry throat; just then it might have been sandpaper. I did not trust myself to ask for a glass of water; I would have been unable to control my tone. One of our aeroplanes, perhaps the only one, had circled and was flying to rejoin the fleet. I made out it had caught my attention, and breathed some very deep breaths. before turning back to him. 'The Twenty-ninth Division, Sir,' I said, 'a division of regular soldiers of many years training, was sent off the Peninsula for a rest. We, apart from some brief sojourns on Lemnos, have had no rest. My own battalion didn't even go to Lemnos. Perhaps that might be as much my fault as anybody else's because I have not pressed for it, but we are not in a fit condition.'

'We considered giving you a spell, Colonel, but your battalion was doing such an essential job, we couldn't see our way clear to relieve you.'

So that was our reward!

'I suppose the brigade could have done with a change of air,' said he. 'Gone back to Egypt, rested and straightened ourselves up, but as you yourself have said, the Englishmen have nowhere near the health and stamina of our boys. Besides the Twenty-ninth, not being so rough and ready as us, need more time to bring their reinforcements up to regular standard.'

Faced with the choice of saying what was in my mind or saying nothing, I said nothing. And what was there to say? His comprehension of the issues involved was that of a schoolboy.

'And remember, Colonel, the credit we have received for *volunteering* ourselves.'

On reflection I have come to the conclusion that if it had not been so serious it would have been laughable. The brigadier is a strange being: decent as a man, hopeless as a soldier. Despite our arguments, he doesn't speak with malice, and unless rattled, his manner is always friendly. It has now become only too plain to me that Brigadier General Johnston was recognised as the fool of the family. He was put into the regular army by his family not because they perceived he had a talent for the calling, but because they believed there was no other profession where he might fit. Once in the army, he made it a home away from home. The only decisions of his own were trivial, and those made by his superiors he never considered.

I went and saw Colonel Young, told him the gist of what had been said, and suggested he accompany me to have another look at where we were to attack. He willingly agreed and we first climbed Walker's Ridge, saw what we could from there, trying to get the lie of the land, particularly the high points. Then we went along North Beach as far as we could to see how it looked from there. We agreed with Johnston in one respect: if Russell and Meldrum could not clear the foothills, nobody could. After that, we concluded *if* Otago, and Canterbury behind them, did not get lost or held up, and *if* the Turk garrison is no stronger than believed and *if* the terrain is as has been described, all should turn out as planned.

Although the difficulties begin at brigade level, they do not end there. I am not vain enough to believe I was the only one to think of a flank attack from the left, nor that I was the first to do so. Goodness gracious I have nothing against my commanding officers personally. General Godley has treated me as well as anybody could be treated. It is he who gave me a command and, I am sure, he who was responsible for my being sent to Quinn's and retained there as its commandant. And it is he who has marked my company commanders for battalion command; if Hart had not been wounded he would now command Auckland and it is Young, my next best, who was appointed there. When Hart returns, I shall lose him when the next command comes up and I expect it will not be long before Cunningham follows. Soon we shall command the whole brigade.

General Birdwood has also been a frequent visitor and unstinting in his praise of the battalion. But why did he not over-rule Johnston's volunteering the brigade? He sees for himself daily the condition of the men. He could have restored us to what we were if we had returned to Egypt to recuperate and reinforce. And the implementation of General Hamilton's plan, with its over-emphasis on finesse and ignoring of unknowns, which Godley and he have devised, is also complex, encouraging hesitation rather than boldness. Of one matter only am I sure: my men and I shall do everything to ensure the attack will not fail.

Mail is being delivered! Only lately do they seem to have it organised; too often it has been sent the most roundabout way possible or held up at base for no reason. It is mail that keeps us going, a reminder that the world of our loved ones is still there and we are still in their minds, cheering us up as nothing else can. I shall absent myself, briefly, with instructions that I am to be disturbed only on matters of urgency.

I put my trust in God and my men. I am prepared to die and if that is to be, I shall die happily. For my frequent absences from my dear loving wife and family, whom I have neglected more than a husband and father should, for when I have been hasty and unkind and indifferent to my fellow mortals, may God forgive me.

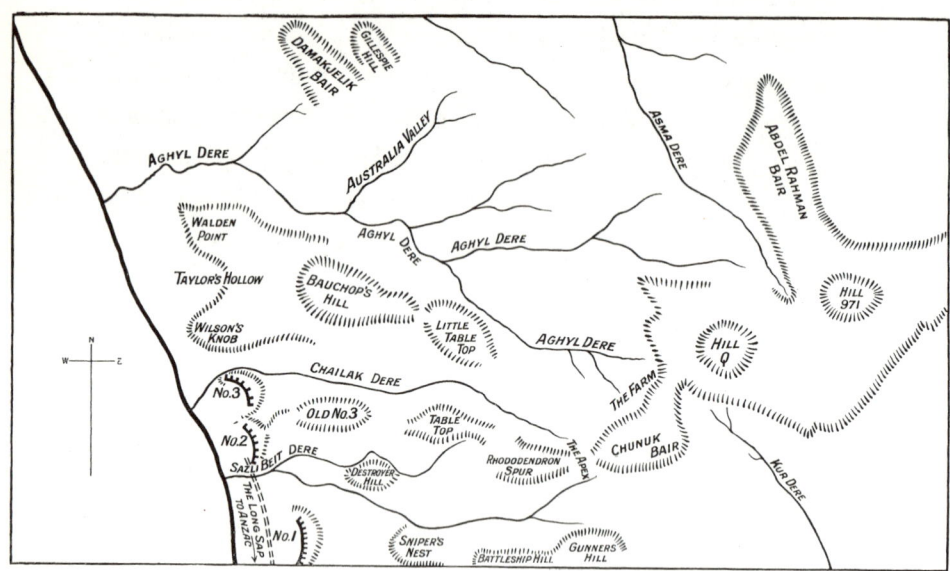

Approaches to Chunuk Bair. *Source: Waite, F.*

HARRY
Chunuk Bair

When I returned to the Wellingtons they had just been relieved from Quinn's. As we moved out of Shrapnel Valley and across to Happy Valley it was a sad sight. Worn out as they were by dysentery, bad food, lack of sleep, stifling heat, and under fire night and day from an enemy whose proximity could be measured in feet, the contrast between them and Headquarters' men like myself was distressingly obvious.

You are not likely to meet many New Zealand infantrymen who fought in the August battles, but if you do, all will have a tale to tell about Rhododendron Spur. As it branches off Chunuk Bair (Hill of War, so ours can't be the first battle for it) its crest narrows to a small peak known as the Pinnacle. Below the Pinnacle the crest drops and rises to another small peak called the Apex. Below the Apex, the crest widens enough to contain a hollow. Beyond the hollow, it broadens out, like the rump of a well-fed horse.

I first went up Rhododendron Spur when, on the afternoon before the Wellington attack, a sniper mate of Jimmy Swan and I covered Jimmy on a forward patrol. He reported that on the crest of Chunuk Bair were two shallow trenches and one machine gun and some riflemen. About three a.m. Wellington formed up, with Hawke's Bay the lead company. The 9th Gloucesters and the 8th Welch Pioneers were to follow. Jimmy and I scouted ahead. No crawling this time, moving from shadow to shadow, alert, gliding will-o'-the-wisp style. No Turk outposts and no noise except Hawke's Bay behind us. It was eerie. One wondered about an ambush.

Darkness was turning grey when we closed on the crest. Jimmy went ahead and I lay with the Mauser at my shoulder. When he waved I joined him to see a rough, disconnected trench. Peering over the parapet were heads, and at one end, a Maxim with its Number One and Number Two ready. We'd been ordered to report back when the enemy was sighted, but with the Maxim there was only one thing to do. Jimmy pointed to the heads, I nodded and we fired.

We expected Hawke's Bay to have rushed up right there with us but they stood *waiting for something to happen.* Jimmy turned and yelled that the Turks were just over the rise. No reply or movement. Something stirred above the parapet and I shot it. Johnny yelled for an officer and again when nobody responded to that, he yelled for them to get a b—— move on and dashed forward as heads appeared. I put them down. Jimmy rushed the Maxim, kicked it over and shot a German NCO who tried to bayonet him. Some Turks let off a shot and ran to another trench. Others tried to surrender. Too often, in the heat of battle, this is not always successful and so it proved here, although we secured another German NCO. Hawke's Bay had at last got a move on and they charged and took the other trench. But there were still no officers evident, otherwise we may well have, as Jimmy wanted, charged to the north and taken the next peak, Hill Q, there being enough of us to overwhelm it.

Warfare is full of ifs, but I really feel that if we had charged while there was still momentum, Hill Q would have been ours and saved a lot of trouble. Who held Hawke's Bay up? Even today when the few survivors of the company get together you will hear talk about whom it was and how his family connections supposedly led to his position. A name is bandied around, but he, like so many, never left Chunuk Bair.

As the sky lightened, the Mudros plain, The Narrows, and where they widened—the passage to Constantinople: our ultimate objective—came into view. We felt privileged, the first British unit to see such a sight. Only a passing glance however. Hard digging. Parties were at once sent to occupy Turk gun pits, unoccupied, below and in front of us on the forward slope. The brighter the light the better we were seen and the enfilading began. Upper Rhododendron Ridge and its slopes received their ration too, the rear of the 7ᵗʰ Gloucesters getting it. When their leaders were hit, they ran, open to any machine gunner within range. Most of their officers and NCOs, brave but no better trained than their men, were soon dead, although a few, I suspect, also ran. A party was mustered and put to work at digging an extension of the crest trench, while their rear companies crowded into the support trench being dug on the reverse slope by Ruahine and Taranaki. There was also the Welsh Pioneer Battalion. They had no show at all, being hit right from the start. Some crowded into our trenches and others tried running.

On the crest our two hundred yard trench did not allow much room for two half battalions even if one of those halves was a remnant, though we soon thinned out. We might have dug out a couple of feet, but no more. Each man had carried two sandbags and once filled they made a low parapet. We badly lacked a machine gun. Turk skirmishers quickly engaged our men in the gun pits. Because of the heavy scrub and the steep slope, our boys had no more than muzzle flashes to aim at. They were also enfiladed. A few climbed up the slope and into our trench.

Although the first wave of the Turks was suicidal for many, it was not without result; when the survivors retired we were fewer to meet the next rush. Then came a grenade attack. The casualties thinned out the shallow and overcrowded trench. Another charge followed, then another deluge of grenades and so it went on. Neither did the fire from our left and right let up. Plenty came across from the Anzac sector, so we knew that whatever diversions or assaults had been made, matters were not going well there either. The low parapet made me reach out and with one hand haul a heavy Turk onto the sandbags. It was mistreating the dead, and if I'd had to move him when quietness reigned it would have taken both hands. But that didn't happen because a grenade did for my foot. It was the left foot, fragments ripping through my boot, opening up the flesh and going in. It took my field dressing and another man's — I never saw him again.

I managed to crawl over the crest and then, on the reverse side, I paused to work out the pattern of Turk rounds hitting the ground. There was no pattern to the overthrown grenades so I had to take my chances but, thanks to the Almighty, none landed near me. Dragging the foot I crawled past the support trench, where the colonel had made his headquarters, into a gully near the head of Chailak Dere. It gave cover from small arms' fire, but not shrapnel. We did what we could for each other, but many were incapable of helping themselves or anybody else. The higher the sun rose, the more the gully became an oven. There were bushes, but they were mostly too low to cast much shade. The only water was what might have remained in water bottles filled the night before. Tongues swelled to fill our mouths. Beside me there was a boy who had been in at the landing, walked away from Helles, gone through Courtney's and Quinn's, and now, with a shattered knee, he had a shoulder torn by shrapnel. The hospital ships, white and clean, and the barges ferrying wounded out to them, could be seen through our swollen eyelids. For many it was their last sight on this earth. As hour followed hour there would be two to three hundred in the gully. It became a pit of agony.

When the numbness wore off the pain in the foot was not light. But I was one of the lucky ones. I could crawl, so as I lay there I bent my mind on how to get out. The foot never eased and I might have been delirious at times but I knew I would have to move. I prayed for strength and watched the shadows as the sun rose and began to fall. The scrub grew in patches or as isolated shrubs. The route which seemed to offer most would be where I would first have to crawl down to a dry watercourse and then zigzag up the slope to the crest of Rhododendron Spur. Unless the shadows were right I would not have to climb up far before I would be in view of the snipers on Sari Bair. Until mid-afternoon, the shadows were too short to provide cover: too much bare clay.

It was hard, waiting. In the meantime I looked north to Suvla Bay. Do not believe those who tell you we could see the New Army troops sitting on the beach, swimming and sunning themselves. In a sight line, it's five miles down there; far enough for the brown plain to take on a tinge of blue. You cannot see what men are doing at that distance. I pondered on how long it would take those New Army troops to advance across that waterless plain and then through the foothills up to the Sari Bair range before the Turks met them. I decided they would be lucky to make the first foothills. A real general would have sent in an experienced fast moving force—Gurkhas, or French colonials up from Helles—with support coming in behind. That, or something like it, might have made a difference. I had plenty of time to think while keeping my interest in the pattern of shadows and with the foot protesting. There was the never-ending rattling din of musketry and throughout the day, men made their way down, some unwounded.

By mid-afternoon, when the midsummer sun was dropping and swinging to the north, the shadows mottled the hillside in a helpful camouflage. I have made easier crawls. I was stiff from lying so long and the leg seized up when, forgetting, I tried to use the foot. I took account of the lie of the land and avoided gutters cut by the spring rains, as it was hard getting out of them. I took rests, and at the foot of the hillside I needed a longer one. Nearby, crouched together, were wounded Turks. As I turned to them, as one they cupped their hands and raised them to their swollen lips. I could only shake my head. Here in the pain and horror, they were no longer the enemy.

I examined the hillside like a rock climber, except that I was not looking for what might assist a climb, but what might obscure it. Part way up, a poor chap lay on his back, hanging grotesquely across a shrub, eyes staring and arms stretched out. Only yards away, two more had fallen, crumpled on the ground, slide marks on the clay and smashed branches in the scrub leading from where they'd been hit. My route had to be in shade and yet gentle for crawling. It would be a long trip and, along the way, I would have to traverse sunlit clay—a fly on a wall.

The lower slope was OK but about halfway up it became cliff-like and cut by fissures that in rock would be called chimneys by a climber. If I'd had the full use of my limbs, these fissures would have provided a good channel to the ridge, as with the declining sun they were shrouded in shadow. To the left there was a shallow gully suitable for my mode of progress, but with few shadows. I had no option but to move into it. Never be hard on the poor old snail, it's going as fast as it can; indeed that may have saved me; progress invisible to any observer. I don't know how long I had been crawling when, near the bottom of a fissure, a pebble dropped on my head. Knowing it would not have come down by itself I went very still. When two more dropped and no damage done, I peered up. Gazing down was Frank.

It would be a cheap remark to say that God was not going to take me that day, but I am sure it was no coincidence that Frank appeared when he did. He held up his hand and disappeared. I lay knowing I would need all I had. When a lump of clay splattered beside me he was halfway down the fissure, on an outcrop of rock, dangling a rope of rifle slings. I knew my arms could not bear my weight but Frank had thought of that: from the last sling there hung a webbing belt and I buckled it around my waist. I crawled up the fissure like a three-legged bear on the end of a chain, with Frank hauling as if he were oblivious to the fact that, in securing a good purchase for his feet, he had put himself in view of anybody with hostile intentions. Clambering up beside him, I sank back into the shade, exhausted, letting the bad leg hang over the edge. He took out his water bottle and handed it to me. Remembering my Field Ambulance days I did not overdo it, much as I was tempted to. Glancing down I saw the Turks. They could see us and were again raising their cupped hands.

'We'll be out of this soon,' I said to Frank.

'Hope so,' he said.

'But those down there, they're stuck there.'

He nodded.

'Those poor beggars, the Turks, I was beside them for a while.'

He nodded again.

'They're suffering terribly.'

Frank must have thought the remark too obvious to warrant a reply.

'Would you mind?'

'Would I mind what?'

I held up the bottle.

'If we let them have this.'

'OK, but I'll have a swallow myself.' It was but a mouthful. Handing the bottle back, he scurried up the fissure.

Despite the inevitability of several dry hours ahead and the possibility there was every chance that he too would be mangled and, like them, lie neglected in a torment of pain and thirst, it was the reply I knew I would get. The officer had been watching and I carefully tossed the water bottle down. He caught it and instead of drinking, lent over a poor fellow and administered the water to his lips.

Above, Frank lay flat and hauled me up. With only one useful leg and my general condition I was not much use to him. Although he had cover, it was not complete. As if I were a gasping fish, he landed me onto the bottom of a shallow trench where a comrade had been gripping his ankles. We crawled out into the hollow below the Apex, still as crowded as in the morning. I expected to be left until dark when I would try — and it would not have been more than that — getting down to the beach. But Frank put his arm across my shoulders and we staggered off until, at a wave from his comrade, Frank halted.

'There's a b —— b ——,' he said, 'in front of us.' It was unusual for Frank to use strong language. 'A quartermaster sergeant,' he said. 'Got himself a soft job in a safe possie.' He picked up an abandoned rifle. 'With this, do you think you could make a hundred yards?'

'All the way.'

'A hundred yards will do.'

Frank waited as I hobbled on ahead and came into view of a gentleman who, with his red, ravaged, but well-fed face had obviously made full use of the opportunities his position offered him. He was in a hole and had just enough of his head out of it to eye passing traffic. He barely noticed me — or anybody else in a similar condition or worse. Frank was another matter.

'Soldier! What do you think you're doing back here?'

'Returning for ammunition.' When provoked, Frank could exercise an enviable skill: firm with a superior, just short of dumb insolence.

'Yeah?'

'Yes, Staff Sergeant.'

'Produce it then.'

'Are you referring to the chit supplied to me by Major Wallingford?' (The officer responsible for ammunition supplies that day.)

'Soldier, you know I am.'

Frank held it out at a distance just far enough for the man to expose himself more than he cared.

'You're going back for ammunition, soldier, leave that man to Field

Ambulance.' It must have been my fresh blood on Frank's trousers that alerted him.

Frank and his comrade strode past me and I hobbled slowly behind. Once I was out of the quartermaster's sight, the two men were waiting for me.

'I shouldn't have got you into that,' I said.

'"Wounded are not to impede the advance or delivery of supplies,"' Frank mimicked. 'Come on.' I protested but he put his arm around my shoulder.

Tripping and stumbling and in places exposed to snipers, we made our way down. From time to time, when warned by Frank's comrade who led the way to warn of a repeat with the quartermaster, we had to separate. Once on the beach I expected to be left at the Casualty Clearing Station but Frank ignored it, escorting me out onto the pier as cool and collected as if he were assisting me off the football field.

I was loaded on a troop transport and laid out on deck. I do not remember seeing a doctor or a nurse but the officers and crew could not have been more caring and gentle. Firemen straight up from the stokehold, black as Negroes, brought us food and drink and the captain and first officer read burials at sea with frequency. On the second day an overworked medical orderly looked at my foot, liberally dousing it in iodine. Fearing submarines, our captain navigated a zigzag course and it was five days before we were disembarked at Alexandria.

Because a broken bone in my foot was re-joining crookedly, it had to be re-broken and set. Being incapacitated too long to be returned to the Peninsula, the last weeks of my recovery were spent in a convalescent home for New Zealand soldiers established by Lady Godley. We were very well fed and equally well looked after. She did her rounds regularly with a brisk word for everyone: 'Private Y how are you this morning? Sergeant X, you must exercise that limb of yours. And Corporal Z we shall soon have you on your way.' She had a keen eye for malingerers, but much to my embarrassment, there was one exception, your humble servant. 'The old girl's a mate of yours?' was the mildest of comments advanced by my fellow patients. Worse was to come. Sweeping in one morning, she announced I had been awarded a Serb decoration. Like many women of her class, her voice carried—on that day, from one end of the building to the other. I had no illusions about the value of the award, but if I had, they would have been promptly dissipated by the public reception her announcement received.

When news came through of the evacuation, I thought deeply and could only come to the conclusion that it had all been for nothing. I soon gathered, from conversations with other men, that I was not alone in this. We were glad to be out of it, let no one doubt that, but why had it taken all those months for the Heads to realise that the landing had been a loser from the start? Its purpose had been to open the 'Narrows' (the channel between Europe and Asia) so that the Navy could steam through and bombard Constantinople until the Turks submitted. But what if we had taken the 'Narrows' and let the Navy through? Would the Turks have given up? Not the ones we fought.

The boys joked about my decoration and I don't blame them because the courage of the New Zealanders on Chunuk Bair was barely recognised: one MC for the Wellington Battalion and nothing, so far as I am able to recall, for anyone else in it, save a mere Mention in Despatches for our colonel. The Gloucesters and Wiltshires, would you believe it, were afloat with decorations. For Lone Pine alone, General Walker's recommendations led to seven Victoria Crosses being awarded to the Australians. New Zealand received one: to Cyril Bassett for keeping the phone line open, under fire all day, from the Apex to the forward trenches. As well deserved as any VC, his actions were likely to have been witnessed by so many that his award could not have been avoided, but let the man himself speak: 'The only crosses my mates got were wooden ones.'

Worse than that, however. When we reassembled in Egypt, it was to learn that among the few New Zealanders who did receive awards was Johnston—Companion of the Order of the Bath! Him! The lowest latrine digger on the Peninsula deserved more than him. But what pleasure it gave him was for no more than two years: shot by a sniper, after his superiors permitted him to return to the front against psychiatric advice.

It has been my privilege to see a side of the Godleys that few others have. Lady Godley need not have worked to establish the convalescent home, nor have kept working to keep it going. Nevertheless it was while convalescing that I came to the conclusion that her husband was not a general. Many years later he was to write he always regretted not going forward himself to Chunuk Bair. Indeed he has every reason to regret that omission. Even more regrettable is that there was to be another time when he should have gone forward and did not. The cost of that would be even greater.

JIM
Chunuk Bair

I should have mentioned this earlier. I have a sister a couple of years older. She's married and she lives in Westport. He husband drives the coal trains that cart the coal from the foot of the Denniston incline to Westport. That's as close as my sister wants to get to the mines. Over the years there has always been a place to go when I needed it. We were not a writing family, but when we needed to, we wrote. The day before we went up the hill I wrote. We had been told that General Birdwood had ordered that neither officer nor other rank was to assist a wounded man to the rear. Nothing new in that except that when it is spelt out to men who've already been through it, you know that even the Heads don't expect it to be a walkover. It was also the day I learned I was to be the colonel's runner for the battle. I took the place of a lad who had put his age up to enlist and who was a friend of the Malone family. Before we moved off Malone gave him a letter to post to his wife if he didn't come back.

Although the Mounteds were doing everything they'd been ordered and on time, Otago fell behind. After waiting at the mouth of Chailak Dere, Malone ordered me to deliver a message to Colonel Moore. I went up Chailak Dere, a valley leading to Rhododendron Spur with a riverbed dry for most of the year. Otagos were scattered all along it. As deres go, Chailak Dere is not that bad. It's broad and doesn't have gullies branching off. If you kept your wits about you, you wouldn't mistake them for the run of the valley. But a lot of channels cut across its bottom. As the moon didn't come up until a couple of hours before dawn, many a man fell flat on his face. I did too.

When I caught up with Moore, he and some officers were standing around as if they were waiting for something to turn up and not expecting to like it when it did.

Moore read the message, and then, speaking to no one in particular, said:

'Colonel Malone requests that I be so good as to inform him when he may bring his battalion forward.' He turned to an officer. 'Do you know when Colonel Malone might bring his battalion forward?'

'Can't be too long, Sir.'

'To be sure, it can't be too long at all.' He turned back to me. 'Tell Colonel Malone it can't be too long before he may be able to bring his battalion forward.'

'You will inform Colonel Malone when he can move his battalion, Sir?'

He didn't like that and I hadn't expected him to.

'You have my reply, Corporal, deliver it!'

'Sir!' and I saluted as if he were His Majesty the fucking King.

When I got back Malone was pacing up and down.

'And that was all Colonel Moore had to say.' He wasn't asking a question. 'Wait here.'

He ordered Harston, his adjutant, to bring up Jimmy Swan to scout ahead, then said to me, 'Lead the way, McDonnell. Otago Battalion Headquarters.'

We set off, no time wasted; the Otagos strung along the valley as good as a paper trail. Moore was where I had left him.

When the colonels met there was saluting but no handshake. As well as there being no moon, it was cloudy and we were in thick scrub. Malone and Moore saw just an outline of each other.

'Good evening, Colonel,' said Malone, 'when might your men be on the move again?'

'Colonel, if I knew that, I would have told you,' said Moore.

Just then we heard cheering.

'Well, Colonel,' said Malone, 'it sounds as though the Mounteds have taken Table Top.' It was a hill garrisoned by the Turks that stood in the way of the attack.

'If so,' said Moore, 'I'll be glad to hear it because then I shall be able to inform you that my battalion is able to advance.' Since the landing, the Mounteds had made a reputation. Otago hadn't. Later, Moore and Temperley claimed that Otago had taken Table Top. It'd be interesting to know who believed them.

Malone kept his mouth shut.

'We are in country, Colonel,' Moore went on, 'that refuses to conform to the map and we are dealing with an enemy who is not supposed to be here.'

'Colonel,' said Malone. 'It is my intention to suggest to brigade that, while you are clearing the valley, the Wellington Battalion pass through and occupy Rhododendron Spur.'

'Suggest to brigade what you like, Colonel. I have plenty to do here.'

'Thank you, Colonel Moore,' said Malone.

'The pleasure is all mine, Colonel.'

It was hard yakker that night. If a company commander wasn't reporting his position I was sent to find out why. If there wasn't a company commander to be checked on, I was sent off to brigade to report how we were doing and where we were. With scouts out front and more covering our flanks, we moved fast and held together.

When the Wellingtons got to the head of Chailak Dere I was sent to report to brigade headquarters that we were advancing as daylight was breaking, were not yet sure of our position, were lining the crests of the surrounding ridges for safety, were reconnoitring forward, and would act on further knowledge and report. Brigade Headquarters were dug into the side of a hill. If you sat down you had some sort of protection from shrapnel. The brigade staff was sitting down. Brigadier Johnston was standing up. He was one of those top-heavy men who look about to fall over. 'A lot of pork and port have gone into you,' I thought, seeing him close up for the first time. Near Johnston was his brigade major, Temperley. He was bareheaded. Maybe it was because of his haircut, the fact that he was going bald and had a bit of a lantern jaw, but front-on he didn't look that far off a baboon.

After Johnston had read the message he gave it to Temperley and

Temperley, standing up and putting on his cap, said they should go and see what Colonel Malone was up to. Johnston nodded. I led them up to the Apex. Neither Johnston nor Temperley said anything on the way.

The battalion was digging trenches in the hollow below the Apex. Above it was the last slope to Chunuk Bair. Nothing was coming down at us but if anyone was seen advancing beyond the Apex a machine gun opened up. Not long after dawn we heard a din on our right: rifles and machine guns going at it hammer and tongs. All we knew was that the Australian Light Horse were making a diversionary assault that had been planned to coincide with the New Zealand infantry attack. The purpose of the Aussie assault was to keep the Turks off our right flank. Because we had taken so long to get up Chailak Dere, we arrived too late to go in at the same time as the Aussies. But they went ahead anyway.

Malone saluted as Johnston approached.

'Good Morning, Colonel, your men are busy, but what order did you receive to occupy them so?'

'Our position needs to be secured, Sir,' Malone replied. 'And to prepare for the attack, the men need rest. They will take it once our defences are secure.' The Wellingtons were sleepwalkers, lifting picks and letting them fall by their own weight, shovels half full.

'The ridge is but five hundred yards away, Malone,' Johnston spoke as if all we had to do was to pick up our rifles and walk.

'Indeed, Sir, and if we had been able to keep to the plan and had attacked before dawn we would have seized it.'

'And Sir,' said Temperley, 'the Turks have the approaches well covered and there is no sign of either the Australian infantry nor of the Indians on the left being in a position to attack Hill Q on Sari Bair. In point of fact, so far, Sir, there is no sign of them. If we went forward now we'd be exposed on three sides.'

'Very well,' the brigadier said, 'I will inform the general.'

Temperley wrote the message. The brigadier signed it. He might have read it and he might not have. A brigade runner was sent off.

I dropped there and then and awoke when the runner returned from Godley's HQ. While I had been asleep the Aucklanders had formed up and a battalion of Ghurkhas were deploying on our left below Hill Q. They had spent the night trying to find it. The Turks were bursting shrapnel overhead. There was also small arms' fire on our flanks. The position was as crowded as a Cairo tram; officers and men were jammed together.

'The order, gentlemen,' Johnston said, 'is to attack. At eleven a.m.'

It was Temperley who spoke first. 'Sir, I am sure that if General Godley were here, he would see how hopeless an attack would be.'

'He is not here, Major, so your remark is well meant but to no purpose.'

'Conditions have changed much for the worse since the general was sent your report, Sir.' You got the feeling that Temperley had done this sort of thing before. 'Could we not ...'

'No, Temperley, arrangements have been made to mount a bombardment of the crest within the next hour. We shall move forward immediately after its conclusion.'

'But ...'

'No arguments, Major.' Brigadier Johnston turned and with a smile said: 'Young ...'

'Sir.' He'd been one of Malone's company commanders. A month before he'd been promoted to command the Aucklands. Before the war he'd been a small-town dentist, so you could say he wasn't doing too badly, although at Quinn's his men called him the Dug-out King. Whether that was fair or not, I don't know. Somebody must have thought he was OK because he finished the war as a brigadier.

'Reconnoitre the ground and prepare your battalion to attack.' Nodding to the Gurkhas' CO, he said: 'we appreciate your presence, Major.' Another smile. 'You will support Colonel Young on his left and I suggest you advance in line.'

'We shall do our best, Sir.' I suppose, that as a British regular, the Ghurkas' CO had no option but to put a brave face on it.

'I suggest I do a recce, Sir,' said Young. No one said no, so taking an officer with him he crossed a patch of dead ground just up from the Apex and dropped to a crawl. It wasn't long before we heard a Turk machine gun open up. Shortly after, Young and the officer came back.

'Sir,' he reported. 'There is scrub, but no real cover. An enemy trench across the spur about a hundred yards forward appears to have been abandoned. The spur is narrow, requiring an advance in column, two platoons up. It is enfiladed from each flank and in direct line of fire from the objective, Sir.'

'Very good. Deploy your men.'

'From what I have observed, Sir, the only chance of success will be to delay the assault until dark. I most earnestly recommend, Sir, that you order a postponement until then.' Young would not have been the only one in the Auckland battalion who wouldn't have minded a nice cosy dugout.

'I'm sorry, Colonel Young, General Godley has issued his order and that will be that.'

'Yes Sir.' Young saluted slowly and looked up towards Chunuk Bair as if trying to see something that wasn't there. He went off and soon the Aucklands were filing through us. They were quiet. So were we.

'Sir!' It was Wallingford, the brigade machine gun officer. One of the instructors from England brought out by Godley, he knew more about machine guns than the rest of them put together. Afterwards there were those who said he should have got a VC.

'Major?'

'Sir. My guns are sited to cover Cheshire Ridge and its approaches. Give me twenty minutes and I'll move them to cover the attack.'

'Sorry Major, you're too late.' And Johnston *was* sorry; no doubt about it.

'I have only just learned that this attack is to be made now, Sir.' Wallingford was making it plain he was stating a fact.

'No fault of yours, Major, but the barrage will commence any minute now. Be satisfied with the excellent work you're doing where you are.'

'Let me try, Sir. I'll get the guns here in double quick time.' And you knew he could.

'Major, be a good chap and leave it,' said Johnston. 'We cannot delay the attack.'

Wallingford was about to speak, stopped, looked up at the ridge, back at the brigadier, saluted, and left.

'Temperley, come with me.' Johnston walked up to the Apex. He stumbled, took a pull at his water bottle, and led Temperley up to the lip of the hollow. Temperley spoke and left quickly. The brigadier had a grandstand view and was a ripe target for a sniper.

The Aucklands formed up, the order given, the whistles blew and up the spur they went. Until they came to the edge of the dead ground. There they stopped and made a sound halfway to a growl.

'Come on boys!' A major ran out waving his pistol. He might have made ten yards, but it got the lead platoons on the move. The lucky ones made it to the empty Turk trench. Others dropped and stayed where they were until dark when, if alive, they crawled to the trench. One was Young. Between the trench and us were the wounded who, if they didn't have cover and tried to move, were targets. On the left flank the Gurkhas, spread out and advancing in line, did a little better but not much. Their white officers were easily picked off. With them gone, the Gurkhas veered into dead ground.

Johnston cheered when the Aucklands charged. When asked to come down he cheered all the more. A lieutenant took his arm, got himself a round, and died the day after. After mopping his brow, Johnston joined Malone. The 7th Gloucesters had come up behind us and it was still crowded.

'Form up your men, Colonel Malone.'

'Sir?'

'Prepare for the attack. And Major Temperley, inform Colonel Hughes that the Canterbury battalion is to support Colonel Malone.'

'I am here, Sir.' It was Hughes, a slight, short man who more often than not had a grin on his face but not this time. 'But, we're no longer a battalion.'

'How many have you?' asked Johnston.

'Fifty, Sir. And three officers.'

'Colonel, I know you lost your way last night and would have lost men coming up this morning, but Hughes, surely, I misheard you.'

'Shelled, Sir. Caught when we were forming up at the end of the Spur.'

'You formed up down there?' Johnston seemed surprised.

'There was no shelling until we formed up and then a barrage hit us. Had our range first time, Sir.'

'We ... we will talk about that later, Colonel Hughes. In the meantime prepare to support Colonel Malone.' Turning to him he said: 'The honour of our brigade now rests with you, Malone.'

'General,' said Malone, 'if we go now, we won't get there. If any do, they won't hold.'

'That is not the issue, Colonel. Indeed there is no issue at all. General Godley has ordered us to advance on Chunuk Bair and advance we shall.'

'With the greatest respect, Sir, there is no point in making an assault if there is no chance of achieving our objective.' Malone's tone was dry.

'The longer we talk here, Colonel,' said Johnston, 'the easier it will be for the Turks to reinforce their defences.'

'We know the terrain, Sir; there it is in front of us, plain as a pikestaff. A night advance will bring no problems and high chances of success. Now, Sir, the chances are nil.' Malone's tone was getting drier.

'Colonel, please! This is no time to dispute General Godley's order!'

Temperley chimed in. 'Sir! Perhaps we may delay a little for Major Wallingford to deploy his machine guns.' He turned to Malone. 'That will give you covering fire.'

Malone didn't hear him. A sort of half-smile flickered on his face. 'General, my men are not attacking in daylight!'

You might say we couldn't believe that a colonel would tell a brigadier general that he was not going to obey his order. But at the same time, none of us who knew the old man were surprised.

Johnston and Malone were face to face.

'Malone! I must have misheard you!'

Malone said nothing.

'This is serious, most serious, Colonel. Unbelievable!' Johnston looked around—as though we'd be on his side.

'Sir!' Malone said. 'My men shall take that hill. They will advance tonight and they shall take it.' He turned away from Johnston. 'Captain Harston! Instruct company commanders to disperse their men.'

'Sir!' Harston about-turned. 'Company commanders!' All obeying, they approached him.

'Colonel Malone, Sir.' It was Temperley. 'You might have a point, but it is a point made without reference to what the rest of the corps is doing, indeed the whole expeditionary force on the Peninsula and the coordination within it. We are already running behind. To delay further will only worsen the situation.'

'Colonel, Major Temperley is right. We must play our part.' Johnston had a hard time keeping his hand away from his water bottle.

'And we shall, Sir, tonight. As for coordination, there is none. No one is attacking Hill Q and Point 971 and the Australian Light Horse have already made their assault.'

'Colonel Malone,' said Johnston. 'You are disobeying an order. General Godley's order.'

'General Godley is not here and I take full responsibility. I am not going to send my men to commit suicide to no purpose.'

From the crowd there came a low muttering. Malone swung round. 'Corporal! Convey to the RSM he is to assist Captain Harston to disperse the battalion. Immediately!'

Like Harston, I didn't have far to go. The RSM had heard and was yelling at the platoon sergeants to get their men out of the hollow and down to a sheltered gully. As the last of the men were filing past, two said 'Thank you, Sir.' Malone didn't answer. If he had he'd have charged them for speaking without permission. He set us digging. Word came back from Godley that the attack would go in before first light with a barrage.

While there was daylight we dug. Trenches and latrines. No matter where we went or what we were there for, latrines were dug. Graves too. There was cover from small arms' fire and high explosives but the shrapnel hit the unlucky. Enough to keep the rest of us digging. The earth was hard, it was midsummer and the sun took a long time sinking. Only when it had, did the Indian transport mules arrive with water. Enough to slake our thirst there and then and fill our water bottles but that was it. They brought ammunition too, but like the water, not enough. It was midnight when the trench line had been dug, machine guns positioned and dug in, and sentries posted. I slept for exactly one hour. Then I was woken to go with Malone to the brigadier. The meeting was short and neither man said more than he had to. An artillery and naval bombardment would start at 3.30 a.m. and finish at 4.15. The leading companies would advance at 4 a.m. sharp so they would be well forward when the bombardment stopped. I was sent to round up the company commanders.

I was ready to drop but Malone set off down the Spur to see the Colonel of the 7th Gloucesters. They were to follow us and, once we had seized the crest, pass through and turn north along the crest to seize Hill Q. It was another New Army battalion. One that had landed at Anzac the past week. Its CO might have known what he was about and maybe the RSM and a couple of others, but the rest, officers and men, were as raw as orange peel. They were cannon fodder and only now beginning to see it. Behind them, towards Cheshire Ridge, were the 8th Welch Pioneers: pick and shovel men with rifles in their hands. Back to brigade to have another word with Johnston and Temperley. Whether more water and ammunition had been promised, I don't know, but we didn't have enough of either and the two of them were told about it and a squad was sent off. It'd be daylight before they'd be back. Then he turned in for a kip. Me too.

Not for long. It was the barrage, four to five hundred yards away, sometimes less. We'd seen it all before but as fireworks it wasn't bad. Not that we expected it to be any more use to us than it had been to the Aucklands. When the orders were yelled and the whistles blew Hawke's Bay and Wellington-West Coast climbed out of their trenches. They were neither keen nor flustered and once out moved towards the barrage. They went as steadily as they could, though they were shaky on their feet because of all that had gone before — the night march, the digging and the dysentery — wanting to get as close to the barrage as possible without being hit before it stopped.

We advanced, being careful not to walk on the fallen Auckland boys. There were some live ones on the ground and in the trench. When something was said it was our boys asking if they'd like to come along and they saying they were happy where they were. When we came upon a hollow, twenty to thirty yards below the crest, Malone decided to dig there.

Being on the reverse slope and well sheltered, it was ideal for a support trench and Battalion HQ. Between it and the crest trench he planned a communication sap, and another to a trench forward of the crest. I say planned, but half an hour was our lot. By then the Turks attacked and there was no time for the trench forward of the crest or the communication sap.

The Gloucesters' colonel and some of his men joined us in the support trench. About a platoon of the Welch Pioneers made it to the dead ground below the lip of the crest. Someone had to go back to the phone at the Apex and report to Johnston. That was Harston. The chances of getting through being fifty-fifty, I was sent too. We went separately. Harston got there first but he was paid more than me. When I caught up he was on the phone and not as polite as he usually was. He could have been talking to Temperley, though by then I wouldn't have been surprised if it had been Johnston.

He put the phone down.

'Finally,' he said, 'they believed me.'

When we went back, Harston crawled too. Grenades landing on the reverse slope kept rolling. You never knew where they'd go off. About noon the boys on the crest were near the end. A machine gun would have made the difference but our pissed-as-a-fart brigadier didn't send one until the counter-attack was under way and only the man with the barrel got through — no tripod, no ammunition.

Malone went up to the crest and I with him. The Turks were heaving their grenades and then charging. When our boys had no time to reload, they would take to them with bayonets or entrenching tools. The old man had a go too. But we didn't have the numbers. We left the crest early afternoon. It was the support trench on the reverse slope that held the Turks. The Turk artillery had no way of sighting it. Not that it was much fun; a lucky shell just might fall on you and there were plenty of grenades. Mostly they bounced past because the fuses were set too long — but not always.

Word got down to our artillery and the navy about the crest. They opened another bombardment. Even at one hundred yards from a barrage, you still lose men from shorts. Our artillery was firing howitzers too. At three thousand yards, a 4.5" howitzer shell has a fifty per cent chance of landing on ground half as long again as a cricket pitch and ten yards wide. But, at thirty yards from the crest, we were within the margin of error of naval guns too. One or the other finished Malone. The Turks sent over a shrapnel barrage, Malone and the Gloucesters' colonel stood up to see the damage, and one of our shells fell short. Harston said he saw the flash of a destroyer's gun; others have said a naval gun's trajectory would have been too flat to hit there and that it was a howitzer.

I was sent to brigade headquarters. When I got there Johnston was sitting, staring at nothing, Temperley beside him, standing, looking out to sea. Behind them a signaller was trying to get his phone to work.

'Yes?' Temperley slowly shifted his gaze from the sea.

'Colonel Malone's dead, Sir. Major Cunningham wounded. Captain Harston commanding, Sir.'

'What about the Gloucesters' colonel?'

'Wounded, Sir.'

'The Welch CO?'

'Don't know, Sir. Maybe missing.'

'*Maybe* missing?'

'Haven't seen him, Sir.'

Temperley looked down at Johnston. 'General!'

Johnston stirred.

'Sir,' said Temperley, 'with your permission I shall visit our position on the crest.'

'Take all necessary steps and let me know what you find,' Johnston mumbled.

'Indeed I shall, Sir. Lead the way, Corporal.'

'Sir,' I said, 'water.' I upended my bottle with the cork out.

'Look smart about it, Corporal.'

When I took the bastard up to Captain Harston in the trench below the crest, I moved quickly. I knew the way and where the dead ground was. If Temperley wanted to stay in one piece he had to stay with me. He was panting when he got there.

'They've given you a pasting, Harston,' he said between breaths.

'Sir.'

'I shall recommend to the general that you be relieved tonight.'

'Yes, Sir.'

'Considering the circumstances, you have held on remarkably well.'

'Thank you, Sir.'

'Hopeless position.'

'Sir?'

'To entrench on a reverse slope? To hold a counter-attack? From such a position?'

'With respect, Major,' said Harston. 'We couldn't have held on the forward slope.'

'What! We'll talk about it under more propitious circumstances. Do not misunderstand me, Captain; you and your men have fought to the best of your ability.'

Harston was quiet.

Temperley looked at him for a moment. 'Harston, you have lost a commander of great determination, who made the Wellington battalion his own. His passing will be regretted by all.'

'Yes, Sir.'

'Good. Prepare your men for relief at nightfall.'

'Sir.' Harston saluted.

Seven hundred and sixty Wellingtons walked up; seventy walked down. We were fit for nothing better than being sent back to Egypt, but we stopped at Cheshire Ridge. It was in the early hours of the morning and we dropped. But in case we had any ideas we might be in for a rest, we were woken at dawn when the Gurkhas had another go. They made it to the crest and were just about to turn on Hill Q when our gunners opened up again. Right on top of them. And the New Army Brigade that was to support them had got lost. Johnston had told its brigadier to take a short cut.

That night the New Army 5th Wiltshires and the 6th Loyal North Lancashires went up to Chunuk Bair. At dawn the Turks charged. The Wiltshires and Lancashires ran. Wallingford and other officers at the Pinnacle used their pistols and Temperley ordered a burst from a machine gun to halt them. The Turks were held at the Pinnacle. We were back to digging: new trenches across Rhododendron ridge. In front of us were the Wiltshires. We were to fire if they found their running shoes again. And we might have let off a round or two if they'd run. Too many of our own left up there.

They made me acting sergeant. I was ordered by an officer fresh out from New Zealand to lead a patrol that night — six men. Until then only snipers had done anything like that so I told him one'd be enough, maybe two. 'The men need the experience, Sergeant, six, and you may choose them' — the last said as if it was a favour. Two I took because they'd been farmers, one a musterer; a third was a seaman I guessed to be handy and having a good eye, and another was a Wanganui lad who'd come over as a sergeant and had demoted himself before being told to. Then there was Frank. Didn't know him all that well — when Harry and he got together they'd talked about people I didn't know and things like religion — but he'd been around long enough to know the score. The others were to turn out OK but he was the only one I could trust to take over if things didn't turn out right. During the day, when the sun sank behind the ridge but it was still bright enough to see, I had them look at the ground, the route out and the route home: our job was to see where the Turks were, not to fight them. Compared to what was to come up in France, we were greener than grass.

We went out in a † formation with the musterer in front, me at the cross with the other farmer on my left and the seaman to my right, the Wanganui lad behind. And in the rear, Frank. Getting near two suspected Turk outposts, I left the boys with Frank and set off. After fixing their positions for the attention of our artillery — such as it was — I returned. When I crept up beside one of the new men he as good as shat himself. Later I told him it was only Ghurkhas who would sneak up and cut your throat. But sit still, I said, and there's a fair chance they'll let you be.

Disease hit us, and the odd man still being bowled, the company was down to less than a platoon. That's how I made acting company commander and Frank my 2i/c. Then I had stabs in the guts, the shakes, cold one minute, boiling the next. But, if you were still standing, you stayed put.

'If you're here any longer,' said Frank, 'that, for you, will be it.'

'Yeah.'

'If you go crook,' he said, 'I'll be OC.'

'And the best of luck.'

'Go crook and I'll have you evacuated.'

'They mightn't like that,' I said.

'It's been my life's ambition to be a company commander. I'd risk my life for it.'

'OK,' I said.

'Lie down.'

He came back with a couple of boys who'd just landed.

'The sergeant is seriously incapacitated. Take him down to the beach. He might last the night and he might not and,' he reached into his pocket and there in his hand, were two half-crowns, 'while you're there, pick up what you can from the canteen.' He gave each a stretcher-bearer brassard and a signed chit.

After I'd been put on a stretcher, he said: 'You will take Sergeant Mc-Donnell directly to the embarkation pier. The Casualty Clearing Station is choked and you will not overload it further. That is an order and on your return you will report to me, personally, that Sergeant McDonnell has been placed on an embarkation barge. Do you understand?'

The way he carried on; you could see the boys wondering if they should call him Sir.

'And Sergeant!'

I couldn't laugh because of my gut.

'Sergeant, the men are not to visit the canteen until they see you safely off the pier.'

When we came to the end of Chailak Dere, the queue waiting for embarkation wasn't as long as it had been—with so few of us left, maybe they were running out of men to go sick. So it didn't take the boys long to get me onto the pier.

I was lucky twice over. Off the Peninsula in double-quick time and put on a barge that took me to a ship for Egypt, not Lemnos. Everyone else aboard had wounds but nobody cared. They told me if it'd had been another day I'd've been a goner. I knew that, but it's one thing to know it and another when a doctor tells you. I went through the mill. Jaundice and dysentery together, and a bit more, I think.

I had three months in an Australian hospital. There they told me the Australian Light Horse were knocked out because when they made their attack we were too late to have made ours from the Apex on Chunuk Bair as planned. And then I was sent to old Lady Godley's convalescent home. It was light and airy, had sheets, soft beds, deck chairs, shady verandas, as much as you could eat. Never known a better jail. Except it wasn't there to keep you in but to kick you out — had to keep the mincing machine going. Harry turned up the same time. We were sitting on the veranda when the old girl came past. We were new and she wanted to know who and what we were. She didn't register when the Matron said Private Patterson, only when Harry said: 'Good morning, Lady Godley,' with that big smile.

'Patterson! No, don't stand up … you poor boy. The general mentioned how gallantly you insisted on going to the front … how you have changed from the lad I remember. Matron, we must restore this young man.'

You could see he'd wished he'd kept his trap shut and when she'd gone we let him know about it. When you're convalescing you're not short of time so there was always someone keeping his eyes and ears open when the old duck did her rounds. Like the day she told him he was getting a ribbon on his chest.

'Patterson, His Majesty the King of Serbia has awarded you a medal. The Order of the White Eagle, Third Class. The general tells me it is for your gallantry at Monash Gully. What a pity it is not from our own dear King.'

FRANK
Corporal (Acting Unpaid) Commanding

The voyage from Lemnos on one of HM's destroyers I remember vividly; we went belting along at thirty knots, funnels belching smoke, spray sweeping the decks — it was diverting enough to keep me from brooding on returning to the Peninsula. Landing on Anzac, August 8, too late to join the Wellingtons on Chunuk Bair, has enabled me to write these memoirs. Harry and Jim were among the very lucky. If I'd been there, the odds against three out of three surviving would have been too great.

When we disembarked at Anzac, the New Zealand battalions were holding Chunuk Bair. After being told to wait we were forgotten. Somebody knew the bivvy of the New Zealand press journalist and after heading there we found a couple of bottles of wine, and seeing he was not there to draw the corks himself, and with his friend assuring us of his hospitality, we set about disposing of them. It was a Lemnos concoction and we persuaded ourselves we were doing its owner a favour.

We sat there, imbibing, gazing seawards, surrounded by the hustle and bustle on the beach below us, the flashes and bangs of the navy and, in a hollow on our right, a howitzer battery doing its own banging. It was the wine and howitzers that did me. I was thirsty, so with a lad from the Auckland battalion, I went off to replenish my water bottle and find a quieter spot. At the water tank the NCO asked what we were doing and, pointing to the Divisional HQ, sent us there. I had the presence of mind to find and fill another water bottle.

The Great Sap was already clogged with wounded, masses of them lay outside the Casualty Clearing Station, and near North Beach pier were hundreds of Turk prisoners. The wounded were hard to walk past. Another water tank was nearby, guarded by armed Sikhs. They let us fill a couple of pannikins and for all I know we might have poured water down the throats of those whose wounds couldn't take it. One was a friend of the Aucklander and he suggested we try and get him into the CCS. We borrowed a stretcher from a pair of exhausted stretcher-bearers.

Waiting our chance, we saw a loaded stretcher carried from a tent and were into it quickly. It was crammed with iron bedsteads end to end. The air was thick, the heat intense and not all were suffering silently. Like its neighbours the bed's mattress was soaked with blood and just about everything else. An orderly, exasperated, dripping sweat, yelled we were jumping the queue, coughed, and collapsed. When we reached him, he was gone, shrapnel slicing through the tent, his back and his heart.

At Divisional HQ we were ordered to carry ammunition and report to the Wellington-West Coast quartermaster sergeant on the Apex. We were also informed of General Godley's orders that reinforcements and ammunition were to have priority on the track and on no account were we to give way to wounded or to support or be delayed by them. Our rifles, gear, and ammunition gave us a heavy load, afternoon sun was directly behind us, and so we were back to husbanding water. Hundreds of men were passing up and down, the latter mostly walking wounded. My Auckland friend learnt what happened to his battalion when he gave a Canterbury man a drink. The Apex was a real mix up so we put the box down to look around. It was then we heard a yell. I hadn't looked forward to working under our QMS and I was not to be disillusioned. The first yell was followed by a second. He was in a deep bivvy.

'Where do you think you're going?'

'Looking for you, Sergeant.' I was answering a head; all else being encased in solid clay.

'Staff Sergeant, next time soldier. Where're you going with that ammunition box?'

'The Regimental Quartermaster sent …'

'I can see that and what do you think you're doing now?'

'Looking for you …'

'Well now you've found me and you'll get that box to Major Walling-ford. He's up there.' He waved towards Chunuk Bair. 'Enquire at the first machine gun post. No hanging around.' The head disappeared, safe and sound until it had the inclination to poke itself out again.

With careful crawling, we reached the post. Wallingford, we were told, was up forward. We could seek him out or wait. We waited. A brisk, efficient man, he arrived about ten minutes later. He noted our regimental badges, asked where we had been and if either of us knew about Vickers guns. When we said no (in 1915, with two machine guns to a battalion, men who knew them were few) he ordered us to leave our rifles and packs with the men of the post and return for more ammunition.

'Sorry,' he said to the Aucklander, 'your battalion can't do much now,' and to me, 'while your battalion could use you, there's no guarantee you'd get to it.'

Writing out a chit, he went on to say, 'every box you bring up is going to serve your mates. If they can hold out till night, there's every chance they'll be relieved.'

We were crawling back to the Apex when I glanced into a gully and saw Harry. The only time I have seen him vulnerable: his face very pale under his tan, his eyes staring and one of his legs finishing in something that looked like butcher's mince. The Aucklander and I hauled him up. After getting him past our QMS friend, we took him down and had him ferried to a ship, getting away with it because we didn't hang around. Going up again, the track was more crowded and the boxes heavy. After delivering to Wallingford, it was dark enough to bring in wounded. There were dead we might have saved if we'd got to them earlier. We could hear the wounded in the gully. We couldn't do anything about them either; it would be two days before they were cleared.

Keith was one who never came down from Chunuk Bair. The condition of the survivors was shocking, but, by the orders of Hamilton, they and the just landed Fifth Reinforcements were to hold Chunuk Bair 'forever'. A count at Cheshire ridge showed, with the Fifth Reinforcements,

Wellington-West Coast Company numbered fifty-one. Without the Fifths, on the night of the seventh, there had been two hundred plus. We stayed five weeks and when we moved out we were much less than fifty-one.

It was a life of monotonous hell. Keeping watch at night, digging in the morning, fly swatting semi-dozing in the afternoon, all heavily punctuated by diarrhoeic emissions. Sores enlarged themselves despite liberal splashes of iodine. Gums bled, sties grew in eyes, and limbs swelled, particularly among the men who had not been off the Peninsula, so had been without fresh food let alone fresh vegetables and fruit. It was scurvy: a disease whose remedy had been identified by the Royal Navy exactly one hundred and twenty years before. The best that could happen to you was to be wounded because then you would be evacuated. Unfortunately the option was not yours to choose. You were sick when you collapsed and nothing could move you. If you were lucky you got a stretcher and if you were very lucky you would wake up in somewhere like Lemnos. It didn't matter how useful you were. Wallingford, after Malone the most useful man in the brigade, was struck down, eventually evacuated, and health ruined, returned to New Zealand.

Because I now qualified as an old hand, it was inevitable Jim and I would notice each other. He had been Harry's spotter, they had bivvied together and each had complete trust in the other, but when Harry and I had met up, Jim usually withdrew into himself or found somewhere else to go. If you were anything other than what he considered working class, you were guilty until you had proved there *might* be occasions when you *might*, in spite of your origins, have some compensatory quality. Dour, rationing his words, with eyes keen and sceptical, and leaving no doubt about his practical capability, Jim, during his lifetime, has made many a man uneasy or, as on Cheshire Ridge, grateful for his presence. One of the first jobs he was given was to lead a patrol into no man's land. When he gathered us together, the first fact he made clear was that we were all superfluous. Each, after that, wondered: then why me? Next, dryly and precisely, we were told the purpose of the patrol, which included an explanation of why we were superfluous, and then, seeing we were there, what each of us had to do, and how to do it. I, we were informed, was his 2 i/c and we were told why. It could have sounded flattering, but it didn't. Nevertheless I knew exactly what he wanted from me, what we might expect and what he would be doing. Thus it worked out. It was my first patrol and confirmed my previous opinion that patrolling was an activity in which I was not overly keen to participate. We went towards the Turk outposts below the crest. Once we were beyond sight and sound of our trenches, Jim dumped us in a semi-safe haven, told us to shut up and stay still and went to look by himself, picking us up again on his way home. They were surprised when, asking if it was like other patrols, I answered I did not know as the distance between forward lines at Quinn's had not been such as to accommodate patrolling.

I was surprised, but not overjoyed, that Jim picked me for the next patrol and again designated me as his 2 i/c. Not that I considered it an overwhelming vote of confidence on his part. Three of us were chosen again plus a pair of new boys. Where we went made the other night out like a picnic. Before we had taken the Apex, the Turks had dug a connecting sap from it down into the gully and then up again to Battleship Hill. Our job was to crawl along it at night to see if there were any signs if it was to be used to mount a raid. This time I was granted the honour of taking the lead. I didn't like it then and I wouldn't like it now. Whether or not it was Jim exercising his wry sense of humour, I have never been sure. He was at my shoulder, covering me, when on meeting a traverse, I peered around the corner. It was a beautiful Mediterranean summer night, stars glittering, the air calm and very dark crawling along the bottom of the sap. In some places the sides had caved in and one never knew whether the resulting pile of clay did not have a rifleman behind it and all one may say about crawling into the remains of a decomposing Turk, is that it was preferable to meeting a live one.

Around this time a memorial service was held for Colonel Malone. His remains, like so many of those at Chunuk Bair, had been overrun by the Turks. With luck they would have been hurriedly covered over. Otherwise they too would have made their contribution to the miasma of the battlefield and the proliferation of flies. The service had been delayed until the line had settled down and we had a position with cover where we could gather. The turnout was excellent considering there were not many left who had known him. I thought about my one meeting with him and how, brief though it was, he had made it clear to me, a boy, what I would be letting myself in for, indeed what the country would be in for. Such knowledge and perception, despite everything that has happened since his passing, continues to be as rare now as it was then. To the survivors of Chunuk Bair, he had become a double hero: as a soldier on the crest and for his point-blank refusal to sacrifice men to no purpose. A man who himself demanded obedience, he would have been fully aware of how his disobedience would affect his future and reputation in a calling he loved and excelled at. Let there be no mistake, I was in no way disappointed that I'd had the experience of standing before him only once because a second time could have been only for an offence. During his reign — for that's what it was — the Fates must have resolved to put me under their protection. It was one of Malone's men who was court-martialled and sentenced to death for sleeping at his post, the only death sentence imposed on a New Zealander at Gallipoli. Hamilton commuted it on the grounds that the man was not relieved when he should have been. Malone's politics too, as they say these days, were well to the right of Genghis Khan. So Colonel Malone is not a man to be sentimental about. But, as I stood there, as the Mass was being conducted, it was fair enough to wonder how we would manage without him, the one senior officer in the brigade who couldn't be faulted. Apart from having no option but to manage, the most important reason we did, was because of the legacy he left: two of his majors were to become brigadiers, some of his junior officers who survived Gallipoli became battalion commanders and, for the rest of us, we won survival because of his leadership and training. We also carried with us the example of a man who, driven by duty, combined courage, capability and principle.

It was not only old hands who were few at the service, but recently landed Fifths too. My own Wellington-West Coast Company was down from two hundred and forty-five on the sixth of August to one officer and twenty-one other ranks within a fortnight or so. Then the officer went and others along with him. In no time I was acting platoon commander. As our numbers dwindled, everyone had to turn out each night, dusk to dawn. Apart from that my responsibilities were hardly onerous, being confined to issuing ammunition, bully beef, biscuits and water for seven. Jim became OC, WWC, and yours truly his 2i/c. When Jim had to be carried out it was with the written authorisation of Butler, F. (Corporal, Acting) OC (Acting) Wellington-West Coy, Wellington Infantry Battalion. Thus, for an exalted twenty-four hours, I commanded a front line rifle company before reverting to Corporal (Acting, Unpaid). Shortly after, our new CO, Colonel Hart, recovered from wounds, returned from hospital in England. He was to be one of the two Wellingtons who finished the war as a brigadier, but nobody would have survived as Malone's 2i/c unless he was approaching perfection.

At irregular and long intervals, our bully beef and biscuits were supplemented with titbits like one stained, Egyptian, pullet's egg to every four men. I was one of the seventy-five per cent who lost the toss, but luckier when bread was first delivered. It was solid, but, unlike my neighbour, I did not bite into a toenail. There were also 'spanish' onions. I couldn't keep mine down, but those made of sterner stuff chewed them like apples. A red-letter day was when all were issued with a mug of flour, a dessertspoon of coffee, and four raisins. Another surprise was fresh mutton, despite not being all that fresh and far from what we knew at home. Towards the end, bread, rice and meat were issued twice a week and onions every other day. After the scurvy symptoms appeared, limejuice trickled in, and now that Malone had gone, dribbles of rum.

It is here I again mention the QMS on the Apex. He was fond of rum and lime; what came our way bore little relationship to what went his. One day he disappeared, sick: the best fed man in the battalion. His successors were a different breed. One was to be killed on the Somme and the other at Messines, each when bringing supplies forward. The new QMS, however, heard I was a teacher. So I must be literate—not always a safe assumption, I know, but that's how it seemed to him. Thus, during our last days on Cheshire, he conscripted me to help deal with the latest mail intake. It was bulky and, being overdue, posted well before the August attack. I had to check envelope after envelope against company rolls and, as appropriate, inscribe Killed, Missing, Wounded, or Evacuated Sick. In almost every case the recipient would have received his mail if it had been delivered punctually. One also thought of the writers whose letters were not redirected to a hospital but returned.

Also in that batch of letters was a bundle from Helen. I hadn't written to her since I had returned from sick leave. I put it down to the strain, the heat, the food and everything else that went with Cheshire Ridge. I wrote to my mother, effort though it was, and nowhere near as regularly as she wrote to me. I held the bundle from Helen in my hand but didn't feel inclined to un-bundle it. Two or three days later I did and read them. They were boring. Her chatter about goings on in Wellington and the church no longer had relevance. I felt unkind about it, but that was how it was. At first I thought I would reply by copying out the letter I was about to post off to my mother, but I couldn't raise the effort to do that. So I just let it slide.

After weeks of sweltering heat, mid-September saw us down on the beach at the brigade dump in the first rain for months. There, clutching ground sheets and wearing rags that passed for shirts and shorts, we waited to collect our warmer gear. On the steel decks of a Greek tramp, we had a night of shivering in rain and shrapnel, until she sailed at dawn for Mudros. Disembarking in the mid-afternoon, we straggled off, not even showing the pretence of a march. Men who fell out were left to follow. On coming to an inlet at low tide, those who felt up to it waded across. Those who knew it was beyond them went around, knowing they'd have another night in the open. At first we felt sorry for them, with our boots off for the first time in six weeks, wading was a delight until it became dragging one foot after another and stumbling, packs and all.

We were driven by the prospect of shelter. Arriving at the camp, there was just enough light to see a bare muddy slope. A thunderstorm and showers had us sodden and shivering, crouching under groundsheets. In the morning we learnt we had come three miles; we would have sworn it was thirty. Stragglers drifted in the rest of the day. When marquees were put up, the battalion easily fitted in; we were less than a hundred. But once the sun shone what a treat! Fresh meat, bread, eggs, as much as we could eat. Keeping those early meals down required persistence. Small local grapes were in season and I ate them by the handful although I could not persuade my gut to accept the island's almost equally small tomatoes. Amazingly, half-pints of stout came our way but, you wouldn't believe it, not enough for one bottle for one man below corporal.

For three days we were flat on our backs in the marquees, the conversation desultory and ceasing before lights out. Cleaning was the next priority. My feet, in boots I had not removed since last in Lemnos, were encased in foul plaster-cast socks. Days passed before we had soap and fresh water. It was a relief to discover a hot spring on the other side of the island. Perhaps it was the change in weather and situation but illness swept through, sending men to hospital. I was one of the few who was free of it. We were paraded before a French bigwig, whether general or admiral, no one was quite sure. The impression we made on him, other than that his antipodean Allies were skin, bone and rags, I cannot tell save that he expressed great pleasure at meeting troops who had fought so bravely and won such fame. We wondered about the latter. The newspapers that came our way mentioned Australians and Anzacs, with emphasis on the A.

We had a church parade on our first Sunday. It was the day I became, at best, an agnostic. The padre was Fielden-Taylor, a friend of Harry's and revered among some in Wellington city. His message to us—half-starved, shivering in the wind—was that no man had done his bit while he had a leg to stand on. A couple of days later we were hauled out to parade for Godley. As this was preceded by two hours of close order drill, and news that the stout issue had ceased and fresh meat had run out, we were not appreciative of his presence. Immaculate as usual, he let his eyes range over the tattered, but perfectly formed, ranks and complimented us on being a fine body of men who, in a month, *once again* would be proving our quality and bravery by being the first in the next great advance and triumphal entry into Constantinople. Lambs being fattened for Christmas, was the gentlest comment: the remainder unprintable. Being fattened, however, entails a not too strenuous life and so it became: two hours close order drill and the rest of the day our own until 6.30 p.m. At the end of September, when the Sixth Reinforcements came, we were occupied four hours a day. During October, night operations were brought in and courses run for machine gunners, signallers, pioneers, stretcher-bearers, scouts, snipers etc. As I neither volunteered nor was pressed for any of these, my life of ease continued: walking the island, trading for local food, hiring boats and cruising around the harbour to trade with our seafaring colleagues. Boredom reared its head; Two-Up and Crown and Anchor flourished, and as with idle young men anywhere, some made trouble.

As for me I had a quiet time. Harry and Jim were in Egypt and I went off by myself a lot. I could have chummed up with someone and sometimes I did but I also wanted a break from the perpetual presence of others that the army inflicts on you. I did a lot of walking, following where I'd gone when I'd been convalescing after my spell in hospital. There was nothing new to see. Not Mudros village, which by then was crowded with soldiers, sailors and others connected with all the soft jobs at base — for the most part an unlovely bunch — all taking advantage of not being on the Peninsula. What I missed most was having all that time on my hands and not a book within miles. When I'd left home I stuffed a Shakespeare and Milton into my haversack — mainly because each had more words to a single volume than anything else I could think of — but they had long since gone, lost in the toing and froing between Rest Gully and Quinn's. I had nothing except week-old newspapers from Egypt or month-old from England. There didn't even seem to be Greek books on the island although there must have been Greek Orthodox Bibles. I could have got an English Bible if I'd wanted it but I had lost interest in all that. Sometimes I would gaze out to sea and attempt to remember poems I'd read. Naturally Byron came to mind, even though it is hardly his greatest:

> The isles of Greece! the isles of Greece!
> Where burning Sappho loved and sung …

Unfortunately Lemnos was the most boring of the archipelago, well to the northwest of Sappho's island. Early in November we embarked for Anzac.

Up at the Apex again it was as though a fairy godmother had descended. Bivvies scraped into hillsides had been replaced by shrapnel-proof dugouts, hastily dug ditches were now a comprehensive trench system, and snipers had to work harder. Flies had almost gone too. They said it was the cold weather, but the dead were less frequently replaced and battle remains rotted or petrified. Wounded and sick were treated and quickly shipped out. The bully beef, no longer liquid and string, was at least reminiscent of real beef, and canned with vegetables, palatable. Above all there was plenty of water. But fairy godmothers cannot do everything and our little grey friends still accepted our fractious hospitality.

They didn't go away when the autumn gales came either. If anything they bedded themselves in. In October there was wind and rain and in November, snowstorms: we were shivering cold, and for some, frostbite substituted itself for flies and thirst. How did they expect us to see the winter through? They didn't. High brass came and went; Hamilton was replaced. In mid-December a latrine rumour circulated about another assault, followed by gloom until a new word went the rounds: evacuation. Amazingly it was confirmed.

No one, however, could imagine being let go unhindered. Rearguards were to hold the forward line until the last man, to allow as many of the force as possible to get to the piers where they would be evacuated. Guess who would comprise the rear guards? We were not proud to be among the chosen. In the meantime we were to carry on as normal. When digging we were ordered to throw the dirt high, our shovels above the parapet, flashing in the sun. Picks thudded into the ground near known or suspected Turk tunnels and listening posts.

On the last day before evacuation, I was ordered to lead a party under cover down to the beach and then, taking care to be observed, to return, apparently laden—if sniped that would be the ultimate success. Our down route was by way of Courtney's, Quinn's, Monash and Shrapnel. We did not find it at all reassuring to see that only the front trenches in our lines were occupied. Talk about the thin red line! The emptiness continued down to the beach: even the Great Sap was vacant. There were great heaps of stores and smashed equipment, soaked with kerosene. Indeed only the night before one of these had been fired, lighting up everything to Chunuk Bair, postponing evacuation for another day. We did not like that.

We were contemplating a pile of smashed half-gallon rum jars, breathing the odour and brooding on the wicked waste of war when an enemy aeroplane swooped low. We took pot shots at it, but after it turned for another sweep, ran for cover, hoping the aviator would think we were a brave few who, after doing our duty, had joined the thousands hiding from it, and that he was otherwise blind. Loaded with large but light burdens we took time off for a sit-down at an Advanced Dressing Station. The CO was a doctor under orders to remain and treat the wounded in the event of a Turk attack which, as all knew by then, would have nothing to impede it. The orders were based on the assumption that the honourable Turk would permit the CO and his staff to continue their duties when overrun. A further assumption was that, once the Turk had completed his advance, he would agree to the evacuation of the ADS on pain of a bombardment. The CO and his team were not happy men.

Our next reminder of our possible future was to encounter, out of sight of Turk lines, a massive hedge of barbed wire, with ten-foot high gates, following the contours of ridges and gullies. The gates were to be closed by the last rear guard party. But if there were an attack while rear guards were still inside, then the gates were to be closed and the rear guards left to fight it out. It was as well we were kept busy moving along the trenches, firing our rifles as though we were on our toes, which we were, and setting up simple devices to fire other rifles, at irregular intervals, after we had vacated the trenches.

The rear guards were three: A, which was to withdraw at dusk; B, at 9.15 p.m. when A should have embarked; and C at 2.15 a.m. when B too should be afloat and out of range. With one hundred and fifty other New Zealanders and nine hundred and fifty Australians I was in B. Everything A left, we destroyed. Save one thing: a portable gramophone too heavy to hump down to the beach. Among its records was a hit of the time, 'The Patriot Turk'. The turntable was wound up, 'The Patriot Turk' placed on it, and the arm set ready. The last few hours were excruciating but right on 9.15 our first man moved off. We were in single file and orders were passed along in a whisper. It was hard to believe, as the track twisted down to Chailak Dere, we would never have to negotiate it again. We moved quickly, deliberately breaking step to muffle the noise and only paused at the cemetery to pay silent tribute to comrades who would never leave, bitterness supplementing our anxiety.

At the mouth of Chailak Dere we thought we were nearly there until we were ordered to make way for the men from Suvla Bay. In the moonlight they passed like ghosts. At the embarkation jetty we had to stop again, for the Monash and Shrapnel men. On the jetty empty sandbags muffled our tread. Waiting for us was a former cross-channel steamer. We were the last aboard and still being crammed into the hold when, her engines thudding and funnel smoking, the vessel cast off, going full speed it seemed, by the end of the pier. For the first time for hours talkers could talk and smokers smoke.

Just before dawn we disembarked onto HMS *Zealandic*. We thought she might take us to the Salonika front. But again, our pessimism was unfulfilled. We were there to receive Royal Navy hospitality; being met by matelots who hurried us down to their Mess decks for hot cocoa, fresh bread and butter and plied us with cigarettes and chocolates bought out of their meagre pay: generosity one never forgets. While they were a little disappointed we didn't have heroic tales to tell, anything we wanted was ours, even, lice ridden though we were, a kip in their hammocks. Tempting, but up on the decks were half-barrels of hot soapy water.

At Mudros we met up with A and C, the latter also unmolested. We marched off, a spring in our step, to the transit camp. Coming to the crest of a rise, we saw a crowd at its gates. Wondering what was going on—had there been a mutiny at last?—we were cheered; everyone had written us off. Dismissed, we were off to the hot springs and by the end of the day there wasn't a louse amongst us. The relief was marvellous. Four days later, on Christmas Eve, we embarked for Alexandria. Christmas Day at sea, the Wellingtons were lucky, being aboard a vessel carrying Australians who wouldn't stand for anything other than a decent Christmas dinner, a celebration of the living. So ended Gallipoli; nothing became our generals as much as their leaving it.

NELLE
1915–16

News of the evacuation of Gallipoli came as a complete surprise. And when it was reported it was in a way that made it seem a sort of victory. Perhaps our annual commemoration since, on the twenty-fifth of April, reflects the way the disaster was first presented to the public. And then there was the death of Colonel Malone. My memory of Hugh Branscombe—and the men who were also in the garden that day—was still fresh and no longer was I blissfully ignorant about what war was about. To hear of the death of Colonel Malone was not quite the surprise it would otherwise have been, especially as we were also hearing rumours that hospitals in south England were taking numbers of men from Gallipoli—the hospitals in Egypt and Malta being overtaxed. Indeed as the year wore on, Lady Bell remarked that it was said there were as many men in English hospitals and convalescent homes as there were on Gallipoli.

When Father learnt Colonel Malone had been killed he was quite upset. As a reserve medical officer, he had been attached to the Wellington-West Coast Regiment of which Colonel Malone commanded the Taranaki Battalion. Although they were not close, Father spoke of him as the most proficient battalion commander he had met and, as well, rather liked him. But Father was also upset because he had, in the course of his duties, met officers from the Wellingtons who claimed that their commander, now that he was safely dead, was being blamed for some grievous blunders. By then the New Zealand Army had established a headquarters in London and when Father made quiet enquiries, he found this was so. Nothing much was *said*, but various failings, something to do with trenches on a ridge, was implied. Father was very angry. He found it impossible to believe that his old acquaintance would commit such errors—especially after he had again spoken with the Wellingtons' officers.

All he could do about that was to call on Mrs Malone to reassure her, if any of these false rumours had reached her ears. He was, however, also concerned about her. She had taken a passage to England early in the war believing that it would be possible to provide a home for her husband and maintain her own and her children's ties with him when he was granted leave. That, however, was not to be. Relatively young, much younger than the colonel, she had been in England but a few months when she received one of those dreadful telegrams. New to the country, she had, as I recall, no relatives, very few friends and two young children.

We called. Father had every reason for his concern. Mrs Malone was completely at a loss, breaking down when her late husband was mentioned. Luckily her isolation had kept her from the rumours and Father's assurances and his passing on of letters of condolences which he had asked the Wellington officers to write, provided her a permanent reassurance if the stories ever did come her way. But, just then, that was almost incidental. That she and her children were surviving her deep sorrow was due to her stepdaughter Norah who, praise be, had accompanied them to England. She hadn't just come for the trip but to join the VAD units of the British Red Cross. That, however, had to be postponed after the death of her father. She was very little older than I, but it was she who had dealt with accommodation matters, organised the household, ensured the army widow's pension was paid immediately, and arranged for the care and education of the two children. In short, she made life less unbearable for all three. Now that everything was functioning adequately, if not entirely happily—the signs were that the widow would carry her loss for a long time—Norah was about to carry out her original aim—although still keeping a watchful, if necessarily a more distant, eye on the household. On leaving the house and travelling home, Father remarked that she was very much the daughter of her father.

I have mentioned how Mother expected me to stay with her in

Marylebone and how I had other ideas. Everyone, it was said, should do one's bit and I must confess I was influenced by what Norah Malone was doing and what I had witnessed at Avon Tyrell. But there was more to it than that: for me the call for king and country carried the scent of freedom. Two of my English friends from Hampshire thought the same and they arranged to spend a year in St Thomas's hospital as probationers and then join the Volunteer Aid Detachments. One was very well connected: so well, that Mother permitted me to accept an invitation to stay with her. Perhaps because they were so well connected, nobody minded if she became a nurse for the duration. When I said I wanted to do the same, Mother objected, nurses being one step above bus conductresses. Father's one comment was that nursing might be too heavy and demanding. Mother seized on this, but when I mentioned my friend and how her family had no doubts about it and that indeed her mother would like to meet my mother, she modified her views. Mother and daughter came to tea, Mother was gratified, and I was enrolled at St Thomas's.

We all trooped off to meet the Matron of St Thomas's who quietly communicated that within the hospital's precincts, she was the superior. In our suitcases was nursing garb attesting that Florence Nightingale and Queen Victoria were very much alive and well. We each had our own bedroom: modelled, one felt, on a prison cell. It was rise at 5.45, breakfast at 6.30 and report to your ward at 7.00. Mine was first a women's surgical ward, and on being handed a broom, my lack of practice provoked considerable comment. From morning to night we fetched and carried: basins, bedpans, sputum cups, dressings, instruments; we filled and emptied hot water bottles, served dinner and teas, and washed up: tableware and cutlery in the kitchen, medical equipment in the sink room, a nauseating place where a scratched hand turned septic. When we were not so occupied we helped to paint wounds, rub chests, bandage and lift patients, the latter sometimes being done alone—turning one man left me in pain for days. Ward Sisters and Staff Nurses could broadly be divided into two: those who used us as charwomen and those who also used us as charwomen but who thought we might be capable of learning something. At 9.15 p.m., after formally wishing the Ward Sister goodnight, we were permitted to drop into our beds.

The half-day a week off was committed to Mother; tolerable when Father also had time off and we would go to Simpsons for afternoon tea. But each day we were given two hours off and they were my own. For the first time in my life, I could go out alone or with people of my choosing. It would be nice to relate we got up to mischief or had romantic meetings with handsome young men, but our outings rarely went beyond tea in Lyons Corner Houses or crossing the Thames to St James's Park. Not many of us could afford more, as being unpaid, we were still dependent on our parents who, in my case waited until I asked and then decided whether I should have it. If we met someone whom we might like to see again, there was no way to arrange it, as we never knew before the day, when time off would be. And the boys, invariably in khaki, were either coming or going.

More beds were needed when soldiers' wards were opened—I was 'too pretty' for the officers' ward. Nursing staff was barely increased so we did duties that had been done by qualified nurses. Some accepted this graciously, but others resented it and rarely forwent an opportunity to show it. I was directed to theatre work. I went with curiosity as Father, when I had enquired after his profession, had not been terribly explicit. Interestingly, when I first witnessed the sweep of a scalpel across a poor woman's belly, I did not flush and become nauseous and faint, the common fate of probationers on their first duty. Despite the oppressive heat, the tension, and the controlled butchery, working in the theatre was a positive change from scurrying about a ward. The most stressful aspect was the trip back to the ward. It always seemed to coincide with an orderly doing his last task of the day and running the trolley at breakneck speed, with me trying to keep up at a sideways trot supporting the patient so there'd be no tongue swallowing, and hoping there would be no early resuscitation to deal with. To my surprise, one day I received a compliment. Then somebody learnt about Father and after that *all was explained.*

I learned what hard, manual, repetitive work performed day after day, week after week, month after month, can do to one. Senses were dulled, mind stultified, ankles swollen, face puffed and hands formed sores. Should we have colds, tummy upsets, no matter what, so long as we might stand on our feet, we worked. Naïvety, dedication, and knowing if one wasn't there one's colleagues would do one's work too, dragged one out of bed in the morning. Night work appealed, the Sisters were mostly more pleasant—whether it was because they were married to husbands rather than to their work, or glad to get away from them, I will not presume to judge. Save in the case of an emergency, it was quieter, but not silent. There was always somebody in pain and sleeping aids being what they were, there was little we could do unless it became impossible for everybody else and a doctor had to be called. And that is another memory I have of the war years: unrelieved pain.

During the last weeks of June we noticed patients being discharged early and wards jammed with extra beds. Early in July we learnt there had been a great victory near a river called the Somme. Two or three days later, in the early hours of the morning in a nearly empty ward and after a quiet night, we heard cries of 'Convoy! Convoy!' I was sent to see. Ambulances were queued outside the hospital. Those in the front had orderlies unloading stretchers, rushing them inside to distribute them along corridors, across dining room tables, and on bed rails after the beds had been pushed together so that a second layer might lie above patients in the beds below. Everybody was called out. The ambulance trains were arriving at Charing Cross almost by the hour. I worked through until the following midnight. Collapsing on top of my bed, I found six a.m. came soon and another eighteen-hour day was ahead, followed by another and another. Only slowly did the working day shorten. The hospital reeked of stinking, filthy, groaning men. Only then did we realise how sanitised had been the wounded we had received before. Because of a general's ghastly mistake, the evacuation system had broken down. We received men who'd had just a quick examination and a label describing their wounds. Their uniforms, plastered onto their bodies by dust, filth and blood, had to be cut off.

We had to clean up after our doctors had made their diagnoses. Once cleaned, some died; others died on the operating table and it was common for those with stomach wounds to die a fortnight later. One man I cared for had tetanus, and all his crockery, cutlery and anything else he *might* have come into contact with, had to be scrupulously sterilised and food leftovers burnt. But it was lighter work than assisting a Sister change dressings where bones had been shattered, often with infection occurring since. One had to hold the limb firmly with a slight outward pull to prevent grating. Soon one's arms would ache, but if one relaxed ever so little, the most stoical patient would shriek.

My probationary year ended soon after the arrival of the Somme wounded, but I couldn't think of leaving. It was another matter when the numbers lessened, and half-dead, I moved in with Mother where, for a fortnight, I did nothing but live a life of leisure: lingering in bed, luxuriating in long hot baths, no institutional meals and happily sleepwalking with Mother to wherever her fancy took her. After a month, when my hands had recovered, my ankles were back to normal, sleep was no longer the be all and end all, and I could look in a mirror without trauma, I was bored to distraction.

My year at St Thomas's meant nothing to Mother; Father, however, was interested. Actually I was in two minds about returning to nursing. Women were driving ambulances. I liked the idea of that. Drivers were out and about with no Sisters breathing down their necks. The problem was: where might I learn to drive? Then I learnt there were VADs who rode in the back of ambulances attending the wounded. That seemed an avenue that might produce something interesting. I was thinking on this when Lady Bell and Vi called.

It was a warm afternoon and tea had just been poured when Lady Bell remarked how well I looked. Mother replied that if she had met me a month earlier, she would not have thought so.

Lady Bell turned to me saying she was sorry I had been ill.

'Badly run down,' said Mother. 'Very badly run down.'

'Oh!'

'It's that year she took it upon herself to spend at St Thomas's.'

'So public-spirited of her,' said Lady Bell.

'Perhaps,' said Mother. 'It was all too much for her.'

'Was it, my dear?' Lady Bell gave me a friendly glance.

'You should have seen her,' said Mother.

'All I needed was a little rest,' I said.

'And the care of your Mother.'

'I wouldn't have missed it for the world,' I said.

'Is that so?' remarked Lady Bell.

'Yes,' said I.

'It is easy for her to say that now,' said Mother.

I kept quiet.

'Would you return?' Lady Bell asked.

'Not St Thomas's, I think.' It would have been rude not to answer our guest.

'And I should think not,' said Mother. 'Next time she might not be so lucky.'

It seemed best not to respond to that too.

'But you are well now?' asked Lady Bell.

'Quite well, thank you,' I said.

'For the time being,' said Mother.

'It will, of course, be your, and Colonel Travis's, decision,' said Lady Bell.

'I'm confused, Lady Bell,' said Mother. 'What decision?'

'It is time, Mrs Travis, that Vi and I made a confession.' Lady Bell glanced across at her daughter. 'Recently she has been a volunteer at Mount Felix at Walton-on-Thames which, you may remember, was founded by the good work and donations from the New Zealand War Contingent Association.'

Lady Bell paused at just the right moment. She was well-practised in the art of persuasion which, when one considers it, is not surprising given that her husband was a politician *and* a lawyer, and that she had spent years managing her brood of eight children.

'Since we last met,' she continued, 'it has been decided that Mount Felix should be taken over by the military. Sadly the demands of this dreadful war have become far beyond anything a private charity may provide. The Government is staffing it with trained nurses from New Zealand, but is unwilling to send girls to assist them. Indeed the only New Zealand VADs we have in England are girls who were already here when the war began or who have made the journey privately. Sir Thomas McKenzie, our High

Commissioner, has been asking everyone to urge young women who are over here to help in our hospitals.'

'No sooner had they decided to call for help than they were at our door. Before we knew it, we were in a car and on our way to Mount Felix,' said Vi, throwing in her twopence worth.

'We have English and Scottish girls,' said Lady Bell, 'and we don't know what we would do without them, but the poor boys respond so well to our own girls.'

'I see,' said Mother who doubted whether she should.

'Of course,' said Lady Bell. 'If you have any concerns, you might consider coming down to Walton. I have taken a small house in the vicinity so that Vi and her friends may visit.'

'They live in?'

'Most of the staff lives on the premises, in the original country house.'

'*Most* of the staff?' said Mother.

'Some have taken rooms in Walton.'

'Oh!' said Mother.

'But closely supervised,' said Lady Bell serenely. 'Since Mount Felix opened, nothing untoward has happened.'

Mother's expression made it clear there was always a first time.

'Please come,' said Vi to me.

'I will have to speak about this with Colonel Travis,' said Mother.

'Violet,' said Lady Bell. 'The decision will be made by Colonel and Mrs Travis, although,' she smiled at Mother, 'I am sure they will take Nelle's wishes into account. But you must come and see for yourself, Mrs Travis. Just recently, their Majesties and the Prince of Wales paid a visit.' It was now my turn. 'Nelle, I know you would be proud to help our brave young men.'

So my future was decided.

SOMME

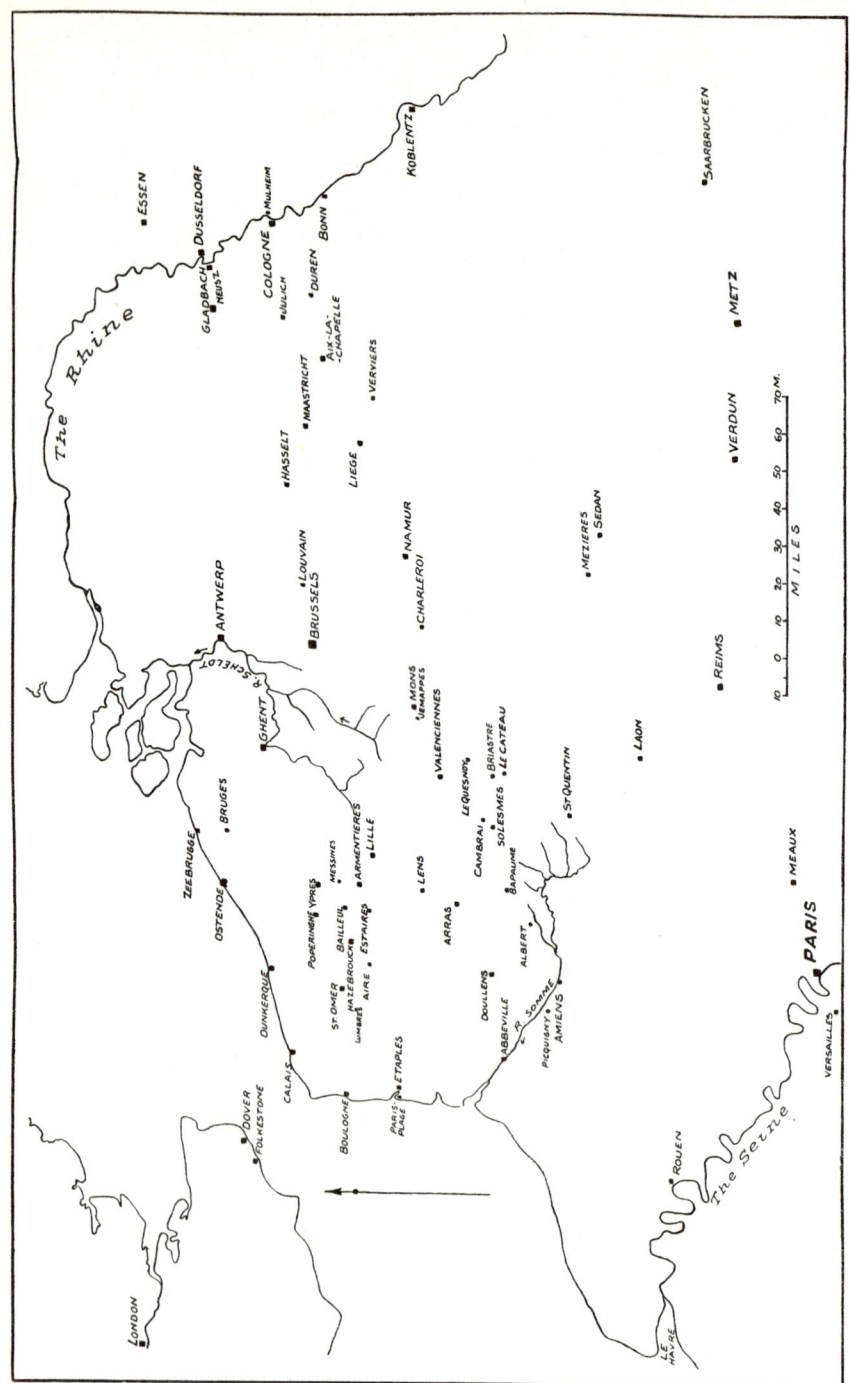

Northern France—Belgium—The Rhine. *Source: Burton, O.E.*

HARRY
Egypt/Armentières

You will understand that much as I appreciated the healing of my wound and the comforts of convalescence, I felt a strong desire to leave at the earliest opportunity and return to my friends and brothers-in-arms. It was with some trepidation that I arrived back, as I wondered whether Jim had told tales about how Lady Godley had carried on. I received some good-natured chaffing for the little piece of tin the Serbs and General Godley had bestowed on me, but nothing otherwise; Jim had exercised the self-restraint that was so much part of him. When I was promoted to platoon sergeant, the position rightfully belonged to Jim but for some ridiculous reason they had taken his stripes away. Jim ribbed me about my elevation and if I had thought he was serious I would have had myself demoted, as a trustworthy friend can never be measured against trappings of office. My saddest discovery was to learn that Frank had been transferred to the Otagos. It was to be some months before we met again. A soldier's world is centred on his platoon and if it goes beyond his company, it mostly stops at his battalion unless he suffers the misfortune of being transferred as Frank was.

Another change I found was that so many eager young New Zealanders had volunteered that it had become possible to form a complete New Zealand division comprising three infantry brigades, 1st, 2nd, and Rifles, of four battalions each, along with a full divisional complement of artillery, engineers, medical etc. The first two brigades had territorial affiliations — e.g. 1st Wellington was in the 1st Brigade — while the Rifles was New Zealand wide. Commanding the Division was Major General

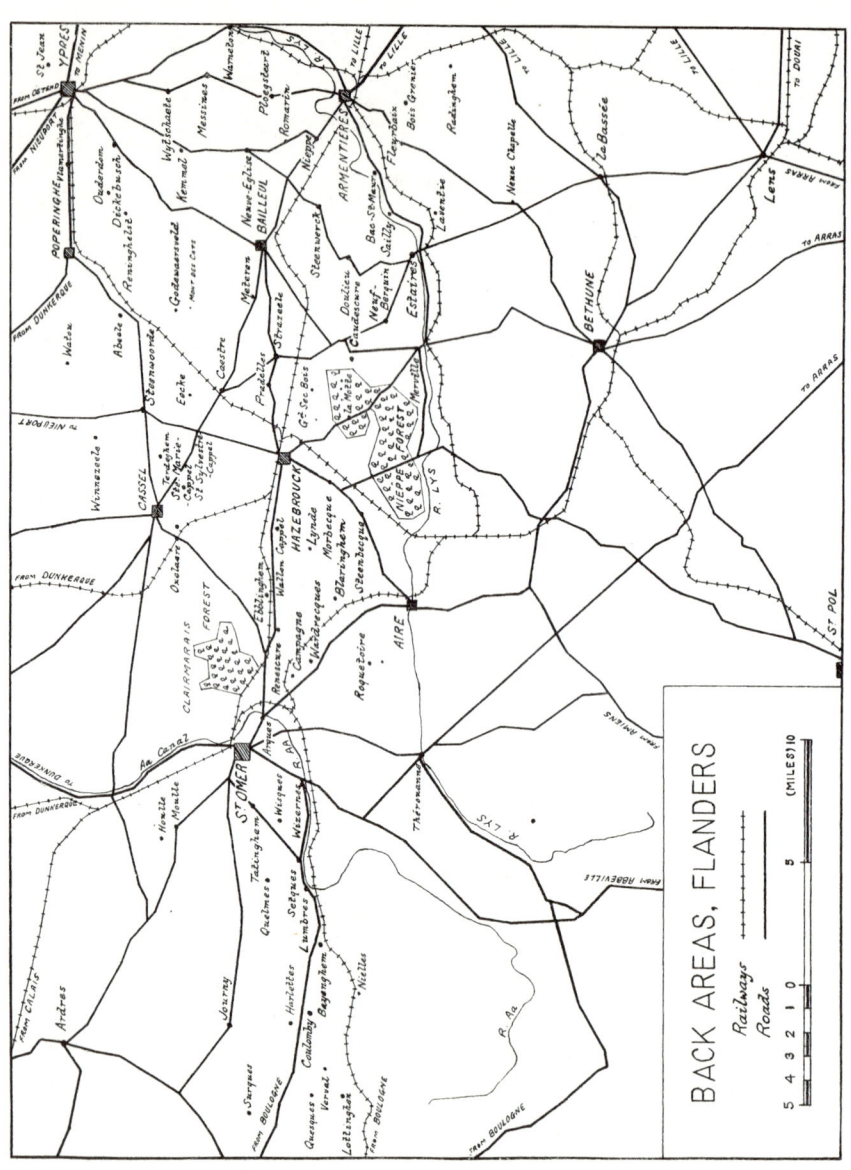

BACK AREAS, FLANDERS

Railways +++++++++++
Roads ――――――

5 4 3 2 1 0   5   10 (MILES)

Behind the lines from Ypres to Armentières. *Source: Ferguson, D.*

Sir Andrew Russell, perhaps the only senior officer who returned from Gallipoli with a higher reputation than when he landed. It is interesting to compare his career with that of the drunkard Johnston. Like him he was educated in England and became a regular officer in the British Army and then served in India. Unlike Johnston, he returned to Hawke's Bay to manage the family farm. Never was a senior rank appointment to prove so justified. He was also a practising member of the Church of England, and firm in his faith. He was to make mistakes, then and later, but, as a humble man aware of his mortal fallibility, he was never too vain to guard against, recognise, and rectify, error.

Our camp was at Moascar, near Ismailiya, with its European quarter laid out in a style we were to recognise once we had crossed the Mediterranean. As for the native quarter—it was as squalid and as rife with vice of the lowest order as anywhere in Egypt. From time to time I was detailed to lead a picket through it. More than once we would rescue one of our lads lying in the street drugged insensible, robbed of anything of worth, and, too often, infected with the foulest of diseases. But our camp had one great advantage, and that was Lake Temsah, one of the Suez Canal lakes. It became the Mecca of the thousands of British troops in the area and what a fine sight it was to see the mass of gleaming white bodies in the pink of physical condition diving and skylarking under the clear blue skies of an Egyptian winter.

We were in the midst of preparations for our departure from Egypt when I was called before Colonel Hart, who taxed me for not having applied for a commission despite being informed I was 'officer material'. Moreover, General Godley had mentioned my name. I explained that if I went to an Officer Training Unit I would be out of action for some months, a bad time to be, as we were on our way to the Western Front, a new style of warfare, where my men would need a platoon sergeant with experience in the field. Neither could he guarantee I would be returned to 1st Wellington. What I did not mention, although I would not be surprised if Colonel Hart had guessed it, was that my platoon commander had been commissioned in New Zealand and had never been in action. There was nothing about him to convince me he was a fit and proper person to lead men beyond a supply dump. Untried officers were resented throughout the Division to the degree that it was taken up with General Godley. He sympathised and put the case to the authorities at home. Beyond that he could do no more and for reasons that defied common sense they continued to arrive. Blatant incompetents were weeded out but it was the high infantry officer casualty rate that opened the gaps for most promotion from the ranks.

I did not regret embarking for France as I had seen enough of Egypt and its hapless inhabitants oppressed by the twin evils of Islam and poverty. After a lively but comfortable voyage across the Mediterranean to Marseilles we boarded a train for the Western Front, trundling along at a rate that might have averaged seven miles an hour. Everything was green and the warm and welcoming women and children healthy and beautiful. But we noticed the men were either old or in uniform, and sometimes both, or were German prisoners of war, working on the wharves or roads and who did not appear dissatisfied with their lot. The young and the not so young Frenchmen were being herded into the terrible slaughterhouse of Verdun.

In due time we drew into a siding whose purpose was starkly apparent, but the immediate prospect turned out better than we expected: our first experience of billeting and, for us off the farm, amongst people with whom we had much in common however differently they might speak, eat and house themselves. While we preferred the animal housing and the products thereof to be at some distance, and rather would not have bedded down with our heads butting against a pigsty fence, we appreciated the warmth of their barns and the fresh produce we were able to purchase and the stubborn courage that cultivated land to the edge of the battlefield and sometimes even within it. With their young men thrown into the cauldron they welcomed us.

Training recommenced and I took courses on the Lewis gun and the Mills bomb hand-grenade, the latter a considerable improvement — if one can apply such a phrase to a weapon of war — on the tin cans and cricket balls of Gallipoli. I made it my business to learn each weapon thoroughly, to gain the authority to instruct my men without the meddling of those who thought they knew better.

In the middle of May 1916 the Division was sent to the Armentières front, a quiet sector mainly because it was low-lying swamp country. The Germans had the advantage over us. A mile behind their front line the ground rose high enough to provide them with an uninterrupted view of our trenches. Elsewhere too, it was not uncommon for the Germans to occupy the high ground. Unlike their German counterparts, our generals throughout the war refused to take advantage of high ground if it involved pulling back a bit. They believed aggressiveness would outweigh the disadvantage of holding overlooked ground. It did not.

Our first tour lasted nine days and although they were quiet we still had a lot to do, the former occupants of the line not being prone to overexertion. We were not in trenches; if they had been, they would have been permanent drains. We built up rather than dug down. Parapets of sandbags rose in front and likewise the parados behind, except when the latter were merely screens to fool the German air observers. Beneath our feet were duckboards that rotted quickly and never ceased to be replaced—as we never stopped rebuilding parapets collapsed by German shelling nor repairing the gaps blown out of the barbed wire. We also improved dugouts that had been merely sandbagged nooks supporting a sheet or two of corrugated iron. What amazed us after the poverty of Anzac was the abundance of building materials. When we weren't building and wiring we were burying telephone cables running back to the artillery and command posts. Another big difference from 1915 was that having and holding in force a continuous firing line, was being replaced by a string of connected strong points positioned to cover each other—with most of the men being held in what we called the support and subsidiary lines. Each of these could cover the line in front of it. Fritz did not like our dedication to putting things right and his shelling increased.

Colonel Hart ordered me to do something about the dominance of German sniping. It was a case of again going out and securing good Mausers. First Wellington had only two optical sights and it took time before our battalion had sufficient telescopes. We were also short of experienced men as Gallipoli had taken our bravest and best. It was a case of looking for quiet patient men with good eyes. Flashy devil-may-care characters seeking a reputation as Hun killers were of no interest to me. Once suitable men were found, they had to be trained in a very short time. Every day that we lacked snipers was another good day for the enemy. It was a combination of needing to train snipers and the prospect of my platoon going into action under the sole leadership of an incompetent that led me to decline leave in England. Word got around I'd gone soft in the head.

All work and no play makes Jack a dull boy so we were given spells of 'resting'. 'Resting' is one of those words the army had made its own. 'Resting' was night work carrying unwrapped coils of barbed wire and other stores to the front, or repairing parapets and parados when our friends on the other side rested not. 'Resting', however, did allow one—possessing the God-given, taken-for-granted energy of the young—to visit Armentières during daylight hours. Although the town was shelled regularly farmers still came on market day to sell their produce. On talking it over with other farm boys, we agreed that if our families were in their shoes, they would do the same. The main attraction for the troops, however, was the estaminets—cafés where, unfortunately, copious quantities of wine were available. There was also a YMCA to mitigate the routines of army life with its quietness, stationery for writing home, newspapers and the cups of tea and cakes so cheaply available. Christians in the battalion soon made use of it for prayer circles.

Towards the end of June we were up at the front again. Because our presence there was to coincide with the opening of Haig's attack on the Somme, we were ordered to make raids to discourage the enemy to divert troops to the Somme. There was also another reason: to keep us from going 'stale'. Haig's order to keep up the pressure was in accord with General Russell's temperament. Orders went out to the battalions to train and plan raids. In preparation our bombardments became much heavier: on one day three thousand shells were fired, more than during our whole time at Anzac. The Germans did not take long to retaliate and it was as well a number of their shells were duds. Not as many as one would wish, alas, and not as many as ours. After about a week of being on the receiving end from Fritz, our support and subsidiary lines caught a packet of accurately placed shells. This was on the day after one of our men deserted to the

Germans and the day before 1st Wellington mounted a raid.

Whatever he might have told them they were not on their guard when we made our raid. Colonel Hart had ensured we prepared carefully and intelligently. There had been two previous raids and Hart had no hesitation in learning from their mistakes. The Otago raid, for example, had been known in and around Armentières beforehand. We took great care to keep ours secret. Hart was also cognisant of one of the oldest laws of military conflict. Attributed to an unfortunate Mr Murphy it states that anything that can go wrong, will. We took measures to deal with this.

The clear starlit night without a moon was a good night for a raid and that was what Hart had planned to take advantage of. Half an hour after midnight our barrage opened up and fired for twenty minutes with the field artillery concentrating on the forward trenches and our three-inch trench mortars on the enemy wire. We went into no man's land and waited in the midst of shelling and counter shelling. It was not what might be called a comfortable experience, but we knew if we had remained in our forward positions we would have received the enemy's retaliatory barrage—as those positions did: three of our strong points being wrecked.

Because we knew to the minute when our barrage would cease and because we were already in no man's land and had little ground to cover, we suffered few casualties in our rush to the enemy trenches. We of the scout squad were in the lead. We had no bother when we came to what had been a thirty feet wide thicket of wire; our mortars had flattened it. Meanwhile our artillery offered protection from enemy reinforcements. We were allowed eight minutes to do our work in the enemy trenches. Before eight minutes had passed we had taken ten prisoners and maps and papers. We were able to confirm that the German defence works were more resistant to shellfire than ours and that their front line was very lightly held. One German officer bravely sacrificed his life rather than surrender and other losses of life occurred to those who refused to exit their dugouts.

So ended the most successful raid in the Armentières sector. When it was all added up it might be claimed the raid was well worth it until one takes into account that there was little learnt that could not have been obtained by a competent reconnaissance patrol and a close reading of aerial photographs.

A raid by 2nd Wellington followed. Unlike us, they did not proceed into no man's land when their supporting bombardment commenced but waited in front of their parapet. They received a shower of German shells. After that they were caught in crossfire. Those who got through it dropped into a vacated trench and while doing so were on the receiving end of grenades thrown from a trench immediately behind. They found nothing of value and their withdrawal was carried out under more crossfire. Twelve were killed, thirty-six wounded, and five were missing. The award of a DCM and a Médaille Militaire to a sergeant major might have recognised one man's courage but that was all that came of it. Other raids were either no better or even more disastrous.

For a raid to have any chance of success it has to be thoroughly planned, with each man highly competent and well-trained for the particular raid. It was the wastefulness of sacrificing these men for so little that condemns those who prescribed raiding on the grounds 'that the aggressive spirit must be maintained'. In other words, men, to be effective, must be kept under stress beyond that imposed by a front line trench. The Germans mounted raids but they were fewer and retaliatory.

A man had deserted, the only one in the war, and although the deserter could have contributed little to the failure of the raids, as is human wont he was blamed and a spy mania took over. Typical of the accusations made was that an old peasant doggedly ploughing his land in sight of the enemy was doing so in a pattern that was signalling a secret message to the Germans. There would have been spies in Armentières certainly and when there was a lot of talk and interesting goings on they would have the means of getting their reports back to their masters, but the real reason the Germans were well informed was they had equipment that could overhear our telephone conversations.

Fritz was largely on the defensive on the Western Front after he failed to prevail at the terrible battles of Verdun, where, as he tried to bleed the French armies to death, he also bled his own. He changed his strategy to first defeat the Russians in the East. Hence the high quality of German defence works on the Western Front including taking measures like cutting the grass short far out into no man's land and at night sending up an abundance of flares and playing searchlights along his own, as well as our, parapets. Cunning booby traps were set in his wire and broadsides of hand-grenades kept ready.

Nevertheless patrols of cool and capable men would enter the German front line long enough to take a prisoner, rat a dugout and get their hands on any documents found. These targets were chosen only after scouts had made a thorough reconnaissance of the lie of the land and the habits and routines of the troops occupying it. Anything gained was at far less cost in matériel and men than a conventional raid. A lot of patrolling was nosing around no man's land to find what Fritz was up to, like fighting patrols sent out to find and destroy a listening post in a shell hole and secure a prisoner.

I got a particular kick of going out after prisoners, despite it being not very healthy if, in seeking for an enemy post, its occupants found you first. Once secured, a prisoner was in fear of his life, unaware that he was of great value to us to the degree that we were risking our own skins to bring him back alive and whole. Of course one could not disabuse the poor fellow. Few possessed the character to be uncooperative and on the rare occasions they told no more than their name, rank and number, their regimental insignia was a helpful guide to our intelligence staff on the quality of the men opposite and how frequently regiments were rotated.

Patrolling became my game. I lived and breathed it. For the rest of the war patrolling was my vocation and I thought myself lucky that I had COs who encouraged it. Part of its appeal was curiosity about 'the other side of the hill'. What does Fritz have in mind today? What's the latest trick he's got up his sleeve? Will he attack? If so, where? Was there any significance to his latest barrage? He's hardly shelled for the last couple of days—why? And is Fritz himself fit and ready to go or is he even more fed up with the war than we are? But that's only part of it. What really gets men into patrolling is the hunt: your skills and cunning against the other fellow's—the stakes at the highest: life and death, him or you. So out you go, out he goes and may the best man win. Patrolling is a distillation of the dreadful fascination of war.

JIM
Egypt/Armentières

I was discharged from the convalescent home before Harry. I told him to stick around and have a good time with her Ladyship. He said it was the doctors keeping him there. Is that what it is? I asked, and pushed off to join the lads just in time for a walkout because they weren't allowed leave to the nearest rat hole. Hopeless from the start, no organisation, nobody who'd sat down and thought it out. Couple of the lads got excited, talked about how it was the start of something big. Big what, where and for what? Frank was there. I wouldn't have been if I'd been him. We walked into town and walked back. Lost my stripes. Didn't worry me much, I never asked for them. What I didn't like was I'd blown my cover: the only NCO who walked. Then Frank was transferred out. His cover blown too, when you come to think of it.

So I kept my head down, put myself in the middle of a platoon, did everything I was told, smartly, and did nothing to rile anyone. Maybe they thought by ordering me around like a private fresh off the boat they were teaching me a lesson. Whatever, it passed and they put me two stripes up, i/c the guard party. Soft option: no fatigues, four hours on, four off. The old hands rallying to their old mate who'd been through it too, I guess; keeping one eye on how much he was a Red, the other for old times' sake, and because they didn't have too many seasoned NCOs.

We guarded the Ismailiya-Cairo railway bridge: us at one end and Indians at the other. They were Baluchis: over six feet, with skinny legs and turbans. Smart as the Guards on parade and as good as anyone when it counted. Had held the line at Wytschaete, First Ypres, 1914. But the damp got to them; Khyber Pass was their country. Hard, hospitable men: if they liked you everything was yours. They didn't like the Tommies. Looked down on them and wouldn't take the wog treatment. We'd meet in the middle of the bridge and they'd ask us over for a feed: chapattis, rice and the rest. We got on with them just as we'd got on with the Gurkhas. Theirs was the only place for miles you'd get a decent cup of char.

The next guard was a Royal Flying Corps aerodrome. That stop was the closest I came to leaving my old mates. After I'd been there a week I'd worked out what went on and hung around. The day came when I noticed the mechanics were cleaning up after working on an engine and a pilot was standing by. I went over and stood where he could see me. By then they all knew who I was. 'Like a flight, Corporal?' the pilot said when the cowling had been screwed down. 'Yes, Sir,' I said and there I was in an open cockpit; the wind whistling by with the smell of burnt oil. We skimmed the canal and this time it was me who looked over the side through goggles and grinned at the poor buggers sweating below before we climbed, looped the loop, took in Cairo and the pyramids, between, not over them, and back home down the Nile. Who'd want a trench after that? I was all set to volunteer. They wanted gunners, and knowing the Vickers, I reckoned it wouldn't take me long to handle the Lewis in the air. After I climbed out of the cockpit, I took a closer look at the plane. The pilot was filling in his logbook. 'Done a lot of flights, Sir?' I asked. He let me look at it: time, date, where to, that sort of thing. He'd transferred out of an English regiment as an observer, and then went on to pilot. Why not me, I thought. Down the left hand side of the page there were these dots, half a dozen, each at the beginning of an entry. 'What are the dots for?' He laughed. 'Crashes. Awfully nice chap, my pilot, but the blighter never really learnt to land. Seemed a good reason to fly the bus myself.' 'Yes, Sir,' I said and looked at the book again. There was a dot when he trained and another after that.

If we had stayed at the airfield I might have gone, but we were sent to guard the camp and the manoeuvre area. Boring after the airfield and in line of sight of generals. One day Birdwood and Godley were out walking, having a good old yak together and I called out the guard to throw the general salute. Birdwood looked up and waved his hand not to bother so I dismissed the guard except for the man on duty. OK. But Birdwood knew what he was doing. It was a way to have the boys think he was a no bullshit man — but if I hadn't called them out, I would have heard about it. This was around the time the Aussies were leaving us and we became the New Zealand Division. Just before they left they cut loose one of our men doing No 1 Field Punishment. Tied to a post in the midday sun. Half passed out and hanging by his ties. There had been a mass meeting about him. Nothing came of it; windbags exercising their lungpower; another mob with no organisation.

Before going to France I had a day's leave and Frank was on the train too. We teamed up and saw the sights together. He'd missed out on the way over so I was able to show him one or two things and he'd read about the mosques supposed to be worth looking at and the Cairo Museum. We met an Egyptian who had spare time and an inclination to talk. He filled us in on how he and all Egyptians, except the ones who made money out of us, wished we'd get out. He was interested when I mentioned workers' international solidarity.

We landed in France as summer was coming on but the best that happened was a spot of leave in the Old Country. There was a free rail pass, so I went to see where my dad came from. He had told me we were known as the McDonnells of Glengarry and there weren't many of us left at Glengarry and how we'd had a raw deal from our chiefs. One had volunteered the clan for Bonnie Prince Charlie. They were done for at Culloden and their houses burnt down. The next chiefs became loyal subjects of King George and cleared the people off, most going to Canada. My dad said his dad wished they had gone too. My dad remembered a lot of shivering over a peat fire in a stone hut and wondering what it'd be like to have a full belly now and then. When he was twelve he took off. They gave him a bag of oats. It was the best they could do and he wondered where they got it. That more or less kept him going as far as Glasgow. Canada was in his mind. He'd thought he might sign on a ship but there was nothing going. With the oats running out it was down to the Lanarkshire coalfields where he might be able to pay his way across the Atlantic. That wouldn't be for a long time with the money they were paying, and he was laid off before he'd saved enough. He finished up in the Yorkshire pits. It would have been an answer to his prayers when he was told about the free passage to New Zealand.

My first stop after London was Fort William, followed by Invergarry. When you go inland from Invergarry you're in the homeland of the Mc-Donnells. I stopped in a pub at Invergarry. The locals made me welcome: I had to fight to pay the bar—and the only whisky they drank was malt. On the second night a man came through the door, closed it, said hello to two men, and looked me up and down. I knew who he was. Same forehead and jaw as my dad but harder eyes.

'Jamie McDonnell.' He looked at me straight, no blinking.

'Jim,' I said.

'Nephew.'

'Uncle.'

'Your father?'

'Passed on.'

He nodded.

'I heard he was in the pits.'

'Roof fall,' I said.

'When?'

'Nineteen-ten. Fourteenth December.'

Another nod, another look at me and he joined the men he'd said hello to. One of them ordered a round. I turned back to the men I was with, one a Canadian from a Canadian Highland regiment. I was the first from New Zealand at Invergarry but he was not the first Canadian. Now and then my uncle would look across at me. He didn't seem to mind me noticing. Went on looking. Before he went out with one of the men he stopped in front of me.

'Settle up here. Tomorrow morning.'

No sleep in, just time for tea and porridge and he was at the door.

'Leave it with Davey.' He pointed to my pack.

The publican put it behind the bar, but I took my greatcoat.

He walked with a long stride, which he kept up all the way. There was a track that leads up to Loch Garry and then for most of the way along the edge of it. We passed where crofters had lived. All but two of their houses were ruins. They were stone and whitewashed but one had never been a croft. It had bow windows in the front, floor to ceiling, and dormer windows coming out of the roof, all with a view of the loch. Nearby was the other house, which was more of a cottage. This is where we stopped. We went to the back door. As a great favour they let me sit just inside the kitchen and gave me a cup of tea while he went inside. When he came out he didn't say anything but it didn't take much to guess it was a call on his boss. What with cutting in and out around the edge of the loch we walked a good fifteen miles before we reached his croft beyond the head of Loch Garry. It was stone, whitewashed and better looking outside than in.

I went off with him every day and got to know the country. We didn't talk much, but like with Dad, when I asked him about the family and the clan he told me. He looked after the deer on the hills and the fish in the loch and he had as good an eye for country as Harry. My auntie fed me as if I were her son and always hungry. Jamie didn't spare the fish or the deer when it came to eating at home. Maybe my dad should have stayed but there was no guarantee he would have got Jamie's job. And while Jamie was good to me I couldn't see my dad working hard to keep poachers away.

As for my auntie treating me like her son, she had one and a daughter. He was with the Cameron Highlanders. From his mum and dad it hadn't taken me long to work out he was a sniper. And from them, and others like the Canadian McDonnell, I learnt it wasn't only in 1914 that other men's wars had done well out of us. Our bones were rotting in Belgium before there was a Belgium and after that it was just about anywhere the Union Jack has been raised. It had either been go and take the King's shilling or, like my dad, just go. And if the King of England wasn't to your taste there was always the King of France, and of Scotland too if you went back far enough.

From the look of the country there wouldn't have been much of a living from it even if the people had been let be. Maybe that chief had done them a favour, getting rid of them like that. It was early spring when I was there. In France and England they had been going into summer. Up there trees were just showing their leaves. Some days were clear, some grey, some a bit of each but none were what you'd call warm. I remembered Dad telling me he'd come from a land of granite, peat and cold. I thought of the poor little bugger crouching over a peat fire. The big house we had passed was called Ardochy. It was where whoever owned the land came to stay. I won't say lived because he only came for holidays. To fish, shoot, and rubberneck. That is what the country had become.

Back at the battalion there was a smarten-up campaign. General Russell put it out we had to salute and walk around as if we were on ten thousand quid a year. A lot of money in those days and not a little today. I don't know how much Russell was paid but I guess it wouldn't be far short of that, especially with his farm and what came out of it. One way of explaining what you want, I suppose. You don't have an army without discipline. Saluting never worried me and I looked the buggers on the other end hard in the eye. Kept them on their toes. A touch of the fascist about Russell, maybe more than a touch: the man who led Massey's Cossacks. But he knew how to run an army, as the Right too often do. The Left get hoity toity about the military and wake up when it is too late, blaming everyone except themselves. Trotsky made his mistakes but that wasn't one of them — and he knew about discipline.

Armentières gave us our first inkling of what Ypres might be like. First Brigade sub-sector was a salient so we got it from the flanks as well as the front. It did not make things any better that we had what was called the Mushroom. It was where our trench system stuck out into no man's land in the shape of a mushroom. Sixty yards separated the head of it from the German line. Nowhere near as bad as Quinn's Post but enough to remind you of it.

One night Ruahine Company was given a turn there. It was too much for one of them because he took off for no man's land leaving his rifle behind. When Ruahine saw his rifle and no sign of him they fired everything they had after him. We heard it and wondered what was going on. We keyed ourselves up for whatever might come our way. But the German trenches stayed quiet. Nor could we see anything in no man's land. Then, after a couple of sweeps from a Vickers, the firing ceased.

Next day we learnt that the Ruahine target had been one of their own. Gone to visit his relatives, it was said—his parents were German born. He must have said something to his new mates that upset them because when morning broke there was a mother and father of a bombardment. I remember it because my tin hat was knocked off with a dent you could put two of your fingers in. A sledgehammer hit and a headache for the rest of the day and night. We didn't have the hats in Gallipoli and when they were issued in France we didn't like them. They were no good against a direct hit. But without one, a glance of shrapnel could slice your skull open. As mine would have been.

Before the 1st Wellington raid our field guns strafed twice. The first on the night before to fool Fritz there was to be a raid that night—although I can't remember too many times when Fritz was fooled. The second, on the night of the raid, to soften up and keep heads down before our boys took off. That was normal. Everybody did it but the colonel decided to make the first strafe more useful than just that. That was how I was called up by the sergeant major and told to take a couple of men to a forward listening post just before the first strafe so that I could report on how the shells fell and on enemy movements. All going well, the listening post would be the start line for the raiding party the next night. If either the German shells or ours fell too near, or on us, the start line would be somewhere else.

'A three man patrol,' I said.

'Yes,' the sergeant major said. 'You could call it that.' This was the first time he'd said anything to me since the walkout. We hadn't got on too badly before. Used to call me Jim.

'Then, Sar'Major, I'll need to pick my own men.'

He nodded.

'Good men will be in the raid,' I said.

'That's the way it goes,' he said.

I said two names.

He said they were in the raid and mentioned three or four more whom I was thinking of.

There weren't many left whom I'd trust. But all that was needed were men who'd sit tight.

'OK,' I said and gave him a couple of names of men who'd joined us in France.

'Good steady blokes,' he said.

We'll see, I thought.

'You'll be relieved at midnight. That party will go and inspect the German line when the bombardment ceases.'

'That's nice. Sar'Major,' I said.

We went out through the sally port into no man's land at 9.30 p.m. to a slump in the ground—about fifty yards from our line and less than a hundred from Fritz. At ten sharp our strafe opened up, and not wasting time, Fritz came back with his. It was full blast in front and behind. The new boys thought they might be better off if they pawed into the mud, but after five minutes they got curious to watch the show, forgetting about the war profiteer's duds that could drop short, or a sentry who could pick out their tin hats against a shell burst. So I said to get their heads down to the lip of the hollow, where there was still something to see. It was worth watching ... Shells going overhead from each direction and us on the edge of where they were bursting, the explosions shaking the ground and lighting up the earth, sandbags and God knows what else thrown into the air. Midnight came and went. The shelling didn't stop and no relief. We didn't mind; the ground between us and our forward trench was not what you'd call peaceful. The forward trench didn't look all that bright either. Then I heard our password being called.

'Sar'Major?' I said.

'Jim, my lad.' He tumbled down beside us.

'Haven't seen much of Fritz,' I said.

'Keeping his head down?'

'Like us,' I said.

'All this shit. The relief party's cancelled. Thought I'd better let you know.'

'You didn't have to,' I said.

'You'll have to stick it out, Jim.'

'Can't think of anywhere worth going just now,' I said.

When barrages began to tail off I gave him a chance to say something.

He didn't so I said: 'In a minute we might give Fritz a look.'

'You do that lad.'

I told the other two how we'd move. I'd already told them but I've never known repeating directions doing any harm.

'I'm coming along, Corporal.'

'Might not be much to see, Sar'Major.'

'I've come this far, lad.'

The new boys hadn't patrolled before so I put them on the flanks and slightly behind me, with the sergeant major between. Parts of the wire had been flattened and we crawled through it. But then a couple of shots came somewhere near us. When the next flare went up we were close enough to see the parapet of the German forward trench and that it had been holed but was manned again. Going back wasn't as easy as going forward. When flares went up the new boys had on-the-job freeze training. They turned out OK. Which was just as well. The sergeant major said it had been interesting.

FRANK
Egypt/Armentières

It was Christmas Eve when Lemnos disappeared over the horizon and there was a sigh of relief all round. Then the sea roughed up and a lot of us spent the night on deck. The Christmas dinner they dished out was pretty ordinary but it was better than nothing. Also better than nothing was a book I'd found jammed between a pair of pipes in the hold: Rider Haggard's African adventure, *King Solomon's Mines*. Not a bad yarn but for me — the first book I'd had in my hand for months — it could have been *War and Peace*.

Disembarking at Alexandria we were soon passing through the Nile delta with its green irrigated fields and fellahin working them. There being no toilets on the train and with dysentery rife, we made our contributions to fertilisation, gripping a rail and hanging over the side of a carriage platform. Those inside kept their windows closed and put up with the heat. Some had acquired liquor. Their grip on the handrail was not always sufficiently secure.

The train kept going east, to Moascar, outside Ismailiya, Ferdinand de Lessep's town halfway along the canal. After marching a couple of miles in the dark and a sandstorm we were halted before piles of timber and a scattering of desert shrubs. Our first job was building our camp, toilets being a priority. We weren't allowed out, either. Why? We had tattered shirts, shorts of doubtful decency, dirt ingrained and were well seasoned with sweat; the White Man's Burden would not permit our public presence.

Neither were we allowed to write letters. So we walked — drifted was more like it — through the tent lines, having no wish to embarrass the sentries. It took a while for the Heads — as we called those who controlled our destinies, at whatever level they might be — to learn what was happening but by then we were enjoying the delights of Ismailiya to the best of our ability, which was limited, as neither had we been paid. They called the rolls during our absence. Jim was reduced to the ranks, and along with the rest of us, chased the bugle and drilled in the noonday sun for ten days or so. Only time I was ever up on charge.

To give a leavening of experience in the Second and Rifle Brigades a selection of experienced officers, NCOs and other ranks, was transferred into them. I was one, but when we arrived at 2nd Otago, we were told that 1st Otago were two short and I was one of the two sent there. I didn't like leaving Harry and Jim but, as I came to discover, I had the consolation of being posted to the 10th (North Otago) Company — OC Jim Hargest. I also came to know Alex Aitken, then a sergeant, about my age and some years off his distinguished career in mathematics; he was a man I was glad to be around: for himself and as an NCO.

Before departing for France we were granted leave. I met up with Jim and we spent three days in Cairo. We climbed the Great Pyramid and admired the view and being a traveller in an antique land I could not help recalling Shelley's lines:

> … 'My name is Ozymandias, king of kings:
> Look on my works, ye Mighty and despair!'
> Nothing beside remains. Round the decay
> Of that colossal wreck, boundless and bare
> The lone and level sands stretch far away.

From the pyramids it was to the Great Mosque of Hasan where one's architectural appreciation was aroused. The Cairo Museum had just got going but it was interesting enough. We arrived there latish in the afternoon and were shown around by an Egyptian our age who didn't mind extending closing time and who showed us far more than if we had been left to our own devices. After leaving the premises, Jim and I paused outside, wondering where to go next, when out came the young man. He nodded, began walking away and then turned back.

'Gentlemen! Do you drink coffee?'

'Yes,' said Jim.

So far as it went, Jim's reply was true, but it did not go very far. Like others at that time in New Zealand, we had hardly ever been given the opportunity either to decline or accept an offer of coffee, and even on the rare occasions we had been given that opportunity, it was invariably adulterated with chicory. So when we went with him to sip the thick black Turkish coffee of the Middle East, it was our first real experience of the brew. Generally after that—until the advent of espresso—other coffee seemed on the watery side.

'My name is Naguib. Not many soldiers visit us.'

'We're a long way from home,' said Jim.

'Are you from London?'

'We're New Zealanders,' I said.

'Ah, Australian.'

Jim picked up his hat, and turned up its left side.

'That's Australian,' he said, 'and that', he flattened the brim again, 'is New Zealand.'

I set about explaining just where we sat on the globe. Looking back, I suspect I puzzled as much as I might have enlightened.

'We don't see many soldiers at the museum. Officers, sometimes, soldiers, hardly ever.'

'Blame him,' Jim nodded towards me.

'More would come,' I said, 'if they knew more about you and where you were.'

'We might have ancient exhibits, but as an institution we are young and we do not get much money.'

'You have marvellous things on show,' I said. 'Your Government should be proud to support you. If they knew about it, people would come from all round the world to see your museum.'

There was a wry smile.

'People do come from all round the world. And they admire our treasures—and take them home.'

We waited for him to say more.

'We are also the bridge between Africa and Asia. We have never lacked visitors.'

'Of which we are the latest?' asked Jim.

'And at least we've kept the Turks out,' I said.

Naguib considered each of us. Then he said:

'Turkish people are respected here.' He noticed our surprise and went on to say, 'The Khedive rule was better than what we have now. And you have taken the Sudan from us.' Then another smile. 'But of course you are not British.'

How to explain the complexities of a New Zealander's identity in 1916? I tried and when I had finished, Naguib asked, 'So you are citizens of the British Empire?'

'Most New Zealanders are proud to be called that,' I said.

'As we were not unhappy with the Ottomans,' he said. 'And you,' he asked, turning to Jim, 'you are proud too?'

'One day there will be no Empires. People will rule themselves. This war is the beginning of it.'

'Is that why you fight in it?'

'I have my reasons.'

I hoped, for a moment, that Naguib would press Jim on this and Jim might just say something about it, Naguib not being one of us, but Naguib just smiled at Jim as if the two of them might share something.

'Are you a revolutionary?' I asked.

He laughed.

'In Egypt we are all revolutionaries. I am a revolutionary for my museum and it was my pleasure to show it to two soldiers of the British Empire. I wish I could have shown you more of our illustrious past, but to do that I would have to take you to London, Paris or Berlin, each of which, in one way or another, you are likely to visit before I do.' He stood up and held out his hand, 'May God be with you.'

Before leaving Cairo I found a bookshop whose Egyptian proprietor included in his stock a number of books in French and I was able to stock up on Hugo's *Les Misérables* and a collection of his poetry. We sailed from Port Said aboard the Cunard Liner *Franconia*. It was unbelievable: we had bunks, sheets and pillows. Unfortunately the voyage was brief and the sea rough. It is grimly ironic that we believed we had come to the Promised Land. It was the spring green hills, fresh blossoms, whitewashed tiled cottages, medieval church spires, chateaux in the hills, the ambience of Provence and the Rhône Valley before the age of the motorcar. We were lucky in our train, although we did not know it: second-class carriages with windows intact. There was even a rail map screwed to the wall so for once we were able to work out where we were and might be going. I lapped it up; I was in France.

Dawn was dirty red, changing to dove grey, followed by drizzle and we began to pass, or be passed by, troop trains. The further north we went, the more frequent they became. Sitting or standing in the open doors of the wagons signed HOMMES 36–40 CHEVAUX 8, the *poilu*, unshaven and pale faced, with eyes we knew at Gallipoli, told us where we were. The map pointed to Paris and I was looking forward to seeing it, even if it would only be glimpses. We really thought we had made it when we halted at a station that proclaimed itself Versailles, but that was as close as we got, having branched off to circumvent the city. Through the drizzle and in the distance, we might have seen the Eiffel Tower.

We went as far west as Boulogne where, the outlines of the white cliffs of Dover coming into view, we allowed ourselves to give credence to the rumour we would be embarking for England for further training, a hope apparently confirmed as we headed towards Calais — everybody knew that Calais is as connected with Dover as Sullivan is with Gilbert. We actually stopped there, but then it was inland, passing trains carrying khaki. We halted again and this time, to thunder-like rumbling and white flashes, we jumped from the carriages into mud.

When we weren't drilling we were instructed in trench warfare and gas. When we were not being drilled or lectured, we hung around or slept. Around us was an abundance of pork, beef, poultry, beer, wine and French bread, but hardly a mouthful of anything outside the cookhouse passed our lips. The reason: there was no money to pay us. No one, in the whole of the New Zealand Division got paid for a fortnight. For once 1st Otago possessed advantages the other battalions lacked. First, we had an old sweat, and by old sweat I mean exactly that, who had long served his King, and his Queen before him. His medal ribbons testified to that—though the less sporting amongst us claimed they commemorated service in campaigns fought simultaneously. Whatever, he was Irish and possessed the silver tongue so often exercised by that race. I was impressed; he didn't so much speak to our colonel, as massage him. It mattered not that everybody knew he had brought himself to the fore as spokesman on account of it being more than twenty-four hours since he had drunk anything other than tea or water. Our second advantage was Downie Stewart, future cabinet minister, then a subaltern, who had personal letters-of-credit credible enough for him to go to Dunkirk and there, through an English bank, secure an advance sufficient to pay us something to go on with.

After the pay had been sorted out, we were granted eight days' leave in England. In London the YMCA ran a leave hostel where there was the unheard of luxury of one hot bath a day. There were also billiards, chess and draughts, and as many cups of tea as you could drink served by upper-crust young ladies who never reappeared two days in succession: purity by discontinuity. All for ninepence a night. The Y also ran a programme of sightseeing tours and I took in a couple and also made my first visits to the National and Tate Galleries—a country cousin, looking, and looking again.

I also visited relatives in Cornwall. Though they could not have been more kind to a young man from twelve thousand miles away the visit was not a success. They lived in a picturesque coastal village and their home was a relaxed one, more like that of my grandparents up on the hill than that of my parents. I was able to give them news and views of my grand-parents whom they had not seen for forty years, and they put themselves completely at my service. Staying with such people might have been a pleasurable and diverting change; one could not have been farther away from the war. But I could only take so much chatter. It was not that they ignored the war; it was beyond their comprehension. One night my great uncle took me to the pub to meet a local boy who had recently joined up, one of the million or so of Kitchener's men who had willingly volunteered. The cream of Britain, they have been called: and I will not quarrel with that. All they asked for was recognition of their worth and leaders worthy of them. Instead they were treated as scum and disposed of as scum is disposed of. I saw all this in his pinched earnest face and uniform that fitted him even worse than ours did.

'Could you give me some tips, Sir,' he said.

'No,' I said.

My great uncle was embarrassed and the boy humiliated.

Rather surprised at my behaviour, I ordered three pints, brushing aside my great uncle's money on the counter. I handed one to the boy, drained mine, and when my great uncle had swallowed his, left with him following. I did not catch the London train the morning after — as I said, they were kind and decent people — but held off until the morning after.

When the Cornwall train drew into Waterloo I had arrived at a decision: I was not going to die a virgin. I headed for Piccadilly Circus because it was at the centre of things. If I were to be a paying customer I might go east if I wished to economise, or west if I were willing to be on the lavish side — though I didn't really envisage venturing as far as Bond Street, let alone Park Lane. For the time being, however, I wondered if there was an alternative of a non-mercantile nature. I began nosing around the pubs in the tenuous hope that there might be a young lady sympathetic to a young soldier going out to die for king and country, but I soon came up against public bars for privates and private bars for officers; naïve as I was I thought I would be more likely to find a woman more to my taste in a private bar. New Zealand troops were noted neither for drinking according to rank nor saluting officers other than their own — and not that assiduous at recognising their own when beyond the bounds of a military area — but I had better things to do than get into a confrontation, especially as I was alone and easy meat for some military busybody.

Proceeding slightly east, along Shaftsbury Avenue, I noticed a couple of theatres were playing revues. It was going be a long night anyway, why not give one of them a go, patronising its bars in the intervals? Knowing I would never have a chance of buying a ticket at that hour of night at a box-office, I hived off to the New Zealand YMCA. I was lucky—a single ticket in the stalls at a discount.

I enjoyed the show and patronised the bars but when I drifted out afterwards I was still single and contemplating that whether I liked it or not, street-bargaining it might have to be. Additional Dutch courage didn't seem a bad idea so I wandered into a pub. It was lavish with the polished mahogany and shining brass common to pubs in that part of town but one sensed a more cosmopolitan atmosphere than the pubs I'd looked at earlier. After buying a beer I looked around for a seat. The most comfortable were well-upholstered bench seats around the walls. There was a gap in one of them, near a corner. I went over to it, weaving my way between tables, and sat down. Immediately to my right, in the corner, was a party of five, two subalterns—as the army refers to junior officers—with three women. One, slightly older than the other two, was about a foot away. The younger ones looked vaguely familiar and then I recognised they were from the chorus of the revue I had just been to.

The subaltern nearest to me stood up to go to the bar. The older woman, who had been talking animatedly to him, rose to let him pass. When she sat down, she and I were not as far as part as we had been. When the subaltern returned and she again rose and sat, she was closer although she resumed the conversation with him.

I glanced around the pub and it seemed the three women might not be the only theatrical people present. No one, however, appeared willing to meet my gaze.

'Would you mind if my friends used your ashtray?' It was the older woman.

'Not at all.' I picked it up and when I gave it to her, our fingers touched.

'You don't smoke?'

With what I believed to be becoming modesty I said I didn't.

'I don't either,' she confided. 'You sound like a colonial.'

I explained.

'Have you been over here long?'

I mentioned Gallipoli and added that I had enjoyed the show.

'You were there?'

'I recognise your two friends. They were in the front row of the chorus.'

She smiled. 'You have a keen eye.'

I nearly said very keen, but instead said: 'I had a good seat. They weren't easy to miss.'

Her smile broadened. 'No,' she said, 'they wouldn't be.'

'And you?' I asked. 'Forgive me, you must have been there, too.'

This time it was a half-smile. 'You don't have to apologise. Until recently I would have been. Now I look after them backstage, wardrobe mistress: the one who makes sure they dress for the part.' The half-smile again. 'As much as they're dressed for any part!' If she exercised as much care on them as she did on herself she was earning her money. Her frock was lilac, and in the style of the time, liberal in material making a full skirt to her ankles, with puffed out sleeves and a deep V-neck that opened over a white lace blouse. The ensemble indicated style and a well-formed woman.

Beyond her, I glimpsed the chorus girls and the subalterns; they were absorbed in each other. I turned to her. An empty glass stood in front of her. 'Care for another?'

'I'd love a bubbly.'

I stood up. To get out I had to brush past her. It was rather pleasant. When I returned and sat down the pleasure was repeated and on handing her the champagne, the back of my hand lightly glided across her front. And once I was seated one of her nice long legs was against one of mine. (Let it be noted I was nowhere near as sure of myself as the above might imply.)

A subaltern went off for more drinks and one of the women leaned forward and said, 'Hilda, introduce us to your friend.'

'His name's Frank, he's from New Zealand.' I liked the way her eyes twinkled.

The remaining subaltern had no option but to recognise my existence.

'You have a Boy Scout hat too,' said the woman who asked my name.

'Keeps the rain off,' I said.

The subaltern eyed me.

'And he's been in France and Gallipoli,' Hilda said.

With their hairless chins and very well pressed uniforms, neither the subaltern who was present nor the one at the bar looked as though they'd been anywhere.

'I enjoyed the show,' I said to the two other women. 'I had an excellent view from the third row. I recognised you as soon as I came in.' Something told me the subalterns hadn't done quite so well when it came to seating.

'Soldier,' began the subaltern, 'you may not have noticed, being a colonial, that you're in the wrong ...'

'And we're glad he enjoyed the show and we're glad he's here.' Hilda did not only cut in; her look conveyed a warning she expected to be heeded. The girl next to him put her hand on his. He reached for his drink. The class war was to be postponed.

'It would be nice to have dinner,' Hilda said to me but once outside she said, 'If you want to come with me, it'll have to be a hotel.' It took a while to find one, but we did.

Later when events had sorted themselves out by warmth, affection and pleasure, there was a quiet spell. Hilda was sitting up and I was lying down admiring the mass of black hair which she had worn piled high but which now tumbled to her waist, when she said, 'Frank. I could have taken you home but there are times when I have to get away from the place.'

'That's OK,' I said. And it was, indeed it was.

'It's not just the neighbours, though they're bad enough. You can't move without their curtains twitching. And when a taxi appears, half the street turns out. Nothing better to do with themselves.' She looked around the room. 'This isn't much, but we're lucky to get it seeing it's late at night and there's a war on, but it's a change. I just have to get out of the house.'

'Do you get out much?'

'Not as much as you might think. Show business isn't all glitz and glitter, not by a long chalk. It's hard work and when we go home at night we're tired.' She turned so that she was looking directly down at me. 'Frank.' She took me by the other hand. 'I'm about to ask you a question, please don't be upset.'

'I won't,' I said, taking her other hand, 'I guarantee it.'

'Frank, how often do write to your fiancée?'

Of all the questions I might have expected that would have been about the last. 'I don't have one,' I said slowly.

'Girlfriend then. You're not a married man, I know that. Don't tell me you don't have one. How often do you write to her?'

'Well …'

'One letter to her three — or four?'

'Maybe.'

'Maybe? Frank, there are some men who do write regularly, but so many just don't.'

Letters, I felt, weren't really what were concerning her. 'We seem to have drifted apart …' I began.

But she had turned away, the wall at the end of the bed apparently engrossing her attention. 'Everything was going swimmingly and then he went: suddenly. And there was no one. You reach out at night and no one's there. You have no idea what it's like: coming home to an empty house every day, the only sound you can hear is yourself. And at night, with the floors creaking, you're wondering if it is just the floors and whether you remembered to lock the doors and when it's morning, again the only noise you hear is yourself. You don't know what it's like, alone.'

'I wouldn't mind it now and again,' I said. 'Army service is hardly known for its solitude. Crowded in with all sorts, shapes and sizes, twenty-four hours a day, seven days a week.'

'Do you know when Dick and I were last together?' She was still speaking to the wall. 'Six months ago and he'd been in France for a year. He was home for four days! And it will be six months before we're together again. This time it'll be a whole ten days. We'll just be settling down and he'll be gone. No one there and we're expected to carry on as normal.'

I sat up, putting my arms around her.

There was a sob. 'And when he writes, do you know what he writes about? The weather, the bloody weather.'

I murmured that it wasn't much fun in a wet trench.

'He writes about the weather and here I am waiting for him!'

I pressed her to me.

'And you, Frank, you'll be off tomorrow, won't you?'

I kept holding her.

The first morning back with the battalion, we went on a route march. Fourteen miles, it was our first experience of *pavé* roads: cobblestones. The curve of each stone concentrates the pressure on a small area of the sole of your foot and puts your leg slightly off balance. Repeat that several thousand times, with each stone having a slightly different shape and size, and soon one is subjected to a refined form of torture. You get used to it, but it takes time. For those with worn soles and/or legs yet to be conditioned to long marches it can become unbearable to the point of making it impossible to go anywhere other than by crawling.

Being well-laden did not help. Seeing no one was doing anything with the Quartermaster's scales for a couple of minutes, I weighed my gear: haversack (rations and other items needed during the day), valise (a larger pack, dumped when moving up to the line, containing greatcoat, other clothing, waterproof sheet, blanket, etc.), webbing, one hundred and twenty rounds, tin hat (unknown at Anzac), two gas helmets (also unknown there), water bottle, entrenching tool, rifle and bayonet, and for me, a book or two. With my books and other personal items, I carried seventy-two pounds; without, sixty-two.

Soon we were marching to Armentières, entering in the evening. Beyond, flares rose and fell and the hard rattle of machine guns could be heard. The new chums looked at each other: you could see them wondering and putting on what they believed was a brave face. I was professionally interested to note that our particular billet was a classroom. The teacher's desk was on a podium and in front of it was a shell hole.

We were billeted in Armentières for a week, time enough to get to know people, most of whom were in the food and drink business running estaminets where wine, beer, eggs and chips were dished out by young ladies who, in worldly wisdom and backchat, left all but a few of us many miles behind. Hovering not too far in the background was the invariably formidable madame. It was rare, however, that her chicks were unable to look after themselves very well thank you. Nobody was fooled, however, about how far anyone could look after herself or himself in Armentières. Near the centre of the city was 'Half-past Eleven Square' so named because that was where a German shell had stopped the town clock and every day there were further reminders of what might be coming your way, but just for the present, was going somebody else's. Nevertheless, after Gallipoli, being billeted in a more or less functioning city within spitting distance of the front line was a luxury we had never envisaged.

If we had returned home after Gallipoli, bodily intact, we could have, largely, put it down to experience. A dangerous experience, but in retrospect, interesting, in that we had learnt things about ourselves, and others, that would have taken years to have learnt otherwise, if at all. Character building, perhaps. But we had not returned home; we were again marching to the sound of the guns.

We went up on the first day of daylight saving. A defused rifle grenade landed with the message, 'Send over the time, please, Anzac.' We were shelled, heavily, we thought, but, in fact, it did no more than flatten a few yards of parapet. Came the dusk and we set about repairing it. We were nearing completion when a machine gun opened up and, before we bit the dirt, hit two of our men. This was Parapet Joe, who would make a precise sweep along the line to connect with anyone working, no matter where or at what angles the line twisted. You never knew when or where Joe might give us a stitch. What you did know, and for sure, was that some time, somewhere, during the night, Joe would feel the urge to sew us up.

The normal pattern of duty was eight days in the trenches and eight days out. Our first eight days—four days in the front and support lines, and four days in the subsidiary line—did not go too badly. In the subsidiary line most of the time you maintained defences. Up in the front and support lines, apart from sentry duty and essential work, which was not infrequent, you did your best to sleep and at night you manned the fire step. I shared a dugout with the platoon commander and two sergeants. As there were four of us, it was double the normal dimensions, i.e. a little small for one man to turn round comfortably. The bed was made of planks, the bedding three waterproof groundsheets and three greatcoats. If you suddenly raised your head it would hit the shelf, which held webbing, ammunition, gas helmets, tin hats, Mess tins, rifles, bread and cheese. Above was corrugated iron that gave adequate protection from sun but not rain.

On the eighth day we were told we weren't going out but taking over a neighbouring sector. It coincided with an increase in shelling that made Gallipoli almost a popgun affair. When it began three of us were in the dugout. One, another Gallipoli man, made a show of cracking jokes, but the other chap and I were preoccupied with shell bursts getting closer. As has been said before, the sound of a shell coming in your direction is like an express train thundering into a station. Such was the shell that fell in front of the dugout. There was the thud as it landed, a split second of nothing, and the explosion—two heavy-weight boxers slamming you flat, so numbing you don't know if anything is wrong or not, black sulphurous, phosphoric fumes, and a burst sandbag smashed in your face. Crushing pressure, you choke, cannot breathe, sandbags have saved your life but now they can smother it. You try to struggle but you are in a vice. Numbness returns, different this time, not that you have much time to notice it, because you are soon out to it. Then you see something in front of you: shapes stacked together, sandbags, and you are in the open, under sky. You ponder; you are breathing because when you inhale your rib-cage hurts. You brood on this. Then you know. You are lucky. You look along the trench. A jumble of sandbags where the dugout was. You are left for a while then you get up and learn that the other Gallipoli man was not lucky.

All battlefields are foul. At Gallipoli it was the unburied dead. At Armentières, and elsewhere in what our forbears termed the Low Countries, it was marshland: stinking mud you were never free of summer or winter. Foul black slush under duckboards had to be hand pumped out day after day into shell holes to soak back where it had come from. Then there was the rat, coming out at night, infesting our dugouts, scurrying into no man's land to get the dead before we could.

It did not help that the battalions on our flanks mounted raids. Each was enough to make Fritz retaliate with a pandemonium of shelling. It was not just the casualties, or the wear and tear of being shelled and mortared but that every sandbag out of place exposed a target for a sniper. And we were now into the longest days of the year. Fed up with filling and stacking sandbags, and with festering sores from replacing wire, I let it be known I had patrolled on the Peninsula. There being no one to vouch for my capability or otherwise, I went crawling around no man's land in the middle of the night. One of the first things we learnt about night work was that if you were out in the open, up on your two hind legs, and a flare went up, the chances were, despite half the countryside being lit up, that if you stood stock still, you would not be spotted. It must have worked, otherwise I would not be here, but I cannot say I would offer to demonstrate it. Infrequent were the nights on the Western Front as sparklingly clear as at Anzac.

Sometimes we met up with our German counterparts but mostly—unless the notorious Darkie Starke was out—it was like ships passing in the night. I can't say I was enthusiastic about seeking an engagement and neither were most men I went out with. Sometimes, at what seemed like a safe distance, we might fire a shot or two, just as most of the Germans, at a similar range, might fire at us. Do not misunderstand me, however. If you were careless, or unlucky, things were not cosy. Towards the end of June, when I was back to Acting Lance Corporal (Unpaid), we went out in front of a wiring party. I had just posted the other two men and was settling down for an hour or two of watching and listening when hand-grenades landed near us. If they had landed a minute or two earlier they'd have got us. Although we couldn't see much we returned the compliment and they responded to that. It all might have lasted two minutes, but we didn't hurry away. Apart from one being wounded, we were OK and so, I guess, by their silence, were the Germans. It gave me something to report on and think about. Not long afterwards another patrol had an encounter, but they came away with a prisoner, the first capture made by New Zealanders of a German. The corporal who led the patrol was given due praise but his feat was overshadowed by the prisoner himself. A bewildered, and initially, frightened Saxon, he found himself an intense object of curiosity and, before he was led away, recipient of enough cigarettes to last him a month.

It was exactly a month after we had gone up to the line that we were relieved. We stumbled out to a stone hall in a hospice, still run by nuns, and collapsed onto the straw-strewn floor. In the morning women and children with eggs, chocolate and English newspapers awakened us. I was happy to purchase all three, but the event of the morning was to be marched off to what had once been a bleach works for the Flanders linen industry and was now the army baths and laundry. There we removed our mud-caked, lice ridden attire, unchanged for a month, to plunge into huge tubs. Behind a line of sacking that was supposed to shield us from their view — though from the comments I picked up, the screening was not a hundred per cent — were mesdemoiselles ironing the seams of our uniforms where our little grey friends loved to reside and reproduce. Cleansed, we received back our uniforms and replacement underwear. Then it was on the town — according to our various inclinations. During our absence Armentières had not been allowed to forget it was on the edge of the front line. A pastry shop we had patronised was marked but still trading, but the girl who had served us had been killed by shrapnel just outside. When she had served us, shells and shrapnel were the last things on our minds.

Here I must mention our colonel. In civil life he was a school inspector. Now I am breaking no professional confidentiality if I state that inspectors are the most disliked arm of the teaching service, sometimes to the point of detestation. Particularly if you are isolated in a sole-charge or a two- or three-teacher school, where you are judged according to what an inspector saw, or thought he saw, on a particular day. It takes a certain type of teacher to become an inspector. A few use it as a stepping-stone to become a principal; others stay, either because they like doing that sort of thing or because once there, no one will have them anywhere else. A hard worker, our colonel was also determined and stubborn, a man of the book, and lucky in the way hard working determined men often are lucky: he was there when a gap had to be filled.

When it was our turn to raid, nothing was to be left to chance. Four parties were detailed: scouts, parapet, assault, and flank. Each of these was trained to the last minute and the final yard; indeed the parapet party had trained on a replica in Armentières. And to be absolutely sure nothing would be left to chance, there was a fifth party, keeping watch against any unforeseen German counterattack. Ten minutes before zero hour, the artillery was to commence a slow rate of fire. At zero hour the artillery and mortars would open up full barrage on the German firing line and the parapet party, preceded by the scouts, was to cross the German firing line and bomb dugouts and shelters to the rear with grenades. Following would be four assault parties to work along the firing line. Twenty minutes after zero hour, the mortars and artillery were to lift and provide cover for everybody to get back to our lines by zero+30. And zero hour: dead on midnight.

On the day before the raid, we were subjected to light shelling that had every sign of being ranging shots. We were the right flanking party. Creeping behind Alex Aitken, we were led to two shell holes that we joined, sandbagged, and deepened as the slow bombardment commenced. Dead on midnight a sheet of light rose behind us, illuminating Armentières and dazzling us. Instantly the Germans, warned by the slow bombardment, got to work. Everyone seemed to be firing at us. Mortar bombs were homing in, exploding and sending up flares to light the ground. As you pressed your head into the earth you could see dew glistening on the grass. Very slightly, I inclined my head. In the flares' bright bluish light, I saw one of our party, up and going through a gap in the wire, a threat to us as much as to him. I yelled at him to freeze. He did not and mortars bracketed us. We crouched low in the holes but if there had been a direct hit, they wouldn't have saved us. We survived because of luck and Aitken's reading of the ground.

Wounded were crawling in and out. Aitken grabbed one who, though wounded in the arm, was crawling into no man's land. Aitken gestured. I crawled up to him.

'He's out of his mind and his friend's out there.'

I nodded again.

'The only way we can keep him from committing suicide, and stop him infecting the others, is to get his friend.'

This time I did not nod.

'Come on.'

I looked down at the man. He was in a state, but so was I.

Aitken gripped my shoulder.

'Come on. I think I know a way.'

So I followed. We wriggled along a line of blasted trunks and brought him in.

'Thanks, but I'm done for,' he said after we had put him beside his now calmer mate.

'Don't think that, they'll fix you up fine.'

'No,' he spoke as a doctor might speak about an absent patient. 'I'm gone.'

He lasted a week.

I don't know of any parapet or assault men who reached their targets. The German shelling died away at dawn, machine guns and snipers took over, and men who were alive at dawn were dead at dusk. It was only when night fell again that an organised effort could be made to bring in the casualties. One, who did more than his fair share, was Darkie Starke. A member of the parapet party, he had come over in the reinforcement after mine. Following several spells of Field Punishment and clink, the colonel had his latest conviction quashed and a five year sentence 'suspended for the time being' because of his expertise with the hand-grenade. This he was not to use with effect until daylight when he wrecked a German machine gun post. With that and the men he had carried in, he probably earned a chest of medals but because of his hatred of authority, impetuosity and refusal to conform to any law, custom or convention when his blood was up, he was never awarded one. The rest of us, no matter how much we detested the niggling, petty, nasty and demeaning sergeant major discipline endemic to the military, conformed. Starke did not. In that respect, I almost had a sneaking regard for him. Otherwise, no. A tall barrel-chested man with the colouring that had determined his sobriquet, Starke was a psychopath. I have no doubt at all that in his younger days if the war had not been fought he would have killed a local or two. The military, however, has its uses for men like him—though not as often as so many who know nothing about the matter care to believe. Starke would risk all to go out and kill. Yes, we must not forget the lives he saved and if I had been one of them I too would have been grateful for the rest of my life; but when you did let him loose, any expectation that he would act rationally would be as ill-founded as expecting restraint from a shark in an aquarium. Those who gravitated towards him tended to be men of weaker character.

First Otago was now down to three companies out of four, but we completed thirty-five days in the front line, performing all the duties of a fully manned battalion. When told we would be going to the Somme the name did not mean much to us.

SOMME
1916

It helps to understand British command in the Great War if we look at its army's previous history. Between Waterloo and Sarajevo, it fought two major campaigns — Crimea and South Africa. In the former, command and organisation were scandalous and, in the latter, man for man, the Boers outfought British forces. In between, the British Army was sent to put down colonial uprisings — recall the redcoats in New Zealand's bundle of skirmishes.

The British Army had run on patronage since the days of knights and squires. The wheels of promotion were oiled by whom you knew. Ability came about second equal, more or less on the same level as riding on the hunting field. (That is not intended to be a joke.) Innovation and enthusiasm were not encouraged, 'shop talk' being out of order. Regular infantry and cavalry officers tended to be well-off gentlemen who took commissions in anticipation of a convivial regimental life and the possibility of adventure in one of England's little wars. Real wealth was required to enter as a subaltern in the guards and the cavalry. Today the world of the cavalry is distant. They screened the infantry and the artillery and enhanced mobility by harassing the enemy's flanks and rear. Above all they exploited a breakthrough. In 1916, of the six highest commanders on the Western Front, four were cavalry, one was guards, and one, Plumer, run-of-the-mill infantry.

A guards or cavalry officer, who didn't mind being tolerated, rather than liked, was practised in keeping his thoughts to himself, and if he possessed ambition, had a fair chance of becoming a general. Haig fulfilled the criteria: his list of qualifications included the family whisky fortune, marriage into the

Royal Household, service in the field with the 7ᵗʰ Hussars, and a conservative cast of mind—he restored the lance to the cavalry after South Africa demonstrated it had become an encumbrance. Possessing an undeviating determination, a keen eye for the main chance, more intelligence than generally given credit for, and the conviction that he had never served under or with anyone whom he couldn't better, Haig would have been a hard man to hold back. One incident that illustrates this is when he cooperated in the unseating of Sir John French, his CO and Commander-in-Chief of the British forces, 1914–15, and then replaced him. Not that French was any great loss.

A major difficulty for the officer class was that the Great War could not be fought without a vast preponderance of civilians. Given its instinct not to trust its regular soldiers, uniformed civilians, whether officers or not, were distrusted even more. Never for a moment would they admit to the implications of one of Britain's greatest generals being Cromwell the farmer.

Then there was the artillery, which went to war believing its 18-pounder field guns would fight over open sights firing shrapnel. By mid 1916 it had been disabused of that. Numbers of guns had increased, as had the numbers of gunners, but expertise was spread thin. Likewise, many more shells were manufactured, especially of high explosive, using factories that previously turned out pots and pans. The wonder is not that there were so many duds, but that there weren't more.

Of all the battles the British fought in the First World War, the First Battle of the Somme will be remembered longest. It began on 1 July 1916 and on that day twenty-thousand of those who advanced to the German trenches were killed and forty-thousand wounded. When the battle petered out in mid-November, around half a million men of the Empire had been killed, wounded or missing. German casualties were about half of that.

While the topography of the Somme might, at first glance, appeal to the eye of the attacker, a second look reveals that its smooth and easy slopes give the advantage to the defender; the reverse slopes offering him cover, and the forward slopes exposing the attacker. For eighteen months the Somme had been quiet. German picks and shovels, however, had not. Deep and large dugouts were excavated. For about fourteen miles, two trench systems faced each other; the German taking advantage of the rise and fall of the land. The Germans had three defence lines, up to two and a half miles apart. Communication saps and deeply buried telephone cables connected them and the artillery. Villages had been turned into strong points, their cellars reinforced.

By 1916, the war involved millions of men. Godley, commanding three divisions, had more men than Wellington ever had. Haig found the implications of that, and weapons such as machine guns, difficult to accept. He believed, for example, his war could be won by a few major battles, as Napoleon initially had won his. They would be won by speed and manoeuvre, in the manner of Stonewall Jackson. The Somme would be the first of these battles, the three lines knocked out in one day; the first being smashed by our artillery, stunned survivors mopped up by our first assault. Immediately behind, the follow up assault would break into the second, make ninety-degree turns to right and left, roll up the line like a red carpet, and allow the cavalry to charge through the third.

Rawlinson, Haig's subordinate, was not the greatest of generals, but being an infantryman, he focused on the trenches. His plan was to concentrate effort on the First Line, take it, consolidate there, move up the field artillery, assault the Second Line, take that, consolidate, and so on, progressing by what became known as 'bite and hold'. To do this he reckoned that the artillery bombardment would have to be long and heavy before each of the lines would be accessible. As Rawlinson's view differed from Haig's, a compromise was reached between commander and subordinate. The bombardment would be long and in the last hour, very heavy. The attack would be mounted, and as dusk descended, the battle would have been won.

At 6 a.m., on the twenty-fourth of June, the weeklong barrage opened up. The artillery, which totalled more than one thousand five hundred guns, seemed a lot, but it wasn't. Calculations were available on how much shell was required to destroy a trench system, but they were ignored. In the enemy dugouts, some ceilings collapsed and shafts fell in, the atmosphere was foul with the packed men and the stink of exploding shells, and the ground shook like a continuing earthquake. The more vulnerable of the occupants showed symptoms, but the majority sat it out—with pounding headaches and wracked with nausea—knowing they were safer below than up top. At night there were calm intervals but there was no relaxation because British patrols and raids were made. Each met intact wire and fully capable troops. Their reports were ignored save by a few. Hunter-Weston announced the wire in front of his sector had been cut and 'the troops could walk in' when his officers had told him otherwise.

At 7.30 a.m., on 1 July, a cloudless morning, the bombardment lifted. No man's land appeared empty and the First Line a wasteland. The British attacked. Some made it. Most, because their artillery had not pulverised the defences, did not. They were unable to reach the German lines before machine gunners came up from their dugouts. Among the worst served was the Newfoundland Regiment, of VIII Corps, 'commanded' by Hunter-Weston, who ordered his heavy artillery to cease firing ten minutes before zero hour and his field artillery to cease two minutes before. In forty minutes the New Foundlanders suffered six hundred and eighty four casualties out of seven hundred and fifty two.

Haig kept attacking. On 14 July Rawlinson was permitted to make his own plan: a night attack—which Haig was sceptical of the troops being able to handle—and a 'bite and hold', concentrating on three miles of German line that overlooked British ground. Every gun available pounded it and the infantry was right up at the edge of the barrage. It worked. But there was no breakthrough.

The New Zealander's battle commenced on 15 September and concluded on 4 October. Their advance was to be closely coordinated with those of 41st and 47th Divisions. Together, they would overrun the German Third Line, enabling, Haig believed, the cavalry to charge across open country for Bapaume, the railhead for this sector of the Somme. Haig may have been learning about tactics but he was still after speed, confident that while each trench system was to be attacked in a separate operation, a twenty-four hour pause between each attack would be sufficient to bring up field artillery. Neither were there to be any fresh infantry divisions waiting in reserve to reinforce such successes as might occur. The reserve divisions were cavalry.

It was General Russell's first divisional battle and he approached it as an intelligent, practical, observant and experienced general would, assessing the ground himself and allowing for unforeseen circumstances. His first objective was the Switch Trench; the second was the Flers System and the third, Gird *system. Second Auckland and 2ⁿᵈ Otago were detailed to take the Switch, and the Rifle Brigade the Flers System.*

The routine orders prior to an attack came into force: burial officers were appointed and grave digging, in the vicinity of Casualty Clearing Stations, commenced; salvage parties for bringing in abandoned but useful equipment were made up; carrying parties were detailed to bring forward ammunition, water, stores and food (in that order); pickets were stationed to police communication trenches for 'stragglers', and the selection of 'B teams' or 'Lobs' (Left Out of Battle) made. These were generally two officers per battalion, two or three senior NCOs, and specialists. Their purpose was to form a core for the re-forming of a battalion in the event of heavy casualties.

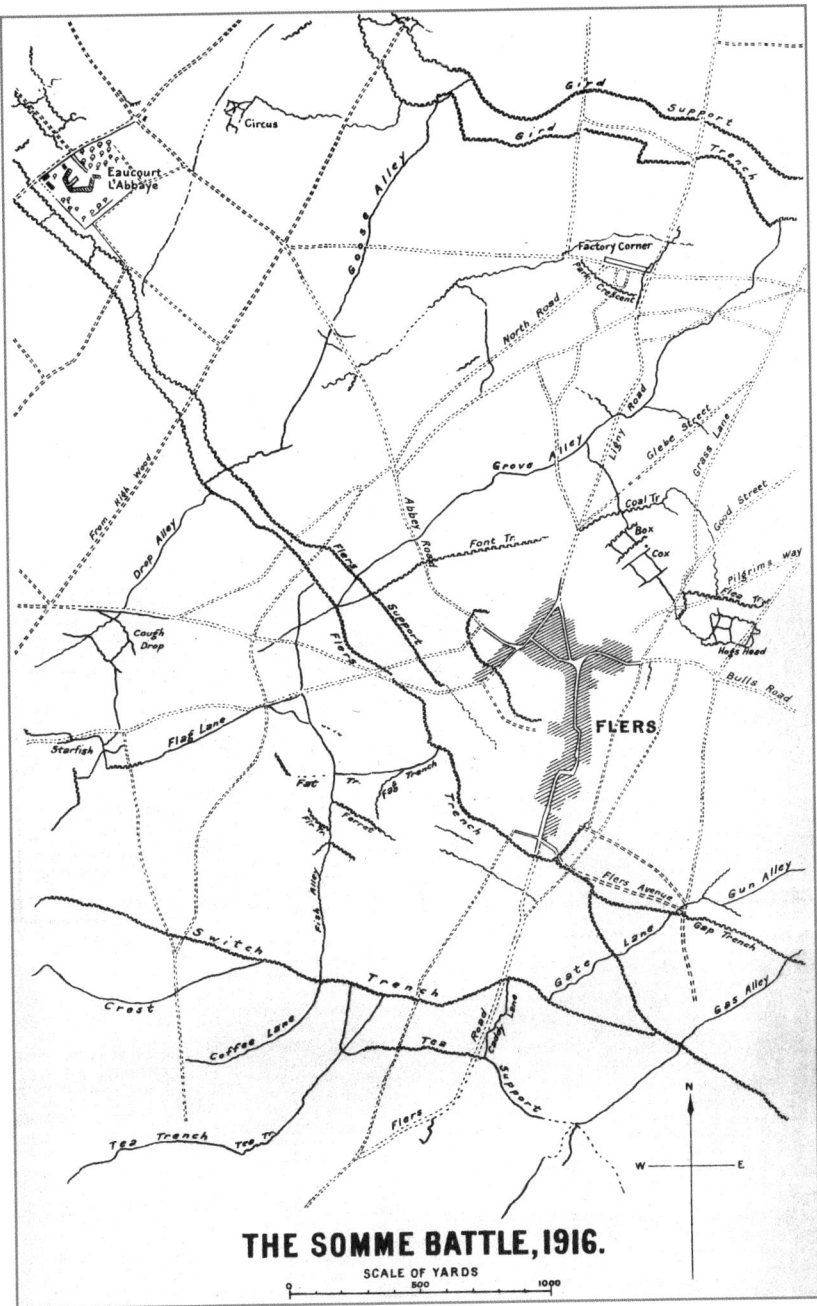

THE SOMME BATTLE, 1916.

SCALE OF YARDS

0   500   1000

New Zealanders at the Somme, 1916. *Source: Burton, O.E.*

JIM
Somme

When we went to the Somme I was back in the Sergeant's Mess. Maybe they decided to let bygones be bygones or there weren't too many platoon commanders who knew what it was about or maybe it was both. Ours was a greenhorn fresh from home. We bivvied in Fricourt Wood, between shattered stumps. At the bottom of the valley below us a road ran six and a half miles to where our assembly positions would be. The Germans had built a railway alongside the road. Sidings ran off into cuttings where there were 9.2 howitzers, sometimes heavier. In between was lighter stuff, mainly 4.5s, sometimes nearly wheel to wheel. I can't remember when there wasn't something firing.

A Hun whiz-bang had the range of a crick in the valley, where it turned north and then east again. Nice and steady but not too regular. A lot of the traffic was nose-to-tail day and night and the whiz-bang knew this. Each time we marched up, we could cut the corners, but the horse traffic had to keep to the road. Parties were ready to clear it after a hit. They shot the horses and hauled the wrecked wagons away before you could say Jack Robinson. We did a spell of keeping the road open and didn't loaf either. The worst was dealing with the horses. The wagon drivers were either dead or taken to the Advanced Dressing Station across the valley. While we cleared the road and filled the shell holes, the banked-up wagon drivers would wait their turn. I never heard of them getting medals.

One morning we heard shooting in the sky. A British aeroplane taking on a Hun. Almost a joke. They were two seaters with a Lewis or a Spandau fired by the observers. These two had a go at two thousand feet or less. Crazy. They called them kites and you could see why. They dipped and dived, turned and spiralled like something on the end of a string. Flat out on a calm day they'd be lucky to make seventy mph. The rest of the war stopped. All eyes, both sides, were on the aeroplanes. Ours was a BE2c, as useless as an aeroplane could be. An artillery spotter and reconnaissance photographer, it put its observer where he could see least: in front of the pilot with one wing above and the other below. To fire the Lewis he had to stand up, turn round and shoot with the barrel six inches above the pilot's head. The pilot had to manoeuvre the plane so that the enemy was behind, within range, and in line of sight of the gun just above him—without getting himself shot down. The German observer had a better view and a better arc of fire because he was in the rear seat, but the two planes were still like two old boxers staggering around a ring, weaving in and out, up and down, throwing more punches in the air than connecting. At last the British plane gained height without getting hit and dived. The German followed, got a blast full on, and kept going down. The British plane flattened out and went for home, low enough for us to see the crew in their cockpits. They were lucky to have the height to pull out.

The RFC lost a lot of fliers, but it would have been the worse for us if they hadn't been there. On 15 September, they bombed and strafed Flers, very low. There was an airfield to our rear and on a fine day you could see them circling to get height before they crossed the lines. It could take a good twenty minutes to get to ten thousand feet. They liked having a go at the German observation balloons, sometimes being fitted with rockets that would explode inside the gasbag. But even with rockets they had to be clever to get them. When a British plane looked interested, the ground crews would get the winches going and down the balloons would come. A balloon being hit was not something you forgot, all that hydrogen going up.

Another day we poked around a hill riddled with German dugouts. I went down seventy feet and that was enough. Some went further but their candles went out. It looked like it had been cleaned out with grenades and phosphorous bombs and was ripe with month-old dead. It would have held hundreds. There'd been a lot of souveniring already but by careful looking we found cans of meat and boxes of cigars and in the officers' quarters, a pair of lady's scants. No expense spared: beds, bunks, tables, chairs, airshafts, and kitchens, even a hospital.

On the fifteenth, the valley filled with smoke from the bombardment. In the afternoon we marched to the reserve trenches near Green Dump where ammunition and other stores were kept. After midnight we were on our way again. It had clouded over and the only light came from German flares and shell bursts. Hard on the eyes and not easy on the nerves. Black as ink. A man behind me had most of his arm torn off while the rest of us, once we'd picked ourselves up, kept on. Next morning we captured Grove Alley. Hawke's Bay had it rough. Their OC got an MC. Nice to know someone benefited.

We had to build a block across Grove Alley. Not easy. Grenades were flying. After the block was up, our new lieutenant must have thought things had calmed down. He was leaning against the side, in a corner, facing a length of open trench. Not where we would have stood. A grenade sailed in, right at his feet; on a cricket pitch it would have been a perfect Yorker. Well timed too. It didn't explode as it landed, nor did it lie long enough for someone to return it. No. He must have heard about tossing grenades back because he bent down and as he bent, it blew his guts out—to put it politely. But not enough to finish him there and then.

It turned to rain. Water soaked into the trench from shell holes. We were up to our knees in mud that ran off your shovel. Fog in the morning, and to get their minds off our sorry lot, I used it to send a party out to rat the packs and pockets of the dead. There weren't as many water bottles as we would have liked, but there were hard rations and cigars. A couple of new boys went to where the Rifle Brigade had hit Flers. A lot of dead they said, both sides, and some of the Germans had scorch marks around their bullet wounds and a couple lay as if they'd been bayoneted with their hands up. 'We don't know, do we?' I said. 'Might have been hand-to-hand stuff.' But I'd heard the Dinks, as the Rifles were known, had had a hard time and gone over the edge because of it.

Soup was brought up to us: warm, going down better than beer. We nearly forgot the shelling, which came in fits and starts. Around 5 a.m. two were wounded. Bad enough but then one went off his head and that was worse. The rain was like the shelling, coming and going, never holding off long enough to take your mind off it. We got colder and the mud deeper. We were relieved around midnight on our second night and it took us four hours to make it to Green Dump where we had a feed of hot stew and were still out in the rain.

One afternoon a bunch of us were given a dose of square bashing. Harry was there too. He couldn't see the joke and that made it funnier. I would have paraded for the rest of the war but it was called off because we couldn't hear the instructor because of the shelling. We also worked on the Lewis. It was our first machine gun that one man could carry—though you needed a number two and three to change and carry ammunition pans. It took a while to get used to. At first we thought it could be used like a Vickers, only not as good, for spraying a target. But you fired it in bursts of four or five rounds, to keep heads down, as covering fire for bombers and riflemen moving on to a strong point. We already knew it didn't like mud—and we wouldn't be allowed to forget it.

The day before we were to get into it again, a new second lieutenant was landed on us. We'd been expecting it just as we expected the chances of his getting through were about fifty-fifty. After sundown he went with us up to Flers to dig another assembly trench. Still raining, and the mud just thick enough to stick to your shovel. As anyone who has swung a shovel knows, wet mud is heavier than dry earth. I don't think the lieutenant knew this any more than he would have known he was dealing with men who'd been where he hadn't and were going back to it. All he knew was how to get a commission in New Zealand.

'The men are loafing, Sergeant.'

'I will speak to them, Sir.'

'We're here to dig a trench, Sergeant.'

'Yes Sir.'

I went and told them what they knew already—the sooner it was done, the sooner we'd be out of it.

A couple of minutes later he was at it again.

'Sergeant, get those men moving!'

'They've been at it five days and nights, Sir. No real break.'

'And having a good rest in the process.'

Making sure they were bending their backs to it, I went up to him.

'Sir, may I request a word with you? On the quiet, Sir?'

'I beg your pardon, Sergeant.'

'A quiet word, Sir.'

'If you have anything worth saying, Sergeant, say it now, right here.'

Another quick look at the boys. They were using their brains; shovelling, all them, as if the lieutenant and I were having a little chat that had nothing to do with them.

'They've had a long spell of it, Sir. The attack on Grove Alley, holding it, and then working parties. No break, Sir.'

'In case you haven't noticed, Sergeant, your men are loafing on the job and they seem accustomed to it.'

'It's heavy work, Sir.'

'Get their backs into it.'

I looked across at them again. They were doing as well as they could.

'You heard me, Sergeant.'

'Yes, Sir.' I went over to the men. 'The lieutenant's keen to get the job done,' I said. Normally I would have picked up a shovel myself, but I didn't want him patting himself on the back.

He came striding through the mud.

'Put some beef into it!'

This time there was muttering but not loud enough to hear what was said.

'You men want to be up on a charge? Is that what you want? For by God you'll get it.'

'F....!'

'Shut up!' I'd expected something like that and drowned the man out.

'What did he say, Sergeant?' This time he spoke quietly.

'I don't know, Sir.'

'That's not good enough, Sergeant.'

I didn't say anything.

'Sergeant, I asked you what that man said.'

'I don't know.'

We heard a shell coming. By then we could tell a lot from its sound. It was coming close. We dropped. He didn't and nothing hit him.

'You cowards,' he said, 'you bloody cowards.'

'And you'll get one between the fucking eyes.'

'Sergeant! Did you hear that? Did you hear it?'

'Yes Sir.'

'Put that man under arrest.'

'What man, Sir?'

A flare had just gone up. Whose it was, ours or Fritz's, I don't know, but it lit him up. He was shaking and his face was a sort of violet colour. Maybe it was the flare, but that's what it looked like.

'His name, Sir?' I said.

He choked.

'You know who …' He was breathing like he'd run a couple of hundred yards. 'You know who … and … you will arrest him!'

'Sir, I don't know.' Though I might've had an idea.

'You, Sergeant, will hear a lot more about this, a lot more. And for you lot,' he yelled, 'there'll be a court martial!'

We all stared. By now he really had the shakes.

After that the only way I could see things turning out was that my stay in the Sergeants' Mess would be shorter than the last time and that there might be something not very nice to go with it. There was also the prospect of going into action with the bastard. So when the company sergeant major called me up to go before the company commander, I wasn't expecting a tea party.

I marched in.

'Sergeant McDonnell!'

'Sir.'

'What is the state of your platoon?'

'Fine, Sir.' Nothing else to say.

'Are you sure, Sergeant?'

'Yes Sir.'

He looked at me hard and I met his gaze.

'Well then, as from now, you will command your platoon until further notice.'

I hadn't expected that but I wasn't going to let him know it so I gave him the usual yes Sir.

'You are confident it is fit to go into action?'

'Yes Sir.' No worse than the rest of the company.

'Sergeant McDonnell?'

'Yes Sir.'

'You'll need an acting sergeant two i/c. Have you a name?'

I gave him a corporal's.

He turned to the CSM. 'What do you think, Sar-Major?'

'A good man, Sir.'

'Seems so to me.' The OC turned back.

'Have you anything further to say, Sergeant?'

'No Sir.'

'OK.' He paused. 'McDonnell, you're an old Gallipoli man and when we go over tomorrow it won't be a picnic.' Another pause. 'You'll need everything you know.'

'Yes Sir.'

'Dismiss.'

Nothing was said about the lieutenant and neither was he seen again. The story went around that he'd gone to the colonel and complained and the colonel, after asking questions that didn't get answers he liked, said he was giving him his running shoes because he had no use for officers who couldn't lead men. Another colonel and it could have gone the other way.

Next day we had it bad from the beginning. A barrage hit our company in the assembly trenches: there were killed, wounded, and men going off their heads. We advanced as far as what was known as Gird Trench and it was there that Harry got his MC. He kept on going after being sniped, leading his platoon to outflank strong points. If his men hadn't got him out quickly he'd have bled to death. Frank was at the Otago RAP, an old pals' reunion.

But Gird Trench was as far as anybody went. Before us was a shallow kidney-shaped hollow. Four to five hundred yards long and two hundred yards across: we hadn't expected it. It was too shallow to be shown on our maps or to show up on aerial photographs. The Germans had dug what we called Gird Support Trench on the edge of its curved northern lip, and Gird Trench on the edge of its southern lip, with four rows of wire in front. Running into the hollow, Goose Alley could be enfiladed from both Gird Trench and Gird Support.

When another attack was called for, our colonel came up and saw for himself that the junction of trenches was in a dip and that all who'd gone into it had been clear targets for the Germans. He also saw that if the Germans tried a counter-attack, they would be targets for us. Until we had enough men and artillery support to attack from the flanks, we would have to stay put. I know of other colonels who would have pushed on there and then. Hart was not like that. He reported the situation to brigade. They knew him and did not argue.

During the three weeks and a couple of days the New Zealand Division served on the Somme it lost fifteen hundred killed and five and a half thousand wounded. Others fared worse, but not many.

FRANK
Somme

Now and again I would remember Hilda. I thought of how we had been together and how I wouldn't mind being with her again. It was some years before I became aware of how lucky I had been that my first experience with a woman was with someone like her and that it had not been, as it was with so many young soldiers, something cold and commercial. It is the nature of youth—and not infrequently their elders—to underestimate just how lucky one is on occasions and to believe a positive event is due to one's inherent charm, style, intelligence etc., and to conveniently overlook that the situation was favourable from the start. But I also thought of her beyond the bedroom door and how she was caught up in the war like the rest of us and how the waste of a good woman was the outcome. Along with that, I wondered what would happen when her man came home—if he did.

The odds were that he would, like most of us, get through it, but it is one thing to have it demonstrated mathematically and quite another to accept it when you're about to go into battle if you have been in a battle before—especially when you witnessed, as we did, walking-wounded from the first attack limping past while we waited for our turn. The new boys saw them too, but their concern was whether they would be 'brave' enough to face it—unaware that, like ninety-nine point nine per cent of the rest us, they would make the best of it. They would also learn that when they were sent into their next battle, 'bravery' would be the least of their concerns. And when they were sent into their third, a deep foreboding would hit them.

About mid-morning we formed fours and marched to the battlefield. Once there, instead of deploying us into an appropriate battlefield formation to lessen the possibility of casualties from the enemy artillery, Colonel Charters kept us marching. To him it mattered not that, as we went down to the Switch Line, it was broad daylight and we were in full view of German observation posts. We marched on even after it became evident we were lost; even when shells began to fall, flinging up geysers of dirt. They were marching too— towards us. Beyond the cratered landscape, we could see fields, villages, and trees, almost a reminder of normality. Almost, but not quite, because out of a clump of trees, a church tower rose—an enemy observation post directing the fall of the shells. It was only when they fell amongst us that our colonel called a halt and ordered us to dig.

A doctor at a Regimental Aid Post, with wounded lying out in the open, untouched until we arrived, abused us for attracting fire. His invective provoked two subalterns to reconnoitre on their own initiative. They saw that the trench we were to relieve was not far away and reported it to their company commander, but the orders were to keep on digging. For a while the shells eased off, but by late afternoon they resumed, eased off again, and resumed, along with snipers and machine guns from High Wood. All day the walking wounded and stretcher-bearers went by.

Eventually we moved to where we were supposed to have been and, yes, again we marched. Our time of arrival did not impress the battalion we relieved. Fire from High Wood was still a menace and we were also sniped from Grove Alley. Driving rain and squalls fell for twenty-four hours. Funk holes were dug into the side of the trench, room for your upper half to sit, with your legs over the side—if you were lucky to have a hole. Mostly you planted your boots in the mud, wrapped your groundsheet around your shoulders, leant against the clay and shivered. What passed for our trench was an ill-functioning drain perpetually caving in. Sandbags were in short supply and mostly used to wrap around our boots. Wind chilled the bones further. The water we drank came up in kerosene (petrol?—or both?) tins, the bread was muddy and only the keenest eyes saw the pork in the canned pork and beans. There was also tea, served like the pork and beans, at rain temperature. When a length of our front line came under a grenade attack from an offshoot of Flers Trench, the battalion bombers were sent to clear it and establish a block. They succeeded and those who were not killed were wounded.

Each battalion had a specialised 'bombing' party. It required men with good hand/eye coordination, quick reflexes and not too great a concern with anything beyond the here and now. It entailed the party entering an enemy trench and throwing grenades from one traverse to the next and then, at the right moment, dashing into the traverse just bombed on the assumption their grenades had cleared it well enough for the bayonet to deal with anyone left. Then more grenades would be thrown to clear the next traverse. The grenades were an early version of the Mills bomb and would occasionally explode before their five seconds fuse expired. The compensation for being a 'bomber' was less square bashing, fewer fatigues, more opportunities to patronise estaminets and, if you were that way inclined, more chance of a medal.

One, who died of his wounds, was a chap I had known since Sunday school, who'd rushed to the colours early and gone to Samoa. Replaced by older men, his contingent landed in Egypt when we returned from Gallipoli. Like me he'd been sent to the Otagos to make up numbers. We'd never been close, I can't even say I liked him; if it hadn't been for the war, neither of us would have bothered to walk across the road for the other and if he had come through neither would we have seen much of each other afterwards. But being in the same platoon it was natural we'd fall in together. We knew people in common and I could enter an estaminet with him without the expectation he'd be blind drunk before we left. But that is somehow trivialising him. It was the appalling circumstances, not sharing of thoughts, which gave our relationship its character. When another man and I had slopped out a hole and covered his pathetic body with mud in the hope the next shell wouldn't blow him out again, I could not see much hope for any of us.

It was nearly midnight when we were relieved. We wandered through the mud like sleepwalkers from one place to another until dawn helped find the trench that led us out, which had just been shelled, so maybe our erratic return might have saved our lives. We were billeted in assembly trenches called Savoy and Carlton—examples of the British sense of humour for those inclined to look for it. The lucky few occupied dugouts, the rest of us made ourselves 'comfortable' in shell holes, sharing ground sheets, which, like us, became more sodden as rainwater dribbled in. Still within artillery range, the shelling we were subjected to might be called desultory. We also received an introduction to tear gas shells. Mail was distributed, however, and for me it was a parcel from home of fruitcake, chocolate, a scarf, balaclava and socks. The three latter I kept, the remainder, as was the custom, shared with the rest in my section—along with the parcel from the parents of the dead bomber.

Four days later we assembled two hundred yards behind Grove Alley to advance on Goose Alley, occupy the junction with Flers Trench and Support, build a block to the north of it, and consolidate. The barrage preceding us was to be precisely timed and it was strongly emphasised we were to adhere to that timing. We, and another company, went in under the overall command of our OC, Jim Hargest. The briefing beforehand was as thorough as any I have known; everyone was part of it from platoon commanders to privates known to carry authority. Hargest was determined that everything he required of his officers and NCOs was etched in their brains. After the briefings he had them in his dugout to go over the whole thing again. What was strange was that before they reappeared, we heard singing. It wasn't exactly a Welsh choir and the songs were what you would expect from young men at the time, but it says something worth remembering about Hargest that he'd have his men sing at a time like that. Next day German shrapnel killed his brother.

We were lucky, but as Goose Alley had been a communication trench, having neither traverses nor wire, and was heavily shelled, a defence trench was needed parallel to it. As we dug and shovelled, the buried dead were exposed. Sentries had the pleasure of peering into no man's land with their noses within an inch of grey clad remains. Shell bursts began throwing up flames, earth, and men thirty feet high. But it was not just artillery; to our left there were German strong-points well manned by machine gunners and snipers. The battering continued into the next day. One consolation was an abundance of brand new German greatcoats, which, along with the youth of their former owners, suggested they had been a raw unit. With the coats were loaves of black bread, which I've been partial to since. We also found German bully beef—no improvement on our own—and bottles of soda water, a luxury compared with the tincture of kerosene we usually received.

Our next attack was mounted against the Gird System, which comprised a well-engineered and well-defended trench known as Gird Trench and, two hundred yards behind it, a support trench known as Gird Support. Gird System ran from west to east. The north end of Goose Alley, which, broadly speaking, ran from south to north, ran into the west ends of Gird Trench and Gird Support, forming a right-angle junction with each. First Otago assembled in Goose Alley, its start line being about a thousand yards distant from Gird Trench. Our company was to advance up Goose Alley and seize the junctions. The other three 1ˢᵗ Otago companies were to fan out from Goose Alley and attack in the line, it being assumed that their most eastern flank would link up with the western flank of 1ˢᵗ Auckland who were on our right.

As soon as the plan of attack was described everybody had his doubts. We were told that artillery support would be limited in quantity and in time. It would fire for a mere eight minutes. Not only would that be of doubtful effectiveness against the defences of the Gird System, it was also far too short a time to cross a thousand yards of a shell-holed, bullet-swept battlefield. (In the assault on Goose the distance had been seven hundred yards, the time twenty-three minutes, and the barrage heavy.) Everyone knew that Gird, the third line of German defence in our sector, would be far more formidable than Goose Alley.

The fate of the three other Otago companies will not occupy us for long: between their departure from Goose Alley and breasting a slight rise, their losses, in staff officer language, were 'moderate'. After that, every officer was hit—and a lot of their men. As our company advanced we received our share, one being our platoon commander. At one hundred and fifty yard intervals, Hargest established strong points. When we topped the rise and surveyed the ground where Goose met Gird, we saw no sign of active khaki uniforms anywhere near us; so Hargest ordered that we stay put and establish the final strong point. Then he took over command of the 1st Otago survivors; organising them into a coordinated unit and ordering them, exhausted though they were, to dig a diagonal trench to the Aucklands, who had gained their Gird objective. By taking those measures he prevented the Germans from mounting a successful counter-attack. His Military Cross was deserved.

By then our RAP had been hit and there were too few regimental stretcher-bearers to cope. When darkness fell our sergeant major ordered me to organise additional stretcher-bearers. Anyone not bespoken, was grabbed, some who'd come in after going to ground. I didn't blame them then, and I don't now, but they were put in a bearer party and sent forward again. I worked with our Regimental Medical Officer, Captain Prior MC. Known for getting a job done, while the new RAP was being established, he tended wounded on the battlefield.

When word got out that 1st Otago was woefully short of bearers, about a hundred men came up to help, bringing with them a couple of hundred blankets to prevent hypothermia. By then I was a walking zombie, programmed to do what needed to be done. I might have slept from time to time, slumping to a fire step or something like that but my memory is vague. I remember saying hello to Jim around 4 a.m. when 1st Wellington came up for their attack, and recognising Harry on a stretcher later, but they were hardly more than passing faces. It was easier when the drizzle cleared and the stars lit up. We brought in most though the ground was under fire. We kept at it into the next day until, along with the last bearers, we dragged ourselves out through communication trench quagmires.

Although out of it, in untouched countryside, I couldn't help thinking of the man I had buried. After sorting things to be returned to his family, I wrote a letter. I could see their uncomprehending faces. Owen's 'Anthem for Doomed Youth' summed it up.

> What passing-bells for these who die as cattle?
> Only the monstrous anger of the guns.
> Only the stuttering rifles' rapid rattle
> Can patter out their hasty orisons.

No mockeries for them from prayers or bells,
Nor any voice of mourning save the choirs, —
The shrill, demented choirs of wailing shells;
And bugles calling for them from sad shires …

The season didn't help. The skies of northern Europe have their days of brilliance but when winter is on its way no one bets on their frequency. No wonder, I thought, Europe has one war after another.

As our sergeant had been wounded I was not overly excited when, as the senior corporal, I was ordered to fill in as i/c of the platoon. We had just been on a route march, for the purpose, we were told, of hardening the old hands and reminding the boys who'd just arrived that the army wasn't all beer and skittles, and I had just dismissed them and was looking forward to a meal and a sleep, when the sergeant major yelled my name.

'!!!'

'Having a dream, Corporal?' For a sergeant major, the tone was friendly. We had struck up a rapport while getting the wounded out and apparently it was still there.

'No such luck, Sar'Major.' He was an old Gallipoli man too.

'No? Where's that spunk, enthusiasm and alertness we expect of our corporals?'

'Be my guest, Sar'Major.'

'Yeah? Seems I'm wasting my time, not to mention Captain Hargest's. Wants to see you. Now. About a promotion.'

'I'm flattered.'

'They're getting to the bottom of the barrel.'

'It's cosier down there.'

'Get over to Captain Hargest,' he said.

I went with mixed feelings. Indeed it was, in many ways, cosier down there. There was also inertia: a by-product of the fatalism that descends when you know the odds must catch up with you and so why do something that will increase those odds? I was beyond boredom: a feature of an infantryman's life surpassed only by fear. Indeed I had grown to welcome inaction, not even bothering to haul a book out of my pack; emptying mind and body of any desire to do anything. I was twenty-two years old and what adult life I'd had, was driving me mad. Not certifiably, not yet. Some of us had been driven stark raving mad, evacuated, and committed before the infection spread. For most it didn't happen like that, but crept up as many afflictions do.

When I entered the Nissen hut where Hargest had his office and came to attention, he was seated at a table, writing. Looking up, he ordered stand at ease, and continued to write. Beside him was a sergeant from Battalion HQ. As he was preoccupied it gave me an opportunity to examine my company commander. When he had raised his head I noticed eyes that were dark brown and very alert. His eyebrows and moustache — it was rare to see an officer without a moustache from 1914–18 — were pronounced and black. His hair was also black and carefully parted in the middle. He quickly signed what he had written, handed it to the sergeant and dismissed him. The tabletop was empty except for a thin file.

'Corporal Butler!'

'Sir!'

'Colonel Charters has instructed me to have a word with you.'

The way he said it made me wonder whether, if it had been left to him, he would have bothered.

'Captain Prior has reported you were of assistance at the Regimental Aid Post. The sergeant major has confirmed this.'

I couldn't think of anything sensible to say so I gave him a 'Yes, Sir'.

'As from today you will be Acting Platoon Sergeant.'

'Thank you, Sir.'

'We'll see. Provided your performance is satisfactory you will be confirmed in the rank.'

'Sir!'

'We are short of experienced men.' It was pronounced as if I had yet to be informed on the matter.

'Yes Sir.'

'However, Sergeant Butler,' here there was a pause and the brown eyes locked in a stare. 'Whilst at Armentières I can't remember you volunteering for a raiding party.'

'You bet you can't,' I thought to myself. Nevertheless it riled me. If he wanted to give one minute and take away the next, he could have the bloody stripes back—all three.

The stare continued and I contemplated yet another return to a stripe-less state and, the way it seemed to be going, latrine fatigues. Behind him there was a trench map on the wall. Before I could work out where it might be, he had picked up the file and flipped back the cover sheet.

'Do you know what the first note on your file is?' As if he didn't know I didn't know.

And I noticed the file was skinny.

'No, Sir.'

'It is not your attestation form. It is a note by the late Colonel Malone.'

'Oh!'

'Unusual. Signed and dated it states: "May have officer potential". Which, Sergeant Butler, makes me wonder why, until now, you have reached nothing higher than a corporal's rank.'

If he had wanted an answer he would have made it a question so again I kept quiet.

'I hope you appreciate the honour of having served under such a fine officer.'

'Colonel Malone was respected by all, Sir.' What else could I have said even if I had thought otherwise?

Hargest flipped a page, read, and flipped another one.

'Nothing much here. Some Confined to Barracks in Egypt.' Another stare. 'That wouldn't have done you any harm. It's also noted that you held a temporary position as lance corporal and were then promoted acting corporal. Nothing further. Why was that, Sergeant?'

'They came and went, Sir.'

'What came and went?'

'The promotions, Sir.'

'I can see that for myself. I asked if you have any idea why.'

'It was when we were on Cheshire Ridge.'

'Go on.' For the first time his look and tone indicated something like curiosity, as if I might just have something of interest to say.

'You might remember, Sir, things were rather raggedy. We went from one day to another. Rank didn't always count for much.'

He sat straighter than even before—my remark was approaching delicate ground. 'You'd better explain that, Sergeant.'

'Well, for a time I was i/c company.'

'So you might say you have had command experience.' If he intended irony, he did not reveal it.

'I wouldn't put it quite like that, Sir.'

'No?' He leant back in his chair. 'So when did you come off?' He was almost speaking man-to-man.

'Last day. B Party.' Shove that in your raiding pocket.

'When did you land?' He was curious.

'Fourth Reinforcement.'

'Any time out?'

'Sick once—Lemnos.'

He put the file down, glanced upwards, paused and then sat up—ramrod straight again. 'Have you thought of a commission, Butler?'

'Now and again, Sir.'

'Have you or haven't you? A man who doesn't know his own mind is no use to anyone. I have a form here. If you have thought about it, take the form, fill it in and deliver it to the company office. If you haven't, forget any future prospects.'

By then I had been around long enough to notice that the life of a junior infantry officer did not tend to be lengthy. And then there were Harry and Jim; I knew I'd never match either in this business. On the other hand, more and more I was being ordered around by men who knew less than I did. Not just that; I was growing tired of the primitive life in the ranks and if it was going to keep me alive longer, how much longer? And if I was going to go—forgive the solecism—why not go with a degree of comfort and privilege and a little more control over one's fate?

'I'll take it, Sir.'

HARRY
Interim

I remember being hit near Gird Trench on the Somme and keeping on my feet a while before dropping in my tracks. After that I have a hazy recollection of being assessed at a Field Hospital as a 'Blighty' case, and then of a succession of trips by ambulance, train, ship, train, and ambulance to Walton-on-Thames to be given a comfortable bed, clean sheets, abundant food, proficient doctors and kind beautiful nurses. One could not have wished for a better fate. Most of us recovered, though some would never return to what they were when they had so gaily volunteered. Healing took its time and the accompanying pain tended to be on the memorable side. Some bore it better than others, but, with a little encouragement and sympathy, even those who suffer greatly may go far towards accepting the trials and tribulations that come their way and emerge better men for it.

Another reason for remembering Walton fondly was meeting Nelle. Given the unpleasant duty of cleaning wounds, she combined deftness with compassion. I have seen more than one boy, going through agony, keeping control of himself by gazing up at her comely features, as frowning in concentration, she bent over his wound then raised her head, responding to his gaze with a smile that said, for the time being anyway, it was all over. As was often the way with the lads, when they were on the mend and perked up about it, they tried to backchat her. Few persisted; the riposte they received was quick, to the point, and much appreciated by neighbours.

By mid November I was transferred to Bulmer Lawn, the officers' convalescent home near our other English hospital, Brockenhurst, on the outskirts of the New Forest. Here one was well pampered. After three weeks I went on a fortnight's leave with a free travel warrant, pleased with the generosity of the powers that be. On reflection, however, one was not yet in a condition to return to the trenches.

It was up to Edinburgh to visit my mother's relatives and then across the Irish Sea to Belfast. Here I must divert a little. The prime instigator of this memoir, as you may remember, is my daughter. Although she cannot help but be very much aware of the effect my war experiences had on me, I doubt she expected I would describe them in the detail I have. Although the war allowed me to visit Scotland and Ireland, I went there because of my family connections. Indeed it is fair to say that my visit had no influence on my war experiences at all. What it did do, however, was to bring home to me where the roots of our family are and that, I think, might be of interest to my daughter and other family members. Moreover, like many of her sex, she is interested in families, being a mother herself, and my stay with our relatives will probably be of greater interest to her than my interminable tale of the trenches. To begin at the beginning: in 1875 my paternal grandparents, with three hundred other Ulster folk, joined an emigration scheme dreamed up by one Charles Vesey Stewart. He sought to transplant Ulster Protestantism to a milder clime and fertile lands at a most reasonable price, a haven where all would prosper and one's neighbours would be of one's faith—or so Mr Stewart led them to believe. Those who lacked capital, but were of proven quality in agricultural work were given a free or a very cheap passage provided they agreed to remain in the community for a specified term. My grandfather was the third son of a tenant of the Earl of Antrim—whose family name, as I rib Jim from time to time, was McDonnell. The first son was destined to take over the tenancy, the second for the church, and my grandfather, like so many Irish born, to seek opportunity beyond the seas. Through the Orange Lodge he heard of Stewart's scheme, applied, and was accepted. Once the settlers had disembarked in Auckland and travelled down to the Bay of Plenty, those who knew land did not like what they saw, and those who didn't were appalled by the isolation. The two classes of people who at once set about their business without complaint were the wastrels—fares etc. paid by their families—and men like my grandfather whose skills were in immediate demand. So through hard work and saving, grandmother and he acquired land of their own—an impossible task if they had stayed at home.

From Belfast I went up the coast to the little village of Glenarm. At first it was as though we were back in England, with the cosy little villages, hedges, and tree lined roads, except that Presbyterian and Methodist churches predominated. Where the road turned inland for a time, it became evident we were in a country with a hard rock underlay. We passed through the village of Glynn and I was assured it was one hundred per cent against the Pope and for King George. Given the abundance of Union Jacks flying, I was in no position to question the matter. So we came to Glenarm, the first of the Nine Glens of Antrim, one of the most beautiful localities of the British Isles. I felt at home, yet not at home. Everything, the village, the topography, the vegetation, the sky, was different, but not quite alien. The people … well it was clear I was amongst those who shared much with those with whom I had grown up. In some ways, they reflected the country in which they and their forbears lived: hard rock underneath, fertile peat on top, and a grey climate—productive if you worked hard and didn't expect too much.

The village, I was told, was the oldest of the Nine Glens villages, which, in that part of the world, means really old. It was noted for its limestone and all buildings were of stone, generally whitewashed, with slate roofs. Most were single storey, but some were double, and I even remember a three-storey building—perhaps it was to house the holiday-makers who flocked to the sweeping stretch of beach in summer. As well as being the home of two of my great uncles, Glenarm is the seat of the Earl of Antrim. He resided in what appeared, at first glance, to be a castle, but closer inspection revealed that its turreted appurtenances had been added as recently as the nineteenth century. I was tempted to knock on the gate and request entrance on the grounds that I had a friend, a relative of theirs, who despite his left-wing convictions was risking life and limb under conditions hardly luxurious so that they and their kind might continue to enjoy their inheritance. But I jest; my relatives assured me the family had a tradition of being fair and generous to their tenants—which, in one way or another, meant everybody in the glen and the village. Unlike so many lords of the manor in that benighted isle, they were not absentees and, moreover, there was not a school, hall, or church they had not contributed to—save the Roman Catholic chapel.

My great uncle on the land kept a farm in good repair and ran healthy stock. I was interested to note that, cold though Ireland might appear to us, it was not necessary to house animals in winter—an advantage they had over their counterparts on the mainland. The farms themselves, I noticed, were long and relatively narrow, running vertically, up from the valley bottom, rather like a ladder. This, it was explained to me, was so that each tenant might have a reasonable share of productive land. But I also greatly enjoyed meeting my other great uncle, the minister of the Presbyterian meeting hall. Built in the eighteen thirties, it was large enough to accommodate five hundred to six hundred people, thus being the largest building in the glen. The services I attended easily filled the body of the church. Nonetheless the church that dominated the village was the Church of Ireland, the church of the Earl and Countess. And undoubtedly the most attractive building in the village.

Anybody who has visited Ireland will not be at all surprised that I was welcomed with great warmth and hospitality, but it was not long before I sensed I was, despite my relative youth, regarded with some deference. This, I came to realise, was because my uniform was that of a British officer and therefore my loyalties must be for king and country. Remember though that this was the year of the Dublin Easter Rising and that Ireland was about to be torn apart into North and South. Whether I was chatting with my farmer great uncle about the land, or seeking to learn from my minister great uncle about pastoral work in the glen and where and how he trained for the ministry, the conversation inevitably gravitated towards Home Rule and associated issues. It was evident this topic exercised their minds more than the war. They found it difficult to comprehend that a relative of theirs, intended for the church, and holding the King's Commission, was little interested in the differences that so divided their country. When asked about the position in New Zealand I could only reply that on a personal level—apart from inter-marriage—there was some, but not much, prejudice against Roman Catholics, and that politically the denominational differences, despite the efforts of bigots (a word they did not really appreciate) on each side, so far as I had noticed, had little effect. I could not help mentioning that it had been my privilege to serve under a brave and most capable soldier who was a committed Roman Catholic and who had sacrificed his life for the Empire. Unfortunately, they reacted as if he were the exception that proved the rule.

Returning to Belfast, I noticed a lemon squeezer in the crowd—it stood out by a mile—and after introducing myself, we decided to see the city together. He was a Rifle Brigade man; a farmer from South Canterbury, and like me was convalescing from a Somme wound. A no nonsense fellow, he was not hesitant in expressing his opinions. He had just visited his uncle who farmed near Strabane, County Tyrone. What he saw of the farming there was contrary to what I had seen: broken down fences, dilapidated buildings, poor pasture, a hundred years behind us, he said. I was amused when he mentioned going to church and putting half-a-crown in the plate and the amazement it created—threepenny bits seemed to be the going rate. 'Not that I blame them,' he added. 'The sermon never ended.' He also advised me to keep out of Roman Catholic pubs because they didn't like khaki. I agreed to restrain myself in that direction. For the first, and only time, we came across open dislike of our origins. 'B——y colonials' was voiced more than once in our hearing. Another matter we could not help noticing, was the large number of young men in civilian clothes. There was no conscription in Ireland and my Rifle Brigade friend had strong opinions on that.

On being advised by just about everybody that the khaki of individual soldiers wandering around Dublin was likely to attract trouble, we decided to return to England. Now, I see it as an opportunity missed. One of my forbears had attended Trinity College—perhaps his family had been Church of Ireland—and I would have loved to visit the hallowed halls of that famous institution. I had also heard about the beauty of the west, but Cork was another city we were expressly warned against. I should have gone and taken my chances. I don't know whether my Rifle Brigade companion regrets our decision, but when one takes into account where we'd been and what we were going back to, our decision was tending to the absurd.

I rejoined my unit in February to discover I had not missed anything much. They had returned to the quiet but rather damp Armentières sector. General Russell, however, tried to cheer everybody up. As each brigade went into reserve, along with the usual parade ground 'bull', a lot of time was spent on rugby, soccer, cross-country running and boxing. He already had the man to organise it, Colonel Plugge: a fine parade-ground soldier, and, after Gallipoli, looking for work. A schoolmaster by profession, he was used to organising sporting events, and if a night of intemperance happened to be too much for him, no lives would be unnecessarily lost after the sun came up. Educational sessions, elocution and literary competitions were organised by the YMCA and a cinema and a concert party were also established. Out of line living conditions were improved too, straw regularly changed in barns, cooks properly trained and the incorrigibly ignorant and filthy of them sent up front where any slacking received short shrift. To enforce these measures, Russell personally inspected the men's quarters and kitchens. Being the sort of general he was, and the soldiers we were, we expected he would pay close attention to our positions and equipment, but we were surprised when his eagle eye fixed on where the men lived and ate.

I have already mentioned how one of the fascinations of war is wondering what is 'on the other side of the hill' and how raids, in seeking to answer the question, more often than not returned with very little to show for their effort. A remarkable event, however, occurred not long before we departed the sector. Second Auckland made the largest raid since our departure from the Somme. It comprised five hundred men and was mounted, I assume, because smaller parties had failed to achieve much and also, I suspect, by the frustration of 2nd Auckland's fiery, most competent, and recently appointed CO. Heavily supported by artillery, they went forward at dawn, occupied enemy front and support lines for half-an-hour, and brought back an officer, forty-three other prisoners and reported killing two hundred others. It cost them eighteen killed, sixty missing (many of whom would have been killed) and seventy wounded. Any raid is a vicious, nasty business; hand-to-hand fighting is when the worst of our natures come to the fore, retaliation is the norm and mercy abhorred. The larger the raid, the worse it becomes. When the 2nd Aucklands returned to their trenches, they believed there would be little prospect of doing anything for their wounded left behind in the confusion and half-light, except to abandon them in the mud and the cold for the rest of the day. Being a Northern European February, it meant they were being left to their last hours on this earth. Imagine 2nd Auckland's surprise, therefore, on turning to look across no man's land, to see German soldiers lining their parapet with their hands up and an officer ordering another to put his rifle down. Surrender? Oh no, not those men who had resisted our boys so fiercely. They were signalling that the wounded might be collected. And so they were. Not right up to the German parapet — they were brought in by those manning it — but everywhere else. Not until no man's land was cleared and a shot fired into the air did war began again. Because the Germans acted immediately after a hot-blood encounter, the aftermath has lingered in my memory.

NELLE

Walton-on-Thames

Mount Felix was a different kettle of fish from St Thomas's. Each was a hospital but there the similarity ended. St Thomas's was English, long established, renowned, built like a prison and completely at home in the middle of a city of millions. Mount Felix was New Zealand for the time being, improvised, and never, despite the efforts of the military, lost its character as a country residence. Lord Plunket had resisted the military takeover. Like the rest of us he would have heard stories from boys in British military hospitals about being ordered by Sisters to lie at attention in bed when superior ranks were planning to enter the ward, not to ruffle the counterpane, or disturb the pillows, and about other stupidities the military get up to. Despite his title, however, Lord Plunket could not resist the reality he was presented with. First, it is beyond the army's comprehension not to have all men under its thumb all the time, and second, with the New Zealanders being sent to the Western Front, a voluntary organisation would be out of its depth coping with the train loads of maimed and sick arriving on its doorstep. So his lordship and his committee gave way gracefully but continued to help by more than just distributing fruit, sweets, cakes and cigarettes. Lady Bell, for example, spent her afternoons mending and she was not alone in that. Huts were laid out as billiard and games rooms and film shows and concerts were arranged. Well-to-do members of the local community were persuaded to volunteer their large motorcars to convey men to the sights and theatres of London and Windsor Castle, where if one were lucky, minor royalty might guide one around the premises. The other civilising influence was Mount

Felix itself with its twenty acres of beautifully laid out gardens to delight the eye. When I arrived they were building prefabs on the front lawn but even they could not disrupt the harmony of house and gardens.

The cold wet day when I started at Mount Felix was appropriate; it coincided with the first convoy of New Zealanders from the Somme. Everyone at the hospital had expected a rush of wounded, and everyone in authority would have known our boys were to be flung into the Somme, so one gets tired of the excuses that those on high have become so adept at making. The evacuations were better organised than they had been in July — even generals might learn a little sometimes — but at our end there were just not enough people. I heard from Ivy that when New Zealand offered VADs (officially known as Volunteer Aid Detachments) in 1914 to the English general in Egypt it was turned down and that it was largely due to the urging of New Zealand trained nurses that they were eventually dispatched. After that there were so many of them who wanted to serve abroad that the Government wasn't going to waste boat space on VADs. In mid-September the Sister to whose ward I was sent had no other trained nurse, just three orderlies and three VADs. Of the latter, one was English, the other a Scot, and their hospital experience consisted of some weeks in the kitchen. I was the third.

On my starting day twenty-eight ambulances arrived with ninety-five men; the day after it was sixty-five men, and so it went on to late October. It became so bad that an SOS was sent out and twelve Sisters from the Canadian hospital nearby were sent to us. Throughout the war New Zealand soldiers could not have been cared for without women from elsewhere in the Empire. Later, after matters had settled down, my ward had three Sisters, two of whom were New Zealanders and one Canadian, and four VADs — English, Scottish, South African, and me. That would be about average for most wards. And so deficient had been the estimation of wounded — hope springs eternal in a general's manly chest — that marquees had to be erected and cold and muddy they were until one by one they were replaced by prefabs.

On the second day, while I was drinking a quick cup of tea with the Sister, she said: 'You've done this before haven't you?' I mentioned my year as a probationer. For the first time I was well regarded — for a VAD that is.

New Zealand nurses were no more tolerant of us than their English sisters. But one can pay a price for even the modicum of respect that came my way. I was put on the 'agony wagon'. When I pushed the trolley into the ward, all that could be heard was the rattle of its instruments except when we had a patient who went off his head at the very sight of it. Even without him the ward did not stay quiet for long, for what one had to do was to clean the deep wounds of the pus that had accumulated in them since the last cleaning. If one did not do this properly, and as often as needed, gangrene or even worse, gas gangrene, could develop. It was a dreadful business probing deep into the wound, the pain for the patient excruciating. One had to clean the wound properly and quickly, and quickly did not mean quick for the patient. However a man might scream (being not infrequently held down by orderlies) one had to meticulously probe and scrape as if he were inanimate. To the men I would have been a cold fish.

Mount Felix was primarily a hospital for 'other ranks', as the army so charmingly puts it, but we did have an officers' ward and when one of the nurses there collapsed through overwork, I was sent up to replace her — no opinion having been voiced on one's appearance. Harry Patterson had just been admitted. A bullet had entered his left sternum, shattered the bone and then exited through a rib, shattering that too. The field dressing hadn't staunched the bleeding and ultimately he fell over and couldn't get up again. When admitted, his pulse weak and beating quicker than it should have been, his skin was cold and clammy. He must have had a second haemorrhage on the train. If it had not been for his very strong constitution, he would have been beyond help. He was given a medal for carrying on but really it was silly for a man in his condition. He could easily have picked up gangrene or tetanus. He was lucky on two counts: that it had been a bullet wound and that his infection had not developed further. Healing was slow so day after day I had to work on him and then flood the wound with Carrel-Dakin solution. Earlier in the war, before Carrel-Dakin came into use, wounds took much longer to heal. It sounds nice that they now healed more speedily until we remember that the sooner soldiers heal, the sooner they are sent back from whence they came.

Later he told me where he had grown up. Although it wasn't far from

Wanganui I didn't know anybody from there, whether friends of the family or girls at school. I noticed he had a Bible on his locker. He was also friendly with the hospital chaplain, a gentleman who had lost a leg at Gallipoli. But Harry sought to be friends with everybody, whether orderly, nurse, doctor or Matron, greeting all with a smile, even if one arrived with the trolley. And while you were going about your business on him, he would chat: how you were, the weather, if a day off was coming up and what you might be doing, and after, what you had done. And you chattered in return, as if you were merely sponging his back, and when you worked on his neighbours, he would chat to them. One, a lieutenant, who today would be described as having a low pain threshold, afterwards felt deeply ashamed of himself, disbelieving when you did your best to assure him no one judged him for it. His turn mostly came after Harry's and although Harry had been through his dose of agony, he would at once chat to the man, like a father, although I doubt if Harry was any older. Harry was as helpful when a man came in with a thigh that had been cut to the bone by a shell splinter. The wound had been sewn up before it had been cleaned properly. When he came to us and we cut away the dressings, solid with dried blood and other matter, a foul stench arose out of bubbling brown pus, provoking even the most hardened to gag — gas gangrene, the severest gangrene of all, where bacteria form gas under the skin. In the hope that it hadn't spread further, an immediate amputation was performed. It had spread, and the man only lived long enough to learn he had lost a leg. It was Harry who made his last hours as bearable as they might be.

Before Harry was discharged, we heard he had been awarded a Military Cross. When people fluffed around him, he told them that better men had never been given anything at all. And when asked about his other medal he said he was given it because the general liked him and that was how most medals were awarded. It didn't sound like false modesty. Feathers were ruffled when, after being asked about how he felt about appearing before the King at Buckingham Palace, he replied that he hoped he was a better man than his son whom he had seen in Egypt and hadn't been impressed by. In those days there was the Holy Trinity and then the King, Queen and Prince of Wales.

By November the rush of the Somme admissions was over. Patients were being discharged. Anxiety replaced pain. How would each man be graded? Would he be assessed as unlikely to be fit for service within six months, and therefore loaded onto a hospital ship and sent home? (I will leave to your imagination the futures of some of those men.) Or would he recover within six months? One cannot forget their faces when a doctor appeared to pronounce their fate. Some lived under suspended judgement: those who, by one means or another, managed to have themselves chosen to remain as orderlies. However, as more Sisters arrived from New Zealand and more English girls were recruited as VADs, and more generals girded their armies for more battles, these men too departed. When they announced they were glad to be getting back to their mates, we replied, 'Yes, of course,' even to the lazybones.

Mount Felix, by admitting only New Zealand soldiers, had sudden eruptions of patients and then relative quiet until another battle. Which is not to say our wards became empty: men were wounded every day—or fell ill. I can vouch that the war put as many diseased into hospitals as wounded. Obvious when one thinks of it; millions of men swilling around in mud, wet, filth, and the cold: a breeding ground for dysentery, influenza, pneumonia and TB, as well as trench foot—a disease not unknown to our Sisters in France. (Wounded tended to be more cheerful than the ill; no doubt because only part of their body was afflicted.)

The November fogs overlapped into December and its frosts. During the day, the steam for heating the wards was also used by the kitchens and suddenly people became interested in kitchen work, but that was the privilege of 'General Service' VADs—clerks, typists, charwomen, etc.—who, besides possessing the opportunity of being warm, were paid considerably more than us. We nurse aides almost became reconciled to thick stockings.

Which reminds me of our uniforms—an improvement on what we had worn at St Thomas's. In the wards it was a blue dress with narrow white stripes and a white apron that had a Red Cross, with a white NZ in the centre, on the bodice. Stockings and shoes were black and the cap—white with a little red cross in front—was a scarf tied back. The cape was navy blue with a royal blue lining. Our walking out uniform, it has to be admitted, was smart—wartime smart. Surprising—or was it?—because it was designed by the wife of the general who commanded our troops in England. It probably did no harm that an English tailor cut it. Navy blue, it had a fitted jacket with royal blue facings on the collar and cuffs worn over a white shirt with a royal blue tie. The buttons were brass with 'RC' on them. The skirt indicated the way skirts were going, above the ankle but not yet near the knees. The navy cap could have been improved on; it looked like a failed imitation of an airman's helmet. On our right cuffs were small light blue chevrons for each year of service. Because of my year as a probationer I was entitled to 'put one up' immediately.

On first going up to London, whilst descending to the Underground at Waterloo, I was politely requested to take the lift down. 'If you will carry my bag, porter,' I replied. A Royal Flying Corps pilot, he had the grace to apologise and then, diffidently, but at once, took me up on my comment. 'Next time,' I said. By then we had descended—the real lift girl having taken the hint—and when I stepped onto the platform my train was there, about to pull out. I jumped in as the doors closed and afterwards wondered why I had been in so much of a hurry.

For Christmas 1916 there was still hope; the Somme had passed, the boys gloried in being alive and we, too, dedicated the day to forgetting about the war. Although none could forget how far they were from home, all were amongst their own folk and that was something to celebrate also. The War Contingent Association and the local citizenry of Walton really did the hospital proud. Add that to the nursing staff dipping into their own pockets and a great deal of improvisation and the result was every ward decorated and every patient waking up to a small present in the morning.

After Christmas it was back to normal and for me it was a disappointment to learn I had not been selected to go on a six-month motor course. In November, Oatlands Park, a hotel about a mile away, had been taken over to accommodate limbless convalescents and tubercular patients. Motor transport was needed between the two and it had been my hope that I might be trained for it, but one of Ivy's friends was chosen instead. 'Sorry, Nelle,' said my Ward Sister, 'you may blame me.' It was nice to be appreciated, but I would have liked the job. This was not just because I wanted a change and was curious about driving and motorcars anyway, but the freedom that went with the job.

Frosty January moved into February snow and for an all too short duration we were in a fairyland that gave us a frozen little lake near the hospital. People came down from London to skate, but mostly those on the lake were locals: staff and walking convalescents from Mount Felix, Oatlands, and the Canadian hospital that had supplied us with Sisters; and servicemen from nearby camps and aerodromes. Canadians and Newfoundlanders outstripped all others on the ice and inhabitants of the southern isles rated at the other end of the scale. Being among the lucky ones who were able to maintain equilibrium without too much loss of dignity, I made the most of it.

The fairyland coincided with a transfer to Oatlands, to the TB ward: something else I did not tell Mother. Moreover, I was put on night shift with more responsibility than usually given to a VAD, transferred by the Matron on the grounds they needed a good person there! At any rate, the work was not as demanding of one's energy and gave me more free time. The ice only lasted a fortnight but it was long enough to meet Albert, last seen in a lift at Waterloo.

'Hello,' he said.

'Oh!' I said, nearly falling over. 'Where have you sprung from?'

'Brooklands,' he said.

I had heard of Brooklands: two of the 'general' VADs had boyfriends who were mechanics there. It was about five miles away. Best known for motor racing, it was also an aerodrome. I had seen airmen amongst the skaters but had never dreamed Albert might be one of them, not really.

As I write this, I have his photograph in front of me, now brown with age—or was it sepia already when, after much asking by me and his demanding one in return, he gave it? I forget. As I look at him I see a boy standing in front of an aeroplane: a child almost, still not quite believing the lethal toy behind him was his. While I wouldn't call him shy, he was diffident, having no idea how handsome he was. He was not tall, but beautifully proportioned with thick black hair falling over a broad forehead, rather full lips and skin unblemished. The Royal Flying Corps uniform with its diagonal row of covered buttons on the right, cavalry trousers, and side cap—two fingers above his right eyebrow—suited him. Unlike other officers he had not grown a moustache. I rather liked that, but he couldn't have even if he'd wanted to, not a proper one. Although he had just been promoted to captain, Albert was not yet twenty. He had returned to England after flying aeroplanes for eighteen months over German lines, latterly the Somme, photographing German trenches. Nothing to bother about, he told me, like driving a No. 10 bus: you fly where you're told to fly, your observer works the camera, then you turn round and come back. He made it sound so simple. I deliberately did not ask myself why it was possible for nineteen year olds in the RFC to attain the rank of captain. At Brooklands he alternated between training student pilots and delivering new aeroplanes to airfields in France and Belgium. I asked him about training pilots: wasn't it dangerous, up in the air with someone still learning? He said the lads were keen and learned quickly; it was a piece of cake except it could become boring, which is why he liked flying across the Channel and having 'a decent time in the air'. That was another thing I learned: as many, if not more, men were killed in training than in action. Any 1914–18 flying was dangerous.

We skated together all that afternoon and for as many afternoons as each of us could manage while the ice lasted. The gods might have been playing with us. His afternoons were free as frequently as mine, except when he had to deliver an aeroplane to France. But he no longer lingered there, not staying for lunch or dinner in the mess, as had been his wont. With the thaw of the ice I wondered what we would do next, but he had the answer. When he suggested his motorbike I was doubtful; the rules at Mount Felix were freer than they had been at St Thomas's (we even had dances and mixed doubles at tennis!) but a VAD seen on the back of a motorbike would soon have the chicken-coop clucking. 'Don't worry,' he said, 'I'll fix it.' And he did because when I met him the next afternoon, there was a flying suit with helmet and goggles bundled up on the pillion. Off we went with me snugly behind him. The flying suit was not just a disguise, but practical too; remember it was February going into March and April. Looking back, he must have been an accomplished motorcyclist because the roads were slippery, but I never once had cause to fear, though when we went around corners the ground was close. Whether I would travel with such equanimity now, is an open question, but then if a charming young man made an offer, who's to say what I might decide?

We would head off into the country, choosing narrow winding lanes. I guess the wartime petrol came from the same place as the flying suit. We had our opportunity and we took it; we did not talk about it. Once he told me about his previous life, not that he had a great deal to tell, and I talked about New Zealand. He said it sounded like a country where a man might spread his wings. I don't think a pun was intended and anyway I said he should come and see for himself and he said he might and we left it at that. Actually I don't remember we talked a great deal; we just were.

On the last afternoon it only needed one look. 'You're leaving.'

'They're forming a new squadron, S.E.5s. They've given me a flight. Mostly fellows like me. Who've been out of it for a bit.'

'When?'

'Tomorrow. Got back last night and there it was. Name up on the board.'

'Tomorrow?'

'There's to be another push. Belgium, I think.'

'You think?'

He shrugged his shoulders.

'Well, I don't really know. Better than Mesopotamia. Once out there, you don't come back for years. So they say.'

'Do they,' I said.

'I'll be due for leave,' he said. 'In no time, spend it in London. Paint the town red.'

'Yes,' I said. 'Red.'

'Should be interesting work.'

'Work? What work?'

'Flying S.E.5s, best there is. I'm jolly lucky, really.'

'Yes,' I said again.

'Not like floating around in a Harry Tate, taking photographs. Sitting ducks, those chaps.'

This was the first time I had heard that. Walking over to the motorbike I began putting on the flying suit.

'Where shall we go?' He was trying to please.

I pulled the helmet over my head and then the goggles.

'Anywhere.' Tears and goggles do not go together. I pulled them off and somewhere along the road I lost them.

Then began a life fraught with anxiety and apprehension. Every day, hour, when not absorbed in work, I wondered; living from one letter to the other which, brief though they were, were still letters. Otherwise I knew nothing. By reading between the newspaper lines, one could guess that matters, in Flanders, for the time being, were 'quiet', but I knew that for Albert and all the other Alberts, the war was quiet only when the weather kept them on the ground. I prayed for rain and cloud and snow and sleet and him and when an expected letter was delayed, I could not do other than fear the worst until my anxieties were relieved. I worked hard and slept little, becoming irritable, exchanging sharp words with whoever crossed my way, whoever they might be.

Despite being as salubrious as any institution of its kind, Oatlands was still what it was. The grounds extended fifty acres, much of them bounded by the Thames. Stories were told of how it had once been a monastery and later one of the country houses of King Charles whose head was chopped off. Royal dukes seem to have made use of it too and the gardens did have something of a ducal grandeur about them. My colleagues found the work interesting and less stressful than nursing at Mount Felix. Although Oatlands had a TB ward, its main purpose was to rehabilitate the limbless. An ideal situation, it was claimed, being so near to the Roehampton hospital, which specialised in research and therapy for the British limbless. So although I was in the TB ward, where young men were coughing their lungs out, as I went to and fro I was confronted with those lacking one, two, sometimes three, and yes, not common, but still it happened, four limbs. Few did not make the effort to be bright and cheerful and were genuinely pleased when, for example, an enthusiastic Sister praised the newly acquired skill at needlework of a labourer who now lacked legs.

PASSCHENDAELE

MESSINES

Messines was a battle fought preliminary to a series of battles later in the year which was called Third Ypres. The assault on the Messines Ridge was successful and if one man could ever be said to be responsible for that victory, it was Plumer: a white-haired, pink-cheeked tubby little man with a walrus moustache, monocle and bulbous watery eyes, and whose Second Army was responsible for the Ypres-Messines sector. The Tommies called him 'Daddy' or 'Old Plum' and younger staff officers, 'Drip'—he had a runny nose. Nonetheless he had proven his ability as an infantryman in the field. He had learnt much about handling civilians in uniform when he was commanding irregular colonials on the veldt: where he had finished up rather liking them, Haig came away with an enduring dislike. Plumer had also learnt that, if time is available, you seize the opportunity to plan meticulously and in so doing you make the most of the talents of your subordinates. Above all, he was his own man: he knew how to put a point of view to a superior, was neither stubborn nor unduly compliant, and knew how to offer his resignation without pique or beating about the bush if he felt his superior had lost confidence in him—as when Haig had criticised him about an earlier battle.

Taking into account the fear Haig routinely engendered in the other generals under his command, it is unlikely he would have been entirely comfortable with Plumer, his most capable subordinate. Neither would Haig have been able to keep his mind free of the talk in higher echelons that if he hadn't succeeded Sir John French, Plumer might have, or—so some held—should have. That it is most unlikely Plumer would have sought Haig's position—let alone in the same manner as Haig had sought French's—would have been difficult for Haig to accept.

After the Somme bogged down, Haig was keen to re-open the battle as soon as weather permitted, but was checked by the worst winter in local memory. Moreover, in February the German High Command, scenting victory over the Russians, gave priority to the Eastern Front. Consequently they went on the defensive on the Western Front and shortened their line on the Somme, withdrawing by up to twenty miles to well-sited and solidly built defensive positions constructed in the rear. They left behind a booby-trapped wilderness. Realising for the time being the Somme was a dead duck, Haig turned his eyes to Belgium. Any attempt to mount an assault in that sector required the acquisition of the Messines-Wytschaete Ridge, the southern cornerstone of the German defences in Flanders.

Plumer had been working on a Flanders offensive for the best part of two years. Reluctantly accepting his staff couldn't come up with a better plan for Messines, Haig had no option but to accept Plumer's version, with minor modifications. It comprised mine shafts, new roads, railways, tramways, communication saps, assembly trenches and other engineering works, much of it already underway. With close coordination between artillery, machine guns and the Royal Flying Corps (RFC) to open up the way for the infantry, it was getting very close to an 'all-arms' battle.

If there is one thing people know about the battle of Messines, it is the blowing of the mines. It helped that German engineers discounted the practicality of mining on the scale achieved by the British and discovered only one shaft—actually, just inside the New Zealand sector.

The Messines-Wytschaete front line ran along the western slopes of the ridge and looked over the British lines. The Germans had spared no expense in the provision of wire and strong-points; some concrete, some timber, some reinforced farm buildings, and some shell holes. Knowing our artillery would target them, the Germans manned their forward defences lightly. The second line had wire, trenches and concrete blockhouses—or 'pillboxes' as we called them—surrounding Messines town, and within it—including heavily reinforced cellars. One and a half miles beyond were further defence works. The German Army also had 'Eingreif' divisions specially trained for counter-attack work, waiting, out of the range of all but the heaviest artillery, ready when needed. Having gone to a lot of trouble organising and building these defences, the German Generals commanding in the Messines sector allowed complacency to cloud their judgement. They underrated British strength and ignored a Canadian mining deserter who spilled the beans and a spy who supplied an accurate description of British intentions.

In the twelve days preceding the assault the British artillery fired three and a half million shells. Because of the stress our barrages put German pillboxes under, their garrisons had to be rotated every two days. That was nothing, however, compared to the morning of the attack when, along with a very heavy bombardment, huge mines under the German forward trenches went up. When the mines were about to be blown, Plumer's staff went outside to see the fireworks while Plumer knelt and prayed for his men.

The New Zealand Division was part of II Anzac Corps, which, at Messines, also included the 3rd and 4th Australian Divisions, and the British 25th Division. Russell's view was that the situation was like the German defenders being on the rim of a saucer with New Zealanders at the bottom. This meant the Germans suffered two disadvantages. It exposed them horribly to our artillery, and the slope our men had to climb up to the rim was concave: dead ground to any German observer not on the rim of the crest or airborne. The RFC worked hard to keep the latter a monopoly—though a low flying enemy strafer did visit our trenches.

After seizing Messines town, the New Zealand Division was to advance by a farther five hundred to six hundred yards where Russell planned to establish machine gun nests. Once these had been completed and manned, he intended to withdraw the bulk of the troops. Drawing on his experience, Russell argued that artillery, mortar, and machine gun barrages held off counter-attacks, not 'hand-to-hand fighting' by infantry. Monash, his 3rd Australian Division counterpart, held the same view, but neither was permitted to withdraw. Conventional wisdom stipulated that forward positions were to be fully manned to fight off the inevitable German counter-attacks. Godley failed to press the point made by his subordinates to Haig. The Anzacs were to pay for that.

An immediate problem had to be resolved: in front of the New Zealand positions was a flat leading to a stream. If a trench were dug there, it would serve as an assembly position that would greatly reduce the advance across open ground, and also would provide a position where the stream and its banks *could be observed. Digging, however, would be right under the eyes of Fritz. The officer chosen to lead the digging was Major James Hargest, 1st Otago. A cool customer, on the night of the thirteenth of April, he led four hundred men out into no man's land to dig the seven hundred and fifty yard trench. He did it without losing a man. A few days later, a sergeant and he penetrated the German front line and confirmed that our barrage had devastated and denuded it of troops except for patrols and working parties.*

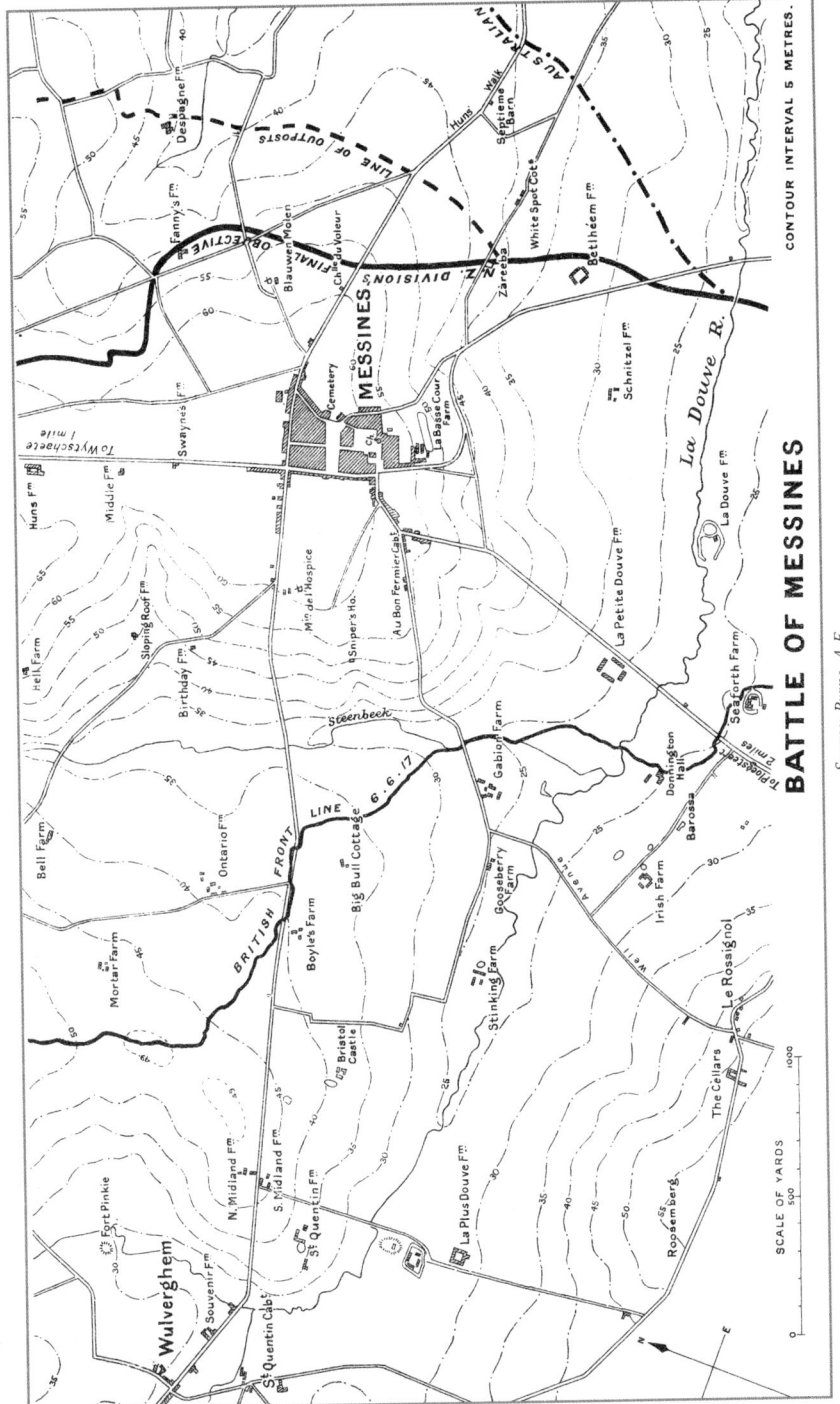

BATTLE OF MESSINES

CONTOUR INTERVAL 5 METRES

Source: Byrne, A.E.

SCALE OF YARDS

HARRY
Messines

I had returned from my leave in Scotland and Ireland and was with the boys when in the middle of May we marched to billets well to the rear. There was a horse show and I was in the saddle again, borrowing a mount from the squadron of the Otago Mounted Rifles that was now part of II Anzac Mounted Regiment on the Western Front. I selected a steed who had more than the eye first noticed. We had time to get to know each other and on the day we performed not too badly, surprising my brothers-in-arms and, if they only knew it, horse and rider.

After that we had twelve days training for Messines, the ground matching what we would be fighting over. Our distant Pacific neighbours, the Canadians, joined us. Recently they had distinguished themselves by capturing the previously unassailable Vimy Ridge in the Arras sector. Like us they were citizen-soldiers who valued initiative and, like us, they learned on the job. Their commander, who never failed to go forward to see for himself, was the most competent Corps Commander in the British forces. Pear-shaped, awkward, a former real estate man whose pre-war handling of unit funds does not bear too close a scrutiny, and under a political master whose prime concern was jobs for the boys, few would have predicted that Arthur Currie would demonstrate outstanding ability on the Western Front and independence of mind. Landing in France shortly before we landed at Gallipoli, Canada had the advantage over us when it came to Western Front experience and it was they who advised on penetrating German defence systems, showing us how the platoon and its sections had become the key to infantry fighting, although we were evolving in that direction.

Each man was taught to be proficient with the rifle and bayonet, the hand-grenade, the rifle-grenade, and the Lewis gun. Each platoon comprised four sections and each of them was a team specialising in the use of a particular weapon. We advanced in section columns and when a machine gun nest, a concrete pillbox or any other strong point had to be taken out, the four teams would deploy: the Lewis gun and the rifle grenadier sections would give covering fire, and the riflemen and 'bomber' teams would use that fire to assist them to envelope the target. Greater demands were made on each man; whether officer, NCO, or ranker. Not all were up to it and changes, some, were made.

On our return to Messines, men who were Left Out of Battle were diverted to a reinforcement camp, among them none other than your humble servant. I may have been left out to give me a rest or my name might have been drawn out of a hat. 'Deserting to the front' is more a concern to those in the rear than those who are not and it probably cost me promotion—hardly issues to keep one awake at night. When 1st Wellington was waiting in the assembly trench on the morning of the seventh of June 1917 so was I.

And now we come to another of the fascinations war has for men: luck, and here I am talking of the luck that preparation allows you to take advantage of. In the darkness, on the other side, in the very early hours just prior to the attack, a changeover of garrisons was taking place. But there was more to it than that: the relieving troops were 'Eingreif' divisions, unfamiliar with the front line, truly in the dark.

At precisely 3.10 a.m. nineteen charges were blown from eleven shafts, the average charge containing twenty tons of explosive. The explosions were heard in London, and Lille thought it an earthquake. It was not just the mines: over two thousand artillery pieces fired. Whole garrisons went up and the survivors were blinded by dust saturating the early morning mist, making our men indistinguishable until they were upon the enemy. The Germans in their subsidiary lines, shelled until the last possible moment, were likewise unable to distinguish their own from ours. When the German artillery responded and shelled our assembly trenches, our troops were clear of them, advancing unaffected and able to pass through the wire unhindered. Because of the shell-pocked ground, however, tanks could not be used.

Men were lost but the advance was of a speed that enabled consolidation beyond the town at 5.20 a.m., to the minute of the appointed time. On the way, Wellington-West Coast distinguished itself by capturing a major strong point, one of the platoons being led by Jim. He was wounded soon after and I obliged by filling his place. (I had been leading a party of ammunition carriers and after sending them back for more, 'got lost'—they had a competent NCO.) I won't say Jim's boys were recalcitrant when I took over his platoon—Jim ran too tight a ship for anything like that to surface—but he had made them a homogeneous unit. I sent off his highly competent 2 i/c to round up stragglers—we were not fussy, among those roped in were a couple of 25th Division men and a chaplain's batman—and when he returned we had a handy little unit for clearing out a machine gun nest and turning it round to establish a useful forward strong point.

I suppose it served me right, but my arrival coincided with a German barrage on our new front line and at about 6 a.m. it increased, continuing for the rest of the morning and getting worse by afternoon. It did not help that the fine view we had over the enemy rear lines was at the price of them having a finer view of us. We were worked over thoroughly: the only purpose we fulfilled was offering ourselves as targets for Fritz. Another factor against us was that, with few exceptions, our staff officers, when mounting an attack, had a penchant for choosing German lines as objectives. The German artillery came to expect this, and having the ranges between those lines and their gun emplacements down to the last metre, shelled with accuracy. At 1.30 p.m. we received their first counter-attack but our artillery and machine gun barrages broke it up as Russell and Monash had said it would. If men had been pulled back as they wanted, hundreds of casualties would have been avoided.

Worse was to follow. The 4th Australians were not only thrashed by the German artillery but were also subjected to one of the most morale breaking experiences a soldier may suffer: 'friendly fire' by our guns who'd been informed they were the enemy — by Godley's staff it seems.

And while I remember it, what should appear riding well forward and exposed for all to see but three cavalry patrols from II Anzac Mounted Regiment, sent by Godley to reconnoitre. One could only commiserate as German artillery and machine guns made a shooting gallery of them. I don't know how many men got back, but we didn't see many horses heading in that direction. I enquired later, and as I feared, among those lost was my gallant steeplechaser. Three days later the mounteds were again sent forward, but this time, abandoning their cavalry pretences, they dismounted when shellfire targeted them, sent their horses to the rear, pushed forward on foot and, fighting as infantry, secured an outpost.

We lost Father McMenamin, killed by shellfire while performing the last rites. By mid-1917 I was finding it harder to comprehend how men who had dedicated themselves as servants of our Lord could belong to a military force. I had also noticed that too often they let the privileges of an officer's rank go to their heads, unaware that if they wanted respect amongst their parishioners, whether officer or man, they had to earn it. Father McMenamin was an honourable exception.

First Wellington lost over seventy killed and over three hundred wounded. All in all the Division lost three thousand seven hundred killed and wounded. Four hundred and thirty eight prisoners were taken, as were one howitzer, ten field guns, thirty-nine machine guns and thirteen trench mortars. Capture of field guns had been one of our aims and to some extent we were successful but the Germans got most of them out.

JIM
Messines

They took us out of the Somme in cattle trucks. The cattle had made themselves at home so we had a job to do. That was in Albert. It was famous for its Hanging Virgin. Fritz had hit the local church but not hard enough to knock her off her perch. The locals said the war would stop when she fell. We watched all day but she was still hanging when the train pulled out. Soaked to the skin, a wet floor, all night to go fifty miles, and a wet march to a barn, it wasn't much of a trip. In the morning half a dozen of us went for a swim. The lice died of the cold. Two days not doing much and it was another train ride, with three hours on the back of an open truck afterwards. We were dropped off outside Armentières and they gave us a schoolroom. It had a wooden floor, the best billet for weeks. Even better in the morning when we went off to the Divisional baths and were given clean underpants and a singlet by the laundry girls. We were in the raw and they laughed and said things in French. We didn't mind. They were the first women we'd seen for weeks. If they liked to measure us up, so much the better.

It was back to duck country again; only the navy could have got through. The front lines were only seventy yards apart but we didn't have much to worry about until our bright sparks in the rear sent up mortar teams that threw a sixty-pound bomb. Plum puddings they were called, because of their shape, not because they were liked. A team would come up, send over its bombs and clear out. We would get the retaliation. One of the first who got it was another old Gallipoli man. It went on like that for about a week. Then came the day when the Hun was waiting: retaliation before the team left. We would have been almost glad if we hadn't got it too and hadn't had to replace smashed parapets and pump out shell holes. We welcomed anything to take our minds off where we were, like when a hedge hopping Hun shot down a barrage balloon, an Archie shell burst around one of our planes and it kept on flying, and, what I saw only once, a plane shot down by a Hun gun.

On most days there was no flying. They issued a blanket, then a leather jerkin, a rain cape and thigh-high boots. Somebody must have got off his arse and come to have a look and then done something about it: unheard of. Dry socks every day too, and whale oil you had to rub your feet with so they could put you up on a charge if you got trench foot. When volunteers were called for raiding they had to hold back the crowd: got you a fortnight out of the trenches and to the rear to train. I thought they were idiots until three raids, one after another, were cancelled because of the weather. So I volunteered.

Whoever dreamt up our raid needs a medal all of his own. Four parties were going out to ambush Fritz. The lead would be a 'bait' party that would move along his front line. Its job would be to draw him to it so that when shots and shouts went up, the three other parties would rush in and ambush him. Two of the parties would be flanking the 'bait' party and keeping pace with it. One of the flank parties would be thirty yards inside Fritz's front line and the other flank party our side of it. Following the 'bait' party at a distance of thirty yards would be the 'Headquarters' party. All of this was to be done at night in the middle of winter in a shell-holed swamp.

The 'bait' party was led by a sergeant about to go to officer school. It was enough for me to be 2 i/c of the 'Headquarters' party. We had a rum issue and out we went. When the 'bait' party went into the German trench it was mud over their knees. The two flanking parties disappeared into the mist and sleet. Our turn came. When we weren't hauling our boots out of knee-high mud, we were sliding into shell holes. Slime soaked to the skin. Cold, never been so cold, none of us had. Not just into your bones, through them. This was January, remember, in France. Then time was up, no shouts, no shots. Back along the trench to wait and freeze. The 'bait' party came back: if Fritz had noticed them, he'd let them slosh around as long as they liked. Then the flankers turned up, and nothing there either. Just as well: we'd wrapped our weapons but they were filled with slime.

Back home they tried a debrief but the only message we had was that you can get so cold that you can't talk. They gave us rum; but not a word, just teeth chattering. It's bad enough for the army when there is nothing to report but it's a lot worse when nobody *can* report. Desperate measures were called for. The colonel brought out his whisky bottle. Looking us over, he fixed his eye on the sergeant who wanted to be an officer. Pouring a very healthy shot of whisky into a mug, he gave it to the sergeant. Down it went. Another shot, another nice swallow, and still another. Maybe the colonel felt sorry for the sergeant. If he did, doing him a favour was all he got out of it because with the rum and everything else the sergeant had to be led away, his teeth still going at it hammer and tongs. But there was nothing to speak about: Fritz held his front line as lightly as a flea. Other bright ideas about raiding were bandied around. One was to fire flares that would fall in front of Fritz's trench so he'd be blinded as you went for him. Another was to go in with machine guns firing over your head so Fritz wouldn't hear you.

We went into Brigade Reserve for a month. Our rest for the Somme. Better late than never. A winter holiday but not what you'd pay money for. Sometimes it snowed, mostly it rained, otherwise it was frost; there was drill in the mornings, sport in the afternoons. Some went on leave. One day we were lined along the edge of a road so General Haig could inspect us from his horse. We polished our brass for that, and before marching out, rolled and unrolled our greatcoats because the weather wouldn't keep to schedule. We didn't complain about being out of the line for Christmas. If you were inclined there were concerts, packed out every night, the pick of what the Division had to offer, with an orchestra that had played in picture theatres in civvy life. You could go into town or visit the farms where they'd turn on eggs and chips for a reasonable price. Coffee too, but Frank said it was chicory. We didn't care, it was warm and hot even if there wasn't any milk and you had to bring your own sugar. The beer was better than you'd expect; we were on the Belgian border where they know about beer.

Harry was back when we were in the line again. He was particular about whom he'd patrol with and sometimes he'd chat me up. He was the only one I'd go with if I had a choice. No rum before you went out with him. When we reported back, they'd give me his nip too, just to see the pain in his eyes.

Another night we had a fright. This time we were a party of four. Fritz sent flares up and they landed amongst us, close, burning magnesium, and took their time to go out. The man next to me was singed. If it had landed on him, everybody would have known about it. Another night one of our raids had a success: brought back three prisoners. It was well into February, frost and snow and, on that night, moonlight. When Fritz's retaliation came, it was one killed, two wounded. Snow and the frost gave working parties a break. Picks and shovels aren't much use when wet ground freezes. We had a sort of holiday but Harry dragged me out when I couldn't find an excuse. Clear nights, you could see where you were going, but had to be careful about tracks in the snow. Each time we'd report empty lines but the mortar teams still came up and the retaliation still came back. One day a Hun plane had a go at strafing Harry's trench. He went up on the parapet with his Mauser and took him on: two Spandaus against one Mauser and Harry, for all the world and every Hun to see; the Hun plane making three passes with the Spandaus and Harry getting one round off each time. I guess he hit the plane: six little holes, three in, three out. The Hun pilot might have had a job to fly low and hit Harry at the same time but Harry's platoon would have liked it better if the two of them had tried to settle their differences somewhere other than above their trench.

In the middle of March we heard about the Russian revolution. It made a bigger hit than the US declaring war. You'd be surprised at the people who were excited that the Tsar and his parasites had been got rid of. Russia might have been on our side but no one had much time for it. It fired us up. The top brass were worried that some of us might be thinking that our turn would come to prune a royal head or two.

At Messines: more hard work, not just trenches, railways and roads too. Everybody, including the Hun, knew why. Our guns sent over a lot and his sent a lot back. It didn't matter whether you were up front or back at a camp, you got it. But we went away for the Messines training; there were warm barns, cows below and us in the loft, ripe at times, but you can't have everything. The weather changed for the better and there was time for football. Harry and I fixed up an inter-platoon match. In my platoon there was a young fellow, not bad, but new and still not knocked into shape. He'd played rep rugby for Wanganui, I think. He played opposite Harry and before the game he told us what he'd do to him. Afterwards Harry said it had been 'hard but fair'. The new boy didn't say anything.

The new boys in Harry's platoon didn't know what to make of him. He'd crime anyone lighting a cigarette outside a funk hole. Neither would he let a rum jar anywhere near the trench when a patrol was going out and yet he'd always put in a word for lads who'd had too much when out on the town and hauled back by the red caps. The only inspection he bothered about was his men's weapons—where they'd be crimed double-quick if their rifles and Lewis guns weren't perfect—the rest he left to his sergeant. If a hymn was being sung or a prayer being said you'd know first off where to find him. But he couldn't have cared less about his boys playing two-up or Crown and Anchor. No one would give an infantryman credit, he said; the most a man could lose would be a fortnight's pay and officers gambled.

They had trouble with his batmen. You could be Harry's batman and never do a day's work and that's what happened at first. He felt sorry for the man, demeaning, he called it, although everyone else knew if you wanted a perk, batman was it. The company commander and the sergeant major got together and the CSM was made OC Harry's batman. If Harry didn't turn out nice and neat the batman was up before him. When 1st Wellington played 2nd Wellington guess who won it and who was the star for 1st Wellington. Then there was the Divisional gymkhana where Harry showed up our toffee-nosed Hawke's Bay and Rangitikei steeple chasers who'd belonged to this club and that club. Some time or other he'd mentioned he'd cleared fences when he'd been working for Godley; I never had the heart to tell him that the horse he rode carried a couple of quid of mine with one of our rear-echelon bookies.

At the start of June we were back at Messines handing in packs, cleaning weapons and, for those who fancied themselves at the game, sharpening bayonets. There was a church parade that finished just in time to see a Hun plane shot down. Good flying weather, really hot, took getting used to. Nice at first, but not when it's gas masks up. That's how it was when we marched up to the assembly positions; gas shells, sweat under the rubber, lungs working overtime and you're still half suffocated. Fritz had our range, HE and gas together: a dozen men down the drain.

After we hopped the bags it could have been worse. Things livened up on the edge of the town. A lot of craters with plenty of enemy in them. While it isn't nice, it's interesting to look back at how the boys took being on the attack again. Some kept my 2 i/c busy by looking for shell holes and a longer life, some went as they should, and some were carried away. A new boy quiet as a mouse, shot a German on his knees crying 'Kamerad, Kamerad' a couple of feet from the end of his bayonet and was ready to do another. One man turned round and bowled three on their way to the rear with their hands up. You stopped it when you could, and learnt whom you'd never send back with prisoners. Hun machine gunners who kept firing and raised their hands at the last minute had no show from anyone. Stretcher-bearers carried our wounded first. Prisoners were told off to carry stretchers, and it was our wounded before theirs. The surprise is not that some prisoners got shot but that more weren't.

They were firing a mixture of HE and shrapnel and it was shrapnel that went through my leg. As good a Blighty as you could get though I wondered at the time. It knocked me over and I couldn't get up. It was my 2 i/c who cut away the trouser leg and poured iodine into the hole and put one field dressing where the shrapnel went in and two where it came out. Then along came Harry. I asked what he was doing and he said he'd been Left Out of Battle. I didn't say he could have fooled me, I wasn't in the mood, but when he said he'd take over, I said the 2 i/c was OK. 'I'll give him a hand, then,' said Harry. 'But first I'll see to you.' A doctor was doing his rounds and Harry sent a man for him. The doctor said I'd need a stretcher. Harry had gone off but now he came back with a German. 'You'll wait forever for a stretcher but our friend here will get you to the

RAP. Won't you lad,' he said. The German didn't understand a word but nodded his head so fast it could have fallen off. He put his arm around my shoulders and I put mine around his and off we went.

His friends shelled all the way back but we were lucky. Every so often we had to stop for a rest. At one of these he had a look at my leg and put his own field dressing on. I asked his name. He showed me his paybook and it said Klaus somebody or other. At the RAP, after they'd replaced the field dressings and given injections for the pain and tetanus, I said I still wanted him. I couldn't do it by myself and a crowd was waiting for stretcher-bearers. It was late afternoon when we made the Advanced Dressing Station. The usual, a lot more lying out in the open than there were surgeons or ambulances. While I was waiting a shell burst and I was sliced across the cheek. Plenty of blood and it brought a doctor. When he'd patched it up and given more morphine, I asked him to write on my wound label that I needed the assistance of the German prisoner until an ambulance could take me. He said I'd risk a haemorrhage with the leg but when I said I'd chance that rather than hang around for when it was my turn for an ambulance, he wrote the note. After a cup of tea Klaus and I couldn't get away quick enough. A young Tommy had a tongue but no jaw, and when the doctor came up, he tried to salute.

Being summer, there was enough daylight to help us along the road to the Casualty Clearing Station. Heavy traffic was going both ways so we kept to the edge, taking it easy but not lingering. When the morphine wore off, we had to give it a rest now and then. I tried talking to Klaus and he tried with me. He mentioned some place he came from but I can't remember it. I didn't have pencil or paper and he didn't either. When I said I was a socialist, he understood and shook my hand. So there we were, two socialists in the middle of all that. The next time we rested a provost came up. 'You got a prisoner there, Sergeant.' 'Yeah,' I said. He read my label. By then we were spending as much time sitting as walking. A truck came along. He stepped onto the road and held up his hand. An officer sat next to the driver. The provost saluted and said he had a badly wounded man and a prisoner who needed to be taken back. The officer, whose uniform was the cleanest I'd seen that day, said they were full and told the driver to get moving. The next truck had no officer and there was no argument. The back was full of standing wounded, getting tired. I joined them and so did Klaus, the provost shoving him up.

It was a solid tyred truck on a dirt road and you felt every bump. We were packed in like sheep, but Klaus kept me upright. The other lads weren't at their best either, some made a noise about it, some didn't. At the Casualty Clearing Station the RAMC sergeant wanted to know what the hell Klaus was doing there and I said he'd saved my fucking life. The last sight I had of him was picking up a stretcher. I hope he got through the next thirty years.

MR BUTLER!

I gave myself three reasons to justify my application for a commission: a desire for respite in England; the wishful thought that the war might be over soon; and because Private John Sweeney was shot by a firing squad, disgust with 1ˢᵗ Otago. Regarding the latter, I am aware of the absurdity of my view when the millions killed are taken into account, especially as, at first sight, the reasons for Sweeney's execution were clear-cut: he had deserted after being ordered up to the line and had previous convictions for AWOL and drunkenness. On the other hand he had volunteered in 1914. A Tasmanian bushman, he had served with the Wellington Mounted Rifles until, prior to Gallipoli, he had been transferred to 1ˢᵗ Otago, and, because of previous mining experience, soon transferred to tunnel under Quinn's and Courtney's. Evacuated sick, he was sent back before he had recovered. He was evacuated again, to Egypt, to be in and out of hospital. We had been in Armentières a month before he rejoined 1ˢᵗ Otago. Rejoined is hardly the word: he'd barely been with us. Moreover he was in his thirties: OK for the Quartermaster's store but not for an infantryman. He disappeared when his company moved up. Six weeks later, when we were at Fricourt, they caught him. I was assigned to his guard and witnessed his court martial. John Sweeney did not get a fair hearing. One explanation might be that a serious court martial, for us at that stage of the war, was a novelty: another that everybody was preoccupied with what would be our most significant engagement since Gallipoli, and—I am sure of this—that nobody cared because Sweeney was unknown. Gallipoli was not mentioned—he told me about it in the guardroom. Neither did a 'friend' officially represent him, as was his right. Speaking for himself, he advanced an excuse that was obviously made up. Neither was he overly intelligent nor—equally significant—had his previous life in the mines and the bush done anying to familiarise him with the procedures of any court, let alone a military court. He, of anyone in the room, had the least idea of what he should and should not say.

The sentence for desertion was death and so it was passed. This is where Charters comes in. Like all commanding officers, Charters was required to comment on the sentence before it was sent up the command chain that ended with General Haig. Of the twenty-eight death sentences passed by New Zealand courts martial, Haig commuted all but five. As Haig sometimes commuted sentences even when commanding officers recommended they be carried out, Charters must have pressed very hard for John Sweeney's death. Moreover, Sweeney was not to be the only 1st Otago man to suffer the penalty: in 1918 another was shot. Of the rest of the Division, four infantry battalions out of twelve had one condemned man each, and among the several thousand other men who comprised the Division, there were none.

As was the custom, men from his own battalion shot John Sweeney at dawn. It was three days after we had been relieved on the Somme. We had been through the worst, and while they weren't enthusiastic about it, so far as the men were concerned, he was a shirker who'd tried to get out of what they and their dead mates had had to put up with. And who can blame them? Knowing I had been one of his guards, two approached me afterwards. The way he had faced them wasn't what they'd expected of a coward. Very thankful I had not been one of them, I told them about Quinn's proximity to the Turkish line and how tunnellers were likewise close to their counterparts, sometimes could hear them—each side out to blow the other or be blown.

What in our lives is burnt
In the fire of this?
The heart's dear granary?
That much we shall miss?

Three lives hath one life –
Iron, honey, gold.
The gold, the honey gone –
Left is the hard and cold.

Iron are our lives
Molten through our youth.
A burnt space through ripe fields
A fair mouth's broken tooth.

I didn't know those lines then; they are from Rosenberg's 'August 1914'. First Otago's discipline was not up to scratch. Transferred from the battalion of Malone and Hart to that of Moore and Charters, I noticed it. Moore's popularity had been due to slackness and Charters, inheriting a mishmash and low morale, set out to clean it up in the only way he knew. Perhaps one might boil down the purpose of the military as the application of controlled cruelty. That cannot be exercised without discipline, and discipline implies leadership and coordination as well as the multitudinous humiliations and irritations inflicted on the individual soldier. Charters was heavy on the latter and light on the former two. And, as I have seen so often in my profession, Charters the schoolteacher, as well as being a rules are rules man, knew how to single out a scapegoat for the discouragement of others.

So far as I know, after the Somme, the Division's court martial procedures were more closely monitored. Injustice was not eliminated, but let us not forget that all 'justice' administered by man is of the rough variety and that military justice has never been noted as a possible exception. First, there is the fact that there comes a time when every soldier, apart from the lunatic, dreads the moment when he must cross the start line. The major reason he keeps going is loyalty to comrades and fear of being shamed in front of them. Sometimes, however, this is not enough. The prime purpose of military training is to brutalise an otherwise normal man so that when ordered, he will kill another otherwise normal man, and will obey orders even when he knows obedience is likely to result in his own demise. From this it follows, as night follows day, that military punishment cannot be other than brutal.

No soldier liked guarding the prisoners at the Field Punishment Centre. Modelled on British and Canadian military prisons, its purpose was to convince inmates it was preferable to risk death than to return for a second dose. The inmates were the dregs of 1 NZEF and there was only one class below them; the NCOs who ran the camp. Volunteers all, they had untrammelled authority. I have a strong suspicion that the reason we were given our tours of duty at the FPC — each unit for about a week if I remember correctly — was to let us see for ourselves what happened to miscreants sent there. We saw, and we also saw NCOs who kept themselves out of the firing line.

Any hopes I might avoid winter at Armentières faded, although there was a brief break when a party of possible officers was sent to be interviewed by General Russell and Brigadier Johnston. 'He's a tough little bugger,' said one of the other interviewees of Russell. 'And intelligent,' I replied. In truth I had been overawed. The questions were crisp, to the point, and demanding of a prompt reply. He wanted men who could lead men, and if that entailed the demise of some or all, that was that, but good men were not to be wasted. Russell expected much of his officers. Of the ten VCs awarded under his command, not one was an officer. In the interview the military mask was close to enveloping; it was only later that I realised I had spoken to a man who was not unsympathetic to the young, and while possessing few illusions about humanity, still retained curiosity about it. Apart from a visage closely matching his collar tabs, Brigadier Johnston did not make an impression except, as I now see, to display openness with neither guile nor malice. Having no idea whether I had impressed the august gentlemen or not, I decided to settle down in the sergeants' mess.

Back at the Armentières front we dug and shovelled in rain alternating with frosts. The most notable event was when the officers' cook drank their whisky, passed out, the officers cooked their own dinner, and the cook woke up in the guardroom. The sick parades grew longer. When we came out on the shortest day of the year I was just capable of reporting sick. Admitted to a British army hospital, stripped and bathed and between clean sheets, I considered myself lucky. It was just as well I did not know where I would have gone if I hadn't gone sick. The same day, my name had been put on a list to depart immediately to join an Officer Cadet Battalion in England. They went off, did their course and instead of returning to France, were sent back to New Zealand to bring out reinforcements. After training and sailing back to England with them, the war was over.

In hospital I was diagnosed with a severe form of 'Trench Fever'. It might have been an early variant of the 1918 influenza and it was a month before it dissipated. I remember Christmas through gaps in the delirium. I was sent to a convalescent camp and halfway through the first week I persuaded the MO, or so it seemed, that I'd be better off taking leave. By the end of the week I was on a civilian express to Paris. At the Gare du Nord I was directed to the British Army and Navy Leave Club. Only when I woke up in the morning did it hit me I was in Paris. That it was mid-winter, the Parisian sky its not too uncommon dove-grey, the trees leafless, and the buildings greyer than the sky, was a matter of small moment. In no time I was in a café—as I was every morning after.

The Leave Club was near the Second Arrondissement and I soon noticed the more I advanced into it, the more stylish everything and everyone became. With one qualification: so many of the women were in mourning. One day I went to Versailles, and although impressed by the opulence, came away feeling that Robespierre might have had a point. I ranged from Montmartre to Chartres, recovering more energy each day, patronising cafés and if the opportunity offered, engaging myself in conversation with whoever happened to be occupying the next table.

A major regret during my visit to Paris was that the Louvre was closed. As a consequence I decided it would be another reason for returning to Paris if I were again afforded an opportunity to do so. So apart from architecture, I saw little art. I did, however, meet an artist. Early in the afternoon, on my second-to-last day, I was enjoying a Burgundy stew just off Boulevard St Germain after my curiosity had led me to wander around the Latin Quarter—by then I knew enough about Paris to be aware of its existence but I can't say I was able to see much of 'La Vie de Bohème' during my brief excursion. While I was tucking into the stew I was also keeping an eye open for anyone with whom I could further exercise my French—hoping to speak to someone who was neither soldier, sailor nor airman. At first it seemed that it would be easy. As with most such establishments, at that time of the day there was an air of jollity, not just because of the food or the prospect of it, but because all of us were warm, out of the wind and sleet, and enjoying what we had come to enjoy. Apart from the sprinkling of blue uniforms, there was no indication we were but seventy miles from shot and shell. It seemed, however, that I might be out of luck so far as conversation was concerned.

All the small tables were occupied either by married couples or lovers my own age. I envied them: if I wanted to have lunch with a girlfriend I would have to travel twelve thousand miles—conveniently forgetting that I now had no interest in the girl I had left behind, and that if I had the choice of being in Wellington or Paris and chose Wellington, it would have nothing to do with the quality of Paris. Closest to me was an elderly couple. When I tried to make eye contact with either of them, each looked past me. They also looked past each other. Nor did they speak. It seemed that whatever they might have wished to say to each other had been said years ago. At another table there was a family: a mother, two young children, and a young officer about my age. They had plenty to say—to each other. Indeed from what I could pick up, the officer had just come on leave. The children were revelling in being with their father: the happiness of their parents was combined with anxiety. Then a group of four caught my attention: two black-clad women and two French soldiers. They would not bear interruption either. They were working even harder than the family at having a good time. I wished I were sitting in the part of the restaurant where everybody was behaving as people normally do when they are eating out. Well into my meal, I noticed there was a young woman sitting at a table in a corner. At once I regretted I hadn't looked around more carefully before I was seated but then I noticed there were no other small tables near her.

Putting down my knife and fork I took a swallow of beaujolais and realised what had first drawn her to my attention: she was the only person neither eating nor drinking. She had a coffee cup in front of her but it was obvious it was there for form's sake. I next noticed her eyes, glancing up, focusing intently, and then looking down again before once more raising them up. As she was doing this, her right arm was also moving, swinging from right to left, back again and up and down. It took me a moment before I appreciated that she was drawing. Not quite surreptitiously, but near it. She was sitting well back from the table and resting on her lap was a board, not much bigger than what today we would call A3 size. It did not project very far above the tabletop. She was oblivious to everything except her subject. I tried to work out which person or group in the café she had chosen but that was not possible.

Finishing my meal, I contemplated her. Being a young, single, unattached male that was inevitable. Above her eyes, which were continually moving, were well-defined dark eyebrows and a broad creamy brow. A thick lock of black hair protruded from underneath her hat, which was black with a wide brim curved slightly up to the right and trimmed with a broad velvet band. Because of the tables of other diners between us, there was little else I could see of her apart from the moving black sleeve. By the time I had ordered coffee and drunk it, I had been there long enough. She was still drawing when I left the café.

I wandered around the rest of the afternoon taking in the tourist sights. It was becoming dark when I felt an inclination to read an English news-paper and surmising there'd be a fair chance they'd be for sale at the Gare du Nord, I took the Metro there. Trains had to be changed at the Gare St-Lazare. On an impulse I went up to the platforms in the hope there would be a newspaper there. I was lucky; there was one, *The Daily Telegraph*. Not what I normally read but good enough. And at a table, outside one of the buffets, was the woman I had seen in the café.

Given what I had been brought up to consider as acceptable behaviour of the time, I normally would have been diffident about addressing an obviously respectable young woman with whom I was not acquainted, but the next day I would be returning to Armentières.

'Good evening, Madame. I hope you have finished your picture.'

She regarded me almost as if I might be a possible subject.

'You are waiting for a train, Sir?'

I turned my head. Unlike what would be seen at the Gare du Nord at this time of day, there was only one khaki figure making his way to a train.

'Tomorrow,' I said.

'If you are not travelling tonight, why are you here?'

'This,' I picked up the *Telegraph*, 'and this,' I picked up the coffee.

Again a close examination.

'And you are waiting for a train?' I said.

'Yes,' she said, 'I am.'

'Do you mind if we talk until your train goes?'

She sipped her coffee.

'No.'

'Thank you,' I said.

There was a brief smile.

'I had hoped to visit the Louvre…' I said.

'It's the war,' she said, 'the war.'

'Yes,' I said, 'Paris is much closer to the Front than London.'

'You are from London?'

'No. But when I visited it, I went to their National Gallery.'

'What did you see?'

I reeled off some of the greats.

'Ah, so you find art interesting?'

I nearly said although I didn't know much about it I knew what I liked. Instead I told her I enjoyed going to galleries and that she was the first French artist I had met.

'What you saw me doing was just a sketch,' she said. 'I would not call it art.'

'No?'

She laughed.

'No.'

'If I knew how, I think I would draw people too.'

'Would you?' she laughed again. 'Then you must learn—and look closely at the great painters you have mentioned.'

'None of them are to be seen where I come from,' I said.

'Then, Sir, you must return to Paris—or London.'

'Here,' I said, 'I'll come back here.' I paused. 'Madame, would you have time for dinner?'

'No,' she said. But my face must have given me away because she added, 'when you came I was deciding whether I might see the ballet and take a later train.'

'So, you must like Degas, too,' I said, as much as anything to show I knew about him and what he painted. Meeting her eyes, I said, 'Would you let me take you to the ballet?'

'That is very kind of you, Sir, but at this hour, only cancelled seats will be available. Single perhaps, but two, no.'

'I can get seats,' I said.

'You?'

'The British Army and Navy Club, they have tickets for soldiers. Is the performance at L'Opéra?'

'Yes,' she said slowly, 'it is.'

'Then let us go.' I had no idea what her answer would be. I was going to add that the sooner we went the greater chance there was of getting tickets, but I didn't.

'Where is this club?'

'Hôtel Moderne, Place de la République.' I then said, 'It's civilised enough.'

She studied the table for what seemed a long time.

'Yes,' she eventually said. 'I will go.'

I stood up, so did she, and for the first time I was looking not just at her face with its broad brow and high cheekbones. She was wearing a black coat that extended to a few inches above her ankles. Hemlines were beginning to climb upwards but for 1917 hers was relatively high. The coat fell from her shoulders in a line that seemed straight but actually nipped in at the waist. Her coat, hat and shoes complemented each other. I wasn't looking at haute couture, but I found it easy to see her choosing her clothes with the same care she had exercised when drawing.

'One moment.' She disappeared with a largish package and when she came back she was without it.

'Let us go, Sir.'

On arriving at the hotel she sat in the lobby while I went into the billiard room. I couldn't see a Kiwi so I went up to an Australian sergeant and asked if he would come with me to the desk so each of us might obtain a ticket as they were allocated one for one.

'I need one for a friend,' I said.

'Sure, mate, where're we going?'

'Ballet,' I said.

'You're joking,' he said, 'You're bloody joking.'

'Not really,' I said.

He gave me the once over.

'Well,' he said, 'it takes all types…'

'I'll need a beer for this,' he said when he handed his over, 'in fact, I'll need two.'

'Done.' I slammed francs into his hand.

'Hey, I wasn't serious.'

'I am,' I said, 'and thanks again.' I turned and went across to her.

'All is forgiven, mate, all is forgiven.' The Aussie accent echoed.

'Who is he?' she said.

'An Australian,' I said.

It would be nice to say that we went to one of the great Diaghilev productions: but not at L'Opéra, not then. It was *Les Sylphides*, and the first ballet I'd seen. It was not a long performance and I asked if she had time for dinner. She said yes without hesitation and that she would choose the restaurant. Unsurprisingly it was a place I would never have picked myself.

'I will order,' she also said and after a while I found a plate of mussels in cream in front of me.

'OK?'

'Never had better.' Which was true.

'It is the cuisine of my home, Normandy.'

'So we might be related.'

'No!!'

'My father likes to claim our people came from Normandy. But I would not bet on it.' I sipped the chardonnay, which I had also asked her to choose.

'And the wine?'

'It's the greatest,' I said and thought of the cash I'd wasted on cheap champagne.

'I am glad to meet an Englishman who likes my country.'

'New Zealand,' I said, 'not England.'

'Pardon? You,' she shrugged her shoulders, 'you have an English uniform, and you speak English.'

'Yes,' I said, 'that's how it is. My grandparents are English. But who cares?'

She laughed, only the third time since we had met. I was enjoying her company and the give and take of conversation. Among other things we talked of Degas and I learnt that, although nearly blind, he was still alive — to die in September of that year, I later discovered. I also learnt I wouldn't have seen him in the Louvre — he sold well to private collectors but not to museums. It was talk a long way from what I had left behind in Wellington and quite different from my interlude with Hilda.

Then she looked up at the clock.

'I am sorry. My train. We must go.'

'Oh.' After a pause I said, 'Like Cinderella.'

'No,' she said.

Not being able to think of anything else to say, I called for the bill and we left.

Entering the Gare St-Lazare, she asked me to wait.

When she came back she was carrying the parcel and held it out.

'It is just a sketch.' Her brown eyes were fixed on mine and then she looked away. 'Your army has a postal service? Then if you wrap it carefully and send it to your family they will have this little memory of France.'

I held it in both hands. A whistle blew. Leaning forward, she placed a black-gloved hand on my cheek.

'From so far away.'

I was as slow walking back to the hotel as I was going to sleep.

I didn't open the parcel until morning, as it was she, not the drawing that was in my mind. When I opened it I saw the young officer's family. In the afternoon, as I boarded the train at the Gare du Nord, outside a station buffet, a British soldier and a French woman were in deep conversation.

When I returned, the two Otago battalions were in Reserve and in the evenings I made a point of going out with the boys rather than brooding on Paris. It took a long time for it to become just a memory, but to quote Robert Herrick, a seventeenth-century country vicar:

> When what is lov'd, is Present, love doth spring;
> But being absent, Love lies languishing.

We marched to Messines to relieve a couple of Irish regiments—each, whether north or south, leaving an equal residue of filth and collapsed earthworks. On the second to last day of March, around twelve noon, Hargest stopped me, the first time we'd exchanged words since the interview.

'Butler! Congratulations.' He shook my hand. 'You've been posted to an Officer Cadet Battalion. Today.'

The warmth with which he spoke surprised me.

'Today? Sir.'

'I said today. Your name's up at Battalion HQ. Get moving.'

'Yes Sir,' I said. 'Thank you, Sir.'

'Good luck, Butler. I know you won't let us down.'

My name was there, along with two others. Time of departure, 2 p.m. Two hours to clear everything and get my kit sorted out. Time to say a hasty goodbye to anyone I might come across, but no more than that. With a great rush we were sent off to a transit camp where we met up with nine others from the Division. Once there, any manifestation of haste disappeared. Thirteen days later we arrived at Cambridge.

Our residence was Trinity College. Some might have deemed our quarters on the austere side but sharing a sitting room with three others, a bathroom of our own, electric light and abundant coal for the open fire was luxury. On Sundays we went to Trinity chapel to hear their choir and the gardens were coming into full bloom of spring. The only reservation was that we were now on civilian rations and in 1917 England only the war profiteers were getting fat. We enjoyed the experience of dining at Trinity, but saw no reason not to enhance it by having someone, during the designated 'study period', slip out and come back laden with the products of a pie-maker. Nobody bothered, or dared, to enquire what was in the pies. Sleeping could be noisy as our dreams were not always free of experiences we would rather not have recalled.

When it came to leadership in the field we weren't instructed in much beyond platoon command; common sense, as the majority of the men I went through with, in one way or another, didn't see the war out. Sport, especially rugby, had a role. Physically fit instructors joined in and those who had lost an arm or a leg watched from the sidelines. If you played hard but not dirty, you were OK. As this was how we were coached at home, those from down-under didn't have a problem so long as close attention wasn't paid to what was, and what was not, dirty. I also tried rowing—which I hadn't bothered with before. Care was also exercised to ensure that we knew how to handle a knife and fork and when to be seen, and not to be seen, with a 'lady' etc. English public school mores were the standard. We had a great farewell dinner in Trinity's dining hall. Professors, grey haired gentlemen with untroubled brows, flanked each cadet. They drew on their cellar, which, after three years of war, still had a remarkable stock. Commencing with passing round a 'loving cup' of port whose age would have been little younger than the professors', we passed on to champagne, assiduously distributed. As good a piss-up as it's been my privilege to participate in. After the award of our parchment King's Commission, we had three weeks' leave facilitated by a first-class rail warrant. Before I took off on my first trip I went down to Walton to see Jim.

'Mr Butler!' The idiosyncratic use by the army of Mister, rather than Lieutenant, when addressing a subaltern would have been too good for him to pass by.

'As you were, Sergeant, as you were.' Whether or not I succeeded in hiding the self-consciousness of a new tailored uniform and a Sam Browne belt shining like lacquered mahogany and seeming to creak at just about every move, I don't know.

'As you bloody were, me old mate. How are you?'

'Glad you enquired. As they say a change is as good as a rest and I've had a rest as well as a change and,' I looked him up and down, 'you don't seem to be doing too badly.' Actually, while he wasn't doing badly, he needed a turn at doing well. When I had last met him on the trip to Cairo just over twelve months before, he had got over the Gallipoli illness, and helped by the Egyptian sun, no doubt, looked as well as any other young man. Now, although his wound had healed enough for him to walk with a stick, he looked as if he had a fair way to go before he was somewhere near the way he had been in Egypt. His eyes were tired, set in a face drawn tight. He was lively enough as we talked but I guess he would have wanted a rest after we parted.

'Yeah. Can't wait to get back and do my bit,' he said.

'You always were a king and country man.'

'Red, white and bloody blue, just look at me.' He was attired in the absurd outfit called 'Hospital Blues'; blue jacket and trousers, white shirt, red tie and, being 1 NZEF, topped by a khaki lemon-squeezer: all to send a message to any purveyor of alcoholic liquor that it would be a criminal offence to serve such a man.

'You look like you could do with a drink,' I said.

'Now what made you think that?'

'A cup of tea,' I said. 'A nice cup of tea.'

'I know just the place for it,' he said.

'Allow me.' I passed him his walking stick. If he hadn't brought it with him we couldn't have gone far.

The teashop people made him welcome and ignored the adulteration of their brew when I added the whisky that I had brought.

Jim sipped.

'Hm,' he said, 'officer quality.'

We chatted, he told me what he'd been doing, I told him what I'd been doing and then the talk moved into politics at home and abroad. Our war came up only when we enquired about the fate and condition of common acquaintances.

I heard a light step behind me.

'Hello,' said Jim. 'Fancy seeing you.'

'Well, well, our Sergeant Anarchist with an officer! How are the mighty fallen!'

It was my turn to look up and decide I would have noticed her anyway. Jim turned to me.

'This is Nelle. Harry's friend.'

'Sergeant!' Her reply was quick. 'I am acquainted with Harry, I like Harry, but I would not describe myself as a friend.'

'Nelle has lots of friends,' said Jim.

'I beg your pardon!'

'Any time,' said Jim with relish.

'And I certainly would never be your friend.'

'She's supposed to be a nurse,' said Jim. 'Being kind and caring for people.'

'Can you imagine anyone caring for him?' She was appealing to me and I liked it.

'No,' I said.

'There you are,' she said to Jim. 'Now you know what your so-called friends think of you. And you haven't introduced him. Too late! Some of us have better things to do. Goodbye Sergeant Anarchist's friend, I will leave you to his tender mercies.'

'Not like you to be on familiar terms with the bourgeoisie,' I said later.

'We've got something in common.'

'I can't wait to hear.'

'Came over in the same ship.'

'Shared the stokehold?'

'That would've been nice,' said Jim, 'but not quite.'

'She knows she wouldn't have got here if it wasn't for the sweat of your brow?'

'I mentioned it. She said first class was boring.'

'Tough luck,' I said.

'Yeah. Next time I'll ask her to do a swap.'

'She could organise for you. The boys'd come flocking in.'

'Her heart might not be in it. She was in Wellington during the trouble and Daddy joined the Cossacks.'

'He wasn't the only one,' I said.

'No, he wasn't, was he? Daddy's somewhere in France now — RAMC colonel.'

'She gives as good as she gets,' I said.

'You could say that.' He sipped his whisky tea. 'Harry was in her ward. Since then she's taken up driving. She comes from around Harry's way.'

'They knew each other?'

'Somehow I don't think so.'

'She's a nurse *and* a driver?'

'VAD.'

'Of course,' I said.

'She does her job and gets bugger all for it. They knew they were onto something when they saw her lot coming.'

'Well, sounds as though she can afford it.'

'The labourer is worthy of his hire, my Presbyterian friend. And,' he poured whisky into his teacup, 'don't forget, the fact that she and her pals are happy to work for the honour of king and country doesn't do much for her working-class sisters who could do the job just as well and need the money.'

'Point taken,' I said, 'but this particular one is very easy on the eye.'

'Just married, RFC.'

'May it be long and happy,' I said.

'Yeah,' said Jim.

I didn't see her in Walton again, despite moving there when I found it had a pub cheaper and better than where I'd been staying in London. I'd go out on a trip to somewhere interesting, come back, and meet up with Jim for whisky and tea and then go out again. Nelle wouldn't have crossed my mind even if she'd been available — the first place I had gone on coming down from Cambridge was to an art shop, where I got them to repack the

French café sketch for posting home. It was delivered in good shape and I still have it. Nevertheless, I did also wonder about Hilda. One night I poked my nose—with mixed motives, I guess—into the pub where I'd met her. At any rate I caught a glimpse of her and she was next to a young officer. I withdrew.

Jim and I went to the teashop the day before I left. After the tea was poured and the good stuff added, he produced a leather case.

'Here,' he said, and pushed it across.

I opened it and pulled out a beautiful pair of Zeiss binoculars.

'I won't ask where you got them, or how,' I said.

'No one seemed to want them,' he said.

'I'm sure,' I said.

'A mate brought them over with my kit. Otherwise they'd never have got here.'

They were small and could fit easily into a tunic pocket. Picking them up, I looked out the shop window to the other side of the street and then over the roofs into the sky and caught a bird flying. Their focus was crystal sharp.

'Nice,' I said as I put them back in the case.

'They're yours.'

'Eh!'

'They're yours. No use to me.'

'Worth a fortune.' Not quite—but they would bring him a lot of spending money and I could never afford anything like them.

'No use here. If I need a pair, I'll get them where I got those.'

He was determined.

'Make it a loan,' I said.

'OK,' he said, 'it's a loan.'

THIRD YPRES

Third Ypres was so called because it was the third battle since 1914 associated with the Belgian town of Ypres. It was fought from 31 July to 10 November 1917, in what was known as the Ypres Salient, where the British front line formed a half-circle that bulged into German territory. The salient, ten miles across and five miles at its deepest, was a vast expanse of shell-holed mud, rusted wire and water-soaked trenches. It was encircled on three sides by German defence works and overlooked by a continuation of the Messines Ridge called Passchendaele Ridge. Because of the salient's vulnerability to German fire, the only people who believed it was worth holding were the politically inclined—not an inch of allied ground to be willingly surrendered to the invader—and Haig. He, ever the cavalry optimist, saw the salient as providing an opportunity for a cavalry breakout once our artillery and infantry had breached the enemy defences.

When Messines fell, Plumer had an attack plan ready for the southern sector of the salient. If Haig had accepted it, Plumer's plan would have taken advantage of the relatively unblemished ground for bringing up matériel and men: favourable weather; the Germans being momentarily knocked off balance; and the momentum that had been created by that. Moreover a secure foothold would then have been captured for assaults that would have coincided with the dry summer weather that eventuated. If Plumer's plan had been implemented, it would have been the first step in a bite-and-hold offensive—which the Battle of Third Ypres turned out to be anyway.

But for Haig, fuddy-duddy old Plumer was not up to it. A dashing cavalryman was required: Gough. If one had ever spoken to an Australian who served under that general, he would tell of battles where they suffered thousands of casualties for minimal gains. General Currie would have resigned rather than serve under Gough. When Gough presented his plan to Haig, the Germans had re-established their defences. Thousands of lives were thus condemned to be lost to no purpose. Generals Petain and Foch were not greatly enamoured of Haig's plans. Petain believed them to be doomed, and Foch thought them futile, but—it is not difficult to visualise the Gallic shrug—if that was what Haig wanted, at least it would tie the Germans down.

Six weeks of excellent campaigning weather passed before Gough made his first attack. It was followed by a second. Getting nowhere fast, and with rain beginning to fall, Haig turned to Plumer. He tried bites and holds and didn't get far either—the advantages that would have come from an attack immediately after Messines having been dissipated. In seven weeks Haig's armies advanced three and a half miles overall at a cost of eighty-six thousand casualties. He pressed on. Eventually over forty divisions were to be thrown in. It was early October when the New Zealand Division took its turn—two months after the battle had commenced.

German engineers had built hundreds of concrete pillboxes and reinforced ruins of farm buildings around the Ypres Salient, their system being designed to suck the attackers in so that the farther they went the stronger defences they would have to face. German artillery was well camouflaged behind the ridgeline and their forward observers had a continuous view of the British positions. German infantry were reinforced, retrained and redeployed; the ratio being increased to twenty German divisions to thirty-four British. The advantage to the British was not as great as it seems, as it is a well-tried Staff College rule that attackers should outnumber defenders 3:1.

The weather was favourable for the New Zealanders' first attack, 4 October, and they gained their objectives. Then the rains came. Haig, however, resolved to press on and Godley, Russell and Monash, heartened by the 4 October success, wanted to repeat the victory at Messines. None appear to have reflected on the fact that Messines had been won by a combination of months of careful preparation, very heavy support from the mines and the artillery plus fine weather. Nor that the 4 October success had been greatly assisted by another coincidence: that the Germans themselves had deployed well forward to mount an attack on the morning of our attack and their deployed men were wiped out by our artillery.

On the eve of the 9 October attack, a press conference was held. One of those present came away with the feeling that our commanders were 'making a great bloody experiment—a huge gamble …'

In the New Zealand sector the English 49th Division attacked on 9 October. Because of the mud, not enough artillery could be brought up. Not a yard was gained. The generals persisted: there was to be another attack on 10 October to seize Bellevue Spur and Passchendaele Ridge. Russell, who normally would have gone forward to see the front line for himself, broke his own rule and never went beyond Spree Farm. From there the view of Bellevue is hazy in the best of weather and a rise called Gravenstafel Spur masks the ground leading up to it.

For the 12 October attack the New Zealand 2nd and 3rd (Rifle) Brigades were sent in—the latter after spending six weeks under fire digging and burying telephone cable with no rest or training for the assault beforehand. Brigadier Napier Johnston, the New Zealand Division's artillery commander, warned Russell and Godley that adequate artillery support would not be available. Afterwards Russell said: '…under no circumstances in war is one justified in assuming anything which can possibly be verified…' In other words, not only had he not gone forward to see for himself, but neither had he called for reports or sent trusted observers forward to report back. The best that might be said about this belated admission is that he made it. Godley never did.

Next it was the turn of the Canadians, our mentors prior to Messines. When General Currie heard of his Corps being transferred there, he protested and refused to attack until all preparatory work that might be done, was done. Haig, although never greatly caring for Currie's independent stance, acquiesced. Currie predicted the seizing of Passchendaele Ridge would cost his men sixteen thousand casualties. He was not quite right; it was fifteen thousand six hundred and thirty-four. In all, Haig's Battle of Third Ypres cost seventy thousand British dead and one hundred and seventy thousand wounded. And when the Germans mounted their offensive in 1918, the Ypres Salient was given up without a fight.

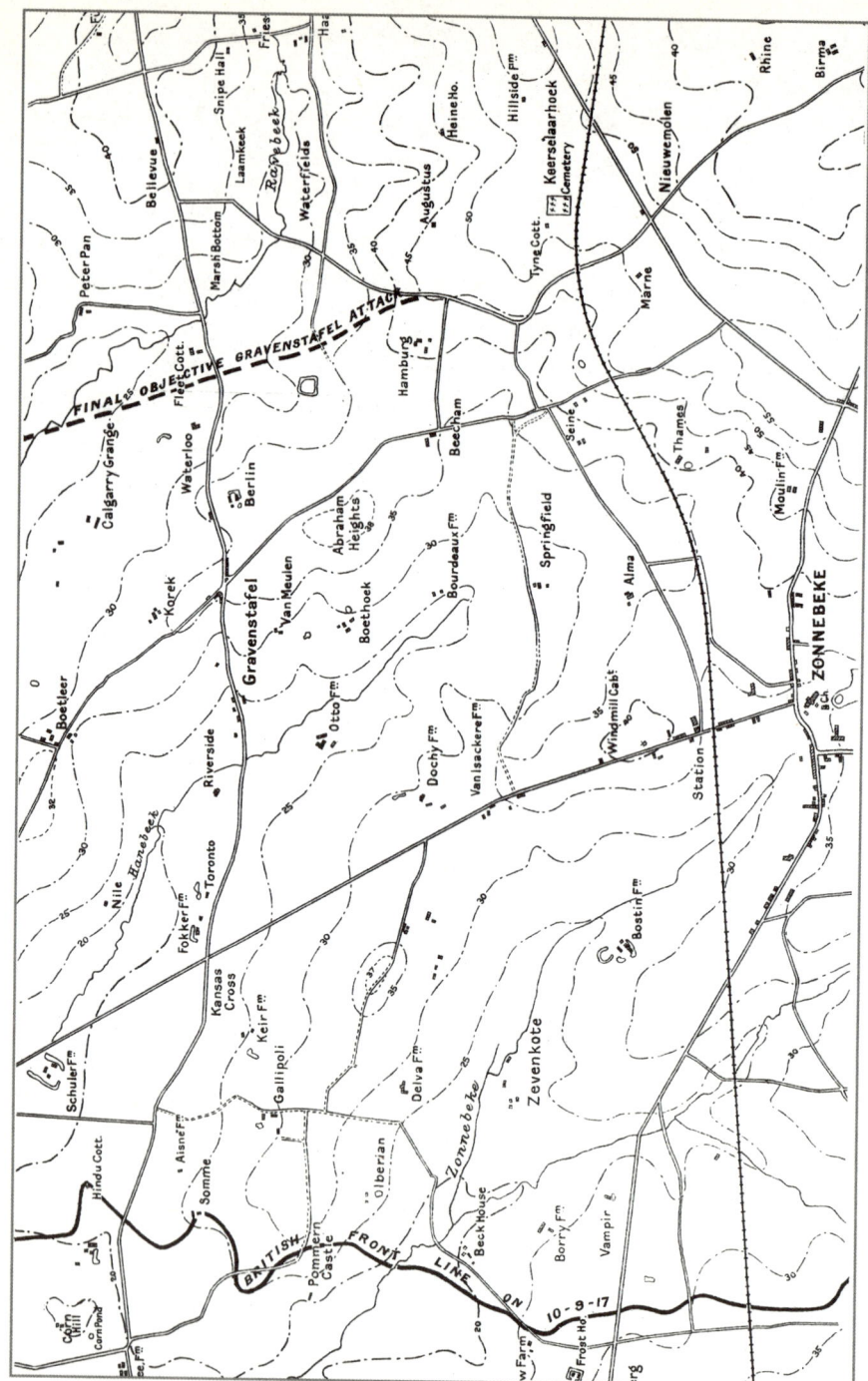

Passchendaele. *Source: Byrne, A.E.*

HARRY
Gravenstafel Spur and John

The most memorable event from when we were in the rear before joining the Battle of Third Ypres was being sent out in the fields to assist
the women folk, the old and the young with the harvest. It was a joy to
be doing real work in such pleasant company. Genuine friendships were
made and they were sad to see us go.

In the middle of September there was a Wellington Regiment church
parade. General Russell was in the congregation, and all were brushed up.
But, try as I might, I could not see how we, dressed for war, could claim to
worship a God of Love.

On a happier note, General Godley held a II Anzac horse show, graced
by the presence of Haig. When a senior officer, possessing a good hunter
and needing a rider, requested my services, I willingly obliged. My conditions were that the horse and I be given time to get know each other and
no competing on a Sunday. These were agreed to and mount and rider
became firm friends. He was a fine animal and deservedly won our event.
As a consequence I was, along with the proud owner, presented to none
other than the Commander-in-Chief.

'May I introduce Patterson, Sir,' said General Godley. 'Once my
orderly.'

'Indeed!'

'Then, Sir, he insisted on going off and distinguishing himself.'

'So I see!'

I suppose he was referring to the pair of ribbons on my chest.

Suddenly a hand was thrust forward.

'Mr Patterson, my congratulations.'

The grip was what you would expect of the man.

'More the horse than me, Sir,' I said.

'Yes, young man, you were given a good mount.' This time there was a smile, and I couldn't help but be surprised to see a twinkle in the eye.

'Sir!' I saluted and stepped back.

His arm swung in response as it had done a dozen times that day, in the days before, and would in the days to come, but the smile remained.

I mention the above meeting because it might show a side of Haig one hears little of; especially as he became the most argued-about general of the twentieth century. It might be that I had the luck to meet him when he was enjoying himself—but then, as he was a cavalryman it is not surprising he did, although I believe that golf was what he liked most. That was the only time I spoke to him but on two other occasions he, I, and about a hundred others, worshipped in the same church. As one who had attended church since birth I was generally able to sense who was in the congregation for appearance's sake and who was there to pay tribute to our Lord. I had no doubt that the Field Marshal was in the latter class.

I am now going to tell John's story. Too rarely are the stories of Johns told. One of the first conscripts, he joined us when we went into Messines and was posted to my platoon but, as you might remember, I was not leading it that day. When I returned, one of the first matters the sergeant raised was John—which was not his real name. Although he had gone over the top with everybody else, he was not there when the platoon dug in. He appeared at nightfall, saying he had got lost. Nothing much could be done other than sending him back to the rear under escort, or putting him under the close eye of a corporal and keeping him busy. As we had lost men, the latter was chosen. Nothing more untoward happened. I stated that John, while having an eye kept on him, should be treated neither better nor worse than anybody else and that when the opportunity offered, I would have a word with him. 'You won't have any trouble with that, Sir, he's one of your mob.' That is, he participated in the prayer meetings, Bible readings, and hymn singing of our Christian fellowship. Although I bided my time, I discreetly observed him. Under shellfire in the working parties after Messines he carried on like the other men. Neither did he show any signs of anxiety when we were out of the line in September.

On moving into the salient, and camping outside Poperinghe, I took an opportunity to visit Toc H. A remarkable institution, it was founded by 'Tubby' Clayton, a Church of England chaplain, as a sanctuary from the horrors of the salient. Talbot House, to give its full name (Toc being the army signallers' code for T) was a three-storey house acquired by the persuasive powers of Tubby. It was furnished for soldiers to pray, worship, relax, converse, drink endless cups of tea, and share meals in fellowship. Over the door of his office, Tubby had the house motto carved: All Rank Abandon Ye Who Enter Here. (Remarkable for an organisation connected with the British Army—or any army.) I made my first visit with Frank, where we caught up with each other and shared news of Jim. On this visit, however, I went up to the third floor, climbed a ladder, and went through a hatch to enter the attic where there was a tiny chapel under the rafters. I clambered in and whom should I see kneeling, but John. He made no sign of noticing me: nor did he when, having made my own devotions, I left. I went down to the sitting room and sat where I had a good view of the door, choosing an easy chair—then and now having perhaps too great a fondness for such furniture—with another beside it. When he paused in the doorway I called out.

'John!'

'Sir!'

'No rank here, thank goodness. You look like you could do with a cup of tea.'

He hesitated.

'I can recommend the seating.' I patted the empty chair next to me.

'Thank you …'

'Harry,' I said, 'or if you want to be formal, Patterson, or really formal, Mr Patterson, but that might be interpreted as recognition of rank. Better make it Harry, John.'

He walked across and when he came to the chair, perched on the edge.

I stood up.

'I'll fetch the tea.'

'But ...' he was getting up himself.

'No,' I said. 'Sit down. Rest your back, John, you'll benefit from it, believe me.'

I was glad to notice, when I returned and handed him a cup, he was putting the chair to its proper purpose.

It was not my intention to talk about what had happened at Messines within the walls of Toc H, but I could see no harm in showing he was in the presence of one who shared his Faith, and at the very least, was willing to present a sympathetic ear. He was shy at first so I led the conversation on matters that we had in common and general chitchat. Being joined for half an hour or so by a lieutenant from a Yorkshire regiment, who was no more interested in talking about the war than we were, helped to put John more at ease. When he departed, John said:

'Sir!'

'I beg your pardon, John.'

'Sorry... Harry.' This was the first time he had addressed me by any name since he had sat down.

'John?'

'If you have the time ... I'd like to speak to you about ... about something.'

'By all means, but first we'll have another cup of tea.'

When I returned he was again perched on the edge of his chair.

'Harry ... do you mind if we speak in private?'

'Of course not.' I settled back in my chair.

He looked around. There were others in the room, talking quietly, but if any had wanted to, they might have picked up our conversation.

'Would you rather speak outside?'

'Well ...'

'Come on.' I put my teacup down. Privately, I would rather have remained and drunk it in the comfort of the chair.

'We'll take a few turns around the square and then we might think of heading back to camp.'

'Sir …'

I was going to tell him, although we were now outside, there wasn't the urgency to resume formalities, but decided if he felt more comfortable that way, to leave him be.

'It'll only take a couple of minutes, Sir,' he said.

'I've plenty of time.'

I was still in my early twenties but knew even then that there are occasions when people speak more freely when walking side by side than sitting face to face: a perception that had come earlier than normal, perhaps, after being with men under long periods of stress.

'I have to tell you this…'

'Yes?'

'I should have before…'

'That's OK, John.'

Looking straight in front, he said: 'Sir, I'm scared.'

We continued walking. I had thought it was going to be this, but equally I was prepared for a confession he might be losing his Faith. After a while I said: 'So?'

'That's it, I'm scared.'

I'd heard that before the war Poperinghe had a population of eleven thousand and now, with the camps surrounding it, it had grown to a quarter of a million. Looking about, it appeared many of the additional populace were crammed into the square.

'I guess that you'll have to put me up on a charge.'

'What for?'

'Being scared.'

'Then I'd have to put the whole battalion up, including myself.'

'I am though, really scared.'

'Everybody's scared,' I said. 'Poor old Fritz, he's scared.'

There was a pause as we crossed a street, dodging horses, wagons, and too many men, and officers, worse for wear.

'I won't be able to face it, I know, next time we go up.'

'None of us will,' I said. 'Apart from the odd brute, there will not be a man who won't be hopping the bags without a dry mouth, a very, very dry mouth. Even,' I turned to him, 'fouling his trousers.'

'But they'll still go over.'

'No man likes appearing a coward in front of his fellows,' I said.

'They know I am. In the platoon, they don't say it but I can see it in their eyes. And the corporal, when anyone's needed for fatigues, it's always me first.'

'Is it because of the fatigues you are mentioning this?'

'No, no, and after Messines, I guess I deserve them. No, I'm not complaining or anything like that. It's that this time, I know I won't be able to leave the trench.'

'You must remember, John, and I cannot repeat it too often, that you are not alone. All, at some time or another, know fear.'

'But they get over it, like you.'

It was difficult not to laugh.

'John, sorry, but you really don't know me.'

'Everybody knows you, Sir. They talk about you — your patrolling, your medals and that you were a sniper on Gallipoli.'

'I wear these ribbons, John, because that is the rule in the army. I am not ashamed of them, but neither, I hope, am I vain. You talk about what everybody knows; well, everybody knows of men who never received medals and who've earned them twice over and those whose medals came up with the rations. Anyway, what did you say your problem is?'

'I freeze up and then, at Messines, I crawled into a hole.'

'First time up?'

'Yes, Sir.'

'War is terrible, John, and evil.'

'I can't go up again, Sir, I know I can't.'

'Why did you go to Toc H?'

'To pray.'

'For guidance?'

'Yes, Sir.'

'Would that other men did.'

'But it doesn't seem to have helped.'

'Have you prayed about it before?'

'No. I thought I might get over it, but now that we're going up again, I know I haven't.'

'How do you know?'

'I just know.'

'You might think you know, John. And seeing you have taken so long to seek our Lord's guidance, why do you expect such a quick response?' I let that sink in whilst we again dodged across another street leading into the square. Once we were on a footpath again I said: 'But perhaps He has, perhaps it is His wish we are speaking now.'

'Perhaps.' He walked on and then stopped and faced me. 'Sir, I'm a coward.'

The poor fellow!

'John!' I looked him in the eye. I nearly said I had yet to meet a coward, as most people understand it, and that if I did seek to find one I would look for one of those immaculate gentlemen in the rear, but that might have diverted him from the issue. 'John, if you are a coward, you're the first I've met who's admitted it, which makes me wonder if you're getting close to spiritual pride.' He looked surprised at this. 'Not the common or garden sort, which all of us, who have Faith, suffer from time to time, but, if you will forgive me for saying so, in a more perverse way. Rather than glorying in your Faith, you are glorying in your lack of it. Indeed you do not just lack faith in yourself, but in the Lord Himself.' I let us walk a good fifty yards in silence before I said: 'John, each one of us, at one time or another, whether in peace or in war, has to go over the top. Sometimes more than once and sometimes you, and I, and the good fellows in the platoon, might have to pass over earlier than we expected, but that, John, is what our Lord has chosen for us.'

Pausing, and face-to-face, I said to him. 'John, what have you and I to fear?' I don't know how many times we circled the centre of Poperinghe but it was more than two or three. 'Justice, John, the Ultimate Justice. And John, whilst it might be postponed, it cannot be avoided.' Again I stopped and faced him. 'For a Christian, there is no issue.' With that, I saw no point in discussing the matter further. I looked at my watch. 'Time we were getting back to camp. Tomorrow morning I shall instruct our good sergeant that you are to be posted beside me during the next few days. Although the brigade is not going forward yet, I warn you that I shall keep you busy. I will need a man I can trust and that man will be you. Now, let us talk of other matters.'

Wishing to gain an advance view of the ground, I had made an arrangement with my company commander to go up to the line the next day.

'Taking him under your wing?' remarked the sergeant in the morning.

'All he needs is encouragement.'

'And you'll keep him busy today?'

'He'll be OK,' I said.

And so it proved. On the way up and back I tested his map reading—which needed improvement. I also instructed him on how and what to judge from the sound of shells and that if you applied your knowledge carefully, you had a good chance of avoiding their immediate consequences, and just as important, when we had to crawl, to keep his head down while keeping an eye out. His ear and eye were not as quick as they might have been, but before the day was out he was getting the hang of it. The company commander and the CO were pleased with the sketches and notes, which, with John's help, I had compiled.

Unlike our training for Messines, our training for the seizure of Gravenstafel Spur was brief, hurried, and did not include work on a replica of the ground. A further disadvantage was that there was only one road up to the front line and along it thousands of troops and their matériel proceeded under bombardment. Shell riven, the battlefield was bleak, monotonous, and evil. Two low spurs, running off Passchendaele Ridge, lay in front of us. The nearest was Gravenstafel. Two miles northeast of it was Bellevue Spur. Mud made the ground impassable for tanks.

We went up to the line that night. Fine and clear, the weather, for the time being, was on our side. Before the sun was up, I seized an opportunity to reconnoitre the swamp that used to be the Hanebeek stream to find where crossings might be made. Then a cold wind from the east brought drizzle. As I said to John, as zero hour approaches, there are lots of dry mouths. It is a relief when the hour strikes. So much fear is anticipation and recollection. When I led the platoon, John was by my side.

There had been a break in the weather that had enabled our artillery to be brought up and sited at effective ranges. Half an hour before zero hour, the enemy fired a barrage but because we had moved up to our assembly positions we were untouched. When we went over the top our guns lit the horizon behind us with all the colours of the rainbow. The light from flares and shellfire revealed German infantry blown into grotesque attitudes, the few survivors weakly raising their hands. Any attempting to resist were quickly dealt with. Soon we came upon massed dead and wounded. The enemy himself was to mount an attack. Like us, he had not wished to advertise his intentions.

As the sky lightened I oversaw the suppression of a pillbox, its garrison firing at us through its loopholes to full advantage. The Lewis gun section dropped into a shell hole, the Number One firing bursts at the loopholes; the Number Two beside him, replacing the pan magazines as they were expended, and other men preparing more pans for use. The Number Two was the first hit; his brains coming out the back of his head, and immediately the Number Three replaced him. Riflemen also set their sights on the loopholes. Meanwhile, rifle grenadiers, 'bombers' and other riflemen were using the Lewis and other fire as cover to outflank the pillbox, but in doing so they knew that on the flanks were other pillboxes, looking out for them and not just pillboxes, defended shell holes too. I looked hard at the pillbox and saw ground to the right of it that looked disturbed not by shells, but a spade. Sure enough I saw a rifle flash. Rifle grenadiers and riflemen were detailed to fire at it until they saw a party rush it, being led, all things going well, by yours truly. One crawled with one's nose millimetres above the foulest mud, edging around one hole to the next and slopping through slush like a crocodile, some dragging rifles, bolts wrapped against the mud, and others with grenades and pistols because we were to be within grenade and pistol range, indeed within bayonet range. The riflemen fixed their bayonets, we threw grenades, rushed, and the hole was ours, its original occupants dead or horribly maimed. Lucky us, all according to plan, textbook stuff, easier to tell than to do, a different story if our party had been spotted.

Now the pillbox, proof against all but the very remote possibility of being hit by all but the heaviest shell, but we had brought ourselves up to the head of the sap that led to its vulnerable rear entrance. We dashed along the sap; out from the pillbox came a German to be bayoneted and instantly, grenades, timed to the second, were tossed in, the throwers springing aside from the entrance to explosions within. Lucky were the occupants who were killed outright. John peered in and vomited. On to the next pillbox, this time the garrison surrendered, but not before poor John was hit in the chest and flung back into the mud. As the Germans came out with their hands up, a man beside me raised his rifle, 'They shot John, the b_____s!' I yelled 'No!' and knocked the rifle down. The prisoners approached, grey faced, stumbling, begging, and we waved them past, someone else could care for them. I bent down to John. Mercifully his passing from this world had been speedy. I took his pay-book and pocket Testament.

The most horrible event of the day happened in a pillbox on our right flank, the largest of a cluster of three. Parties took them out by advancing under our creeping barrage—a tactic, understandably, many were reluctant to employ—and then tossing grenades through the entrances. The sergeant leading the attack entered the large pillbox to see shredded flesh and blood across walls and ceiling and about thirty men dead or bleeding from eyes, ears and noses. Noticing an entrance to an inner chamber, he rushed in—it must have been a command post, with desks, shelves, and paper—to glimpse a German officer throw a lighted match at a desk soaked with an inflammable liquid, and a sheet of flame flare up and out to the larger room. The sergeant managed to get out. We heard the men inside. For the rest of the morning sickly black smoke emanated from it.

With great confidence 1st Wellington advanced to consolidate positions on Gravenstafel Spur. The afternoon was quiet, indeed there was an unofficial truce where each side collected casualties—we could see the field-grey stretcher-bearers on the slopes of Bellevue. When what passed for daylight faded, with rain and shelling it became another miserable night in a war of miserable nights. Our cover was so meagre we had to fall to our hands and knees. When the shelling tailed off we heard the inevitable cries for stretcher-bearers but all that could be done was share our precious water with the wounded, wrap them in a ground sheet and leave them to bear their pain, hoping their cries did not, for our sake as well as theirs, last too long.

We were there all the next day and so was the rain. Ration and ammunition parties came up, and along with them, stretcher-bearers and engineers. But it was the food we were most interested in. We weren't expecting much and we were not disappointed: bully beef and biscuit, the latter with reddish-brown splashes that, on closer examination turned out to be blood. Telling ourselves it must be from a horse or a mule, we bit into it. Mud matted our hair, caked on our faces, noses and eyes. When, that evening, we retuned to the rear, the only way to rid our uniforms of it was to scrape them with a bayonet. I made time, however, to write to John's mother, enclosing his pocket Testament. My letter was sincere, but not what I would write now. One sentiment would remain unchanged: the privilege of having known a brave man.

The rain continued and before we knew it they had sent us up to lay telephone lines. Nevertheless, feeling the elation of having survived and won, we felt pleased with ourselves.

FRANK
Bellevue

I don't want to be a soldier,
I don't want to go to war.
I'd rather stay at home,
Around the streets to roam,
And live on the earnings of a well-paid whore.
I don't want a bayonet up my arsehole,
I don't want my ballocks shot away.
I'd rather stay in England,
In merry, merry England
And fuck my bloody life away.

And so said all of us—not just the British Tommies, who sang it out of the hearing of those who hadn't 'authorised' it. Before boarding the leave train, I purchased thick woollen underwear, a superior quality groundsheet, and wire cutters with hardened blades. Aware I would be new, and junior, in whatever Mess I would be returning to, I took the precaution of also buying a hamper of fruitcake, chocolate, and whisky. I had put in for a transfer to the Field Ambulance, but when I reached the Divisional training area, I was disappointed to learn I was returning to my previous battalion. This was unusual; new officers were rarely returned to units where they had been rankers: familiarity breeds contempt. I was in a different company however. In my absence, Hargest had been promoted to Major and 2 i/c of the battalion. In the Mess that night, he greeted me abruptly and moved on; a new subaltern is at the bottom of the pile.

The day after, Brigadier Braithwaite, CO 2nd Brigade, descended unannounced and inspected the battalion. Unimpressed, he slated officers and men. The consequence was our company commander, Major Tracy, criming the men wholesale and me being welcomed with the remark that my platoon was slack and I was expected to fix it, now. Two days later, Brigadier Braithwaite appeared again, but this time, no comment. Afterwards there was an inter-company rugby match that we won six nil. I'd taken the place of a wing who'd gone sick and in the Mess that night Major Tracy actually spoke to me.

But I wasn't at my best; fatalism can take you only so far. I slept fitfully and became irritable and worse. An example of the short temper: on a hot day, during manoeuvres, I saw a man drinking from a creek, which was forbidden unless permission had been granted beforehand, as we had to learn to conserve drinking water and you drank only what had been tested. When I ordered him to be put under open arrest, his corporal protested that no orders had been issued about water. I had already sized up the corporal as someone with brains, a sense of humour, and not afraid to speak out: the sort of man who, if I'd been in the ranks, I would have liked. The sensible thing would have been to enquire of the sergeant when the men had been instructed about water. If I had, I would have learnt the answer was none who'd been posted to the battalion since Messines. Instead, unabashedly, I ordered the corporal to be put under open arrest 'for neglect of duty by failing to acquaint himself with orders'. I partially came to my senses when Tracy said he had lectured the corporal severely before dismissing the case. 'I'm glad you've taken me at my word, Butler,' he said. 'You'll find the corporal a good man, good enough to be battalion marker. And now that he and the men know where they stand with you, you should have the makings of a first-rate platoon.' Many years later the corporal and I met. He had become a prominent lawyer and was on his way to the bench. He remembered me but it took him a moment to remember the incident; when he did he had the grace to laugh. 'The catch all of all catch alls,' he said. 'We called you The Teacher.'

On a September morning we moved up to a camp outside Poperinghe, where I met up with Harry. He said he had somewhere to take me. I visualised repairing to a decent café and partaking of real coffee and fresh pastries but instead it was a visit to Toc H. That sort of thing was no longer my cup of tea, and it was tea, of the canteen variety, which we drank. Never mind, that was Harry, and we had a good couple of hours over the overdrawn beverage exchanging news from home, bringing him up to date on Jim, etc. He had to return early, so, after we parted, I paused to look across the town square for a restaurant that might turn up a decent dinner that would not be eggs and chips and at not too outrageous a price.

'Butler!'

I was surprised. It was Major Hargest. Only the night before the Mess had farewelled him at a stag party. Today he was supposed to be on a train to be married in England and then off to attend a senior officers' course at Aldershot. That's how things in wartime operated: your battalion might be about to go into battle but if you're down for something like a senior officers' course, off you go. As for wartime marriages: you fitted them in when you could.

'Bloody train,' he said. 'Three hour delay.'

I commiserated.

'And what are you doing here?'

'Looking for a decent meal, Sir.'

'You don't know this town?'

'No, Sir.'

'Time you did.'

'I guess that'll come.'

'And no time like the present.'

He turned and I turned with him. Who was I to argue with a major on his way to a higher officers' course?

'No one else from the battalion in town?'

'The march. Time for a rest, I guess,' I said. 'And the party ...'

'Can't take it, eh! Not like us Gallipoli men.' He grinned. 'Ah, here we are.' He went through an entrance from which loud talk and laughter emanated and the smoke hit you like a wall. It was the notorious Skindles, purveyor of alcoholic and spiritous liquors to holders of the King's Commission unfortunate enough to be posted to the Ypres Salient, and, for same, access to accommodating young ladies with a business sense. As the room was crowded with tables that were equally crowded, it was fortunate that a young lady, and her current companion, rose from a table for two as we entered.

'No, dear,' said Hargest to one of her colleagues. 'As for the lieutenant, he doesn't want to be bothered. Not now.' The waiter, however, was welcomed and sent off for a couple of Scotches, doubles. He noticed me looking around. 'Not that I know this place well,' he said. 'Not at all. Indeed I know it hardly at all and certainly won't be entering it again.' A nod in the direction of the woman he had turned away. 'Not for that, anyway.' The homily was presented in such a severe and solemn tone, and the accompanying frown so pronounced, that I could not believe a word of it. Until then I had not seen past the hard man, the intrepid patroller and raider who would be first on the CO's list, if the CO wanted something done, and who, if he hadn't been an officer in Russell's division, would have been a VC for sure. But now, as I took a good look at the full lips, the knowing eyes, the chubby countenance, I had to work hard not to laugh out loud.

As one does not laugh at a superior officer unless encouragement has been indicated, I took in our surroundings. What had recently been a dining room of a dowdy provincial Belgian hotel had become a Wild West saloon crammed with officers of about every regiment in the salient. All, whoever they were, behaved as if there was no tomorrow, as indeed, for many, there wouldn't be. The menu was likewise adapted to the clientele: eggs and chips, or, for those who were flush, steak and 'French' mustard. Through the fug of smoke where the lights shone dimly, the occasional woman was discernable.

'No shortage of well-heeled customers, Sir.' Guards and cavalry were evident.

'Not cheap, no, but you get what you pay for.'

The whisky arrived.

'Cheers!' We drank. 'Well, how do you like being an officer?'

'Getting used to it, Sir.' Our conversation was at half-shout.

'Major Tracy speaks well of you. Told you to get stuck in and you did. The advantage of having been an NCO. Served me well too. I wasn't commissioned until the war. Mounteds in those days — served with them on the Peninsula till I got it on the eighth of August. We could have done it you know, if better men had relieved us. Bad business. A sideshow though; here's where the war's being fought. They gave me a trip home. Wanted to keep me there. Nice to see my mum and all that, but nothing doing, not for me. Able to work it to get back to Egypt and a transfer to the infantry.' He pushed a packet of cigarettes in my direction. I didn't usually, but it wasn't every day that a lowly lieutenant finds himself tête-à-tête with a colonel-to-be. And, as with so many with energy to spare and the gift of the gab, Hargest was great pub company.

He pushed The Scotch glasses were empty so I ordered two more.

He puffed his cigarette. I did too and coughed.

'You took your time coming back,' he said.

'Once they had us moving, they weren't in a hurry. Nor to send us back.'

'Good leave?'

'Haven't had a bad one, Sir.'

'Lots of girls, bright lights, all the trimmings?'

'Not too bad.' While I didn't have an interlude like the one with Hilda, nor the frisson of the encounter in Paris, all things considered it wasn't too bad a leave.

'Make the most of it, lad, you only live once.'

As I have mentioned, Hargest wasn't all that older than me — maybe two years, three at the most. 'Yes,' I said. If he was issuing an invitation to enlarge on my leaves, I didn't take it up. It was years before I explained the Paris café sketch other than by stating it came from Paris; and as for Hilda, it was even longer before I so much as mentioned her.

'And this course you were on, they taught you to knock the Hun for a six?' He lit another cigarette.

'Helped my rugby.'

'Ha, ha, good to know you got something out of it.' He drank and so did I.

'How they teach war at a university, I don't know, but then, I'm straight off the farm.'

'Many of our instructors, Sir,' I said, 'were there because of their wounds.'

'Poor blighters.' A sip of the whisky and a moment of reflection as he looked into his glass. 'OK Butler, you're an officer now. You don't have to be the best soldier in your unit, though it helps, don't let anyone fool you about that, but these days we have to settle for what we've got.' Here I received a look that might be described as 'searching'. Toying with his glass he continued, 'It's knowing what to do with the best soldiers that counts. Sort out who they are, use them for what they're good at, and look after them. You mightn't like them but some of the worst reprobates I know are just what you need when the chips are down. But don't let them get away with anything so far as *you're* concerned. You lose their respect; you've lost them for good. And that goes for all of them. Once respect is lost, you may as well pack up and go home.'

I saw no point in mentioning that packing up and going home might not be an unattractive alternative.

He took another swallow of whisky and this time put down the glass firmly. Leaning forward, he said, 'Gain their respect and hold it, Butler. That means getting out in front. If you go forward and they're not behind you, that'll be your fault and, nine times out of ten, it'll be too late to fix it. That's where respect comes in. There are some unhealthy places out there and they have to know that while you might not be the best soldier, you'll go forward if it has to be done. At the same time don't be bloody stupid; if you are you'll be out on your own no matter what.'

I couldn't fault his opinion on that.

He focused his eyes on mine, the whisky and a smouldering cigarette ignored. 'You'll be going up to the line in a couple of days and when you're there, patrol. Any officer who doesn't know what's in front of him, isn't worth his salt.' Lifting up his glass he swallowed what was left and I ordered two more whiskies. 'I learnt that on the Peninsula. Great days.'

A novel view of the Peninsula.

'You've got to know what's out there, Butler, and no one can tell you better than yourself, but take a good man with you. And don't forget to let Fritz know who's boss. In no time, when you want to know what's going on, you can wander out and see for yourself.'

'I don't know about wandering, Sir.'

'What?' He shot back his chair and laughed. 'You know, Butler,' he said ruminatively, 'if you get through the next lot, you might have a future.'

I was happy to be reassured.

'Don't take offence, Butler,' he was kindness itself, 'you've been through as much as any man, more than most when you come to think of it, but I can see you as an adjutant. I've done it, and not too badly I might add, but not really my cup of tea. You though, might be the man for it.'

'That's a few rungs up the ladder, Sir.' He was speaking of the position held by the officer who does the administrative work for his CO. When things go wrong he tends to get the blame and when they don't, either no one notices or the CO is complimented. I ordered two more whiskies. 'Some time away yet,' I added.

'Who knows how long the war'll go on.' It was a statement rather than a question.

The waiter returned. We were getting lightning service.

Summing up as much enthusiasm as I could muster, I said it could go on for quite a while.

'Exactly. Now that the Hun has finished the Russians, everything'll be turned on us. The Americans are taking their time, the French are having a rest, so, for you and me, it's lively times ahead.'

'Gets a bit tiring, Sir, now and then.'

'In ten years,' he said, 'we'll look back on it as the best time of our lives.'

I didn't comment that they might be the last years of our lives. Instead we chatted about this and that and drank more whisky until he looked at his watch and announced he had to go.

'Good luck, Butler,' he said, putting some cash on the table and holding out his hand. 'And,' this time there was a grin, 'don't do anything I wouldn't do.'

No hope of that. He'd left more than his share, but after paying the balance, no eating out for me, not even eggs and chips.

The day before we went up, I joined the party of officers to examine maps and view a model of where we were to attack; it was the first time we were supplied with any direct information about the ground and its defences. I also called on the quartermaster sergeant and acquired a private's uniform for the front. Changing into the heavy underwear I had purchased, I added a thick cardigan I had just received from one of my parent's neighbours. The wire cutters, groundsheet, and binoculars were a given. On 11 October we marched to the sound of the guns.

The objective was the seizure of Passchendaele Ridge. Second Otago Battalion would advance to the crest of Bellevue Spur and we would leapfrog them to advance to the ridge. We had a long way to go, because, as the 49th Division went nowhere, generals simply added their objectives onto ours.

Trucks took us as far as they could and after that it was a five and a half hour slog. At about 3 a.m. we took up a position behind 2nd Otago, on the lee of Abraham Heights, the highest point of Gravenstafel Spur. The 49th Division had no desire to linger. No one likes to hang around, but with them one sensed something different. After they had left, and sentries posted, we tried, as best as we could, to settle in. It was between gaps in the shelling that we heard the chilling sounds made by wounded: men the 49th Division had abandoned.

In the dark there was nothing we could do, except to hope that those for whom there was no hope would go quickly, that daylight would come soon for the rest, and wonder what might be in store for us. With dawn they were visible but we could do little except share food and water, put to work our regimental stretcher-bearers, and send back signals that Field Ambulance men would have to come up. They did and with our men worked hard, but by the end of the day not all were brought in. Those who could be reached, had their wounds dressed, were fed and given water. Exposed to the elements, they were in the line of our coming attack. After dark, medical personnel worked until the latest hour. They were exhausted and, like us, after a night in the cold, the wet, and the rain, would be expected to continue their duties when the attack went in. Who would be in a fit state to look after us? In my mind I could hear the last verse of a Tommy marching song; its singing being much discouraged by senior officers:

If you want to find the old battalion,
I know where they are, I know where they are.
If you want to find the old battalion,
I know where they are,
They're hanging on the old barbed wire.
I've seen 'em, I've seen 'em,
Hanging on the old barbed wire,
I've seen 'em, I've seen 'em,
Hanging on the old barbed wire.

The words and the tune kept repeating themselves. Wherever one looked there was nothing but undulations of mud and the detritus of war. Mile after mile of Belgium had been churned and blended with unexploded shells, tangled wire and human remains. Shell holes overlapped with broken and slippery duckboards meandering between. Because of the high water table and shattered streambeds, foul black liquid lapped high up in the shell holes with viscous mud that sucked men under. Blown out of the ground, and mingled with bloated corpses of the current battle, were the blackened bones and mouldering boots of 1914 and 1915.

During the night, Dick Travis (who by then had a DCM but was yet to earn his VC and MM) and his 2nd Otago scouts, had penetrated the German lines and reported there were at least six intact pillboxes, unbroken wire, and manned earthworks. A request was sent back for a barrage to deal with it. No response.

In the late afternoon I took Jim's binoculars to the crest of Abraham Heights and viewed Bellevue Spur in the rays of the setting sun. Shelling had created a morass out of the stream between Abraham Heights and Bellevue Spur. Aptly named Marsh Bottom, it was as good as a moat. Bellevue rose from Marsh Bottom to a small plateau. Under its brow were entanglements that looked as solid as a wall and trenches. Identifying one pillbox after another, I concluded that a more objective frame of mind than mine might have complimented the German Army on its professionalism. Dusk fell at 6 p.m. and we moved to dig in on the forward slope of Abraham Heights. Heavy drizzle began.

We had been told there was to be a barrage that would open large gaps in the wire and knock the pillboxes about. But, on the morning of 12 October 1917, it failed to deliver; indeed it did a good job on 2nd Otago, men being blown sky-high. The enemy retaliation was swift and heavy. At dawn, 2nd Otago, falling quickly, advanced to thick wire and unmarked pillboxes.

Overcome by an intense and deep detestation of the pig-ignorance and stupidity of those who had put us where we were, I leapt, yelled, and swore.

'Sir! Sir!' It was the corporal.

I flopped down.

'You were rather exposed there.' He managed a grin. 'Something upset you?'

'Not at all.' Our eyes met. Then, turning my head, I saw the last of 2nd Otago about to cross Marsh Bottom. 'Where's the sergeant?'

'I'll fetch him.'

'Do that.'

'Here, Sir.' He was an experienced NCO; I was lucky to have him.

'Gather the men. Don't waste time, get who you can, and bring up the rear. Corporal, I want your section behind me and you behind it.'

If I had decided to withdraw we would still have been under fire; I would have faced a court-martial and the men would have just been sent forward again. The least bad choice was to keep going. Somewhere under the brow of Bellevue there might be a shell hole that hadn't been there when the Germans had built their defences. There was a chance—but I wasn't banking on it—that we might meet up with a 2nd Otago unit, and together take out a pillbox and shelter in it.

Early in the morning, 2nd Otago had put a duckboard bridge across Marsh Bottom. Though broken here and there it supported us. Some took their chances staying behind. I had thought of them, but hadn't wanted to risk the sergeant mustering them. And I had decided that, whatever decisions they might make, they couldn't be worse than those made by red-tabbed gentlemen safely in the rear. Indeed once at the foot of Bellevue I was surprised at the number still with us, though one no longer had an elbow and another was there because his mates had caught him as he was hit and kept from drowning. And I was glad to see the Lewis gunner and his weapon, along with the rifle grenadiers. Though, with all the slime around, I wasn't overly optimistic about the Lewis. We cowered in the shallow ditches on each side of what remained of the Bellevue length of the Ypres-Gravenstafel-Passchendaele road.

Taking a slight curve to the right it ran up and over the brow. Its regular gradient, though recently shelled, ironed out the usual bumps in the landscape so that the pillbox on the brow had a clear field of fire down it. For the time being, so long as we kept our heads down, on our side of the road where rain had deepened the ditch, we were in dead ground. But the men on the other side of the road were sniped; the man who had been saved from drowning hit again, this time for good.

The only 2nd Otagos we met were dead. Normally — if there were such a thing as normality on a battlefield — we would have dug in, but on the edge of Marsh Bottom, half the depth of a spade would take us into mush. Sliding to the left, I saw clear ground covered by a pillbox. I wondered, if we deployed properly, whether we might take it out but changed my mind when I looked up the slope and saw another pillbox covered its approaches. Rolling over, I looked right. An empty shallow trench ran parallel with the edge of Marsh Bottom. It too was covered from above but it had a low parapet, not bullet proof, but high enough to mask anybody crawling below its reverse side. Beyond the trench was the pivotal pillbox at the eastern extremity of Bellevue. Between it and us was a thick band of concertina wire. To ensure better protection of the pillbox the German field engineers had extended bands of wire to make an enclosed rectangle in front of it, about the size a of quarter acre section. In this rectangle there was a recent shell hole that might give cover for digging in.

Crawling over to the sergeant and the corporal I pointed to it.

'I'll take a man and see about cutting the wire.'

'I'll come,' said the sergeant.

'OK,' I had intended someone else, but I was more than happy to have him along.

'Corporal, if the sergeant and I get through, bring up the men. If we don't, find somewhere to dig in.'

'We'll cover you,' said the corporal.

'OK, but fire only if you see what you're firing at.'

'Yes, Sir.'

I didn't rate the chances of the corporal and the men much above the sergeant's and mine.

The sergeant and I crawled off, worms in mud. We discovered the rain had cut a channel under the wire, deep enough, with some cutting, for a man to crawl through and into the shell hole. We managed it, and so did the men, screened, I guess, not just by the trench parapet but the thickness of the entanglements and the rain. We burrowed down in the shell hole. It was getting on for an hour, the water rising, the cold soaking in, the war being fought around us, when the sergeant said, 'Sir, I think I know a better hole.'

'Go on.'

'Over there.' He nodded towards the pillbox. 'They've been doing a lot of shooting—mostly at nothing much—and now they seem to be slackening off. Could be they're getting cocky.'

'Maybe,' I said.

'If we go up the hill and cut through the wire, we could take them from the back door.'

'We might,' I said.

'You never know,' said the sergeant, 'it could be worth having a go.'

Whether I would have had 'a go' if he hadn't raised it, I don't know. Where we were had its limitations, and as well as the rising water, there was the fact that snipers weren't always stationary. While taking the pillbox did not have a lot going for it, once in, we'd have the protection of concrete.

'Right.' I called up the corporal, and the Number Ones of the Lewis gun and the rifle grenadiers, and explained what the sergeant and I would be attempting. In the meantime they were to give covering fire if the pillbox noticed us. When we were through the wire, the platoon would follow and we would deploy to attack. They were to keep an eye out for snipers, but there was to be no, repeat, no, pointless drawing of attention to our presence.

The sergeant and I crawled up the slope. It was slippery and when we reached the wire, I reached for my expensive cutters. 'Give them to me, Sir.' The sergeant had been a sawmiller or roadman: someone who'd used his hands. Crawling forward, he cut and I bent the wire away. We did quite well and were almost through when we heard shots from the pillbox. Two men in khaki, clutching grenades, under a burst of covering fire, were running at the pillbox. Splinters of concrete flew as Lewis gun rounds splattered in and about the loopholes, but each man was hit before he could throw. Firing ceased, all over in less than a minute. The sergeant and I lay long enough, we hoped, for matters to settle, before he resumed. We were just about to emerge from the wire when he must have raised his head a little too high and his helmet was knocked awry and half his brains blown into my face.

A single shot; it hadn't come from the pillbox. I lay wondering how long would it take the sniper to draw a bead on me when there was a sledgehammer whack on the side of the head. For I don't know how long there was nothing. My guess is that being knocked cold saved my life. The round had skimmed the frontal of the skull under my helmet and entered the left upper arm, fracturing it. A steel hammer pounded my head.

The arm wasn't so bright either. My first thought was to wonder whether, using my feet and legs, I could push back under the wire. That was dismissed. It might be raining but if I could see mud and wire, some-one could see me. I lay, cold penetrating my bones and soaking up from the ground. Whether it dulled the pain of the fracture, I don't know. It hurt a lot but maybe could have hurt more. When coming to, I had felt pain, dull and sharp at the same time, but as the hours went by it became sharper. And I wanted to wipe my face. Then there was thirst, but I'd have to move to get at a water bottle. There was cramp in my right arm but I wasn't moving that either. All I could do was move my toes inside my boots, so I worked on that and waited as each minute followed the one be-fore. I wondered about the corporal and the boys back in the shell hole but knew all they could see of me through the wire would be a very still body.

About an hour passed and, although I heard shots around the pillbox, I didn't try to find out why. In the afternoon our artillery fired, feebly, but enough for shrapnel to smash a boot heel, cutting into the bone below the ankle. Again there was the hard blow, numbness and then increasing pain. I tried to fool myself that after the 'barrage' there would be an advance and they'd find me when they got to the wire. When night came, by using my good arm and leg, I moved clear of the barbs, drank, and wiped my face. After that I placed a field dressing on my arm and retrieved another for the foot from the sergeant as well as his water bottle. Moving exhausted me, but not enough for sleep. Before the second hit, I hadn't written myself off. Now I did. I cried, from the pain, hopelessness, and my ridiculous 1914 naïveté. Why hadn't I stayed in the shell hole? I tried praying but that soon worked itself out. I might have groaned. I'm sure I did. I thought of the sergeant and that if he'd lived, I'd have put him up for a commission. A Jim Hargest man if ever there was one and then I thought of how many Jim Hargest men would be dead before they were promoted and how many would die after they were. I thought of the woman in Paris. That might have been good for ten minutes. I remembered books I had read and tried to re-read them. I recited French irregular verbs and even tried to resuscitate my German to welcome their stretcher-bearers, but throughout there was the aching, throbbing pain and the cold and the wet. The only mental exercise which had continuity was to note the sound of a gun and identify whose it was, its calibre and where its shell was likely to fall. At intervals there would be a systematic sweep by the German machine gunners. Very little, indeed hardly any, of the same came from our side. Sometimes there would be a rifle shot and one wondered who of our own was finishing himself off. I hadn't brought my revolver (the gun was one of the ways a sniper might identify an officer) but I wondered if I should have. My Lee Enfield was out of reach, as was the sergeant's, and I wasn't keen to blunder about in barbed wire looking for either. There were grenades in the pockets of my tunic, but using them would be messy and there was no guarantee they'd be quick. I guess I must have dozed off or lost consciousness from time to time.

My watch had stopped so I don't know when dawn broke, changing the sky from pitch black to heavy grey. The rain now alternated with hail, and wind had come up. The shelling continued, intermittent, and it might have been because of this that it was about an hour before I noticed the small arms' fire seemed to have quietened. I wondered if, along with everything else, I'd gone deaf, but a shell explosion not too far away reassured me about that. During the night I had moved to a position, which, I hoped, would give better cover. Now, on top of the aching throbs and raw pain in the arm and foot, there was cramp in the good leg but I didn't move because, now that morning had come, the sniper surely would be back in his possie. Harry, I thought, was a sniper and went on about loving one's neighbour as oneself. Brooding on it took my mind off things for a good two minutes. The pain, the cold and the wet did not let up. I watched hail bouncing off the sergeant's boot. Why, I thought, hadn't I tried crawling back through the wire during the night despite the barbs? Could I crawl now? Was I able to crawl? If I could, how far could I go? If I crawled would I be sniped? It was quiet but not that quiet. Time passed. But if I didn't move, I'd be a goner anyway. I pondered on that. I had one good arm and one good leg and I was in mud, stinking greasy mud. I'd have to go through the wire again. Maybe there was a truce—unofficial and local—where each could go out on his side of the wire for wounded but anyone not wounded or a stretcher-bearer, was still fair game. There was no sign of an advance overnight. I was on the Hun side and by now it would be surprising if they had wounded to bring in. I could chance it, they might see me, and they might come and get me and they might not. The shelling, although desultory, had not let up. Giving the guns a rest was not the done thing for generals, no 'relieving pressure on the enemy' for them. So why should a Hun stretcher party come out for the likes of me?

It was either take the chance of a truce, crawl, and maybe die, or stay and die for sure. There was trepidation at the last moment. After that, I put it out of my mind, not all the time, but most of it. The concern was that neither the good leg nor arm were bursting with energy. The grenades were got rid of, worse than useless now. But I kept the binoculars! Then it was the wire. We had cut it for men with their full complement of limbs. I felt barbs when I was part way through and remembered I had left the cutters with the sergeant. I didn't go back and when I came out I had lacerations. But I was not quite as cold.

This time the slope helped, but it was a slow business, crawling, pause,

370   MARCH TO THE SOUND OF THE GUNS

crawling, pause, slumping into the mud. On the brink of the shell hole I flopped down, not sure whether I would move again. Filled with water, it was unoccupied, save for two of my men, lying as if casually tossed aside.

I looked to Abraham Heights. Stretcher parties were out. One had crossed Marsh Bottom, heading for the belt of wire we had first crawled under. Indeed they were close to the drain we had used. I raised myself with my good arm, but when I did I had nothing to wave with and as soon as I was up, I fell down. I then tried, from the ground, a sort of half-hearted flip of my hand that was noticed no more than such a gesture usually receives. I could only lie and watch. They were approaching with a purpose and on the other side of the wire I saw, now that they had stopped beside it, that what I had thought to be just a mound of mud, was a man. I tried calling but all I could manage was a croak. I watched as he was loaded onto the stretcher and slowly, legs sinking into the mud, carried away.

I was reaching the stage when I knew the pain would subside and dying would be easy. Maybe I kept going because it was tantalising to be so near yet so far, after all the effort. The ground had been churned into waves like heavy sea and I had to cross them, with thrills of pain from the wounded limbs, but they might have kept me out of a coma. It was early afternoon before I made the next entanglements. But the drain under the wire was still there; indeed it was deeper. Once through I lay like a dead frog.

But I could see another stretcher party. Again I tried calling and again all I could raise was a croak but I kept trying. At first it seemed to be working because the party was moving closer. I was hopeful until I noticed the bearers were looking from left to right, and when in my direction, their eyes were not focusing. Putting all I could into it I pushed up to a half sitting position, couldn't keep it, and fell back. The stretcher party had stopped and, if they were wondering where to go next, it certainly wasn't towards me. I whimpered.

'Englander!' A shout from Bellevue, under the brow, loud, impatient, and German. 'Englander!'

He fired twice, the rounds splashing mud—some of it over me.

The stretcher party dropped.

'Englander!' He'd had me in his sights all day.

Desperation helped me flap an arm. 'Here … please …' My teeth were chattering; it was hard to get the words out. 'Here … please!'

But the sniper had shown me. Doubtfully, and who can blame them, the bearers rose to their feet. Six of them, Ali Sloper's Cavalry, taken off their wagons and away from their horses. The sound of their squelching boots has remained.

'You're lucky,' one said.

As the crow flies it was not quite a mile to Waterloo Farm. It took three hours. Once there they carried back a patient higher in the queue, barely having the energy to do it. Waterloo, a complex of pillboxes and buttressed buildings, served as the 2nd Brigade HQ and Regimental Aid Post. There being no room in the RAP, I was laid in the open, examined by a doctor, had dressings changed, given a tetanus injection and a shot of morphine. No direct hits but the combination of the weather, shrapnel and blast resulted in there being fewer of us in the morning. Around dawn, I think, I could hear an English accent, peremptorily ordering someone to deliver a message to General Russell himself. The speaker was obviously a senior officer, and angry, but I didn't take much notice, there being plenty to make a senior officer, or anybody else, angry. It was Brigadier Braithwaite, never a man to mince words. Earlier he had informed Russell that a second attack on Bellevue would increase casualties even further and go nowhere. Russell had no option but to cancel it. But that was not the only communication Braithwaite had with Russell. What I had overheard was the sending of a later message despatched at 5.45 a.m. The official history of the Otago Regiment recounts it in full and so shall I.

> In spite of frequent appeals to every branch of Staff, and the ADMS [Assistant Director of Medical Services] three times, the 75 stretcher cases at Waterloo, which I asked the ADMS to arrange the removal of at 12 noon yesterday, are still lying there; 40 of them still lying out in the open under shell fire the whole night. I am powerless to do more than I have done. As a last extremity, I appeal to you personally.

They are also the words of a man who has just about had enough. And so it proved. Towards the end of the year he was sent back to England, no longer the man he was. As one of the forty left out in the mud, I am biased, but if there is one red-tab who comes out with honour in the sordid mess of Passchendaele, it is Braithwaite. Rumours circulated he'd been sent back because he cared too much for his men.

As a consequence, sufficient stretcher-bearers were sent to carry us three miles to Spree Farm, the nearest Advanced Dressing Station. It took five to six hours. For the first mile, there were no duckboards. Since we had gone up, the mud had liquefied and become deeper. Wading as well as walking, the bearers sank to the waist and edged around mud filled craters that sucked men to their death. Jerking, falling, tipping, slipping, sliding, slopping through sludge, they carried on. It was my lucky day.

1918

1918

On 21 March, a terrific bombardment fell on Gough's 5th Army dispersed across the Somme. It was the start of 'Operation Michael', the first of five offensives the German High Command mounted to win the war. In the space of a few days the Germans advanced twenty to thirty miles. The 5th Army fought brave-ly, but being spread thinly and not having made the tactical changes necessary for an effective fighting withdrawal, the resistance it offered, while sufficient to put the German timetable out of joint, could not prevent unit after unit being overrun. 'It was either him or me,' said Haig after he sacked Gough — who for once was not really to blame. The offensive was also the catalyst for the French Marshall Foch to be appointed Generalissimo to coordinate the operations of all Allied Forces on the Western Front — long overdue.

By late March, 'Michael' reached the outskirts of Amiens. It went no fur-ther. Reinforcements rushed in to defend the city. The New Zealanders, the Australians, and probably the Canadians too, have claimed responsibility for stopping it. Actually all did, including the Divisions from the British Isles who, of course, comprised the bulk of the defenders — and the 2nd Army that took the initial shock and upset German calculations.

Nevertheless, although 'Michael' was halted, the other offensives continued to thrust into France. Haig felt impelled to issue a 'Special Order of the Day'.

TO ALL RANKS OF THE BRITISH ARMY IN FRANCE
AND FLANDERS

'Three weeks ago today the enemy began his terrific attacks against us on a fifty-mile front. His objects are to separate us from the French, to take the Channel Ports and destroy the British Army.

'In spite of throwing already 106 Divisions into the battle and enduring the most reckless sacrifice of life, he has yet made little progress towards his goals.

We owe this to the determined fighting and self-sacrifice of our own troops. Words fail me to express the admiration which I feel for the splendid resistance offered by all ranks of our Army under the most trying circumstances.

'Many amongst us are now tired. To those I would say that Victory will belong to the side which holds out the longest. The French Army is moving rapidly and in great force to our support.

'There is no course open to us but to fight it out. Every position must be held to the last man; there must be no retirement. With our backs to the wall and believing in the justice of our cause each one of us must fight on to the end. The safety of our homes and the Freedom of mankind alike depend upon the conduct of each one of us at this critical moment.

'D. Haig, F.M.,
'Commander-in-Chief
'British Armies in France.
'General Headquarters,
'Thursday, April 11th, 1918.'

It was natural that among those bearing the brunt of the offensive some should ask, 'Where's the fucking wall?' But on the whole, Haig's Special Order inspired a lot of people, and reminded many who had previously taken it for granted that the Allies would eventually win, that victory could not be a foregone conclusion.

Indeed it was not: yet as the weeks went by it became apparent that the German High Command had made the last throws of its dice. Matters were not going well for Germany. Its lack of resources and men was beginning to reveal itself: exemplified by the incapacity to bring up sufficient artillery, supply trains and men at the speed necessary to keep the British forces on the run. And then there were the storm troops — not to be confused with the Nazi brutes who stole their name. The elite of the German Army, the storm troops had been specifically trained to become masters of the breakthrough, but, as is invariably the case when elites are sent into action, their casualty rate was high and as more and more fell, there were less and less men of such calibre to stiffen the German ranks. Last but not least, the advancing troops failed to resist the temptations of success. British Army food dumps and abandoned wine cellars were overrun. Having been on hard rations for much of the war, men halted to gorge and drink rather than pressing on to maintain the momentum essential for the High Command strategy to succeed. Moreover, the opposition they met, with few exceptions, was determined and effective. When the offensives petered out, the German High Command was left with a vulnerable salient eighty miles long and up to forty miles deep.

And now we come to August 1918 when Haig came into his own. Foch, on perceiving that Haig meant to fight hard, supported him. Haig had also become more confident in his Army commanders and allowed them to get on with the job so long as they did so with boldness and speed: e.g. in 1918 when he offered them cavalry, sometimes they accepted and sometimes they didn't. The enemy never knew where the next attack would come from, except that it would surely come. In his Staff College days, Haig—along with his contemporaries—had been instructed about the great American Civil War general, Stonewall Jackson: 'Always mystify, mislead, and surprise the enemy, if possible; and when you strike and overcome him, never let up in the pursuit so long as your men have the strength to follow …' Earlier Haig had tried this; except he never mystified or misled and rarely surprised. Now he did. And Haig was one of the very few who judged the war could be won in a matter of months—a view that underwrote all his 1918 decisions.

On 8 August, supported by a record number of tanks and artillery and dominance in the air, the Australians and Canadians of Rawlinson's 4th Army, smashed through German lines to advance a record eight miles in one day: the beginning of an advance that would finish the war. The 1st, 2nd, and 3rd British Armies were also on the move. To the southeast, the French and the Americans made their attacks, driving north. Although the casualty rates were no less than they had been during the years of stalemate and futile attacks, at least it might be argued they were now sacrificed for a purpose.

Along with other divisions in the 1ˢᵗ, 3ʳᵈ, and 4ᵗʰ Armies, the New Zealanders were faced with the Hindenburg Line. Three to four miles deep, it comprised six to nine belts of barbed wire and expertly placed trenches, observation posts, strong-points, etc. In the rear of the Hindenburg Line, supply dumps, aerodromes, railheads, and heavy artillery positions had been established to serve it. If the British forces had assaulted it a year earlier there would have been a bloody defeat. But now the numbers, matériel and tactics were in the British favour, as was Haig's strategy of mounting multiple attacks to divert the enemy and maintain momentum. It was a three-pronged attack that made the initial breach. Most notable in the attack was the 46ᵗʰ (Midland) Division, which, with a combination of a careful and intelligent assessment of the issues involved, close and concentrated artillery support, dash and improvisation, swept across the deeply cut St Quentin Canal. From then on there was no let up; the British Armies swept northwards until the Germans sued for an armistice and the guns fell silent at 11 a.m. 11 November 1918.

HARRY
1918

When the 1st and 2nd Otagos and those with them had their backs broken at Bellevue, we in the 1st Brigade were sent up to take their place and hold the line. Our artillery, impotent when needed for the attack on Bellevue, now bombarded. The Germans retaliated — on us. One of our guns demolished a pillbox on the crest. The first shots were near misses, sufficient to send the garrison scattering to the rear, then one scored a direct hit. A cheer went up along our line. After that there was silence, for out of the smoke and debris there arose a human being. He was not running but walking — towards us. Small arms on each side went silent. He stumbled, sometimes skidding and falling, but picking himself up and keeping on coming. At Marsh Bottom he disappeared and we thought he might have fallen in, but after a while we saw him again. Coming to waves in the ground, he disappeared and reappeared more than once. He was waving his arms, like a voluble Frenchman and we sensed he was carrying on an intense conversation with himself. He walked dead straight towards us, deviating only when he had to circumvent a shell hole, but resuming as if there were a path he must adhere to. When he came to our wire we could hear him complaining as, frustrated, he walked up and down, until, finding a gap, he crawled through and standing on the parapet, addressed us. It was as if he were in a pulpit, discoursing on a matter of importance, and concluding with a question. After pausing for a reply and not receiving one, but unbothered, he clambered into the trench and, as if they were well acquainted, spoke to one of the men. My platoon was a hard-bitten bunch, but they were nonplussed. The man he was speaking to, however, did exactly the right thing; he pulled out a packet of cigarettes and offered one. The thanks were voluble. Another man lit it, and between his draws on the cigarette, we were presented with what was now some sort of friendly lecture: perhaps another sermon. Another man opened a tin of bully. At once the cigarette was stubbed, pocketed, not thrown away, and the tin seized; the despised product of the Argentinean pampas going down like the most succulent of stews. A shell came close enough for all but him to take cover. He was stone deaf. I had the man who'd given him the cigarette take him back to Battalion HQ. He talked all the way.

After being relieved by the Canadians we spent ten days in the rear where we took on reinforcements and returned to the most miserable four months on the Western Front: cable laying, digging communication saps, wiring and salvaging anything possibly useful from the detritus scattered over that foul and desolate Flanders plain. The month of March caught us by surprise. We were sent to billets twenty miles behind the lines, where there were people with friendly faces, and a light haze of green overlaid the woods. Most important was leave to Blighty. My turn came up and, as nothing appeared to be in the offing, I went. Passing through London, and knowing Frank had been posted there, I met him. Benefiting from a well-earned rest from the frontline, he regaled me with tales about base wallahs who were even worse than what I'd imagined. On my return I ran into Jim at Abeele. The conversation we had was not just thought provoking but was to have more significance in my life than I was aware of at the time.

I returned in time to be with the New Zealand Division when it was sent to meet the great German offensive. On the afternoon of 24 March, we boarded trains for Amiens to join Byng's 3rd Army on the northern Somme. After Amiens, we had a hard march up and down hills along a very dusty road. Disorganised troops coming the other way, working hard to increase the distance between themselves and the enemy, passed us. Women, old men, and children bowed down with burdens, and cows, horses, carts, wheelbarrows, babies' prams, anything that might convey food and a few treasured possessions, were also on the road. If anything made us raise our heads and lift our step it was these.

It was no longer the rigid warfare we had become accustomed to; now we had to show flexibility, improvisation and the ability to assess and respond quickly. We joined up with 2nd Auckland and the 4th Rifles to seize a smoothly rounded ridgeline with La Signy Farm at its apex, which Fritz had made into a strong point and observation post. Preceded by a short sharp barrage that we followed closely, and obscured by the heavy rain, we were halfway from the start line before the Germans knew what was happening. Our losses being light, we were a happy band, especially as the defensive works were already there: concrete dugouts, reinforced cellars and well-dug trenches that needed little modification for our purposes. And now *we* looked over *them*.

We held our line from April to August, a period of stability rather than tranquillity. Patrols and counter patrols and attacks and counter-attacks: fierce skirmishes at close quarters, particularly notorious being Rossignol Wood, or Copse 125 as our field-grey friends called it, where New Zealander and German fought man to man. (If you want a real war story, pick up Ernst Junger's *Storm of Steel* or *Copse 125*. Forget *All Quiet on the Western Front*—Junger served throughout the war and was awarded his nation's highest military order for valour in the field.)

When, late in August, the New Zealand Division began its advance, it learned that an enemy retreat is not necessarily an enemy defeat. First Wellington was involved in the capture of Bapaume—distantly glimpsed in September 1916. It commenced with an inauspicious capture of a small wood where our leading platoons had no support barrage, but was followed by a successful envelopment of Bapaume—yours truly leading a patrol into the town to find it had been abandoned. This was not the case, however, when we ran up against three villages beyond, and an entrenched crest. We captured them, but the enemy made a fighting withdrawal where we encountered the full implications of that phrase. Sergeant John Grant of Taranaki Company won a well earned VC when he took out three of a line of five machine gun posts.

By mid-September we were assaulting Trescault Ridge. A preliminary defence of the Hindenburg Line, with two parallel trench systems, well connected by saps, we were subjected to hand grenade counter-attacks, a flame-thrower, and mortar bombs. Engaging with a Jaeger regiment, led us, for the first time, to feel we might have met our match. 'Jaeger', I believe, is German for 'hunter'. First choice as assault troops; in the final months, they were rearguard men. Brave, adept, resilient, thrown in where most needed: few would have seen the year out.

We benefited from a spell of two to three weeks back at Bapaume absorbing reinforcements, training, and generally brushing ourselves up. Educational work also had come to play a larger part during our time out of the line, and the Christian community made time for fellowship. And lest I be accused of omitting important events, Wellington again showed Auckland how to play rugby. After the dank Flanders plain, we appreciated the gentle undulations of the countryside. It has been described as ideal tank country. I suppose so, but its fertile soil, nourished and cultivated for hundreds of years, its carefully nurtured woods, the delightful villages tucked into the valleys or presiding over crests, demonstrated what can be achieved when man and God work together; as the devastation made manifest man's failure to heed his Creator.

I remember standing on the crest of a hillside and looking down where the Scheldt River and canal run parallel with each other, rarely more than a quarter mile apart, sometimes separated by nothing more than an embankment. Together they were the last barrier of the Hindenburg Line. Their bridges were intact. In the country beyond were green swards, ploughed paddocks, woods, streams, and cosy villages. Even the sight of the enemy artillery limbering up preparatory to bombarding us, and infantry digging in on our objectives, did not dull one's appreciation of the Creation.

First Wellington and 2nd Auckland were detailed to seize the bridges. That did not eventuate, however. Every old soldier has experienced Murphy's Law and it was to be applied to us. It had been necessary to move quickly and brigade orders to 1st Wellington and 2nd Auckland were issued at short notice. Telephones were out and the orders had to be carried by runners who, owing to heavy rain, darkness, and crossing unknown churned-up country, did not reach the battalions until 11.15 p.m. This allowed a mere six hours for the battalion COs to plan their attacks and issue their verbal instructions—there being no time for written orders—to company

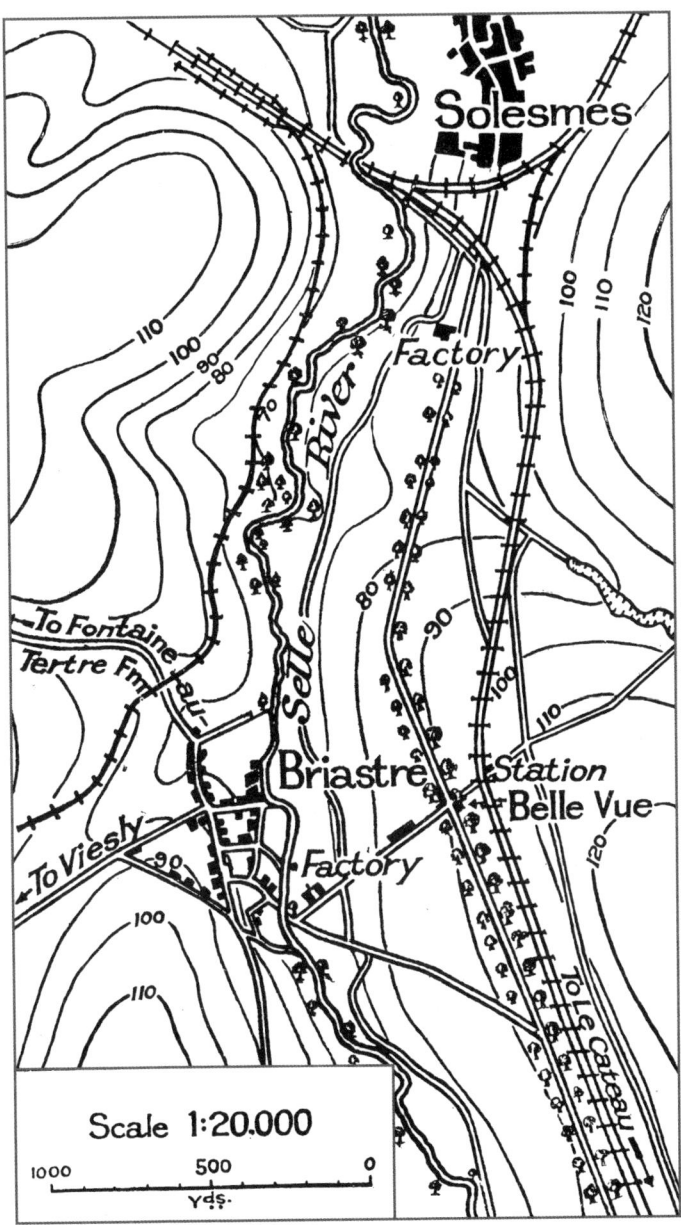

Briastre and the Selle River. *Source: Stewart, H.*

commanders. They too had to verbally instruct their platoon commanders and senior NCOs and have all ready for a dawn attack at 5.45 a.m. In the inevitable toing and froing, at night with heavy rain, confusion resulted. Our CO, for example, mistakenly thought the attack would be at 5.00 a.m. and that artillery would support our company. The consequence was that although we stopped the enemy from blowing the bridges, we stayed on our side of the river until successful crossings were made to the north.

We were not called upon for a week and much use was made of the divisional baths. There was good news too — Messines and its surrounding villages had been re-captured and the Second Army was pushing on. Also I was informed I was to be sent on a company commander's course, a profitable experience for those who like it, but I was happy where I was — my company commander was a patrol enthusiast who allowed me latitude. The upshot was when we went into action again I went too. While I wasn't overtly welcomed, nobody, at the front, complained. Our objective was the railway station just across the Selle River from Briastre, a village about ten miles east of Cambrai.

Briastre is in a valley and sits on a river-flat about two hundred to three hundred yards wide, its main street running parallel with the river that runs north/south. There is a road off it that crosses a bridge and, climbing east up a gentle but consistent slope, connects with the railway station, which looks across the valley, down on the village. The railway and a road run parallel, north/south just below the eastern crest. The river is eight to ten yards across, edged with vertical banks, and too deep to wade. As farming country, it's good for grazing and ploughable, and if you were retreating and inclined to make matters difficult for your pursuers, you too would have positive feelings about it. With grassed slopes on each side of the valley, and with the river cutting across your enemy's advance, it would not take you long to decide to blow the bridge and use the road and railway on the eastern slope to site your strong-points, each with a wide arc of fire across the meadows. Behind the east crest, on the reverse slope, your artillery would have the attackers' range to a T. Then you'd put Jaegers in.

We descended the west slope around 1.00 a.m. Being 'surplus to requirements', I gathered a patrol together, and with another party, worked through the village to ascertain whether it was clear or not. The remaining Germans, however, had no desire to die for the Fatherland. They were as glad to see us as the villagers were. Well, not quite. The villagers had been hiding in their cellars for days. There were young women, but old women, old men, and children outnumbered them. Few of us, at that stage of the war, had over-sensitive olfactory organs—we might have been softened up through recently availing ourselves of the divisional baths—but when a grateful citizen envelopes you in her/his embrace, and she/he has spent some days in a cellar of a French village that has suffered four years of privation, and she/he is unlikely to be over-concerned with soap and water anyway, one's appreciation of the gratitude expressed tends to be tempered.

There being no temptation to linger, we joined our company which, along with Hawke's Bay, had, after a search, found a Royal Engineer span, half a mile to the south. It could not be crossed speedily and on the other side, we had to deploy in the dark on unfamiliar ground and head for the railway station across open fields with no cover. Hawke's Bay Company had their left flank against the river, but the right flank of my platoon was open to the road and railway, a hundred yards away. Dawn broke. Ruahine got it. I was hit, and but for the Grace of God, I would have bled to death. The slightest movement, let alone applying a field dressing, and I would have been a target. Although I had a touchline view of the little battle, my observation had lapses, there being occasions when the wound made itself felt. One had to control one's vocal chords in case a not unkind Fritz heard and thought to put me out of my misery.

With the grim irony that occurs in war, the railway station, and a cluster of farm buildings near it, was called Bellevue. Late in the afternoon the German artillery shelled Briastre heavily. Night passed and just before dawn, the British division on our right attacked, as did a couple of our platoons on Bellevue. I was in the frustrating position of being able to see what they were up against but unable to let them know how strong it was. They reached the station but were driven back by the enfilading fire from the farm buildings. They might have been able to hold on if the British division had not been prevented from extending its flank and advancing up the road and railway. The Jaegers made a counter-attack that forced the platoons back. Briastre was again heavily shelled. We responded in kind. Being in the middle, I have been in happier circumstances. One of our shells made a direct hit on the railway station and men were thrown into the air in a sheet of flame. No explanation, other than God's Grace, can explain why the same did not happen to me. In the end we prevailed, but I can tell you little of it as by then brave men had brought me in and I was on my way out of it.

JIM
1918

I was four months at Walton hospital. The sergeant of the motor pool was a Denniston man. When I was up on my feet, he gave me a job. Better than Passchendaele and I knew he could only keep me for so long. They sent me out with Nelle Carrington for driving practice. I was wary at first, with the way she talked and where she came from, but my mate knew her better than I did. When I left they pasted in my paybook: driver — lorry, light car, Ford car.

I was posted to Sling where reinforcements from home were trained. They made me an instructor: a railway pass to London and warm accommodation went with it. But if I wanted to keep it I'd have to go on a British Army instructor's course. That wasn't me, and neither was the Sergeants' Mess. Not too many had done their spell in the trenches, a few treated men like men, and the rest weren't happy without criming a couple a day. One or two liked going into the guardroom of an evening for a one-way punch up.

I applied for a transfer to the ASC and they sent me to Etaples. Like Sling only worse. Everybody went through Etaples. If you were returning from leave, it would be a couple of days. If you were a reinforcement, it would be a couple of weeks, or less if they wanted you in a hurry, and more if there was nothing coming up. Every division had its bullring, where drill sergeants yelled in the sand and snow. Everyone was still talking about the mutiny in September. New Zealanders had been involved and my only surprise was there hadn't been another before or since. There were lectures in the evenings. I remember one where a padre and a doctor talked about paying a prostitute and the consequences thereof. The boys only became interested when the doctor used words we spoke every day and the Padre objected. When the New Zealand Camp Commandant performed, we didn't mind too much. Hoppy Mitchell's civilian job had been a 'Wholesale Business Manager'—Hoppy's version of commercial traveller. He could've sold the Sydney Harbour Bridge to an Aussie. One night he told us about 'Care of the Feet', and the next, 'Love'. When he got going on 'Why we fight' the reinforcements couldn't wait for the sweet and lovely prospect of going over the top.

He'd gone to the Boer war. After that it had been Gallipoli where he'd got it in the face and leg. The face was more or less fixed up but the leg wasn't. Because he kicked up a fuss about going home, they sent him to Etaples. They gave him a DSO for it. One day he called me up.

'McDonnell, I have your file here.'

'Yes, Sir.'

'We need an instructor.'

No reply.

'It says here you were instructing at Sling.'

'Yes, Sir.'

'Then you were posted.'

'Not my cup of tea, Sir.'

'You've applied for the ASC.'

'They do good work, Sir.'

'I'm not denying that, Sergeant.' He looked down at the file again. 'I see you're a qualified driver.' He looked up. 'A handy ticket to have.'

'Yes, Sir.'

'McDonnell, if I ordered it, you would remain here as an instructor. Your battalion might object but unless they moved heaven and earth, here you'd stay.'

'Sir.'

'If you became an instructor, there would be an immediate promotion and not too long after that, going by your record, CSM. You are due for promotion to staff sergeant anyway.'

'I'm happy in my rank, Sir.'

'You've been a platoon commander but I see your file is silent about being commissioned.'

'With respect, Sir, not my line.'

'We are at war, Sergeant, as you well know, and we do things whether it's our line or not.' He closed the file. 'That's all, Sergeant.'

A couple of days later he called me up again and as I went over to his office I was wondering how to get word to the Wellingtons about getting me back.

'McDonnell!'

'Sir.'

'I need a driver. I'd have a job justifying a staff sergeant in that position. You understand?'

'Yes, Sir.'

'Indeed I may well be questioned about having a sergeant driving my staff car, but we'll deal with that if we have to. Meantime you're on a fortnight's trial.'

'Yes, Sir.'

The fortnight went OK but by then he'd been made CO New Zealand Entrenchment Group. Maybe he'd known it was coming up.

Our base was Abeele, ten miles west of Ypres. The Entrenchment Group was made up of reinforcements, released men from the Field Punishment Centre and VD units, and odds and sods from ASC, artillery, sappers, signallers, cooks, bottle-washers, anything. Not much you could do with them apart from pick and shovel work, one step down from the Pioneer Battalion. Men came and went. You needed someone like Hoppy for a crowd like that.

So he got the conchies. Fourteen had been shipped from New Zealand to England and from there to France. It took me back to my days with the Passive Resisters' Union and Ripa Island. Most were religious and socialists. My dad would have been one. They'd been given a hard time and that, combined with a silver tongue or two, narrowed them down to four. One was in HM Military Prison, Dunkirk; another, after being dragged along duckboards and through shell holes, was shipped home unfit, and then there were two, Kirwin and Baxter. After Hoppy got nowhere with them he sent them to Mud Farm, the Field Punishment Centre. Just inside the wire it had a line of posts, like fence posts but about six foot high, in full view of the road: Number One Field Punishment. Prisoners were supposed to be tied securely, but not cutting off circulation, and allowing a little movement. Two hours was the maximum. When they passed, local farmers and villagers looked the other way and normal traffic drove on. One day, when snow was being blown around, and I was taking a staff officer up to Brigade HQ, we came into sight of Mud Farm. Two men were tied up, and the officer, after telling me to slow down, said they wouldn't forget today in a hurry.

The road up was shelled, we had to wait until it was cleared, and I had to take him on from Brigade HQ to Divisional Artillery HQ where he stayed. On the way back there was a lot of foot and mule traffic and the weather hadn't got any better, so it was four hours later before Mud Farm appeared again. I gave it a glance, looked again, and stopped. The snow-storm had thickened but there was something funny about the posts. I got out for a closer look. The men were still there. The sentry, recognising the staff car, let me through. The men's heads were hanging over their chests, the rest of them hanging too, held by the cords around their wrists and ankles. The posts were not straight in the ground; they leaned forward, and each man was tied on the inside of the angle. The ground where their feet should have been standing sloped away. In the morning they'd kept upright by bracing themselves against the post. But you can't keep that up for four hours and their feet had splayed, with no purchase for their boots; the bindings, around their wrists and ankles, carried all the weight. Their hands were blue-black, faces pale and the tips of their noses turning white. The snow blew straight onto them, camouflaging. It needed a closer look to see one was wearing a greatcoat and the other just his tunic. I could smell coffee.

I went to a hut and it was coffee all right. The door was part open, away from the wind, and just wide enough, if you were inside and minded, to keep an eye on the posts. A sergeant and a corporal, sitting in front of a red-hot stove, having a yarn and drinking coffee, were not minded. I kicked the door wide and a blast of heat hit me.

They jumped like rabbits.

'Get out here.'

'What?'

'Get the fuck out here.'

The sergeant came to the door. The corporal stayed where he was.

'Who the hell are you?'

'Cut those men down.'

'They're conchies.'

'I don't care who the fuck they are.'

'Refusing to obey a legal order.'

'I don't care what they've done. It's what you've done.'

'None of your business.'

'Murder.'

'Yeah?'

'Yes, you bastard.'

'No one talks to me like that.'

'You murdering bastard,' I said.

'We know how to deal with your sort, right here.'

'You want a court martial, you'll get a fucking court martial.'

'I'm following orders.'

'Two men left to die. In the presence of a witness.'

'I was on my way out,' he said. 'To check on them.'

I nearly laughed.

'Cut them down. Now.'

'OK. And,' he said slowly, 'I don't forget faces.'

And I have not forgotten his: podgy, splotched with red, plastered by a black moustache above a thin upper lip that sat just inside the thick lower one, and eyes peering out that never focused on yours but somewhere below and to the side.

We went over. The wrists and ankles had swollen. The cords had too, and I watched him cut. The men fell in the snow and had to be helped up. Not by him. Nothing more I could do except to make sure they got back to their tents. Weaving around, they did.

'Where's your officer?'

'What?' This time he seemed to be looking at the left side of my neck.

'You'll report to your officer. Where is he?'

'This won't do you any good.' His gaze shifted down around my left elbow.

'No?' I wasn't going to let him know he might be right. 'We'll see about that.'

The officers kept away from the dirty stuff. We went out the gate, the snow swirling in our faces. We crossed the road. I wondered what I had got myself into. So I sorted out my story for the provost officer. He had a nice cosy hut with a red-hot stove too. He was reading the *Daily Mail* or some other shit.

'Sir, this sergeant entered the compound and said he'd report me if I didn't release the men on Number One Field Punishment.'

'How long had they been out there, Sergeant?'

'An hour or two, Sir.'

'A little too long, Sergeant, in this weather.' The provost officer knew the side his bread was buttered on.

'Sir.'

'And who are you?' the officer asked.

'Sergeant James McDonnell, Colonel Mitchell's driver, Sir.'

'And what caused you to take a sudden interest in the Field Punishment Centre?'

'I was ordered by Colonel Mitchell this morning to take an officer up to First Brigade Headquarters. On the way up, the officer ordered me to slow down so that he might observe the two men undergoing punishment. It's been snowing all day. Shellfire and heavy traffic and the snow caused delays on the road. It was some hours before I passed the compound again on my return. The men were still tied.'

'Well, Sergeant, I shall report this to my commander. And you might remember we have all sorts of men passing through here. We do not like what we do, but it has to be done. Dismiss.'

Mitchell didn't say anything until the best part of a week later. I'd taken him down to Etaples, and was bringing him back when a village came up.

'I don't know about you, Jim, but I could do with a cognac. Stop outside the estaminet.'

So it was to be Jim, rather than Sergeant.

'Smoke?' He pushed a packet over. We lit up and the cognacs arrived.

'Cheers.' He lifted his glass.

I lifted mine.

'You saved us from an embarrassment the other day.'

I didn't say anything.

'We've got to make an example of them, Jim, or every second Tom, Dick or Harry will go walkabout. But the bastards know how to get the word around. Friends in high places. That's why we had to get them out of England. Breaking the law, they said. Breaking the law! We've come from the ends of the earth to fight for king and country and they tell us we're breaking their bloody law. Very soft you know, our English cousins. A man calls himself a conchie, they send him to court and the court sends him to work on a fucking farm!' His brandy went down a second time. 'I've no more time for the Provost Corps than you have. If it weren't for the few bad eggs the army inevitably seems to pick up, we wouldn't need provosts at all. Scum clobbering scum. And they're bloody stupid; the way they run their show. Could've got us in a hell of a mess.' He looked out the window. 'It's a cold ride home; like one for the road?'

'Wouldn't mind.'

He ordered two more brandies.

'Those two, Kirwin and Baxter: they're the last of the incorrigibles. As for the rest — and I don't mind claiming a little credit for it — they're serving king and country; stretcher-bearers, right up with the boys. Doing well, I'm told, but if they don't last, they'll have a taste of Dunkirk prison.'

'They'll last. As long as any other men. Maybe longer.'

'You reckon?'

'If they say they'll go, they'll go.'

'You seem sure about that.'

I'd said enough.

He pushed his cigarette pack across. Players, better than the Woodbines that came our way.

I lit one.

'Anyway, you saved the lives of two conchies. What do you think of that, Sergeant McDonnell, veteran of Gallipoli, the Somme, Messines and God knows what else?'

I blew a smoke ring and watched it.

'Think of all the good lads who willingly served now rotting on some Godforsaken battlefield.'

'That's how it is, Colonel,' I said.

He left it at that. But a week or so later he sat in the front beside me, and once we were on our way, said, 'You remember Kirwin? He's caved in. Never had much time for him; sends you up the wall. Not like Baxter. Baxter listens; you can have a reasoned argument with the man. But Kirwin's a different kettle of fish. He agreed to do medical work. He's at one of our hospitals over here—not fit for anything else. What do you know? If he's a conchie they want more. No boozing, no loafing, puts his head down and keeps going. Won't take any pay. Against his principles.'

'Nice to know the army's making on the deal,' I said.

'Eh? Ha, ha. He and his mates have cost us plenty. Though it's paying off with the stretcher-bearers. Did I tell you about Gear? Poor blighter, killed in action.'

'And Baxter, Sir?' I asked because I'd heard they'd put him on an ammunitions dump and left him there, untied. Fritz's artillery was making a search for it, shell by shell. Only needed one hit. Got near, but Baxter stayed. They couldn't work that out either.

'Off his head; admits he had trouble before the war.'

'Yeah?'

'Yes.'

'He'd be crazy to admit it,' I said.

'McDonnell, I can see why you were never commissioned.'

So we got on OK. Soon after, Harry looked me up. We spoke of this and that and he asked about the conchies. I told him, and about the stretcher-bearers. He said they were all brave men, whether still objecting, or in the field. I said I supposed so.

Everything comes to him who waits and it came for Hoppy when the Germans broke through. When he paraded the Second Entrenchment Battalion and let forth, there wasn't a man who didn't believe the war depended on him. Our firepower was rifles and a dozen Lewis guns. We went up in buses. Unheard of for a labour battalion. Then a forced march and digging, no artillery; half had never fired a shot outside a rifle range and more than I like to think hadn't done that. I was shoved in as a platoon commander. It was a sharp little action. We stood our ground although the hardest hit company was enveloped and lost a hundred prisoners. I guess they didn't know how to withdraw.

It was in August, after the big breakthrough across the St Quentin Canal and other places and Harry and his boys had cleared Bapaume, that Hoppy and I had another chat. This time it was in an estaminet in Amiens. The place had been bombed a bit from the air and Fritz had got near but we'd held him off. For a city in Northern France it was as close to normal as you could get.

'The way things are going, Jim, the Hun can't last. Maybe not this year, but he'll be gone by next.'

'You don't sound too happy about it, Sir.'

'All right for you. You've done your bit, and you've come through pretty much as when you went in.'

'Luck helps.'

'Yes, McDonnell, it does. Anyway what'll you do when it's all over?'

'Go home.'

'And then?'

'Don't know.'

'Ever thought of having a go at the Bolsheviks?'

'Can't say I have, Sir.'

'They're calling for volunteers, advisors, North Russian Intervention Force, experienced NCOs, to give the Whites a helping hand. There'd be promotion in it, maybe a medal.'

'North Russia?'

'Murmansk and Archangel.'

'Sounds a bit on the cold side, Sir.'

'Summers are delightful, I hear. If you're interested, let me know.'

I had a little laugh to myself, but I also saw it as a sign that Hoppy and I might be about to part. I wasn't wrong. Divisional Mechanical Transport wanted a senior NCO. Hoppy told me he couldn't justify an experienced NCO as his driver any longer and that DMT's need was greater than his. I was made a staff sergeant. It turned out a nice little number. The booze had got to their sergeant major. When they saw I could do the job, he was shipped home and I was given a crown at the bottom of my sleeve. Not a bad rank as ranks go. Divisional Mechanical Transport was a lot different in 1918. Anyone who knew anything about cars and trucks you could count on one hand. We were the ones who kept motor transport on the road: servicing vehicles and getting troops up to the line in a hurry. As long as it rolled they left you alone. We did it over roads that weren't all that much even for horses and wagons. I got around on a motorbike, sorting things out, like when a vehicle broke down and the provosts and ASC wanted to ditch it to keep the horse transport moving. The mechanics were a great mob. They liked nothing better than getting under a bonnet. They taught me a lot.

Early November we stopped in Solesmes, just north of Briastre, and it was there we heard about Turkey and Austria throwing it in. Then it was talk of the German Government sending delegates through the lines. We heard the guns until the last minute. Old habits die hard; it was not surrender, but an armistice: no one knew how long it would last, so you kept firing until the last minute. Then for the first time in four years the guns stopped: no sound. The silence was strange. We didn't shout and cheer. Just looked at each other and went and had a beer or two, maybe more, but we didn't need an excuse for that. I can only say again; it was strange.

The Division marched off to Germany. Took three weeks up to the German border. It had all been under German occupation and it was at Namur, in Belgium, when I was arranging billets that I was asked if we were on our way to Germany. I said we were. They introduced a man from Dinant, a town to the south. He could speak English. In 1914 he'd seen the Germans line up a hundred men and women in the town square, men in one row, women in another, kneeling back to back, and shoot the lot; then another five hundred. The Germans said Belgian civilians had been shooting at them. It might not seem much but the Germans had a thing about brass; if you had any brass in your house, from a doorknob to a lamp stand, if a German saw it, it was his. In Louvain, the Oxford of Belgium, they destroyed the university and the town, killed a couple of hundred people and threw the rest out to shift for themselves. Passing through the Ardennes we saw the forests on the Belgian side heavily cut. Over the border was hardly touched—and no ruins.

We weren't in the best of moods when we marched into Cologne and they didn't like us either. No fraternisation, side arms to be worn, and, apart from the red-light district, the order was obeyed. When you walked along the street they got out of the way, looking past you or at the ground. Sometimes a side look showed what they'd like to do to you. But soldiers are a sentimental lot. Couldn't say no to the kids. They weren't starving, not where we were, but working people knew what it was to be hungry and had a washed out look. There wasn't much in the food shops: black bread and meat that looked like horse, and there were long queues. Once you're friends with the kids, you look further and the obvious rears its head. Who cares if she's German? And a lot of us, senior NCOs and officers, were billeted out. Frosty at first but if you brought home the bacon now and then, you weren't minded too much.

We lived well enough. Our general had a palace and the rest of us made out in comparison. I wasn't the only one who lived better than at home. I was in and out of the general's palace: oak, marble, and brass everywhere you turned. We had been told Cologne was a big city but we had no idea how big until we marched over the Hohenzollern Bridge and saw the cathedral and buildings like the Opera House. With guard work and parades, garrison life is boring but it was better than what we'd come from. There were physical training courses and educational programmes. Some were interesting and others were about things like 'The Bolshevik Menace'. Afternoons and early evening were free so I did things I didn't usually do like viewing the cathedral from top to bottom and taking tram trips down the Rhine to Coblenz or up it to Düsseldorf. At first the only people I knew were army. Some went to the opera. On Boxing Day I went to *Carmen*. I guess *Carmen* was as good as any to begin with. When I went to four hours of *Tannhäuser* that nearly turned me off although on the way home on the tram a couple of English officers told us it was the best they'd been to and almost got me interested. I went to others, mainly Italian, and have since.

But I was curious about what was going on in Germany. We'd heard about the mutiny of the sailors at Kiel and how they moved on to Berlin, Bremen and Hamburg and how Workers' and Soldiers' Councils took over. Because he was no more use to them, the generals kicked the Kaiser out. They and the 'socialist' Government got friendly. The 'socialists' were frightened of the Left, like the Independent Socialists who wanted a real socialist government. More to the left were the Spartacists. They wanted a revolution like in Russia. The Independent Socialists had a government in Bavaria until their prime minister was assassinated to the yell of 'Death to the Israelite'. As happens more often than not, the Right were much better at getting a combat force together than the Left and the Left paid for it.

Now I was part of an army that wasn't just holding a bridgehead for the Allies, but also keeping the Reds under. I didn't like it. I went round the beer halls and cafés looking for my own kind. Some called me a spy. Can't say I blamed them. We'd just left off trying to kill each other. When I ran into men who'd been on the Somme 1916 or Messines, it was easier, but I couldn't find many. We talked in the French I had picked up our side and the French they had picked up on theirs. Soon I was picking up German. Some still wore their uniforms, some half and half, some were in civvies and most had no more than what they stood up in. Some had deserted; others had marched home with flags flying and rifles at the slope. Some had lost a leg or an arm or were not all there. I was told 'You never beat us in the field,' which was what the 'socialist' prime minister said at a march-past in Berlin. Some blamed the generals and some the Kaiser. The Right spoke of 'the stab in the back' and blamed the Left.

Then I met an opposite number, about my age and rank, an Oberfeldwebel. He'd been a platoon commander, but in the German Army that was more common than not. He'd served on the fronts I had and fought the French too. He was looking for a job. His father had a job, driving a locomotive, but about all you could say about the German railways was that they weren't likely to sack you. Gerhard said the choice for a returned soldier was, if you were lucky and had a dad in the railways, labouring on the rail track for a near starvation wage, or going really hungry. If you didn't like either of those, there was the Freikorps with plenty to eat and plenty of action. You could go east and shoot Poles or stay at home and shoot Reds. There were thousands of them, and unlike the Reds, they were not short of money.

Gerhard was a socialist and so was his old man. His dad had always been a union man and if his union could bump his wages up that'd be enough for him. He wanted the old ways, only better. That made him, I guess, when you look back on it, one of the great mass of Germans. There were arguments at home. Gerhard and his sister were of the generation who, Left or Right, were fed up with the Germany of the Kaiser, the Junkers, and the bourgeoisie. We know where the Right of that generation took Germany. The Left, because they had no military, missed out. Gerhard was an Independent Socialist, Helga a Spartacist. Before the war she'd worked in a cotton mill, starting young, and I guess she was a socialist about an hour later and joined the union next morning. She got hold of the *Communist Manifesto* and never forgot that workers have nothing to lose but their chains and the world to win. She'd been brought up a Catholic and one of the first things she did was to throw that out the window and with it the idea of getting married. The job in the cotton mill lasted until she was sacked as an activist.

When Helga was eighteen, Rosa Luxemburg came to Cologne. In the early years of the century Rosa was up there with Lenin, being a great orator and writer. Lenin and she respected each other but with one big difference. For him the revolution would never get anywhere unless the Central Committee of the Party set the party line, to be obeyed by all. Rosa Luxemburg believed the proletariat was fit to lead itself. After the Social Democrats had cut a deal with the generals, Rosa joined the Spartacists. They allowed themselves to be holed up in a Berlin building. After the Freikorps brought up mortars, a couple of howitzers, a captured British tank and flamethrowers, they surrendered; three hundred—those not beaten to death—shot. Rosa hadn't been near the fighting but was beaten and shot.

All this coincided with Helga moving in with me. We weren't to know about Rosa's differences with Lenin until the 1920s. In 1919 all we knew was the murder, and that the Soviet Union, the only socialist revolutionary regime in the world, was being attacked by enemies within and without. We heard about the terror, but we'd also heard about White terror and we knew first-hand about Freikorps terror in Germany. In November 1918 Helga had believed the days of the capitalists, the Junkers, and the generals were over. Now she knew it would be as it had been in the past.

I met Helga when Gerhard took me to a café where she was a waitress. It was a big café and she organised a union there, but they didn't sack her until they hired another good waitress. When the union protested her sacking, everyone was sacked, including her replacement. But Helga had been living like that for years. Like Rosa she had been against the war because it was workers killing workers. She became interested in me because I was a socialist who came from a country she'd never heard of. She wanted to know how far we were along the socialist road. I told her about my dad, the War Resisters, and the 1913 strike.

I'd rented a room near the general's palace. I liked giving shelter to a revolutionary under his nose. Moving in with me gave her time for her real work. All underground by then. A lot of it was with the union movement because the big unions had gone along with the Government and made a deal with the bosses and the generals. I would have married Helga if she'd been willing. I would have stayed in Germany without getting married but there was no future for a deserter in occupied Cologne. It was a hard parting. I used up my cash to pay six months' room rent. If I'd given it to her she'd have given it away in a week. Her last words were to tell the New Zealand workers what I had seen of self-interest, division, and nationalism. She might have lasted out the twenties; in the thirties they would have got her for sure.

We arrived at Sling just after the riots. The authorities had been buggering about with ships and which men had priority. For the ships they blamed strikes. It must have been hard to come up with that one. As for priority, someone in a cosy office in Wellington had worked out that 'pivotal' men would go first; those who had married in England, coal miners, apprentices, farmers, university graduates, etc. If you were a single man like me with no trade, you were at the bottom. Made no difference if you'd joined up in 1914. I didn't care that much but a lot did and so there were riots. The army handled it well enough. It had no option. Underneath the bull, if an army doesn't have the consent of the men, it has nothing. The schedule was altered to first in, first out, and we were given better leave. I could have returned early but I ran into Frank and he got me into a mechanic's course at Sling and three months at the Morris works at Oxford; interesting from a union point of view.

On my second-to-last day in England, at the Divisional Discharge Depot, a British Army recruiter called me up. He said my name had been mentioned for a job they had: Auxiliary Police for Ireland, since known as the Black and Tans. Good money and all found.

I'd been back in Wellington for a couple of months when I ran into Hoppy Mitchell.

'Jim! Good to see you.' He seized my hand. 'Where've you been?'

I spoke of Cologne and how I was now working at a garage.

'You didn't take the offer?'

'What offer?'

'Ireland.'

'Should've known you were behind it.'

He grinned.

'I know you, Jim my lad.'

'Thank you very bloody much.'

'In a year you'll be bored out of your tree. Just make sure it's the right mob.'

'You can count on me, Hoppy.'

NELLE
1918

A great victory had been won at Messines so we knew we'd be busy. I was moved back into surgical where Jim was. His wound was suppurating and twice a day I had to clean it. It was *almost* unnerving because there was not a whimper. Although I have no idea whether it helped or not, I made a point of saying good morning or good afternoon to each patient with, I hoped, a smile. Nearly all returned the greeting. Jim did too but usually it took the form of a semi-Neanderthal grunt so, after a rather gruesome session, I was startled to hear him address me.

'You don't muck about.'

'I wish I could do it more quickly.' It was the first thing that came into my head.

'So do I,' he said, and smiled.

I felt privileged.

It was twelve to fourteen hours a day, seven days a week. These things build up and it was not until the work tapered off that I went up to London to see Father, who had come back from France on a temporary posting. I went to bed feeling not at all well and in the morning I could hardly move for aches and pains. Father took a quick look and called a colleague. Influenza, but not yet a killer. Afterwards he sat beside me and asked what I had been doing. He was surprised and, I think, a little proud, but stated I would be in no condition to return to the TB ward, as had been intended. I begged him not to tell Mother of the TB work. He quietly said he would not. This made me very happy because it meant I was now an adult worthy of keeping a confidence. We had little sessions together when I would tell him more of what I had been doing and he would tell me what he did.

I told him I wished to drive an ambulance in France, even though it would mean joining the English VADs. At first he tried to discourage me. This was not because VADs drove up to the front—they didn't: as in England they conveyed the wounded between railway stations and hospitals—but because the conditions in France were much harsher. I persisted, arguing that it could not be worse than nursing in a TB ward. (Although I was tempted to tell him about how it might bring me closer to Albert, I knew that the time was not ripe for that yet.) At length he consented: partially because he could see I was determined and partially because of his sense of duty. But it was on one condition: that I had experience in England first. If I agreed, he would do all he could to help me. I gave him a huge hug.

He had the use of a car while he was in London and went as far as letting me learn in it. If he had a spare moment he would give me a lesson; when he had not, and the car was not needed for other duties, his driver did. She was a New Zealand VAD and we got on well. She, and Father, remarked on how quickly I learnt. Even though I had told Father much, I had yet to spill the beans on Albert, who had taught me how to keep a motorbike on the road—or rather, keep it from running off the road—by sitting in front of him, half on the seat and half on the petrol tank. He would start the engine and I would steer, his arms long enough, if he snuggled up close, to reach the handlebars if needed. It was mad but it was fun and nice to have him close as we bounced along the road.

Father called the Walton Commandant—one colonel to another—and, after telling him my convalescence had been put to good use, suggested I be sent on the required motor maintenance course. The Walton Commandant, who would not have known me if he had fallen over me, agreed. Some of my nursing colleagues were nice when I returned as a driver, some were not; the latter pointedly remarking on the advantages of having a colonel for a father, quite overlooking that no other aide had spent as much time in the wards as I had.

I returned to Walton for experience and assuredly I gained it. Especially with the car; most definitely especially with the car, but we shall return to her later. Being the most recent arrival, I chauffeured the hospital Padre. Old enough to be my grandfather, the Padre had first gone to war in South Africa. Unlike Father, who wore khaki because there was a war on, the Padre believed himself a soldier who happened to be a padre. If he'd had any doubts about this, which is unlikely, they were refuted at Gallipoli, where his leg was cut off. He came to Walton accompanied by his wife and daughter. I drove him between Mount Felix and Oatlands, Walton village and the railway station, and into London to buy comforts for the patients, or sometimes further afield, to the other New Zealand hospital at Brockenhurst in the New Forest, or to Sling Camp in Hampshire. Distributing cigarettes and chocolates to patients in the wards kept him busy, but he also fussed around New Zealand War Contingent Association people. I welcomed it when I was needed to carry patients who didn't need an ambulance ('sitters', we called them) between Mount Felix and Oatlands or from the railway station when an ambulance train steamed in. The Padre was unhappy when the patients' needs overrode his.

I was not sure why I was never enamoured of the Padre until his daughter was sent a Christmas cake. Miss L, as I shall call her, was older than most VADs, in her late twenties or early thirties, who, at first, worked as a VAD kitchen hand, the Padre forbidding her to transfer to the wards. She was soon promoted to wait on the Matron-in-Chief's table. The Matron-in-Chief grew fond of her—as we all did—and discovered she had always wanted to be a nursing VAD. The Matron-in-Chief, being a strong-minded woman—has one ever heard of a Matron-in-Chief not being a strong-minded woman?—overruled the Padre. He, like everybody else, seeing no future in crossing the Matron-in-Chief, had to accept her decision. When a Christmas cake from New Zealand was delivered to Miss L, she announced she would hold a little party in the ward to share it. In England, late 1917, real Christmas cakes were rare indeed. Set down in the middle of the ward, it made everybody marvel and just as Miss L was to make the first cut, the Padre's batman arrived, picked up the cake and proclaimed it was to be cut up by the Padre for all patients—a loaves and fishes in reverse. Poor Miss L, we felt for her. Aware of the awe in which she held her father, comments were restrained. Equally sad is that Miss L came to believe her father was right. Years later, I was visiting Auckland, and hearing her name mentioned, I called on her. We shared memories. For her, Walton was the highlight of her life. After the war her father died and for years she served her mother, whom she described as 'frail'.

I could write a book about my Model T Ford. High off the ground, not easy for the wooden-legged Padre to climb into—though he was never reluctant about it—Lizzie Ford (for years the Model T was known as a Tin Liz) was a trial for us all. For the garage men she was as stubborn as an army mule; for me she was the bane of my life. Lavishing care and consideration made not the slightest difference. The sheer obstinacy began in the morning, every morning, when she was cranked. If she responded, which was rarely, there would be a shattering backfire and a lashing back of the crank handle—and a bruised wrist for the next twenty-four hours. When she didn't respond, the crank handle had to be turned and turned with not even a cough from her engine. Thoroughly worn out, I had no alternative but to seek the assistance of garage hands. The pantomime of pushing would commence; with me clinging to the steering wheel, a foot gingerly planted on the gear pedal—Model Ts changed gears with a pedal—and swearing men behind (though keyed up in anticipation, I barely heard them). We would roll forward and at the cry 'Now!' I would plunge the gear pedal down. If she decided to fire, there would be a loud explosion, the first of many, and a charge at anything in her path. If she did not, she would jar to a shuddering halt. Once we were on the road, it was not the end of the story, by any means; indeed the days when Lizzie resolved to be tractable were rare and cherished. Lizzie was sensitive about her 'mixture', which, if not to her taste, would make her stall, petulantly, especially if I failed to adjust the lever designated for the purpose immediately after she had condescended to start. Sometimes she would express her dissatisfaction on the open road, or a favourite, when one was about to return home. Another of her penchants was for punctures: productive of barked knuckles and blackened nails, and invariably happening miles from anywhere. On the not infrequent occasions when the spare blew too, one bumped home on the rim. A favourite trick, when bowling along the road, was for her to heave a sigh and roll quietly to a stop. Out I would climb, rain or fine, while the Padre, under cover and in his greatcoat, would alternate complaints with useless advice. I knew the drill well: first, clean the carburettor, hope, and crank; second, check the feed for blockage, hope, and crank; third, unscrew each sparkplug, clean, hope, and crank, and all the time knowing the longer it took, the cooler Lizzie became, and the less inclination she would have to start. If all was to no avail, I would flag down the first mode of transport passing in the direction of Mount Felix. If that failed, you waited until the garage hands decided a joyride might be diverting, and came to the rescue.

They were a cheerful lot in the garage and, as long as I did not let them get away with too much, kept their banter within bounds. If they had a spare moment they might wander across for a chat when I was cleaning Lizzie's engine or washing her less than elegant body—the Padre had the irritating habit of wanting Lizzie when she was halfway through a wash. And so long as I was willing to stand by and hand out tools, they'd do a repair job rather than have her wait in the queue. Being a cut above the Walton orderlies, they were attractive to the 'general' VADs—and it was not unknown for drivers and nurse aides to seek their company either. Under the guise of a 'test drive' a mechanic and VAD would go out for a joyride, to the chagrin of certain military policemen on gate duty. If the VAD was not a driver there was nothing to stop her from walking out the gate in her off duty hours and being picked up around the corner. Because of the Zeppelins there were also the air raid shelters.

I drove in latish one night and, after parking Lizzie, noticed a corporal mechanic descending into the shelter near the garage, carrying something. Lizzie had not being making the right noises, and to my experienced ear, that boded ill. I hurried after the corporal, descended into the dugout, and without thinking, drew aside the curtain. Before me was the corporal holding a teapot. Behind him, lying back on a stretcher was a startled VAD, rather lightly covered.

'A cup of tea, Miss Travis?' He might have been a kindly waiter.

'Oh! Thank you! No!' My face glowing like a lantern, I departed.

Test drives, however, had positive uses. On my return to Mount Felix

I discovered that Jim, as soon as he was classed as convalescent, had gone to the garage and spoken to the sergeant—a kind and competent man as I recall, and he persuaded the sergeant—one sergeant to another—that he needed help in his garage. Before the week was out he had donned overalls and was working. When the garage sergeant noticed Jim and I were acquainted, he said would I mind if Jim might take a few turns around the grounds in Lizzie. I said Jim could take Lizzie to Land's End and leave her there. After a moment I suggested the next time Lizzie was due for a test drive—sooner rather than later, as we knew—perhaps Jim, in his overalls, might accompany me. Once out on the open road ... For a change the war had taught Jim something other than killing men.

Which was not so in everybody's case. In my darker moments I would wonder why, of all people, I had fallen in love with a fighter pilot. Indeed my willingness to spend extra time on the road with Jim was because it took my mind off Albert. I wrote every day and he, for a man, was a good, if erratic, correspondent. It depended on when he was flying, and flying depended upon the weather. I prayed for low cloud and rain. Three letters were delivered in three days; that was when they were moving aerodromes. He rarely wrote anything about what he did in the air, although he frequently mentioned what a fine bunch of chaps his pilots were. A little too often, he told me about 'old' so and so, who'd had 'rotten luck'. He had to mention it to someone I suppose, but these, and others like them, were passing remarks. What he wrote was love: shared with an aeroplane.

Albert's first letter had been a proposal. Not unexpected, indeed at the last minute, on the platform at Victoria he had blurted out, 'Time to make it permanent, what?' and I had said something like 'Marvellous' and no more, feeling there were better times and places to receive a proposal than in the midst of the British Expeditionary Force en route for France. And, since the meeting on the ice—sounds awfully Russian doesn't it?—I knew it would be him. It was easy to compose a reply; the hard part was waiting. An interminable three months passed before, unbelievably, he stepped off the train at Victoria.

Two fearful prospects awaited me: informing Mother and meeting Mater. Although I tried to warn him, Albert had not the slightest trepidation about meeting either of my parents. I 'prepared' Mother by writing to Father. So great was her shock that I was actually called to answer the sole staff telephone at Mount Felix. She went on forever. Albert wrote to Father asking his permission — Father said it could have been a request to borrow his horse — but I knew the two would get on, although Father, knowing about the RFC, kept his fears to himself. We arrived and before Mother could say a word, Father shepherded Albert into his study. They remained there for so long I began to wonder if my confidence might have been misplaced. They came out all smiles and indications of whisky. It was all very well for them; I had to put up with Mother and cold tea.

The best I might say about Mother is that she was more impossible than expected. She commenced with the iciest condescension and questions that made one yearn for the ground to open up and envelop one. Father was a great help, sitting to one side of Mother and a little behind her, his smile for Albert a plea for tolerance, if not unconditional appreciation. Little by little, each question more blatant than the one preceding it, she melted, concluding with an announcement to the effect that perhaps I had made a better catch than any reasonable person might have expected.

That I might soon suffer a similar ordeal did not cheer me. Albert was no help at all. 'Are you prepared for the old dragon? My sister is bad enough, but just wait until you meet Mater,' and he suggested we go down to Hampshire by motorbike, 'much more fun'. There I put my foot down. Dragon or not, her first sight of a future daughter-in-law most certainly was not going to be astride a motorbike. 'Besides,' I said, 'what about my suitcase and hatbox?' 'We're only going for a weekend.' 'Quite,' I said, 'that's why there's only a suitcase and a hatbox.' As the Carrington home was on the edge of the New Forest near the village of Ripley we took the train to the south coast. Neither of us could leave our war behind. When the train stopped at Beaulieu, we noticed an RFC airfield next to the abbey, and after that was Brockenhurst, where, on the platforms, were the Boy Scout hats of New Zealanders from our other large hospital. I was more reassured when, alighting at Christchurch, there was a pleasant looking young woman in the driver's seat of a car who Albert introduced as Monica, his sister.

After I had met Mater, and Albert and I had a moment to ourselves, I had a piece of him for raising utterly groundless fears about her: a beautiful and gracious woman who greeted me as the loving friend she was to become. After I had changed she showed me around her garden. We were into late summer, the early fruit trees were bearing, and in the conservatory there were grapes, which, in the past three years, I had only dreamed of. The vegetable garden we viewed over the hedge, its custodian, Mater explained, having made plain that if the household wished to benefit from it, they had best keep out. We were, however, permitted to pick the fruit and admire his lawns and flowerbeds, although as Mater explained, he was not really happy with them, there being no young man to help him because of the war. He was not the only ancient on the property. The women in the house were similarly advanced; the younger women of the village being needed for the land or munition factories, and as for the younger men, we knew where they were.

Mater was a widow, her husband having died of fever whilst serving in the South African war. While not overly wealthy by English standards, she was comfortably off, the family land being leased to farmers. One approached the house by a tree-lined gravel drive. I caught a glimpse of water as we crossed over a stone bridge to draw up in front of the house. It was not a stream, but a moat—a fashionable accessory for an Elizabethan Manor House. After Mount Felix, it was a pleasant change to be gently awakened for a cup of tea and called for a bath. On Sunday, Monica and I spent a morning together. She was younger than Albert, and I envied her as she was about to be sent to France as a VAD ambulance driver.

On the insistence of Mother the wedding was held in St George's, off Hanover Square; a fine edifice, then less than a decade short of two hundred years old, but I would much rather have been married in All Saints, Thorney Hill; a dear little church built only recently by Lord Manners, a neighbour of Mrs Carrington's, as a memorial to a daughter who died young. Mother would have none of it; what more rewarding way was there to celebrate my departure from her household than a Mayfair wedding? An acquaintance was dragooned to open her house in South Audley Street for me to prepare and be married from and my aunt in

Norfolk was despatched to comb the country for relatives, none seen before or since, to fill the bride's pews. Two of Father's colleagues came, as well as the Commandant and Matron-in-Chief from Walton, as many of the friends I had made at Walton who could be spared, and although I was barely aware of it, Frank Butler was dragged in too. What the bride's side lacked in numbers it compensated for in uniforms. When we stepped into the portico it was under the swords of Albert's Flying Corps and cavalry friends. The breakfast would have been war austerity if it had not been for the bounty delivered from the Carrington farms and gardens. What I remember most vividly about the service is how the sun suddenly shone through the stained glass above the altar.

Our honeymoon was four days in London. I daresay we painted the town red but it seemed almost overnight when Mrs Albert Carrington farewelled her husband.

Mother announced it was time to resign as a VAD and commence a respectable life. Father, knowing I now needed the work more than it needed me, and that there was no surplus of drivers, took my side. I was lucky on my return to Walton. An ambulance driver had had to resign to return home to care for a sick mother—a not uncommon reason for departure amongst VADs, and I am forever grateful that I never had to be one. Ambulance driving was not easy. The grim grey trains with their red crosses arrived at any time of the day or night and one drove until they were unloaded. In the good times, the patients arrived having been treated and cleaned at a Base Hospital. In the bad they came direct from the Casualty Clearing Station with trains arriving one after another. Mostly we would shuttle between Walton station and the hospital, but there were days and nights when we had to drive to Charing Cross. The ambulances were not well sprung and for some men the trip was agony—what it must have been like for them on the roads at the front hardly bears thinking about. The groans and screams of the men in the greatest pain would set the other men off; the only way to deal with that was to concentrate on driving.

As we went into winter, everything and everybody was grey and dowdy, food was meagre and monotonous, and there was a change in the men. Even those who had recovered fully had a hopeless air about them. People hadn't given up, but no longer was there the confidence that had carried us thus far. Mother nearly drove me out of my mind. During her residence in London she had joined a circle of acquaintances. Now a respectable personage, on my duty visits I was introduced as, 'My daughter Mrs Carrington; her husband is a major in the Royal Flying Corps, you know.' The conversation was rarely about anything other than their trials and tribulations; always there was the problem that never ends: servants. The war was especially to blame: the 'wicked' wages paid to women as a consequence of it, bus conductresses, female coal-heavers, and munition workers being high on the list. When I suggested that acquiring a munition worker's yellow complexion could hardly be termed a perquisite, it elicited the comment that if they made themselves more familiar with soap and water they might not have to make such exhibitions of themselves, which led me to the brink of stating that if any of us fell on hard times we had a future before us in either munitions or coal, taking into account we would have no problems with soap and water.

And then I was pregnant; the four days in London having accomplished more than had met the eye. Mixed feelings: the child is for a lifetime but how long for the father? I wrote four letters; the first to Albert and the second to Mater. Albert's was the quickest reply ever; if she were a girl she would be as beautiful as her mother and if he were a boy he couldn't wait to teach him to fly. Not knowing whether to laugh or cry I laughed *and* cried. Mater's great pleasure at having a grandchild did not surprise and neither, on reflection, did her invitation to spend my pregnancy with her. The third letter was to Father and he replied he was happy indeed to become a grandfather and attached a letter of introduction to a London obstetrician. Mother insisted I resign from 'that job' immediately. I resigned when a replacement driver arrived. I left my life as a VAD with neither reluctance nor relief; but with gratitude for what it had taught me.

When I told Mother I was going to Mater's, she said 'No Zeppelin bombs will drop on *you*.' Mater kindly invited Mother to visit. And so she did, and more than once, in response, as I now realise, to Mater's carefully spaced invitations. Save for the absence of a husband, and all that goes with being pregnant, life could not have passed more pleasantly, for aside from carrying the baby, I was able to rest and relax for the first time since I had walked so innocently into St Thomas's. But it did not dull the fear and foreboding. I did not brood, indeed I kept myself occupied, but I could not banish thoughts about Albert. It did not happen every night but three o'clock in the morning was always a bad time: so much so that I came to dread it. On a bad night, try as I might, I could not rid myself of the fears that would drive out any other thoughts. By then I was close enough to Mater to confide in her. A horsewoman herself, she recommended riding, and allowing for my pregnancy, chose a gentle beast to exercise on and if she did not accompany me herself, sent one of the old grooms with me. The worst moments during the day were hearing the crunching of gravel when an unexpected caller came up the drive.

Mater, who had never lacked domestic help, spent three to four hours a day, six days a week, and sometimes seven, scrubbing floors, washing up, and working in the kitchen, not in her own home, but that of her neighbour's. I have already mentioned the Manners family and Avon Tyrell. Although it was now filled with convalescent New Zealand officers, the family continued to live there. Their daughter, Agnes, was appointed Matron and she was assisted by numerous volunteers, of whom Mater was one. While they would not let me do heavy work—usually a duster was proffered—I accompanied Mater to the house where, at the end of the day, if the weather were fine, Mater and I would drive into the New Forest to gather heather and myrtle for the vases of Avon Tyrell.

It was late one afternoon after returning from such an expedition, when darkness was falling, that Mater and I were sitting before a fire enjoying a cup of tea when Ethel, who had just brought us the tray, entered the room again and handed Mater an envelope. Mater held it between finger and thumb, looked at it, did not open it, and quietly passed it to me.

For once I was not thinking of anything, just enjoying the warmth of the fire and sipping the tea, so I reached across for a paper knife, cut the envelope and took out a small sheet of paper.

'Regret to inform you Major ATJ Carrington DSO MC killed in action December 11.'

I rose, walked firmly across to Mater, handed her the telegram, and when she brushed it aside as if she were fending off a blow, I collapsed, my head in her lap. She clasped me close, drawing my face up to hers, our tears intermingling. How long we were like that I do not know. When we had recovered ourselves, as well as we were capable, dear Ethel was there with a fresh pot of tea.

'He was a lovely lad, Mr Albert,' she said to Mater, and when she had passed a cup to me, this normally reserved woman, her kind old eyes meeting mine, placed her hand on my shoulder.

It may sound peculiar, but the first night was one of the easiest. We sat in front of the fire and I told Mater how Albert and I met and she reminisced of him as a little boy. In the small hours, exhausted, we dragged ourselves to bed. I awoke early; still tired, but restless, I dressed and went for a long walk. At first I berated myself for ignoring my feeling that it could end only in this way. Why, I asked myself, hadn't I been sensible or just had an affair, farewelled him and if he returned, taken it from there and left plans of permanence until the war ended, if the war was ever going to end? And perhaps it was a mistake, perhaps there was another Major AJT Carrington DSO MC, and the telegram had been sent to the wrong widow. But it was so sudden, and when I gazed about the garden everything was so alive.

We met at breakfast, Mater as worn out as I and I told her how I would not have been able to bear it by myself; how grateful I was for her invitation.

'Nelle,' she said, 'my dear Nelle, it would be unbearable if you were not here.'

A diversion was the number of callers. Albert had been especially popular and when Mater held a memorial service for him at All Saints, the church overflowed. After the service there were days of emptiness, and moments when one forgot, as when an aeroplane flew low over the house, and one wondered, as one had done, whether it was Albert, about to land at Beaulieu or Brooklands, and soon to surprise us on his motorbike.

There were several letters, including one from his commanding officer, stating what a fine pilot Albert had been, and another from Albert's batman saying he was the kindest officer he had ever served. I invited each to visit and enclosed a railway fare for the batman. It was the custom to return a deceased officer's uniform to his closest relatives. Albert had had two, one to fly in and wear around the aerodrome and the other he had been married in. I received only the latter, with his medals and personal possessions and, a great comfort, my letters. But no 'flying' uniform, made me wonder. Soon after, I met a poor woman whose husband had been killed in the trenches. She told me that when she received her husband's uniform, she had to have it burnt immediately; its stench being overpowering. I found myself wanting, yet not wanting, to know where the second uniform was.

Some weeks later, the commanding officer kindly paid us a visit. He told us no more than what had been in his letter. When I raised the matter of the uniform, he apologised for it not being sent, and said that he would look into it on his return. I had nearly given up on the batman, but arrive he did, on leave, the first he'd had in a year. He was a decent conscientious young man, with a touch of humour in his eyes; I could see why Albert and he got on. After thanking me for the rail fare, he said he'd never heard a cross word from Albert, a real gentleman.

'It was a very sad day, Madam, when I laid out the effects of Major Carrington. He was very unlucky and luck is important for a pilot. For about a week over the salient the weather had been heavy with rain and when it wasn't raining the clouds were very low. Not flying weather. Then came a break, blue skies, you could hardly believe it. A lot of catching up to do. Major Carrington's squadron was very busy. But Jerry, he was also busy. I heard the engines revving up and I went outside to watch Major Carrington and his pilots take off for the third patrol of the day, in the afternoon. They were still climbing when a Jerry patrol dived on them. Out of the sun. Precious little you can do when that happens except do your best to get out of their way. Major Carrington was a very good pilot and we thought he had. But two Jerries attacked him, together. I think he winged one, but the other must have got close enough to hit him.'

'And then?'

'I think he had trouble controlling his aeroplane.'

'You do?'

He looked down at his tea cup.

'I don't think Major Carrington suffered long, Madam, I really don't.'

I had to take out my handkerchief.

'Mrs Carrington, he would not have suffered.'

'No,' I said, 'No, I don't suppose he would.'

'He used to speak about you: even to me.'

'Thank you.' Another recourse to the handkerchief. 'So kind of you to tell me.'

'I liked bringing him your letters.'

I looked up.

'Mr Purdy, you mentioned laying out his effects… You know he had two uniforms…'

'I only laid out what was in his tent. And then it was for the officers to decide what would be done.'

'So you don't know what happened to the uniform he was wearing?'

'I guess that would have been for the funeral, Madam. It was a beautiful funeral. I have not known a better — if I might put it that way. All the squadron were there, not just the pilots, all of us, batmen, mechanics, fitters, Mess stewards, all of us.'

'So you don't know.'

'Madam, the Major's uniform would have been treated with the greatest respect.'

I knew as much as I would ever want to.

Young Albert was born late February. A first birth, not an easy one, but how many are? He would not have been christened anything other than Albert, but even the first look at the crumpled little face revealed his father. The joy he brought helped restore equilibrium in our lives. Life went on, Mater went to Avon Tyrrell, and I, with the help of a nanny, looked after Albert, and drove convalescents between Avon Tyrrell and Brockenhurst.

Then came August, hot, dry and dusty. With it came Spanish Influenza. There was a telegram from Mother. She had just been informed about Father; he was gravely ill. At the time of the wedding he had been very run down. Our soldiers paid a heavy toll in 1918 and Father, although the hospital commandant, began and ended his day in the operating theatre, performing his commandant duties in between. It was too much for his immune system; he succumbed.

A foreboding he might not survive, the death of Albert, and the birth of young Albert, I think, led him to alter his will. The inheritance was split: one farm to be sold and the proceeds, plus a sum equivalent to the value of the Wanganui house, going to Mother. To me went the other farm and the Wanganui house. He knew Mother would not want to return to New Zealand. Mother said I was too irresponsible to be left the farm and the house. She was informed there was nothing she could do about it.

Mater told me to look upon her house as a second home and that she too had settled an income on us. Sadly I said that England had become a place of sorrow for me, and that she might like to reconsider, as I had decided to return to New Zealand. She said it made no difference and if Albert and I might make return visits, and if she might visit us from time to time, she would be very happy. In the meantime, we would stay with her until a passage was available to New Zealand—which would not be soon. Lord and Lady Manners encouraged me to join in the life at Avon Tyrrell even if it was just chatting with the convalescents and driving them to and fro. Harry had been wounded yet again and duly became one of them. Being Harry, he could not rest for long and as soon as he was able to get about, he was off to the New Forest, making friends with the foresters and satisfying his curiosity about their ponies roaming the highways and byways.

In September the flu ebbed, but with the coming of winter it burst forth again, taking the edge off the end of the war. Because of little Albert I was careful about venturing out, as it was the young and the old who were most vulnerable. Another English winter followed and Monica returned, utterly exhausted. Her tales of ambulance driving along rutted mud-ridden roads in France, carrying screaming, raving, dying men who had been delivered straight from the front, and of how after every trip the ambulance had to be hosed and scrubbed with disinfectant to get rid of the blood, vomit and filth, all under the domination of tyrannical Matrons, made my experiences almost restful. We became close and I was determined that Albert would grow up with the Hampshire house his second home. At last, as 1919 was coming to a close, there was a passage on the *Remuera*. Despite my love for Mater and the Manor House, I needed to leave England.

I had to leave because so much had happened in my four years there. Peace had come, but I needed quietness too. One might say the Manor House in Hampshire was quiet—but, for the time being anyway, its associations were not. In New Zealand a house and a farm were waiting for me—my own. There would have been nothing to stop me selling them, but the fact was that they were there and I had grown up with them—and New Zealand was as far away as I could get from all that had gone on. And then there was young Albert: his father had remarked that New Zealand seemed the sort of country where a man might spread his wings: that is, a country where *he* might feel at home. When he had met Father he had warmed to him, and also to the New Zealanders he had met at the wedding—fleeting though the meetings were. I knew he would be happy if young Albert was to be brought up here.

FRANK
1918

I was lucky on two counts: I held a King's Commission and I had 'lesions' from the hits I'd taken at Bellevue Spur. If I'd had neither, I could have ended up dead or in a lunatic asylum. A ranker without 'lesions', and acting funny, unless he was stark staring mad, would be suspected of malingering. I was also lucky that it was near the end of the war because by then Freud had become known and although most psychiatrists disagreed with his theories, they saw the sense in getting a patient to talk about what had upset him — and as soon as possible after the event. My surgeon, noting the symptoms of 'neurasthenia' — in my case trembling hands, withdrawal, apathy — had a psychiatrist working with me right from the start. Treatment continued and I was sent to a country house and put in the care of a Scot whose Calvinist regime had me out with the others: early rising on cold mornings, a run in the frost, a cold bath, physical jerks after breakfast, a team game in the afternoon, and a bean-spilling conversation with him some time during the day.

When I had recovered enough to appear before a Medical Board, they decided to send me home — but if Passchendaele had been my first action, I think it would have been France again. Again I was lucky; one of the board remembered that Brigadier Richardson, GOC New Zealand Forces in Britain, had just issued an order for the compilation of a nominal roll of officers and men qualified to lecture in economics, science, or general educational subjects.

From late April 1918 I was on the staff of New Zealand Headquarters, on Southampton Row. My first job was to organise a conference on how educational opportunity might best be offered to the men of the Division. My report went up the line to be presented to Brigadier Richardson. Soon afterwards, I was ordered to present myself to him. Brigadiers generally speak with subalterns to rebuke them, so I wondered what was wrong.

Sprucing myself up, I marched into his antechamber. Sitting on an office high stool, like a Dickensian clerk, was a lieutenant colonel. I came to attention, assuming he was standing in for Richardson, though the stool surprised me. This gentleman, however, although bearing the grand title of Chief-of-Staff, was, in fact, Brigadier Richardson's receptionist and dogsbody, a job normally held by a corporal. He duly instructed me to enter.

'Butler!' The greeting was stern — what you'd expect of a former NCO Brigadier.

'Sir!' I came to attention again.

'Sit down.'

I sat — at attention. Given the chair, there wasn't any other way.

'Your report is succinct and well-organised.'

'Thank you, Sir.'

'You are correct in recommending compulsory education classes for all men when there is time available.'

'Sir!' All I had done was record the feeling of the conference.

'In fact Butler, you have made an excellent job of it. Welcome aboard.' It was then I remembered it was he who organised the Royal Naval Division from surplus naval personnel in 1914. 'But ...' he said. There is always a but. 'But you must put more emphasis on civics, economics, and science. Although we proclaim we are in the industrial age, Butler, we are really just on the brink of it. Science drives industry; it's essential that our men gain knowledge of science.'

'Sir.'

'I don't know how much you have followed current events lately, but they have been momentous. And I am not just talking about our argument with the Kaiser.'

'No, Sir.'

'You are not wholly ignorant of the Bolshevik revolution?'

'Not wholly, Sir.'

'The most pernicious event of the twentieth century. The Germans are interested only in conquest. The Bolsheviks not only intend to conquer; they seek to destroy the very roots of our life. No country, no matter how remote it may be—and few are as remote as our own—can ignore them. Do you understand, Butler?'

'Yes, Sir.'

'You see why civics and economics must be at the top of the list?'

'Yes, Sir.'

'In war Bolshevism infiltrates; in peace it consolidates.' He paused. 'A great opportunity has been presented. We have over twelve thousand men gathered together, disciplined, and ready to be educated by the best minds our country has to offer.'

'Indeed, Sir.'

'Otherwise, an excellent report. Our men have given four years for their country. They deserve every assistance it is in our power to give. Particularly I am thinking of the poor blighters that have to be re-educated. You know who I mean, the farmer who's blind, the stockman without any legs, the butcher who's lost his hands. They have priority. You rightly mention that, when peace is declared, as it will be, there will also be thousands of men awaiting repatriation. Can't train them all the time and to what purpose would that be anyway? Education must fill that gap, Butler. That's where you've hit the nail on the head.'

As had everyone else at the conference.

Richardson had begun his adult life as a teenage private in the Royal Artillery. He had been sent to New Zealand in the early years of the century as an NCO instructor. From there he had worked his way up to become the chief administrator in the New Zealand Army. He was an autodidact, and like others I have known, he was genuinely concerned that ordinary people be granted access to education.

He suffered, however, from the affliction too often found in the military; sentimentality towards the man who conforms to army mores in every respect except that he's useless. Hence the Lieutenant Colonel Dogsbody who, before the war, had worked in a stock and station agency and been a spare-time major in the Volunteers. Managing a transfer to the Territorials, Dogsbody was sent overseas, where it needed only one look by those who knew that he must never, ever, command men beyond the English Channel. Uninhibited by his wife and family in Wellington, and on a healthy income, Dogsbody's off duty hours were devoted to the fairer sex. Never missing an opportunity to respond to a country house invitation, issued by lords and ladies through the New Zealand War Contingent Association, he would, as the opportunity offered, arrive with a 'niece'. Rumour had it that when funds were running low, he borrowed his batman's uniform and went on the town at a cheaper rate. It was the ambition of Dogsbody's colleagues to attain a similar status. The crème de la crème of this lot was the assistant provost marshall. The one characteristic he shared with Richardson was that he had gone out to New Zealand as an NCO instructor, in his case from the Guards. When war broke out he was commissioned with the Aucklands. Appearing reluctant to lead his platoon forward at Gallipoli, he was sent to England where, apparently considered suitable for the position, he was promoted to captain, APM. London being on the expensive side, he embezzled. Just prior to discovery, he lit out for Ireland where, it is alleged, he made a present of his talents to the Fenians. There were exceptions at Southampton Row and they tended to be men who had joined and trained with the expectation of becoming fighting soldiers. Despising their position, they sought to get away. But as they were invariably the hardworking and the conscientious; they did not find it easy to obtain a release.

Our first priority was convalescents: organising classes for them in carpentry, farming, mechanical engineering and, let us not forget, science, civics and economics. Each centre had its own characteristics: like the high VD rate at the soldiers' convalescent home at Hornchurch on the edge of London, the consequences of celebrating their return to health; and the embarkation centre at Torquay, in the cider country, noted for the number of men evincing a sudden desire for work experience in the manufacture of the beverage. There was also a conference on what should be done at the end of the war with the twelve thousand men while they waited to be shipped home. After it, I drafted a policy, a constitution, job descriptions, etc., and met with Richardson. He made me a captain.

Being a wounded officer, I was on the receiving end of free tickets to the theatre, and when asked to attend a reception at Buckingham Palace, curiosity made me accept, thus speaking a total of five words with His Majesty. Another time I went to a similar function at Clarence House and met one of his sons, where even fewer words were exchanged. Normally there would have been a queue of HQ staff for these invitations, but each was restricted to wounded officers and HQ, although overflowing with officers, was not over-supplied with wounded. I also attended another reception.

When asked to attend the wedding of the daughter of the commandant of one of our hospitals in France to make up numbers, I was not enthusiastic until I noticed she was Nelle Travis. I thought maybe I should go to one Mayfair wedding in my life even if it was just an army one. At the breakfast I was at a table of strangers and when I heard a rustle of silk beside me, I barely gave her a glance except to note the woman was wearing black. We did not speak until someone asked a question that might have been addressed to either of us, and each replied. Black is usually becoming: but not to her, not then; she was too pale and there were faint rings under her eyes. She was not dowdy, she could never be that, but her beauty that day was camouflaged. For the sake of something to say I enquired if she, Mrs Varden according to her card, were bride or groom.

'My husband was a distant relative of Major Cunningham.'

'I'm bride, met her once at Walton, and I'm here to make up numbers.'

'Walton?'

'On Thames, we have a military hospital there. She's VAD. Not many New Zealand VADs over here.'

She nodded.

'We rally round on occasions like this,' I went on.

'She's a beautiful bride,' she said.

'Yes,' I said.

I realised she was as much a stranger at the table as I was. We were included in their conversation from time to time but mostly they talked amongst themselves.

Boredom, as much as anything, impelled me to ask if she were interested in the theatre.

'Are you, Captain Butler?'

'Well, Mrs Varden, I'm wondering whether the Old Vic might be worth a trip tonight.'

'I'm afraid I've lost touch,' she said.

I could think of nothing better to say than the other plays they'd put on had been worth seeing.

'I'm glad you're enjoying our theatre, Captain Butler, but it's quite some time since I've been to Shakespeare.'

Despite the gentle refusal, the topic appeared to have animated her a little.

I mentioned that where I came from it was a privilege to have so wide a choice.

'Is it?' she said.

'In my first week in London I went four times.'

'Goodness!'

'I go to just about everything. And you, Mrs Varden, are you fond of the theatre?'

'Am I fond of the theatre?' A half-smile appeared. 'Yes, Captain Butler, I suppose I am.'

At that instant a man across from us remarked on the long run of *Chu Chin Chow* and that it showed little sign of closing. My neighbour agreed and they talked about it, despite the fact that she hadn't seen it. After that there were the usual speeches and I arranged an early escape. It had started to rain and what with that and a war being on, it was a long wait for a taxi. When my name was called I noticed my erstwhile neighbour requesting a taxi. On an impulse, I went up to her and told her I'd be willing to share. She accepted. On the way she thanked me, saying she had a child who was about to be put to bed. I left her outside a block of flats in Knightsbridge.

Accidents happen when a number of events that are never meant to coincide, coincide. What should not happen, does—and it is not always negative. Becoming tired of seeing shows either alone or with a fellow officer, but unsure whether she was on the phone, I sent her an invitation by telegram that I had two tickets for *Chu Chin Chow* in a week's time. It was not until the night before that I received a reply—accepting. The show was enjoyable enough and she appeared not to dislike it. Although she declined to go somewhere afterwards, it was not in a manner to put me off. When I asked her to dinner a week later she accepted on the condition that it was somewhere quiet.

During it, she asked, diffidently, where I had got the small gold wound-stripe on my sleeve. As she did so, she touched it.

'Passchendaele, Mrs Varden.'

'Oh!' she said, 'Oh!' She was upset.

'I'm sorry...' I said.

'No, no. It ... it ... was at Passchendaele that my husband lost his life.'

'It was not a good place, Mrs Varden.'

'Edward went through so much. He'd done his bit but they insisted on sending him back. I pleaded and pleaded with him to ask for a second opinion. He wasn't himself and a good doctor would have diagnosed it, but when they said he should go back, he went.' Taking out her handkerchief, she dabbed her eyes. 'It wasn't right, Captain Butler, it wasn't right.'

There wasn't much I could say to that.

We went to the Old Vic again, to a revue and to another dinner. During it I asked with whom her husband had served.

'The Royal Naval Division. He volunteered in nineteen-fourteen, the day after war was declared.'

'Some of us were pretty keen then,' I said.

'Did you also?'

'Not the day after war was declared, but pretty soon, yes.'

'What made you do it Captain Butler? Why?'

'Why did any of us?' I shrugged my shoulders.

'Edward thought it would be over by Christmas.'

'He wasn't the only one.'

'He put his name forward for a commission in Major Cunningham's regiment—I think—but they said he'd have to wait as there were so many applying. But his friends knew Mr Churchill and that he could get them commissioned at once.'

'Oh yes.'

'Yes, Edward had been at Cambridge with Rupert Brooke and he knew Herbert Asquith; you know, the poet, and the prime minister's son.'

'I've read a little Brooke.'

'And Edward? He wrote too and so does Herbert Asquith.'

'I'd be interested to read him, Mrs Varden.'

'I will give you a copy of his poems. He had them published just after Gallipoli. He couldn't write any more after that.'

'I would very much like to read them.' I paused. 'The Royal Naval Division was at Gallipoli when we were.'

'You were there too, Captain Butler? You might have met.'

'Privates don't mix with officers; not even in the New Zealand Army, or very rarely.'

'You were a private?' She was not so much surprised, as puzzled.

'We all have to begin somewhere,' I said, 'but I'm interested that your husband was a poet.'

'Actually he was due to be called to the bar, but writing poems was his other interest.' She looked at me closely. 'Frank.' Things were more formal those days and this was the first time she had spoken my Christian name. 'Frank, I think you might understand. Other people … they have no idea …' This time four fingers were placed on my sleeve and her thumb lightly stroked it.

'I'm one of the lucky ones.' Yes indeed I am, I thought as I put my hand on hers.

> 'Soldier, soldier come from the wars,
> Do you bring no sign from my true love?'
> 'I bring a lock of 'air that 'e allus used to wear,
> An' you'd best go look for a new love.'

'Soldier, soldier come from the wars,
O then I know it's true I've lost my true love!'
'An' I tell you the truth again—when you've lost the
feel o' pain
You'd best take me for your true love.'

True love! New love!
Best take 'im for a new love,
The dead they cannot rise, an' you'd better
dry your eyes,
An' you'd best take 'im for your true love.

Although I was far too enamoured at the time to recall it, Kipling, as he so often did, had it right in his 'Soldier, Soldier'.

Soon afterwards, at another dinner, she asked if I knew the New Zealander Bernard Freyberg. I said no, because although we had had gone to the same school, he was five years ahead of me.

'Edward invited him to our wedding. A very tall man. Edward admired him as I think he admired few other men.'

'He was awarded a VC at the Somme,' I said.

'He was Edward's company commander at Gallipoli and afterwards, when Edward was promoted to company commander, he commanded Edward's battalion.'

One of the staff at HQ happened to have been senior to me at Wellington College. He was also one of the few who'd been in action. We sometimes repaired to a pub for lunch and a chat. Dora Varden having roused my curiosity, I asked what he knew about Freyberg.

'Ha ha!' He said. 'Haven't seen him since Egypt.' He gave a grin. 'He's moved up in the world. He was on the move then—not just promotion, socially too.'

'Go on.'

'I got whacked at Helles. Managed to get through it,' he swallowed a beer appreciatively. 'And I was on convalescent leave in Alexandria. Went for a flutter at the Kursal. Remember it?' By the look on his face, his memories of it were pleasant.

'All I know about Alex is what I saw from a ship or a train.'

'Well it's unlikely any of us'll ever go back there, but if you are, it's worth a visit. Another pint?' I had work to do and I shook my head. 'Yes, well, I ran into Freyberg. Had known him at school so we arranged to meet. When we did he had a tale to tell. He was convalescing too and had just been awarded his first DSO — for swimming inshore on the morning of the Landing.'

'I've heard that,' I said. 'Some say he'd have been lucky to get an MC if he'd been with his own crowd.'

'They don't know Freyberg.' His face went serious. 'The man's a natural — if ever there was one.'

'I believe he's a brigadier now,' I said.

'And he'll go further — if his luck holds. But what was interesting about our conversation in Alex was that he said he'd cleared off to Mexico in early nineteen-fourteen to fight for the rebels. Only one explanation for that: if there was a war on he wanted to be there. I mean to say, what other interest could he have in joining those bandits?' He picked up his empty glass. 'If you're not going to have another, I will.'

'Make it a half.' I wanted to hear more about Freyberg.

'War being declared, he got himself over here,' he sat down as he returned with his pint and my half. 'Must have cleared out from that Villa fellow and somehow made his way across country and up to New York where he took a passage to Liverpool. I would have liked to know how he got out of Mexico, being both a rebel and a deserter, neither side would have liked him much, but he was not interested in enlarging upon it. From Liverpool he came down here and looked up Richardson. He'd known Richardson in the Territorials and Richardson introduced him to Churchill. Freyberg was in the Antwerp landing in nineteen-fourteen. Like Gallipoli it was a Churchill idea.' Another deep swallow of Best Bitter. 'A disaster, Freyberg said, from the start.'

'A dry run for Gallipoli,' I said.

'Exactly, you'd think Churchill might have learnt, but obviously when it comes to the Big Idea, he gets carried away.' He looked over his beer. 'Anyway, it couldn't have worried Freyberg too much because he told me he got to know Churchill, and the Duchess of Marlborough: all that crowd.' The pint pot was put down. 'Spoke of them like old friends. And, I guess, when he's not winning more medals, he's seeing even more of them.' The grin appeared again. 'Not bad for a Wellington lad.'

'Not bad at all,' I said.

Dora was telling me about herself, and Edward. In her teens she had acted in school and amateur plays well enough for her parents to send her to a drama school. Early in the war she had sung at a concert for soldiers and was such a hit that she was offered a part in a revue. A year ago she married and gave it all up. The RN Division had been in the Battle of Arras, was hammered, and Edward wounded for the third time. He was on convalescent leave when he'd gone to a Charlot revue. (Charlot and Cochran, names forgotten now, were the West End revue producers during the war.) One of the singers was Dora, not a star, but easily noticed. It coincided with Edward being left a small legacy, intended to provide for his entry into the bar. Instead he spent it courting Dora. It began with a front stall seat every night, heavily tipping ushers and other flunkies, and from there sweeping her off to after-show parties, nightclubs and champagne dinners to culminate in a wedding breakfast at the Savoy—chiefly remembered by Dora when Edward was touched up for a hundred by an 'Honourable' whose subsistence depended on such gratuities. The last of the legacy went on a lavish party the night before she saw him off at Victoria.

'I loved him and would have married him anyway.'

But she was resentful about his extravagance. Edward's behaviour was not responsible, but neither is war. By then he had three wound stripes, his battalion had been posted to the salient, the RN Division's turn was coming up again, and there are few men walking around with four wound stripes. It would have been useless to try to explain this to Dora. She gave me a copy of his poems, pre-autographed, a slim volume, more Brooke than Owen: no wonder he went dry after Gallipoli.

By the standards I had grown up with, Dora could have been a lot worse off. She had the widow's pension of a major, and his relatives would pay for the public school education of her boy, even if not enthusiastically. When we met, a nanny looked after him, and she could, just, afford a small flat in Knightsbridge. However it was not what she and her circle were accustomed to — perhaps had become accustomed to — her family were solicitors in the north of England, and, I gathered, not unduly affluent. I met her mother once and noticed she spoke with a slight touch of Yorkshire. Dora's was fluent Shaftsbury Avenue.

As Dora's enthusiasm for theatre revived, the frequency with which we went to it increased, and we dined out a lot. Dora, a beautiful war widow with theatrical connections, had as easy access to free tickets as I. I hadn't spent much of my pay since 1914 and had free accommodation and cheap Mess fees, thus, for a period, I was able to live in a style to which I was unaccustomed. And she didn't demand the fashionable — so long as I warned her where we were going and she could dress accordingly.

It was dress that brought the first change. She continued to wear mourning; it didn't become her, she knew it, but felt she should. One day I said Passchendaele was in the past, I could speak to that, and she wouldn't do anybody any harm if she left it behind. She was doubtful. I persisted, telling her that if she dressed herself up to the nines, I would take her anywhere, hang the expense.

'Are you sure?'

'Very, very sure. I want to see you at your best.'

'And what about you?' she asked.

'I'll do my best to match you,' I said. 'I shall try, that is. And,' I grinned, 'perhaps fail.'

'I've never seen you in evening dress.'

'You'd be surprised,' and so would I, wondering how I'd get it, having an inkling, that if worn once, it'd be worn again.

'Thank you,' she said. 'We'll go somewhere nice and quiet where we won't meet many old friends. I don't think I could bear plunging back amongst them all at once.'

'Tell me where.'

'The Ritz,' she said.

I nearly laughed out loud.

'Fine,' I said. 'Couldn't think of a better.'

I could afford a white tie, but had to hunt for the tails. I went to the

Secretary of the NZ War Contingent Association, and appealing to her romantic instincts, told her I was taking a beautiful young lady to the Ritz; did she know anybody who might lend me suitable attire? She thought for a moment and then said she might be able to help me. And so she did, 'A gift,' she said, 'keep it.' Having a good idea of where it would have come from I didn't enquire further.

When I went to collect Dora, I was prepared for a change, but not the stunning spectacle before me. 'You're marvellous, really marvellous,' and I gave her a hug that sent her back to rearrange herself.

On entering the Ritz, all eyes were upon us: my first lesson in squiring beauty. The second, which came with little delay, was that every man was after her. After that we were at every opening night and the parties afterwards, when it wasn't an opening. A favourite was the Cave of the Golden Calf. Founded by Strindberg's second wife, and decorated by Epstein and Wyndham Lewis, it'd be hard to match anywhere. Dora's dressmaker got in touch, offering one creation after the other, for showing herself around. I fell not just for her, but also for the whole milieu. Although not of their rank, Dora was good enough to have understudied Beatrice Lillee and Gertrude Lawrence. Each was fond of her and made her welcome. It was normal to be chitchatting with the young Noel Coward, Jack Buchanan, and the older Edith Evans, George du Maurier and Mrs Patrick Campbell. To my regret I never came across Shaw but I did meet Wells, who was showing more than an avuncular interest in one of Dora's friends. It wasn't only the notables who captured me: it was the milieu itself and everyone in it—which up until then I only had heard, read or wondered about.

By then she and I were even talking about a future. I fantasised about getting into the theatre, on the management side, and she about domesticating herself again. In New Zealand! We'll become a pair, I said, you onstage, and me off. If Diaghilev could do it, why not me? We all have to begin somewhere. The mind boggles at the youthful vanity but one *was* young and having a time so great that one was barely aware how great it was. Reality's first intrusion was not long delayed. It occurred at a basement club, just off Oxford Street. A trio was playing: piano, drums and a guitar. I was chatting with an actor who'd had a part in a Shaw play and had been directed by him. Curious about the great man, I pumped him. It may have been a chord from the guitar that made me turn round later to see the guitarist kneeling in front of Dora — a Siren in reverse. I sensed people were interested to see what I would do, but I went to the pianist and put a pound on his keyboard.

'Play,' I said. 'Loud.'

The pound, and the possible alternative, prompted his pianist fingers, and with a leer at the drummer, he launched into a number, loudly. That night was our first row. Matters were more or less normal for a couple of weeks and then I had to go off on a tour of the camps and over to France. I returned late in the evening and went straight to work the next morning. Being tied up all day and into the evening, it was not until latish the next day that I saw Dora again. When I entered I noticed a different feel about the flat.

'Sit down, Frank, I have something to tell you.'

I sat.

'Cochran heard I was about again and offered me a part in his latest revue. Of course I accepted.'

'Of course.'

'It won't make any difference to us, Frank.'

'Why should it?'

'Exactly. We start rehearsals on Monday, but apart from our theatre trips, there will still be time for us to see each other.'

'Yes,' I said.

'Mother has kindly agreed to take Antony. I couldn't really cope … not now anyway.'

'Of course not,' I said.

That was that and it didn't make any difference until I had to go down to Torquay, two nights away. When I returned, the flat was full of flowers.

'You seem to have made a friend.'

'Frank!'

'Smells like a funeral.'

'He doesn't mean a thing to me, not a thing.'

It didn't help when I looked at my bank account, or maybe it did. I was broke. I suppose I could have tried staying on, become a poodle to Dora: one of the tolerated, ineffectual little men, drinking when other people paid and who always kept their place except for the occasional outburst of rage—also ineffectual. Although I was blinded, I was not that blind. It was getting well into 1919 and I was told if I was to return it had to be now.

We parted in tears.

'Dear Frank, dear, dear Frank, it's so sad that they are sending you back now.'

'I might miss you too,' I said, 'just a bit.'

'Just a bit! Oh Frank, how could you! It's been heavenly, it really has.'

'Yes,' I said, 'it has.'

Another huge hug with more tears.

'Come back, Frank, come back soon.'

'When I've made lots of money: like we do in the colonies.'

'Just come back, Frank.'

My eyes had become no drier than hers, couldn't help it.

'I'll never forget you,' I said. And I never have.

The voyage was boring and I slept a lot. Anticipation, not necessarily optimism, was the order of the day. Whatever might happen at home would be a change from the last four years—but what would happen? And no Dora.

Whether you return to Wellington, by land, sea, or air, it's always spectacular. Entering between Pencarrow and Barrett's Reef and the rugged hills with the Tararuas in the distance, it was almost enough to quell my apprehensions. But when the pilot boarded, followed by home service officers in their woolshed-sewn uniforms, and then gliding around Point Halswell to be presented with corrugated iron roofs, weatherboards, and clay-banked roads cut into the hillsides, one could not but think that one had left a city and returned to a shantytown.

On the wharf there were hugs from my mother and sister and a handshake from my father and much chatter as we walked home and up our garden path. As we entered the house there was a lull in the talk and I looked around: there was the hall, the sitting room to the left, my parents' bedroom to the right, and down at the end of the hall, the bathroom with the kitchen next to it; after all that had happened in the last four years, here, *nothing had changed*. We had a sort of celebratory dinner. Breakfast in the morning was as if I had never left. When my mother, in the afternoon, brightly asked about one or two things, I replied accordingly. This went on for a couple of hours. Then she told me how worried they had been about my wound at Passchendaele. What was Passchendaele? I told her.

Next day, before going to work, my father, seeing me lounging in the sitting room, normally only used for visitors, came in and asked me not to upset my mother again.

'What about!'

'What you said yesterday. We know it was nasty but your mother gets upset when you tell her things like that.'

'OK,' I said.

It was as well I went to see my grandparents up in Kelburn. My grandmother, warm and affectionate, supplying us with scones just out of the oven and cups of tea, while the old sea captain and I sat on the veranda, gazed over harbour and hills, and yarned.

At dinner the night after, my mother mentioned that Helen, the girl I had been seeing before I went away, had recently married.

'Good on her,' I said.

'A very nice woman.'

'I know.'

'It's sad in a way.'

'What is?'

'That ... that she's married someone else.'

'What's wrong with him?'

'I don't mean anything like that, he's a fine young man and will make a good husband.'

'That's OK then,' I said.

'Frank, she was very upset when you stopped writing to her. You might remember me mentioning it.'

I did have some recollection.

'She came to see me about it.'

'Oh yes.'

'Why did you stop writing to her, Frank?'

'There was nothing to write about.' I left the table, and went out, hoping I'd meet someone off the ship. I would have gone to a pub but pubs closed at six o'clock.

On Sunday my father said we would be leaving for church early so that we might be in a front pew when the minister and congregation welcomed me, and another man, back.

'What?'

'Every man who returns is welcomed back.'

'Gibb?'

'Doctor Gibb has gone Home for a visit.'

'He's picked his time well,' I said.

'Frank!'

'Not me.'

'Frank …' said my mother.

'Not me,' I said.

My mother began to cry so I left the table.

My father followed and said my mother had been talking about it since the armistice. So I went. On Monday morning I couldn't get down to the Education Department quick enough.

'Here's my name, here's my record, I want a job, now. Outside Wellington. Doesn't matter where.'

'Teaching vacancies don't just happen; not in the middle of term. You know that.'

'See what you've got,' I said.

'You returned soldiers, you're in such a hurry.' He looked me up and down. I was still wearing my uniform. Nothing I'd left behind fitted me. 'You were in the crowd who arrived last week?'

'That's right.'

'Why don't you enjoy your leave?'

I didn't say anything.

He flipped through one file after another and then he paused.

'There is one. Sole charge, about twenty kids. Normally goes to someone straight out of Teachers' College. They had a teacher but he put a local up the duff and he's gone God knows where. Meantime they're having to wait until the end of the year for a replacement. A farmer's daughter filling in. Maybe she's the one up the duff. They're a fertile lot in that part of the world. No electricity. Gets dark early. I'd watch it if I were you. They count your army service, so you qualify for a higher job than this.'

'That's OK.'

'Have you done your country service? No? You'll get your country service there, Captain Butler, guarantee it. Very isolated. Back of Wanganui, long way back.'

'I'll take it.'

HARRY
Peace

On Armistice Day I was in Brockenhurst Hospital still recovering from the wound at Briastre. I had always expected when the day came there would be thanksgiving and jollity. But, as I had yet to learn, anticipation rarely equals expectation. The day began with rumours none of us believed, but at noon the Matron appeared. She had a young doctor in tow and announced, 'The war is over. This is not a rumour. This is official. An armistice has been signed.' She paused, looking at our blank faces. '*The war is over*,' she insisted before sweeping out, the young doctor one deferential step behind her. We heard no cheers from the next ward, just as we'd heard none before she entered ours. Our first reaction was, I believe, a telling one; although we had dreamed of the day when peace would come, we did not know how to deal with it. Little by little, men bestirred themselves and those who were capable, including some who were not quite, hopped out of their beds to see what mischief and mayhem they might commit. Being young men, they needed little stimulus to evoke catcalls, pillows flung, etc., as we could hear from other wards. Drink, unfortunately, took its toll.

I was one whose exertions were limited to sitting a little closer to the vertical than normal. I chatted with others similarly confined to Barracks; a popular topic being how soon it would be before we were shipped home, while, in my mind, I thought of those for whom this day had come too late. When an opportunity arose, I prayed for them, and for we who had been granted life, and carried the responsibilities of peace.

Not long afterwards, my battalion commander, Frank Turnbull, who had just had his promotion confirmed to lieutenant colonel, visited me. I appreciated his visit because of my respect for him as a CO who had known what he was doing, and because he cared enough for his men to visit them. When I congratulated him on his promotion his reply surprised me.

'Thank you, Harry; it was a long time coming.'

'Oh?'

'I was held back, you know.'

'You were?' Never having been overly concerned about promotion myself, from time to time I had to be reminded it mattered to other people.

'It goes back to Malone.'

'He held you back!' I thought of Turnbull as just the sort of man Malone would have liked.

'Well he did and he didn't.'

'So?'

'You were a Main Body man, weren't you? You might remember when we landed in Egypt he worked the very devil out of us.'

'I was Field Ambulance.'

'Were you? Really! Well he drove us hard and by hard I mean hard. It paid off, of course. But at the time, we couldn't see the point of it. There was brigade training and there was Malone training and we did both. When the rest of the brigade was sampling the delights of Cairo we were out in the desert.

'He was hard on his subalterns, very hard; at times we felt his opinion of us bordered on contempt. That was how we received his order; we were to parade early each morning for physical drill, additional to everything else the battalion was doing. Then we learned our neighbours, the Aucklands, treated their subalterns no different from anyone else.'

'That doesn't surprise me,' I said.

'Yes, well, they were hardly a good example of a well-commanded battalion, but we had yet to learn that.'

'Quite,' I said. Got rid of at Gallipoli, but retaining his rank and holding one soft job after another, the original Auckland CO had become the manager of the NZEF rugby team.

'We got together and decided not to present ourselves to the physical training instructor. As expected, we were promptly ordered to parade before Malone.' Turnbull's smile was wry. 'What he had to say was to the point: we had committed conspiracy to mutiny. Either he would leave the battalion or we would.

'We knew enough about The King's Regulations to know they did not look kindly on conspiracy to mutiny. He approached the first in line and asked why he had not paraded. His reply was evasive. The second was asked and his reply was the same. Then it was my turn and I saw no reason to beat about the bush. "I do not think it is fair, Sir." "You do not?" "We have to parade an extra hour that no one else does." He gave me one of his looks, you know what they were like, and went down the line, asking the same question of each. Some gave him an honest answer, some didn't.

'From then on I felt that no matter what I did, I was out of favour with him, his manner being brusque and cold whenever he had reason to speak to me. Then came Chunuk Bair and we were up at the Apex, before dawn, in the morning …'

'I remember that,' I said.

'… formed up, ready to move, and he came up to me. "Mr Turnbull, I wish to tell you that I hold nothing against you over what happened in Egypt. I like a man who speaks the truth. I do not think I shall survive this day but my work is done for I command the best battalion on the Peninsula."'

'You couldn't ask for fairer than that,' I said.

'Yes,' said Turnbull. 'But news of the incident had got about and I feel I have been under a cloud since.'

'With respect, Sir,' I said, 'I doubt it.'

'Do you?' Turnbull smiled and held out his hand. 'Harry, I'm here to thank you for your constant devotion to duty; not just for myself but on behalf of other First Wellington commanders, including our revered Malone.'

If gossip were foreign to one man, it would be Malone. If he *had* said anything about Turnbull it would have been what Turnbull was: a solid reliable officer who exercised initiative in the field and who spoke his mind. Turnbull began the war as a subaltern and finished it as a battalion commander. Throw in a DSO and an MC and one wonders what he was concerned about; the Wellington officers who became brigadiers, Hart and Young, began the war as a major and a captain. Ambition exacts its fee.

From Brockenhurst I was sent to Avon Tyrrell and it was not my cup of tea. An enormous edifice built from racecourse winnings, it was a monument to the prodigality of wealth. It would be unkind to criticise the genteel ladies who waited on us—some had titles that stuck in my throat—as they meant well, but one did wonder whether they might have made better use of their wealth if they had distributed it to the poor rather than donating their spare time caring for commissioned officers on the road to recovery. It was, however, a treat to meet Nelle again. I could only admire the way she coped with being a wife, a widow and a mother in such short order and how she put to it a brave and cheerful face. It was she who introduced me to the New Forest, driving me there in an open car before my feet were functioning again.

As soon as I was fit to walk I was out of Avon Tyrrell and exploring the forest and the countryside around it. Each day I could progress that little bit farther, until, just before I left, I was out from daylight to dark. The first of the forest's inhabitants I met were its ponies, scrubby little beasts that were a smaller version of the wild horses of our pumice lands. They used to venture out regularly to crop the grass on the verges of the roads even to the edge of Brockenhurst town. The Foresters, however, only appeared on market days. I struck up an acquaintance with an elder of the community, but had little success in meeting his gypsy-like relatives.

The Foresters were not the only people who were wary of speaking to strangers. The farmers on the edge of the forest were almost as unforthcoming—my uniform was no different from the army vets who had come to commandeer their horses. Good prices were paid, but any reasonable horse, draft or hack, had been taken whether the farmer had liked it or not. It was only when I went out of my way with one family—by demonstrating my own farming background—that I learnt there was more to it than that. When we were sitting down to a hearty dinner, I was introduced to the son. He had not served in the war. The reason he had not served was because he had not registered, and by keeping out of the way, he had not prompted anybody to come and get him. His father showed me a fine draughthorse: 'We hid him too. He was too good to be sent into all that—like our lad.'

Being a 1914 man with three wounds, I was well up on the list for being sent home but there were still a number of weeks in England left. Through the good offices of Frank, I was able to have myself sent to an Anglican church in the East End that was noted for its work amongst poverty-stricken boys. The driving force behind it, as he was for so many worthy and practical causes, was the great George Lansbury, a man who is little known today, even though he consorted with the so-called great and the good. The son of a railway navvy, brought up in the East End and never living anywhere else; a Labour MP and dedicated Church of England layman; tall, handsome, with a beautiful wife and twelve children; possessing a commanding presence and a powerful voice, George Lansbury was a natural aristocrat who treated all men as his equal, including royalty. A Christian Socialist, a tireless worker for the poor both in Parliament and out, an advocate of women's suffrage from his earliest days; throughout his life Lansbury never ceased to devote his talent and time to building Jerusalem in England's dark, satanic mills and eradicating the scourge of war. I mention him because we were to correspond with each other regularly until his death in 1940. He kept me in touch with events in his part of the world and his support and understanding were to be of great help.

My weeks in the East End coincided with Lloyd George's 'khaki' election. It is almost insulting to Lansbury to mention the two men in the same breath. Each had great talents; indeed one might say they were two sides of the same coin, so similarly were they blessed at birth. One worked to better the poor and downtrodden; the other to better himself. I take the liberty of mentioning Lloyd George because the election he called, and his conducting of it, revealed to me the forces driving him and others of his ilk. Like many other young Christian men in the Empire, early in the war I believed Lloyd George was one who shared our Faith; it being known he had once been a God-fearing Baptist lay-preacher and had opposed the Boer war. As his political career progressed, however, he led a scandalous private life and became a dedicated seeker of power; caring little for propriety and trustworthiness. In less than a week after the armistice, ever one to strike while the iron was hot, he called a general election, campaigning for the return of his Conservative dominated wartime coalition Government. No one would have guessed that he and his cronies, but a few months previously, had proclaimed we were fighting for 'civilisation'. What they shouted now was 'Hang the Kaiser', 'Search their pockets', 'Make them pay,' 'Squeeze them till the pips squeak'. When they added, 'To make a home fit for heroes to live in,' it seemed an afterthought, not to be taken seriously—as indeed it turned out to be.

We had one hope and that was President Wilson's 'Fourteen Points', which, offered in the closing months of the war—and taken note of by the Germans—we presumed would be the basis of the peace settlement. Promulgated were guarantees for the reduction of armaments; national self-determination, and the formation of a League of Nations to afford 'mutual guarantees of political independence and territorial integrity to great and small states'. There was no mention of reparations.

In the meantime I returned to New Zealand. The YMCA was interested in my East End work and on the voyage home I was their ship's representative. It was a happy voyage for all concerned. To help pass the time I sought to educate and entertain the boys by organising lectures and concerts, etc. I gave some lectures myself and among them was one on the liquor industry. I stated the effects it had on the individual, the poor, women and children, but to my sorrow, the young men, in a vote afterwards, carried 'personal choice'. In another lecture I spoke on what then appeared to be the positive aspects of the Russian revolution—all to be horribly annulled.

I will never forget, after rising early from my ship's bunk, witnessing The Land of the Long White Cloud slowly rising on the horizon, and as we steamed closer, seeing the outlines of those familiar razor-back hills under the blue skies and fluffy clouds. As we came alongside the wharf, what a delight it was to feel that dear old Wellington wind on one's cheek. We had a right royal welcome, bands playing and the crowd spreading beyond the wharf gates. We lined the rails, the rigging, and protruded from portholes, alert to spot loved ones below, our battlefield eyes being put to a positive purpose. I had not expected Mum, Dad and the family to come all the way down, but there they were — kindly neighbours were back at the farm, milking the Patterson cows. There was but one gangplank, and we came off one by one and, after some unchristian, I must confess, frustration, we were hugging and kissing. It was nearly five long years of separation, and I was amazed by how the young ones had grown. We had a crowded night with the grandparents, and then caught the early morning train up to Wanganui and from there to the farm. Again I rose early and climbed the ridge from which I had watched the dawn rise before going to Wellington — but this time I carried no weapon. I thought of the old twelve pointer, and as the sun came up, I looked for the clearing. At first I was disappointed to see the entire hillside had been cleared, and sheep grazing between stumps. But the hills beyond were still bush.

As there was work to do I was soon back in Wellington. At church, however, on my first Sunday morning, I met Janet again. We had known one another during our Bible Class days, had sought each other's company, and had gone no further than that, but at this meeting there was a stirring in each of us. Before the year was out we were to be married, the wisest step I ever took. No idle statement: it is impossible to imagine the rest of my life without her. No other explanation for us being joined together is conceivable other than it was our Lord's will.

The obvious reason for my desire to return home as soon as possible had been the same as everybody else's — home is home. But it was not just that: 1919 was the year when there was to be a referendum on the prohibition or continuance of the availability of liquor in New Zealand. Our prospects appeared bright: in the 1911 referendum prohibition was almost carried. Spurred on by the negative vote on the ship, I plunged into the fray: travelling the country from top to bottom, learning much about the acoustics of churches and their halls, finding my feet — if I may put it that way — as a soapbox 'orator'. Sadly we missed out by a mere three thousand votes of the sixty per cent majority the politicians demanded — although they were content enough with the fifty per cent majority needed to elect *them*.

After the referendum, needing the money, and having a job kept open, I returned to the Defence Department. It was convenient, and would provide an income while I went to university part-time. The YMCA was also offering me a position and I was considering that too.

Throughout I had been following the progress of the Paris Peace Conference. Thus from the beginning I was aware of the outrageous decision to exclude Germany from it—the Allies being indifferent to the fact that it had a government—albeit mildly socialist—committed to democracy and individual freedom. Beset by authoritarian forces both Left and Right, the German Government needed all the support it could get from nations that allegedly held very similar values. If we had not been fighting for a government like that, I thought, what had we been fighting for?

I called on my old mentor, Dr Gibb. I said because of their courage and sacrifice I could not repudiate my comrades. He said I need not; but that he too was having doubts, especially since the casualty rates of 1917. He would be sailing to Britain, he said, in a matter of days, and that one purpose of his visit was not just to catch up on developments in church and theology, but also to seek out informed opinion on the war. Apart from that, he didn't tell me anything I didn't know, but what he did give me, in our sharing of views, was an opportunity to begin clarifying my own.

I went to work every morning and returned to my grandparents' house in the evening, just like the old days. On Monday morning, 30 June—I shall never forget it—I was, as usual, eating the breakfast my grandmother kindly made me, when, as was her custom, she laid *The Dominion* on the table. I picked it up as I did every morning to glance at the headlines to note what I might read during my lunch hour and, if she wished it, discuss a topic my grandmother had noticed. I turned to the page where most of the overseas news was printed and stopped short: Germany had signed the Treaty of Versailles. It took only a glance to see the intent of the treaty: Germany was to be humiliated and pay huge reparations. 'Look,' I said to my grandmother, 'Look.' She did and then gazed at me. I stood up. 'I must go,' I said. 'I must go now.' She was perplexed but something stopped her from questioning me.

So I left for work, except I never went to work. My grandparents lived in the upper reaches of Newtown and when I reached the end of their street, instead of turning right and going into town, I turned left for Island Bay and the open sea. Once there I sat on the beach and looked across Cook Strait to the white peaks of the South Island. Then I stood up, turned left and proceeded to walk along the beach and over the rocks to the harbour heads. From there I walked round the entire coast of Wellington's eastern peninsula before I returned to Newtown in the evening. All the way I gazed at the sea and the hills that are Wellington.

> I will lift up mine eyes unto the hills,
> From whence cometh my help.
> My help cometh from the Lord,
> Which made heaven and earth.

As I walked and gazed I pondered on the last four years of my life. The farther I went the more I knew that I had to confront a dreadful truth: four years of my life committed to slaughter and ruin. A better world and a war to end wars? The war I had fought might have ended, but what about the others? Even as the 'Peace' treaty was signed there was civil war in Russia, Poland was fighting Germans in the west and the Russians in the east, Hungary was fighting the Czechs and the Rumanians, the Turks and Greeks were at war and there was war in Ireland. A better world? How could a better world be created with a treaty like that? I thought of Baxter and Kirwin, who had known from the beginning what stand to take. I thought of how brave men on each side had been manipulated by chauvinists with delusions of grandeur, whose only values were power and the increasing of it at the expense of the dead, the insane, and the maimed. I thought of the wanton destruction, of the suppurating wound slashed across Europe: beautiful farmland and villages ruined for years to come. And I had *enjoyed* it: the thrill of patrolling under the enemy's nose so that we might better bring about his destruction; the hunter's delight in stalking prey, and when stalked, stalking the stalker; and the exhilaration of survival when the odds were against it. I thought of the men I had killed, with loved ones who grieved, whom I could no more repudiate than my own comrades. I thought of how we all, whether volunteers, conscripts or civilians, did not 'go' to war but were caught up in it. Courage, audacity, fortitude, self-discipline, plain-speaking and self-sacrifice had been trumpeted. They were the qualities a good soldier shares with a good Christian, but they had been used to bring death, destruction, and misery. God is love but where for the Christian had been the love? As for the peace; with horrid irony it was indeed a 'peace that passeth all understanding'.

Like Paul on the road to Damascus I walked a road and as I walked the scales fell from my eyes and I was given 'sight forthwith'.

> But I say unto you which hear. Love your enemies, do good to them which hate you, bless them that curse you, and pray for them which despitefully use you. And unto them that smiteth thee on the one cheek offer also the other; and him that taketh away thy cloke forbid not to take thy coat also.

There it was. A true follower of our Lord must be an apostle of love and labour for peace.

ABBREVIATIONS/GLOSSARY

2i/c	Second-in-command.
2NZEF	Second New Zealand Expeditionary Force—the New Zealand army force sent overseas 1939–45.
Adjutant	The officer responsible to a CO for administrative and other executive duties.
ADC or Aide	Aide-de-camp—a junior officer who personally assists an officer of high rank.
ADS	Advanced Dressing Station—a medical post to the rear of the RAP where wounded soldiers were taken over by the Field Ambulance for further attention and evacuation.
ANZAC	Australia and New Zealand Army Corps—first applied at Gallipoli where Australian and New Zealand troops fought together. Also the name of the cove where the Anzacs first landed. In Europe the name was applied, for a time, to two army corps, I Anzac and II Anzac, the latter including the New Zealand Division and the former with no New Zealanders and predominantly Australian.
Army	When used with a capital A (as in First Army, Second Army etc.) an Army is a formation comprising several corps and is commanded by an officer with the full rank of general.
ASC	Army Service Corps, later Royal Army Service Corps—it comprised the units responsible for logistic support. Sometimes maligned by the infantry—after their spell in Egypt—as Ali Sloper's Cavalry.
Battalion	At full strength an infantry organisation of just over a thousand men.
Battery	An artillery sub-unit of four or more guns.
Beak	A magistrate—equivalent to today's District Court Judge.
Blighty	A wound of sufficient severity to have you evacuated across the Channel to a hospital in England—thus prolonging your absence from the front line and perhaps even permanently.
Brigade	Commanded in 1914 by a full colonel, but later, and since, by a brigadier general. An infantry brigade comprises 3–4 battalions.
Brigade major	The officer responsible to the brigadier general for coordination within his brigade.
CB	If you were being rewarded for service as a senior officer, you might receive a Companion of the Order of the Bath. If you were a ranker and had been naughty, you were liable to be sentenced to Confined to Barracks for a specified number of days when you had to report, during your normally free time, at regular intervals and be liable for extra, and generally unpleasant, fatigues.
CCS	Casualty Clearing Station—the most forward behind-the-line medical post where operations were performed and the wounded were classified into 'slight', 'dangerous', and 'return to England/Egypt'.
CO	Commanding Officer—generally a lieutenant colonel commanding a battalion or a unit of an equivalent size.
Company	Commanded by a major, at full strength it had around 220 men.

Corporal	A junior NCO who, in the infantry, was responsible for a section.
Corps	A corps comprises two or more divisions and is commanded by a lieutenant general.
CRA	Commander, Royal Artillery—the officer commanding the artillery within a division. In the New Zealand Division it was Brigadier General N. A. Johnston.
Criming	To charge with an offence.
CSM	Company sergeant major—the senior NCO in a company.
Division	Often a predominantly infantry formation (although alternatively it might centre around cavalry or armour) it also includes field artillery, engineers, medical, signals, logistic support etc., so that it is as self-sufficient as an army formation can be. It is nearly always commanded by a major general and comprises 20–30,000 men.
DCM	Distinguished Conduct Medal—the second highest bravery award for non-commissioned soldiers.
DSO	Distinguished Service Order—the second highest award for officers. It is either awarded for single acts of bravery (especially for junior officers) or for distinguished active service by senior officers.
Fatigues	Chores—at which all privates had to take their turn: peeling potatoes, sweeping and scrubbing, cleaning and maintaining toilet facilities, etc.
Field Ambulance	The divisional RAMC teams in the field that were responsible for the treatment and evacuation of casualties from the ADS to the rear.
Field Gun	In World War I in the NZEF it was either an 18-pounder (indicating the weight of the shell) gun or a 4.5-inch (indicating the diameter of the shell) howitzer. Each was an artillery piece that was brought up as far forward into the field of battle as might be managed—in contrast to medium (e.g. firing 6"–8" shells) or heavy (up to 15" or more) artillery, which had longer range and were mostly placed well back from the front line. The difference between a 'gun' and a 'howitzer' is that a gun is designed to fire a high velocity shell on a relatively flat trajectory and a howitzer to fire high and drop steeply, thus being more likely to fall into trenches and on strong-points. At Gallipoli, with its ridges and gullies, howitzers were more effective than guns. Guns, however, were more accurate than howitzers. Other belligerents had equivalent artillery.
FPC	Field Punishment Centre—a divisional military prison.
FRCS	Fellow of the Royal College of Surgeons.
Funk Hole	A dugout or some other useful shelter on a battlefield.
GOC	General Officer Commanding a division (see above).
Grenade	In World War I, a bomb small enough to be thrown by hand or shot from the muzzle of a rifle. The most common British grenade on the Western Front was the Mills Bomb, which, before throwing, had to have its detonator time fuse set by withdrawing a pin. When the grenade left the thrower's hand, the time fuse would commence to operate. If the grenade was accidentally dropped after the pin had been withdrawn the thrower and his neighbours would be in danger.
HE	High explosive—generally refers to shells that explode when they hit their target with the intention of destroying it. The other type of shell contained shrapnel.

Hopping the bags See – **Over the Top.**

i/c	in command or in charge.
IFSDRW	International Federation of Ship, Dock and River Workers—the union of London 'dockers' that in 1889 held a successful strike—unusual for so-called unskilled workers at the time.
IWW	Industrial Workers of the World—Formed in Chicago in 1905, its aim was to unite all workers, skilled and unskilled, to overthrow capitalism and bring in socialism on a workers' union basis.
Lewis Gun	A light machine gun/automatic rifle used by infantry on the battlefield from the middle of the war. Not as accurate as it might have been and sensitive to mud, it nevertheless helped revolutionise infantry tactics. It required a crew to carry the quantity of ammunition needed.
Loophole	A narrow opening in a defensive work for shooting through.
Main Body	The first New Zealand contingent to sail for the northern hemisphere in October 1914. It comprised an infantry brigade, a mounted rifles brigade, plus field artillery and ancillary units: 8,000+ men.
MC	Military Cross—the third highest bravery award for an officer.
MM	Military Medal—the third highest bravery award for an NCO or private.
MO	Medical Officer—a qualified medical doctor.
Mortar	Trench mortars were like small, *very* light howitzers that had light un-rifled pipe-like barrels. They were fired from a trench by dropping the shell down the muzzle to ignite a propellant when the shell base hit the bottom of the barrel. This would shoot the shell out again.
MP	Military Police—enforcers of military law, including traffic control and punishment centres. Sometimes referred to as provosts, red caps or the Corps of the Bastards.
New Army	British units and formations comprised largely of recent recruits who went into action poorly trained and led.
NCO	Non-Commissioned Officer—a corporal, sergeant, staff sergeant, sergeant major, etc. As they were not granted a royal commission their holding of rank was more tenuous than that of commissioned officers. From sergeants upwards they ate and slept separately from the men. Nevertheless they were much closer to the men than commissioned officers and exercised considerable authority over their day-to-day life.
No man's land	The ground between your trenches and the enemy's. Often apparently empty, it usually harboured snipers. At night each side would send out patrols over this ground.
NZEF	New Zealand Expeditionary Force—the army New Zealand sent overseas in World War I.
Oberfeldwebel	A senior German NCO, equivalent to a staff sergeant.
OC	Officer Commanding—in the infantry it could be the officer commanding a company.
Orderly	A soldier who personally assists an officer of high rank such as carrying his map case and overcoat when touring field positions. In the medical corps it is a low ranking soldier who performs basic duties in a hospital or medical post.
Orderly Officer	An officer selected by rota to perform certain inspections and other duties in the battalion for 24 hours when out of the line.
	Similarly for orderly sergeant.

Orderly room	The administrative office of a unit and where orders are posted.
Other ranks	NCOs and privates.
Over the top;	Also Over, or Hopping, the [sand]Bags — Climbing out of a trench, often under fire, to make an attack across no man's land .
Parados	The rearward equivalent of a parapet.
Parapet	A protective wall of varying height, facing the enemy, running parallel to a trench and generally made of sandbags.
Pillbox	A heavily constructed battlefield strong-point generally made of concrete, armed with machine guns and riflemen and used to defend forward lines.
Platoon	An infantry sub-unit that in World War I comprised four sections that could be sometimes up to 50 men but mostly less, commanded by a junior officer (second lieutenant or lieutenant) and, on rare occasions, a sergeant.
Possie	A position or place in which an individual soldier has some degree of shelter.
Private	The lowest rank in the army.
Provosts	Short for provost marshals — military police.
Puttee	Part of a World War I soldier's uniform. It is a strip of cloth that was wound around his leg from the top of his boot to his knee.
PWMU	Presbyterian Women's Missionary Union.
QMS	Quartermaster sergeant. A staff sergeant who carries out quartermaster duties for a company.
Quartermaster	Responsible for food supplies, clothing, stores.
RA	Royal Artillery
RAMC	Royal Army Medical Corps
RAP	Regimental Aid Post — the most forward medical post, generally manned by a doctor and stretcher-bearers permanently attached to the fighting unit, generally an infantry battalion. The primary task was to examine and assess wounds prior to evacuation to an ADS .
Regiment	In the infantry a term that generally encompasses a unit that has battalions that share a common origin: e.g. after the evacuation from Gallipoli the Wellington Regiment had 1st and 2nd Battalions and later, for a time, a 3rd Battalion. In 1914, however, the New Zealand infantry regiments that sailed overseas, comprised only one battalion each. A mounted rifles regiment was the equivalent of a single infantry battalion but with fewer men.
RFC	Royal Flying Corps — precursor to the Royal Air Force and heavily used in World War I as army support.
RMLI	Royal Marine Light Infantry — On Gallipoli these were mainly former British civilians who had volunteered for the navy, but being surplus to requirements, were drafted to fight as soldiers after a very brief period of training.
RMO	Regimental medical officer — the medical officer attached to an infantry battalion or an equivalent unit.
RSM	Regimental sergeant major — The senior NCO of a battalion or similar unit and responsible to the CO for discipline and drill.
Salient	The part of a trench system that exposed itself on three sides by jutting towards, or into, enemy territory.

Sap	Broadly speaking it is a trench that is used for communication and connection to an emplacement such as an observation post, latrine, company HQ, etc.
SB	Stretcher-Bearer—Soldiers designated as such wore a white armband with letters SB in red.
Section	Part of a platoon under a corporal comprising ±10 men.
Sergeant	In the infantry a senior NCO second in charge of a platoon. Occasionally he might command a platoon but not often except when the platoon commander is put out of action.
Shrapnel	Is a number of small round bullets. It is contained within a shell designed to burst not long before it would hit the ground so that the men below where it is aimed are sprayed with the bullets.
SMLE	Short Magazine Lee Enfield—The standard British .303 inch calibre infantry rifle used for most of the war.
Square Bashing	Parade ground drill under the command of an NCO.
Strong-point	A battlefield infantry position designed, manned and armed to resist attack and to provide support to other positions in a trench system.
Strafe	These days an attack by low flying aircraft, but in World War I it originally meant bombardment by shells.
Subaltern	A junior army officer below the rank of captain.
Territorials	In peacetime they were part-time soldiers whose units were drawn from the districts where they lived. When war came they tended to be amongst the earliest to be involved.
Trench	An earthwork dug primarily for shelter from enemy fire but also used for assembling soldiers prior to their going over the top for an attack.
Trench System	A complex pattern of interrelated and mutually supportive trenches, strong-points and saps designed to provide effective defence.
VAD	Volunteer Aid Detachment—an organisation (either Territorial Army or British Red Cross) primarily remembered for its low paid dedicated women volunteers who provided essential support to army medical services particularly in hospitals and ambulances. Non-nursing VAD workers (kitchen hands, cleaners, etc.) were paid rates more closely related to rates elsewhere and were thus better paid than nurse aides and ambulance drivers. They also tended to be of a lower social class than the nursing/driving VADs.
Vickers Gun	Classified as a medium machine gun, it was rather heavy, requiring one man to carry the barrel, another the tripod, and yet more its ammunition. Used by specialised soldiers, accurate and firing 500 rounds a minute, it and its German equivalent were highly effective against mass attacks and for providing covering fire in other situations. The MMG was among the factors that made World War I so different from the European wars that had preceded it.
VC	The highest award for bravery.
WWC	Wellington-West Coast—the designation of the peacetime territorial infantry battalion that drew its men from the Wanganui area. During the war it designated one company each in the 1st and 2nd Battalions of the Wellington Regiment.
Yorker	A cricketing term for when a bowler (generally a fast bowler) bowls a ball that lands (and subsequently bounces) very near the batsman's feet. High skills are needed to deliver it and batsmen need to be equally skilled to score off it.

BIBLIOGRAPHY

LOCATIONS FOR MANUSCRIPTS AND ARCHIVES:

AR   Auckland War Memorial Museum Library.

RUAM   Queen Elizabeth II Army Museum Military Archive and Research Library, Waiouru.

HU   University of Waikato, Hamilton.

WARC   Archives New Zealand, Wellington.

WTU   Alexander Turnbull Library, Wellington.

SOURCES SPECIFIC TO LISTED TOPICS

* Heavily used

NEW ZEALAND

AD1 10/9. WARC

AD1 10/67. WARC

AD1 10/162. WARC

AD 12/38 WARC

Alley, G.T. & Hall, D.O.W. *The Farmer in New Zealand*, Wellington: Department of Internal Affairs, 1941.

Appendices to the Journals of the House of Representatives ... H19. 1911, 1912, 1913, 1914.

Appendices to the Journals of the House of Representatives ... H19a. 1914.

Appendices to the Journals of the House of Representatives ... H44a. 'The Coal Industry ...' 1919.

Barrowman, R. 'Who Were Massey's Cossacks?' unpublished essay, History 316 paper, Victoria University of Wellington 1983, used courtesy of the author.

Beattie, G.C. MS Papers — 3908-3. WTU

Bell Family. MS Papers — 5210-036. WTU

Clayton, G. *Defence not Defiance: The Shaping of the New Zealand Volunteer Force*, unpublished doctoral thesis, University of Waikato, Hamilton. HU

Clayton, G. *The New Zealand Army* ... Christchurch: NZ Army, 1990.

Crawford, J. 'Overt and Covert Military Involvement in the 1890 Maritime Strike and 1913 Waterfront Strike in New Zealand', *Labour History*, 60, May 1991.

Dreaver, A.J. *Horowhenua County and its People: A Centennial History*, Levin: Dunmore Press, 1984.

Gardner, W.J. *A Pastoral Kingdom Divided: Cheviot, 1889–94*, Wellington: Bridget Williams Books, 1992.

Hawdon, S.E. *New Zealanders and the Boer War* ... Christchurch, Gordon and Gotch, [1902(?)]

*Henderson, G.F.R. *Science of War*, London: Longmans, Green, 1905. (Annotated by W.G. Malone)

Hill, Richard S. *The Iron Hand in the Velvet Glove … Policing in New Zealand 1886–1917*, Palmerston North: Dunmore, 1995.

Home Mission Work in the Dominion of New Zealand … Dunedin: Otago Daily Times, 1907.

Howe, K.R. *Singer in a Songless Land: A Life of Edward Tregear 1846–1931*, Auckland: Auckland University Press, 1991.

Johnston, F.E. (Personal File.) 10/512A. NZ Army Base Records.

Keating. J.J. MS Papers — 6887. WTU

Lea, P. *Sunday Soldiers: A Brief History of the Wellington Regiment, City of Wellington's Own*, Wellington: Wellington Regiment, 1982.

Linklater, J. *On Active Service in South Africa with 'The Silent Sixth'* … Wellington: McKee Print, 1904.

McAloon, J. 'Militarist Campaigns in New Zealand 1899: Trade and Imperialism', paper presented at the New Zealand Historical Association Conference, Victoria University of Wellington, Wellington, February 1996.

McGibbon, I. *The Path to Gallipoli* … Wellington: Govt. Print., 1991.

Malone, E.P. 'The New Zealand School Journal and the Imperial Ideology', *The New Zealand Journal of History*, April 1973, pp.12–27.

*Malone, W.G. (Field Notebook)

*Malone, W.G. (Personal file) 10/1039. NZ Army Base Records.

New Zealand Military Journal … Wellington: 1912–14.

O'Farrell, P. 'Politics and Coal: The Socialist Vanguard, 1904–8' in *Miners and Militants: Politics in Westland 1865–1918*, Christchurch: Whitcoulls, 1975.

Olssen, Erik, 'The Great Strike of 1913', *New Zealand's Heritage*, Vol.5, Part 73.

*Olssen, Erik. *The Red Feds: Revolutionary Industrial Unionism and the New Zealand Federation of Labour*, Auckland: Oxford UP. 1988.

O'Shea, P. 'Robin, Alfred William 1860–1935' in *Dictionary of New Zealand Biography* Vol. 3, ed. by Claudia Orange, Auckland: Auckland University Press, 1996.

O'Sullivan, Vincent. *Long Journey to the Border…* Auckland: Penguin, 2003.

Penn, W.J. *The Taranaki Rifle Volunteers* … New Plymouth: Avery, 1909.

Pettit, P.N. *The Wellington Watersiders: The story of their Industrial Organisation*, Wellington: Wellington Branch of the NZ Watersiders Union, 1948.

*Pugsley, C. *Gallipoli: The New Zealand Story*, Auckland: Hodder & Stoughton, 1984.

Pugsley, C. 'Malone, William George, 1859–1915' in *Dictionary of New Zealand Biography* Vol. 3, ed. by Claudia Orange, Auckland: Auckland University Press, 1996.

Richardson, L. *Coal, Class & Community: The United Mine Workers of New Zealand 1880–1960*, Auckland: Auckland University Press, 1995.

Richardson, L. *The Denniston Miners' Union: A Centennial History*, Westport: Denniston Miners' Union Centennial Committee, 1984.

Rosanawski, J. 'Politics and Railways: The Midland Line, 1887–1918,' in *Miners and Militants: Politics in Westland 1865–1918*, Christchurch: Whitcoulls, 1975.

St. John's Church, Willis St., Wellington, Diamond Jubilee Souvenir, 1853–1913. Wellington, 1913.

Taranaki Herald, 12 August, 1915.

Twistleton, F.W. *With the New Zealanders at the Front: A Story of Twelve Months Campaigning in South Africa* … Christchurch: Whitcombe & Tombs, 1902.

*Weitzel, R.L. 'Pacifists and Militants in New Zealand, 1909–1914', *New Zealand Journal of History*, October 1973.

GALLIPOLI

*Aitken, A. *From Gallipoli to the Somme*, London: Oxford, 1963.

Anderson, W. Diary, 1915. RUAM.

Brereton, C.B. *Tales of Three Campaigns*, London: Selwyn & Blount, 1926.

Burness, P. *The Nek* … Kenthurst: Kangaroo Press, 1996.

Chasseaude, D. & Boyle, P. *Grasping Gallipoli: Terrain, Maps and Failure at the Dardanelles*, 1915, Staplehurst: Spellmount, 2005.

*Clark, C. *Interview* with C. Pugsley, TVNZ, Oral Histories, 1982. RUAM.

East, W. *Interview* with C. Pugsley, TVNZ, Oral Histories, 1982. RUAM

Foster, S.W.B. Diary, 1915. RUAM

Grover, R. 'Meldrum, William 1865–1964' in *Dictionary of New Zealand Biography* Vol. 3, ed. by Claudia Orange, Auckland: Auckland University Press, 1996.

Harper, Barbara, (ed.) *Letters From Gunner 7/516 and Gunner 7/517*, Wellington: Anchor Communications, 1978.

Howard, M. *The Franco-Prussian War* … London: Methuen, 1981.

Idress, I. *The Desert Column* … Sydney: Angus & Robertson, 1937.

Johns H. *Interview*. C. Pugsley/TVNZ, Oral Histories, 1982. RUAM.

Leary, L. *Interview*. C. Pugsley/TVNZ, Oral Histories, 1982. RUAM

*Malthus, C. *Anzac: A Retrospect*, Christchurch: Whitcombe & Tombs, 1965.

*Pugsley, C. *Gallipoli: The New Zealand Story*, Auckland: Hodder & Stoughton, 1984.

Steele, N. *Gallipoli*. Barnsley: Cooper, 1999.

*Swann, J.R. Diary/Letters, 1915. RUAM

*Temperley, A.C. *A Personal Narrative of the Battle of Chunuk Bair* … RUAM

Von Sanders, L. *Five Years in Turkey*, London: Balliere, 1927.

*Waite, F. *The New Zealanders at Gallipoli* … Wellington: Whitcombe & Tombs, 1919.

Walton-on-Thames Visitors' Book. FMS-211. WTU

Weston, C.H. *Three Years with the New Zealanders*, London: Skeffington, 1918.

SOMME

AD 1/49/34 Nurses for NZEF... 1914–15. WARC

AD 1/49/34/1 Nurses for NZEF. Offers by N.Z. Government 1916. WARC

AD 1/116 Hospital – Walton-on-Thames. 1915–16. WARC

AD 1/116/1 Hospital – Walton-on-Thames 1917–22. WARC

AD 1/160 VAD & Female Staff – Hospitals NZEF. 1916–22. WARC

*Aitken, A. *From Gallipoli to the Somme*, London: Oxford, 1963.

Day, Angelique, (ed.), *Parishes of County Antrim IV 1830–8 Glens of Antrim*. Ordnance Survey Memoirs of Ireland: Vol. 13, Belfast: Institute of Irish Studies, 1992.

Farrar-Hockley, A.H. *Death of an Army*, London: Barker, 1967.

Farrar-Hockley, A.H. *The Somme*, London: Batsford, 1964.

Hart, H.E. Diaries. Micro MS 552. WTU

Kippenberger, H.K. Diary. 1916.

Knight, G.B., Letters 10-24/6/16, Battalion. MS Papers—5548-05 (Order C132... 1st Bn Otago Regiment 12/6/16.) WTU

*Macdonald, L. *Somme*, London: Michael Joseph, 1983.

*Malthus, C. *Armentières and the Somme*, Auckland: Reed, 2002.

Middlebrook, M. *First Day on the Somme*, London: Penguin Press, 1971.

*Norman, T. *The Hell They Called High Wood: The Somme 1916*, London: Kimber, 1984.

Pidgeon, T. *The Tanks at Flers: An Account of the First Use of Tanks in War in the Battle of Flers – Courcellette, the Somme 15 September 1916*, Vol. 2, Cobham, Surrey: Fairmile Books, 1995.

*Prior, R. & Wilson, T. *The Somme*, New Haven and London: Yale University Press, 2005.

*Sheffield, G. *The Somme*, London: Cassell, 2003.

Swinton, E.D. *Eyewitness ... Including the Genesis of the Tank*, London: Hodder & Stoughton, 1932.

Varnham, F.S. MS Papers 4303/1. WTU

<http://www.electricscotland.com/webclans/m/macdonn2.html>

<http://www.electricscotland.com/history/scotreg/camerons>

PASSCHENDAELE

*Beattie, G.C. MS Papers 3908–2. WTU

Braithwaite, W.G. (Personal File). NZ Army Base Records.

Boyack, N. & Tolerton, J. *In the Shadow of War ...* Auckland: Penguin, 1990.

Cave, N. *Passchendaele: the Fight for the Village*, Ypres, London: Cooper, 1997.

Clayton, P.B. *Plain Tales From Flanders*, London: Longmans Green, 1929.

Ekins, A. 'The Australians at Passchendaele' in *Passchendaele in Perspective*, ed. by Peter H. Liddle, London: Cooper, 1997.

Graves, R. *Goodbye To All That*, London: Cassell, 1977.

Grover, R.F. 'Johnston, Brigadier George Napier (20 August 1868–3 April 1947)' in *Oxford Companion to New Zealand Military History ...* Auckland: Oxford University Press, 2000.

Harper, G. *Massacre at Passchendaele: The New Zealand Story*, Auckland: HarperCollins, 2000.

Ingram, N.M. *Anzac Diary: A Nonentity in Khaki*, Christchurch: Treharne, [n.d.]

Jervis, V. Diary. MS Papers 2241. WTU

Johnston, G. N. Diary 7/10/17–24/10/17. Typed transcript supplied by NZ Ministry of Culture & Heritage.

Johnston, G. N. (Personal File). 1/322 NZ Army Base Records.

*Macdonald, L. *They Called it Passchendaele: The Story of the Third Battle of Ypres and the Men Who Fought it*, London: Macmillan, 1983.

McKeon, W.J. *The Fruitful Years* ... Wellington: Express Print, [n.d.]

*Martin, C.H. MS Papers 2125 [Diary, 1917].WTU

Millen, J. *Over the Top With the Best of Luck ... Roy Gipson Millen*, 1890–1962, Wellington: Serpent Press, 1992.

'Monash, General John (27 June 1865–8 October 1931' in *The Oxford Companion to Australian Military History* ... Melbourne: Oxford University Press, 1995.

Monash, J. *War Letters of General Monash*, ed. by F.M. Cutlack, Sydney: Angus & Robertson, 1934.

Paine, C.H. MS Papers 4288. WTU (Paris visit)

*Passingham, I. *Pillars of Fire: The Battles of Messines Ridge*, June 1917, Stroud: Sutton, 1998.

Powell, G. *Plumer: The Soldiers' General: A Biography of Field-Marshal Viscount Plumer of Messines*, London: Cooper, 1990.

*Prior, R. & Wilson, W. *Passchendaele: The Untold Story*, New Haven & London: Yale, 1996.

*Pugsley, C. 'The New Zealand Division at Passchendaele' in *Passchendaele in Perspective*, ed. by Peter H. Liddle, London: Cooper, 1979.

*Sheffield, G.D. *Leadership in the Trenches* ... London: Macmillan, 1999.

WA 252/4 WARC

WO 95/1032 National Archives, U.K.

WO 158/2008 National Archives, U.K.

WO 158/215 National Archives, U.K.

1918

*Baxter, A. *We Will Not Cease*, Auckland: Cole Catley, 2003.

Beattie, G.C. MS Papers—3908–3. WTU

*Blythe, R. *The Age of Illusion* ... Harmondsworth: Penguin, 1964.

Colbran, B.C. Diaries. MS–Copy–Micro–0037. WTU

Coop, N. Diary ... 1918–19. RUAM

Crane, E. *I Can Do No Other* ... Auckland: Hodder & Stoughton, 1986

Dallas, G. *1918* ... Woodstock & New York: Overlook, 2001.

Döblin, A. *Karl and Rosa*. New York: Fromm, 1983.

Döblin, A. *A People Betrayed* ... New York: Fromm, 1983.

Drew, H.T.B., (ed.), *The War Effort in New Zealand*, Auckland: Whitcombe & Tombs, 1923.

*Ettinger, E. *Rosa Luxemburg* ... London: Harrap, 1987.

Feuchtwanger, E.J. *From Weimar to Hitler: Germany 1918–33*, Basingstoke: MacMillan, 1993.

Foot, O.P.N. Diaries. 1918–19. MSX – 4334. WTU

Grant, D. 'Baxter, Archibald ... 1881–1970' in *Dictionary of New Zealand Biography* Vol. 3, ed. by Claudia Orange, Auckland: Auckland University Press, 1996.

Grant, D. 'Briggs, Mark. 1884–1965' in *Dictionary of New Zealand Biography* Vol. 3, ed. by Claudia Orange, Auckland: Auckland University Press, 1996.

Grover, R.F. 'Westmacott, Herbert Horatio Spencer 1885–1960' in *Dictionary of New Zealand Biography* Vol. 3, ed. by Claudia Orange, Auckland: Auckland University Press, 1996.

Keating, J.J. MS Papers—6887. WTU

Koch, H.W. *Hitler Youth* ... New York: Ballantine, 1972.

McCallum. D.G. Unofficial History. MS Papers 6099—2. WTU.

Peters, E.A. *1st War Pocket Diary*. 1917–19. RUAM

*Prior, R. & Wilson, T. *Command on the Western Front: The Military Career of Sir Henry Rawlinson 1914–18*, Oxford: Blackwell, 1992.

Rawlins, S.W.H. A History of the Development of the British Artillery in France, 1914–1918; typescript of record completed from records in the office of the MGRA at GHQ. Designated 'Unofficial. For Private Reference ... (Pt vii – Tactical Developments.) (Ministry of Culture & Heritage)

Rhind, A.E.M., MS Papers—3772. WTU

The Reader's Bible ... London: Oxford, 1951.

Rogers, S.S. MS Papers—55535–5. WTU.

Scott, W.B. MSX–3211. WTU

Shephard, B. *A War of Nerves*, London: Cape, 2000.

Simpkin, P. 'Co-Stars or Supporting Cast? British Divisions in the Hundred Days, 1918' in *British Fighting Methods in the Great War*, ed. by P. Griffith, London: Cass, 1996.

Smith, H.Z. *Not So Quiet: Stepdaughters of War*, London: Marrriot, 1930.

Stokes, B. MS Papers—4683–12. WTU

Taylor, D.P. Diary 1917. MS 2000/20. Auckland Institute & Museum.

Trussler, S. *The Cambridge Illustrated History of the British Theatre*, Cambridge: Cambridge University Press, 1994.

Vansittart, P. *Voices From the Great War*, London: Cape, 1981.

WA 1. 1/3/24, 10/65. Riots, Sling 1919. WARC

WA 1. 1/3/25, 10/76. Conscientious Objectors 1918–1919. WARC

WA 9. 9/4/27. HQ Entrenching Group. WARC

WA 9/4/36. NZEF – Details – North Russian Expedition July 1918–July 1919. WARC

WA 17. II Anzac Corps. Senior Mechanical Transport Officer. War Diary Nov 1917. WARC

Weintraub, S. *A Stillness Heard Round the World*, New York: Oxford University Press, 1985.

Westmacott, H.H.S. Micro-MS-0847. WTU.

<http://www.avontyrrell.org.uk>

<http://www.Stgeorge'shanoversquare.org/History2.htm>

<http://www.strollingguides.co.uk/books/newForest/places/1999-All Saints-Main.php>

SOURCES USED THROUGHOUT THE BOOK BUT NOT THOSE LISTED UNDER 'SOURCES SPECIFIC TO TOPICS LISTED'.

*Applegate, R. *Scouting and Patrolling* ... Boulder: Paladin, 1980.

Arthur, M. *When this Bloody War is Over: Soldiers' Songs of the First World War*, London: Piatkus, 2001.

Atkinson, C.F. 'Army' in *Encyclopaedia Britannica* ...ed. by Hugh Chisholm, 11th edn, Cambridge: University Press, 1910–11.

Atkinson, C.F. 'Artillery' in *Encyclopaedia Britannica* ... ed. by Hugh Chisholm,11th edn, Cambridge: University Press, 1910–11.

Atkinson, C.F. 'Infantry' in *Encyclopaedia Britannica* ... ed. by Hugh Chisholm, 11th edn, Cambridge: University Press, 1910–11.

*Bagnall, A.G. (ed.), *New Zealand National Bibliography to the Year 1960*, Wellington: Govt. Print, 1969–80.

Barber, L. 'Gibb, James, 1857–1935' in *Dictionary of New Zealand Biography* Vol. 2, ed. by Claudia Orange, Wellington: Bridget Williams Books, 1993.

Barbusse, H. *Under Fire*, London: Dent, 1955.

Barnett, C. *The Swordbearers* ... London: Hodder & Stoughton, 1986.

Behrend, A. *As From Kemmel Hill* ... London: Eyre & Spottiswoode, 1963.

*Bidwell, S. & Graham, D. *Firepower: British Army Weapons and Theories of War, 1904–45*, London: Allen & Unwin, 1982.

Binding, R. *A Fatalist at War*, London: Allen & Unwin, 1929.

Bion, W.R. *The Long Weekend 1897–1919* ... London: Free Association Books, 1986.

Birdwood, W.R. *Khaki and Gown*, London: Ward Lock, 1941.

Blunden, E. *Undertones of War*, London: Penguin, 1936.

Bourke, J. *Dismembering the Male* ... London: Reaktion Books, 1999.

Boyack, N. & Tolerton, J. *In the Shadow of War*, Auckland: Penguin, 1990.

*Brittain, V. *Testament of Youth: An Autobiographical Study of the Years 1900–1925*, London: Virago, 1993.

*Brittain, V. *War Diary 1913–1917: Chronicle of Youth*, ed. by Alan Bishop, London: Gollancz, 1981.

*Brophy, J. & Partridge, E. *The Long, Long Trail: What the British Soldier Sang and Said in 1914–1918*. New York: London House & Maxwell, 1965.

Brown, M. *The Imperial War Museum Book of the Western Front*, London: Sidgwick & Jackson, 1993.

Bruce, A. *An Illustrated Companion to the First World War*, London: Michael Joseph, 1989.

Burns, R. (ed.), *The World War One Album*, London: Bison Books, 1991.

Burton, O.E. *The Auckland Regiment* ... Auckland: Whitcombe & Tombs, 1922.

*Burton, O.E. (Personal File) 2/8229. NZ Army Base Records.

*Burton, O.E. *A Rich Old Man*, MS – Copy – Micro – 0144. WTU

*Burton, O. *The Silent Division* ... Sydney: Angus & Robertson, 1935.

*Byrne, A.E. *Official History of the Otago Regiment* ... Dunedin: Wilkie Print, 1921.

Byrne, J.R. *New Zealand Artillery in the Field 1914–1918*, Auckland: Whitcombe & Tombs, 1922.

*Carbery, A.R.D. *The New Zealand Medical Service in the Great War 1914–1918* ... Auckland: Whitcombe & Tombs, 1924.

Carrington, Charles. *Soldier From the Wars Returning*. London: Hutchinson, 1965.

Cendrars, B. *Lice*, London: Peter Owen, 1973.

Chapman, G. *A Passionate Prodigality*, London: Mayflower-Dell, 1967.

Coppard, G. *With a Machine Gun to Cambrai*, London: HMSO, 1969.

Crawford, J.A.B. 'Hart, Herbert Ernest 1882–1968' in *Dictionary of New Zealand Biography* Vol. 3, ed. by Claudia Orange, Auckland: Auckland University Press, 1996.

Cross, T. *The Lost Voices of World War I*, London: Bloomsbury, 1988.

*Cunningham, W.H., Treadwell, C.A.L., Hanna, J.S. *The Wellington Regiment* ... Wellington; Ferguson & Osborn, 1928.

De Groot, G. *Douglas Haig, 1861–1928*, London: Unwin Hyman, 1988.

Dennis, P. (ed.), *Oxford Companion to Australian Military History*, Melbourne: Oxford University Press, 1995.

Dyer, G. *War*, London: Bodley Head, 1985.

Eksteins, M. *Rites of Spring: the Great War and the Birth of the Modern Age*, New York: Doubleday, 1990.

Essame, H. *The Battle for Europe 1918*, New York: Charles Scribner's Sons, 1972.

Essex, Tony and Gordon Watkins, producers, *The Great War* for BBC-TV *Tonight*. DVD edition. North Harrow: DD Video, 2001.

Evans, M.M. *1918: Year of Victories*, London: Arcturus, 2003.

Ex-Private X. *War is War*, London: Gollancz, 1930.

Featherstone, D. *Weapons and Equipment of the Victorian Soldier*, Poole: Blandford, 1978.

Ferguson, N. *The Pity of War*, Penguin: Harmondsworth, 1999.

Fussell, P. *The Great War and Modern Memory*, London: Oxford University Press, 1977.

Gilbert, A. *Stalk and Kill* ... London: Sidgwick & Jackson, 1997.

Giono, J. *To the Slaughterhouse*, St. Albans: Panther, 1973.

*Godley, A. *Life of an Irish Soldier*, London: Murray, 1939.

Grant, D. 'Burton, Ormond Edward, 1893–1974' in *Dictionary of New Zealand Biography* Vol. 5, ed. by Claudia Orange, Auckland: Auckland University Press, 2000.

Graves, R. *Goodbye To All That*, London: Cassell, 1977.

Griffith, L.W. *Alec*, unpublished typescript of 1964 BBC recording held by Gerald Gliddon.

Griffith, L.W. *Autobiography,* unpublished typescript of text referring to A. Godley held by Gerald Gliddon.

Griffith, L.W. *Up To Mametz,* Norwich: Norfolk, 1988.

*Griffith, P. *Battle Tactics on the Western Front: The British Army's Art of Attack 1916–1918,* New Haven and London: Yale UP, 1994.

Griffith, P. *Forward into Battle* ... Chichester: Antony Bird, 1981.

Griffith, P. (ed.), *British Fighting Methods in the Great War,* London: Cass, 1996.

Grossman, D. *On Killing* ... Boston: Little Brown, 1995.

*Great Britain. General Staff. War Office. *Infantry Training 1911,* London: HMSO, 1911.

Grover, R.F. 'Burton, Second Lieutenant Ormond Edward (16 January 1893–7 January 1974)' in *Oxford Companion to New Zealand Military History,* Auckland: Oxford University Press, 2000.

Grover, R.F. 'Godley, Alexander John 1867–1957' in *Dictionary of New Zealand Biography* Vol. 3, ed. by Claudia Orange, Auckland: Auckland University Press, 1996.

Grover, R.F. 'Johnston, Brigadier-General Francis Earle (1 October 1871–7 August 1917)' in *Oxford Companion to New Zealand Military History,* Auckland: Oxford University Press, 2000.

*Haig, D. *Douglas Haig: War Diaries and Letters 1914–1918,* ed. by Gary Sheffield and John Bourne, London: Weidenfeld & Nicolson, 2005.

Haig, D. Papers, National Library of Scotland.

Haig, D. *Private Papers of Douglas Haig 1914–1919* ... ed. by Robert Blake, London: Eyre & Spottiswoode, 1952.

Hart, B.H.L. *History of the First World War,* London: Cassell, 1970.

Hasek, J. *The Good Soldier Svejk* ... London: Heinemann, 1973.

Haythornthwaite, P.J. *Photohistory of World War One,* London: Arms and Armour, 1994.

Herbert, A.P. *The Secret Battle,* London: Methuen, 1936.

Hogg, I.V. *The Guns 1914–18.* London: Pan/Ballantine, 1973.

*Holmes, R. (ed.), *Oxford Companion to Military History,* Oxford: Oxford University Press, 2001.

Hope, T.S. *Rage of Battle.* London: Universal-Tandem, 1972.

Houseman, L. (ed.) *War Letters of Fallen Englishmen,* London: Gollancz, 1930.

Hunter, E.J. & Prince, T. 'Stress and the Combat Leader' in *Marine Corps Gazette,* August 1988.

*Hyatt, A.M.J. *General Sir Arthur Currie: A Military Biography,* Toronto: University of Toronto Press/Canadian War Museum, 1987.

Hyde, R. *Passport to Hell* (1936) ... ed. by D.I.B. Smith. Auckland: AUP, 1986. Introduction and notes by D.I.B. Smith.

Hynes, S. *Soldiers' Tale* ... New York: Allen Lane, 1997.

James, R.R. *Gallipoli,* London: Batsford, 1965.

Jones, I. *King of the Air Fighters,* London: Greenhill Books, 1989.

Jones, P.M. (ed.), *Modern Verse 1900–1940,* London: Oxford, 1948.

Junger, E. *Copse 125*, New York: Fertig, 1993.

Junger, E. *Storm of Steel*, London: Allen Lane, 2003.

Keegan, J. *The Face of Battle*, London: Barrie & Jenkins, 1988.

Keegan, J. *The First World War*, London: Hutchinson, 1998.

Keegan, J. *A History of Warfare*, New York: Knopf, 1993.

Keegan, J. *The Mask of Command*, New York: Viking, 1987.

Keegan, J. *Opening Moves August 1914*, London: Pan/Ballantine, 1973.

Kendall, S. & Corbett, D. *New Zealand Military Nursing* ... Auckland: [n.p.], 1991.

Kipling, R. *Barrack Room Ballads* ... London: Methuen, 1896.

Koch, H.W. *History of Warfare*, London: Bison, 1987.

Laffin, J. *The Western Front Illustrated 1914–1918*, Kenthurst; Kangaroo Press, 1993.

Lee, J.A. *Civilian into Soldier*, Auckland: Oxford, 1985.

Lewis, C. *Sagittarius Rising*, Harrisburg: Stackpole, 1963.

Livesey, L. *Great Battles of World War I* ... London: Greenwich Editions, 1997.

Lloyd, A. *The War in the Trenches*, London: Hart-Davis, 1976.

Lussu, E. *Sardinian Brigade*, Harrisburg: Stackpole, 1967.

*Luxford, G.V. *How I Came To Be Interested in War and Why I Went to World War One* ...
    WTU

*McBride, H.W. *A Rifleman Went to War* ... *With Particular Emphasis Upon the Use of the
    Military Rifle in Sniping* ... Mt. Ida: Lancer Militaria, 1987.

McDonald, L. *1914*, Harmondsworth: Penguin, 1989.

*Macdonald, L. *The Roses of No Man's Land*, London: Macmillan, 1984.

McGibbon, I. *New Zealand Battlefields and Memorials of the Western Front*, Auckland:
    Oxford University Press, 2001.

McGibbon, I. (ed.), *Oxford Companion to New Zealand Military History*, Auckland:
    Oxford University Press, 2000.

Macksey, K. *Vimy Ridge 1914–18*, London: Pan/Ballantine, 1973.

Manning, F. *The Middle Parts of Fortune: Somme & Ancre, 1916*, London: Peter Davies,
    1977.

Marwick, A. *The Deluge: British Society and the First World War*, Harmondsworth:
    Penguin, 1967.

Maude, F.N. 'Cavalry' in *Encyclopaedia Britannica* ... ed. by Hugh Chisholm, 11th edn,
    Cambridge: University Press, 1910–11.

Maude, F.N. 'Strategy' in *Encyclopaedia Britannica* ... ed. by Hugh Chisholm 11th edn,
    Cambridge: University Press, 1910–11.

Messenger, C. *Trench Fighting 1914–18*, London: Pan/Ballantine, 1973.

Middlebrook, M. *The Kaiser's Battle* ... London: Allen Lane, 1978.

Montague, C.E. *Disenchantment*, London; Chatto & Windus, 1922.

Moorhouse, G. *Hell's Foundations* ... London: Sceptre, 1993.

Moran, C.M.W. *Anatomy of Courage*, London: Constable, 1945.

Mottram, R.H. T*he Spanish Farm Trilogy 1914–1918*, London: Chatto & Windus, 1927.

Murray, J. *Gallipoli 1915*, London: New English Library, 1977.

Myrivilis, S. *Life in the Tomb*, Hanover: University Press of New England, 1977.

Nash, T.A.M. *The Diary of an Unprofessional Soldier*, Chippenham: Picton, 1991.

Neill, M. 'Tactics' in *Encyclopaedia Britannica* ... ed. by Hugh Chisholm, 11th edn, Cambridge: University Press, 1910–11.

*New Zealand Army. New Zealand Expeditionary Force. *War, 1914–1918 ... Its Provision and Maintenance* ... Wellington: Govt. Print, 1919.

Orgill, D. *Armoured Onslaught 8th August 1918*, New York: Ballantine, 1972.

O'Shea, S. *Back to the Front* ... London: Robson, 1997.

O'Sullivan, Vincent, (ed.), *An Anthology of Twentieth Century New Zealand Poetry*, Auckland: Oxford, 1983.

Owen, W. *The Poems of Wilfred Owen*, ed. by Edmund Blunden, London: Chatto & Windus, 1946.

*Pengelly, E. *Nursing in Peace and War*, Wellington: 1956.

*Pugsley, C. *The Anzac Experience* ... Auckland: Reed, 2004.

*Pugsley. C. *On the Fringe of Hell* ... Auckland: Hodder, 1991.

Pitt, B. *1918: The Last Act*, London: Macmillan, 1984.

Reith, J. *Wearing Spurs*, London: Hutchinson, 1966.

Renn, L. *War*, London: Martin Secker, 1929.

Richards, F. *Old Soldiers Never Die*, London: Faber, 1964.

Robertson, J.I. *Stonewall Jackson* ... New York: Macmillan, 1997.

*Rogers, A. *While You're Away: New Zealand Nurses at War 1899–1948*, Auckland: Auckland University Press, 2003.

Romains, J. *Verdun*, St. Albans: Mayflower, 1973.

*Russell, J.M. MS Papers 1696. WTU

*Salmond, M. *Bright Armour: Memories of Four Years of War*, London: Faber, 1935.

Sassoon, S. *Memoirs of a Fox-hunting Man*, London: Folio, 1971.

Sassoon, S. *Memoirs of an Infantry Officer*, London: Faber, 1931.

Sassoon, S. *Sherston's Progress*, London: Faber, 1936.

Sassoon, S. *Siegfried's Journey 1916–1920*, London: Faber, 1945.

*Sheffield, G. *Forgotten Victory* ... London: Headline, 2001.

Sherriff, R.C. *Journey's End*, Harmondsworth: Penguin, 1983.

*Silkin, J. (ed.), *The Penguin Book of First World War Poetry*, Harmondsworth: Penguin, 1979.

Sixsmith, E.K.G. *British Generalship in the Twentieth Century*, London: Arms and Armour, 1970.

Smithers, A.J. *Sir John Monash*, London: Cooper, 1973.

Stewart, D. *Springtime in Taranaki* ... Auckland: Hodder, 1983.

*Stewart. H. *The New Zealand Division 1916–1919* ... Auckland: Whitcombe & Tombs, 1921.

Terraine, J. *Douglas Haig: The Educated Soldier*, London: Hutchinson, 1963.

Terraine, J. *The Road to Passchendaele* ... London: Cooper, 1977.

Terraine, J. *White Heat* ... London: Sidgwick & Jackson, 1982.

Vansittart, P. *Voices From the Great War*, London: Cape, 1981.

Vaughan, E.C. *Some Desperate Glory* ... New York: Simon & Schuster, 1989.

Wade. A. *The War of the Guns*, London: Batsford, 1936.

Warner, P. *Passchendaele* ... London: Sidgwick & Jackson, 1987.

Weintraub, S. *A Stillness Heard Round the World* ... New York: Oxford University Press, 1985.

Williamson, H. *The Patriot's Progress* ... London: Macdonald & Janes, 1976.

Williamson, H. *The Wet Flanders Plain*, Norwich: Gliddon, 1987.

*Wilson, W.K. Diary. 1915–1919. RUAM

*Winter, D. *Death's Men: Soldiers of the Great War*, Harmondsworth: Penguin, 1979.

Winter, D. *The First of the Few: Fighter Pilots of the First World War*, London: Alan Lane, 1982.

Winter, D. *Haig's Command: A Reassessment*, London: Viking, 1991.

Wittlin, J. *Salt of the Earth*, Harrisburg: Stackpole, 1970.

Wolff, L. *In Flanders Fields* ... London: Longmans, 1959.

*Wynne, G.C. *If Germany Attacks: The Battle in Depth in the West*, London: Faber, 1940.

Yeates, V.M. *Winged Victory*, London: Sphere, 1969.

Zilhahy, L. *Two Prisoners*, Harrisburg: Stackpole, 1968.

Zweig, A. *The Case of Sergeant Grischa*, Harrisburg: Stackpole, 1969.